P9-CLO-505

HARVEST IN TRANSLATION

THE LOVER

Books by A. B. Yehoshua

MR. MANI

FIVE SEASONS

A LATE DIVORCE

BETWEEN RIGHT AND RIGHT

THE LOVER

EARLY IN THE SUMMER OF 1970

THREE DAYS AND A CHILD

THE LOVER

by A. B. Yehoshua

TRANSLATED FROM THE HEBREW BY PHILIP SIMPSON

A HARVEST BOOK
HARCOURT BRACE & COMPANY
San Diego New York London

Reprinted by arrangement with Doubleday,
a division of Bantam Doubleday Dell Publishing Group, Inc.

Library of Congress Catalog Card Number: 84-72787

ISBN 0-15-653912-8

Printed in the United States of America

First Harvest edition 1993

A B C D E

For my children
Sivan, Gideon and Nahum

THE LOVER

PART ONE

ADAM

And in the last war we lost a lover. We used to have a lover, and since the war he is gone. Just disappeared. He and his grandmother's old Morris. And more than six months have passed and there has been no sign from him. We are always saying it's a small, intimate country, if you try hard enough you'll discover links between the most distant people–and now it's as if the man has been swallowed up by the earth, disappeared without trace, and all the searches have been fruitless. If I was sure he had been killed, I would give up the search. What right have we to be stubborn about a dead lover, there are some people who have lost all that is dear–sons, fathers and husbands. But, how can I put it, still I'm convinced that he hasn't been killed. Not him. I'm sure that he never even reached the front. And even if he was killed, where is the car, where has that disappeared to? You can't just hide a car in the sand.

There was a war. That's right. It came upon us a complete surprise. Again and again I read the confused accounts of what happened, trying to get to the bottom of the chaos that ruled then. After all, he wasn't the only one who disappeared. To this day there is before us a list of so many missing, so many mysteries. And next of kin are still gathering last remnants–scraps of clothing, bits of charred documents, twisted pens, bullet-ridden wallets, melted wedding rings. Chasing after elusive eyewitnesses, after the shadow of a man who heard a rumor, trying in the mist to piece together a picture of their loved one. But even they are giving up the search. So what right have we to persist. After all, he's a stranger to us. A doubtful Israeli, a deserter in fact, who returned to the country for a short visit to sort out some inheritance and stayed, perhaps also on our account. I don't know, I can't be sure. But I repeat, he hasn't been killed. Of that I'm convinced. And that is the cause of the unease that has been eating at me these last months, that gives me no rest, that sends me out on the road in search of him. More than that: strange ideas occur to me on his account, that in the thick of the battle, in the confusion and disorder of units disbanding and regrouping, there were some–let's say two or three–who took advantage of this confusion to break off and disappear. I mean, they simply decided not to return home, to abandon their old ties and go elsewhere.

It may seem a crazy idea, but not to me. You could say I've become an expert on this subject of missing persons.

Boaz, for example. Again and again since the cease-fire there has been that announcement in the papers about Boaz, who disappeared. Something like this: Mom and Dad are looking for Boaz. And a picture of a young man, a child almost, with short hair, a young soldier in the Tank Corps, and some astonishing details. At the beginning of the war on such and such a date he was seen in action in his tank in the front line in such and such a place. But ten days later, toward the end of the war, a childhood friend, a trusted friend, met him at a crossroads far from the front. They had a short conversation, and parted. And from that point on, Boaz's traces have vanished.

A real mystery—

But we have hardened, reading announcements such as these in the papers, pausing for a moment and continuing with a weary glance to flick through the pages. This last war has made us numb.

But Boaz's parents persist, and why shouldn't they? For years they brought up a son, walked with him to the nursery, ran with him to the doctor, made sandwiches for him in the morning when he went away to the youth camp, waited for him at the railway station when he returned from a school trip. They washed and ironed and worried the whole time. Suddenly he disappears. And nobody can tell them where he is, what has happened to him. The whole system, nation, society, which absorbed him so voraciously, now begins to falter. And when the parents persist, and why shouldn't they, a young officer is sent to them, well meaning no doubt but lacking experience. He arrives in a jeep and takes them, on a bright winter's day, on a journey to the middle of the desert, driving long hours in silence deep into the wilderness, on roads that are not roads, through the dust and the desolation to a bare unmarked little mound of sand, vast emptiness all around. This officer boy goes red, stammers, here is where he was seen for the last time. See, even the dry rocks are broken in mourning. How is it possible . . .

And I say, these parents who do not give up, who are not content with this sandy conclusion beside a lonely hill, who glare with hatred at the young officer, who from sheer anger and disappointment are ready to attack him, these parents demand further explanation, for who can assure them that their Boaz, Boaz their son, is not sitting at this very moment, in summer clothes, with long hair, on a distant beach, in the port of a far-off country, watching the landscape that lies open before him and sipping a soft drink. Perhaps he had reasons for not returning home, even at the price of his parents' misery. He grew suddenly disgusted by something, or something scared him. And if his parents would only study the problem from such an angle, instead of scurrying from one army office to another, there might be a chance of picking up his trail.

But how could they–

I too once visited such an army office, searching for him, and I saw how hopeless it was, in spite of the smiles and the willingness and the sympathy. But that was only after two months or more, when we realized that the lover had really disappeared, that he wasn't going to return. Until then we had said, he must still be on the move, caught up in new experiences, confused by encounters with unfamiliar things. What does he know about the real Israel. Besides, we were so busy that we hardly had the leisure to think about him. Asya was at the school all the time, filling in for teachers who had been called up, running around in the evenings between meetings of the emergency committees, visiting the parents of pupils from the senior grades who had been killed or wounded. At night she used to come home exhausted, collapse on the bed and fall asleep right away. And I had a heavy load of work also, the garage was full of cars already in the first days of the war. Some of my customers were on their way to the front, already in uniform, and they brought their cars in for major repairs, thinking that the war would be a short one, a quick journey of adventure, a good opportunity to have the engine overhauled or the bearings changed, or get a new coat of paint, and in a few days they would be returning home, picking up their cars and going back to their business.

But they didn't return so quickly. My parking lot filled up. One of my customers didn't return at all. I had to return the car personally to his parents' house, to shake hands with the mourners, to mumble some words of condolence and, of course, to cancel the fee, which amounted to several hundred pounds. The other cars were taken away by the wives, those of them who knew how to drive. I never had so much to do with women as in those weeks immediately after the war. They took the cars over, and slowly but surely they ruined them. Driving without water, without oil, even forgetting to look at the fuel gauge. In the middle of the night the phone would ring, and a woman's voice appeal for my help. And I would drag myself out in the middle of the night, roaming the darkened city to find in a narrow side street a young woman, a child really, standing panic-stricken beside a huge luxury car with an empty fuel tank.

But that disruption also came to an end, and life began to return to normal. The men came back from the army, wandering about in the mornings in their khaki clothes and heavy boots, buying supplies in the grocers' shops, dust in their eyes, looking dazed, stammering a little. They came and collected their cars and postponed payment. A hard winter was setting in. Dull days, sodden with rain. It became harder and harder for us to sleep at night. Waking in the middle of the night to the sound of thunder, going to the bathroom, switching on the radio for a moment. So it was that I discovered the extent of Dafi's insomnia. The lover's disappearance began to penetrate. Yearning for him, wondering where he is. Asya knows no peace, running to the phone every time it rings. She says nothing, but I catch her look–

In the mornings I have taken to driving to the garage by a roundabout route, by way of the lower city, passing his grandmother's house, looking for a sign of life behind the sealed shutters with their peeling paint. Sometimes even parking the car for a moment and running up the deserted staircase to examine the broken letter box that hangs there precariously, to see if there's a letter or a message for him, or from him. Can we abandon him, forget him? After all, who but us could know he is gone?

DAFI

Dafi, my dear, it's a white night, there's no point in trying. You'll only end up crying again, kid. I know you, I heard you whimpering under the blanket. It's only when you try too hard to sleep that all these things get on your nerves–the faint snoring of Daddy or Mommy, the noise of a car in the street, the wind rattling the shutter in the bathroom. It's already past midnight. You thought you'd get away with it, pudgy, but tonight is a night without sleep. There's no choice. Stop, enough turning the pillow and tossing from side to side, playing dead. No more fooling. Who are you trying to kid? Open your eyes, please, pull yourself together, sit up and put on the light and make a plan for killing the time that's left between now and morning.

I knew this afternoon that tonight there'd be problems, that I wouldn't be able to sleep. It's a strange thing, this premonition. Tali and Osnat came around this afternoon and stayed until the evening.

We had a good time, chatting and laughing and gossiping, about the teachers to begin with, but about the boys most of all. Osnat's completely crazy, she's been like this since the beginning of the year, she's got nothing else to talk about, just boys. Every few weeks she falls in love with someone new, goes right off her head. Usually boys from the seventh and eighth grades who don't even know they've been fallen in love with. But that doesn't stop her from making a fantastic story out of it, every time it happens. I really love her. She's ugly and thin, wears glasses, and she's got a tongue like a sharp knife. Tali and I roared with laughter at her descriptions, we made such a row that Daddy opened the door to see what was going on, but he closed it again in a hurry because Tali had taken off her shoes and her sweater, opened her blouse, let her hair down and lay down on my bed. Wherever she goes she's always taking something off and getting into other people's beds. Completely unbalanced. A real looker and a good friend.

We had fun. Osnat was standing in the middle of the room with her glasses pushed down on her nose, imitating Shwartzy, and suddenly in the middle of all the fun and excitement, beyond Osnat's head, outside the big window, there's a little purple cloud, a night cloud, floating very low, actually touching the rooftops. And a little lightning flash ignites inside me, deep inside my head, a physical sensation. Tonight I won't be able to sleep, a prophetic warning. When Tali and Osnat are fast asleep, I shall be tossing about here on my bed. But I said nothing, I went on chatting and laughing, and there was just that obstinate little flame burning away inside me, like the little pilot flame that's always alight in our oven. No sleep for you, Dafi. Afterward I forget about all this, or I pretend to forget. In the evening they went away and I sat down to do my homework, still expecting a normal night. I did a quick analysis of the two prophecies of wrath in Jeremiah and compared them. I soon polished off the images of death and destruction in *The City of Slaughter*. Stupid questions. But as soon as I opened the math book, I started yawning. I suddenly felt terribly tired. Maybe I should've laid down on the bed and slept, made the most of it.

But I was silly and went on trying to understand the questions, and then Daddy called me to come and eat supper. When he gets the meal ready and I don't come straightaway it always puts him in a foul mood. He's in such a hurry to eat that he finishes off the meal before he's finished preparing it.

Mommy hasn't come in yet—

I sat beside him even though I wasn't hungry, just to make him feel that he wasn't alone. We hardly talked because it was the evening news on the radio and he was glued to it. He cooked me some scrambled eggs that I didn't want. The food that he cooks never has any taste to it, although he's sure he knows how to cook. When he saw I wasn't eating the eggs, he ate them himself and left the kitchen. I threw some of the food in the garbage, put the rest back in the fridge, promised to wash the dishes and went to watch TV. It was a program in Arabic, but I sat and watched it, rather than go back to my room and find the math book waiting for me there. Daddy tried at first to read the paper and watch TV at the same time. In the end he got up and went off to bed. A strange man. Deserves a close look, sometime. Who is he really? Is he just a garage boss who doesn't talk and goes to bed at 9:30 in the evening?

Mommy still hasn't come in—

I switched off the TV and went to have a shower. When I'm naked under the running water I really feel as if I'm drugged, time becomes sweet and shapeless, I could stand like this for hours. Once Daddy broke down the door because Mommy thought I'd fainted or something. I'd been standing there maybe an hour and I hadn't heard them calling me. Now the water slowly goes cold. I've emptied the tank. Mommy will be mad at me. I dry myself, put on my pajamas and switch off the lights in the house. I go into their bedroom, put out Daddy's bedside lamp and pull the newspaper from underneath him. His beard is big and bushy, there are white hairs in it, glinting in the light from the passage. I feel sorry for him as I watch him sleeping, and it isn't natural for children to pity their parents. I go into my room, take another look at the math homework, perhaps inspiration will come from heaven, but the sky is dark, without a single star, and there's a light rain falling. Since our math teacher was killed in the war and they brought in that kid from the Technion I've lost all interest in the subject. It isn't for me. I can't even begin to understand the questions, never mind the answers.

I pull down the blinds and switch on the transistor, it's that crooner Sarussi. Slowly I pack my school bag, leaving out the math book on purpose. I'll say I forgot it, that'll be the fourth time this month. Next time I'll have to think up a new excuse. At the moment Baby Face doesn't say anything, he blushes as if he's the one who's lying, not me. He's still a bit nervous, scared of getting involved, but he's beginning to gain some confidence–there are disturbing signs. Mommy still hasn't come home. Such a long teachers' meeting. They must be hatching great plots against us.

It's quiet in the house. Deep silence. And then the phone rings. I run to it but Daddy answers before I get to it. Since that man disappeared I've never been able to get to the phone first, Mommy or Daddy always pounce on it, they've even got an extension beside their bed.

I pick up the receiver in the study, and I hear Daddy talking to Tali. She's startled to hear his sleepy voice. I join in the conversation at once. "What happened?" She's forgotten what the history test tomorrow is about. That's what she and Osnat came around for this afternoon, to learn some history, and somehow they forgot all about it. Me too. But I'm not worried about history, maybe it's the only subject that I'm pretty sure about, a talent I got from Mommy; all sorts of pointless and trivial facts stick to me. I tell her the page numbers and she starts to protest, as if I'm the history teacher. "That's far too much, what's the big idea? Can't do all that."

Then she calms down, starts whispering something about Osnat, but a strange whisper rises from the phone, like heavy breathing. Daddy's fallen asleep with the receiver. Tali shrieks. The girl's a total hysteric. I put the phone down, hurry to Daddy, take the receiver from the pillow and put it back in its place. If only I had a fraction of his ability to sleep.

"Go to sleep . . ." he says suddenly.

"Yes, right away . . . Mommy hasn't come in yet."

"She'll be home soon. Don't wait up for her. You'll be worn out in the morning."

Back to my room. I start to sort it out, to turn over the day, scraps, feelings, words and laughter, all are like a thin layer of rubbish that I gather up and throw into the basket. I start tidying up the bed, airing it, I find Osnat's purse and a Tampon in a nylon bag that must be Tali's, she carries it around with her everywhere. At last the room has some sort of shape. I put out the main light, switch on the bedside lamp. I pick up the book on the Age of Enlightenment and get into bed with it, to prepare for the test. The letters go blurred, my head goes heavy, my breathing heavy too, the moment of grace, grab it, wonderful, I'm asleep.

And then Mommy arrives, her footsteps so quick on the stairs sound as if she's returning from an orgy, not a teachers' meeting. The door opens. At once I call out, "Mommy?" She comes into my room, her coat is wet, a stack of papers under her arm, her face gray, she's very tired.

"Asleep yet?"

"Not me."

"What's happened?"

"Nothing."

"Then go to sleep."

"Mommy?"

"Not now . . . you can see I'm exhausted."

Lately that's been her constant refrain. A terrible exhaustion. You can't talk to her, she's always busy, as if she were running the whole world. Now her quick footsteps in the house, moving about in the dim light, taking something out of the fridge, undressing in the bathroom, tries to shower but turns it off immediately. Quickly I switch off the light so she won't come in and shout at me for using all the hot water. She goes into the dark bedroom, Daddy mutters something, she answers, and they are silent.

A quiet married life–

The last light in the house has gone out. I close my eyes, still hoping. Everything is quiet. My mind at rest, my school bag packed, the house locked, the shutters closed. The street is quiet. Everything is right for sleep and maybe I really have slept for a minute or two and then time passes, and I understand that I'm really not asleep, that the little flame burning down inside the soul won't leave me alone. I begin to stir restlessly and the strange wakefulness gets stronger. I turn the pillow over, change position every quarter of an hour, then every few minutes. An hour passes. The luminous hands touch midnight. That's it. You might just as well get up, my dear. Poor Dafi, it's a white night and there's no point in fighting it, get up and wake up.

The path of light on sleepless nights. First the small light beside the bed, then the main light in the bedroom, the light in the passage, and the white light in the kitchen and last of all the light inside the fridge.

Midnight feast. What use is a diet during the day if at night you gobble up four hundred calories on the quiet? A slice of cake, cheese, a piece of chocolate and the last of the milk. Then, heavy and drowsy, I sink down on the sofa in the dark sitting room, facing the big window, opposite me is a mighty ship, a brightly lit palace, under the mountain on the invisible sea. A wonderful vision of people awake. I go to fetch a pillow and a blanket, I come back and the ship has already vanished, she's gone before you even realize she's moving.

Once I managed to get some sleep on the sofa in the sitting room, but not tonight. The upholstery scratches me. I lie there for a quarter of an hour, half an hour. I reach out for the radio. What language is this? Greek? Turkish? Yugoslav? The songs are nice. And the disc jockey has a sexy voice, chattering away. Old women are talking to him on the phone, their voices shaky, they make him laugh, he's in fits of laughter, quite uninhibited. I almost join in. Well, it seems not everyone's asleep. Suddenly he fades out, there's an ad for Coca-Cola, for Fiat, a last song, an announcer's voice, she sounds half asleep, seems to be saying good night. A whistle. The station's closed down. It's already after one o'clock.

The clock creeps on, five hours at least until first light. I sit in the chair, I can't even lie down, I'm close to tears. What about the man who types? I almost forgot him. The man who types at night in the house across the wadi. I go to the bathroom and through the little window that looks out across the wadi I search for his lighted window. There he is, that's him. Three cheers for the man who types at night. Sitting at his desk and working hard, my nocturnal friend.

I discovered him by chance a few weeks ago. A bachelor? Married? I know nothing about him. In the daytime the curtains are drawn, he appears only at night, alone there in the light, working at something, writing without a break. Every time I see him I'm determined to visit the neighborhood across the wadi, find out which is his house and what his name is. I'd phone him and say, "Mr. Typist, I watch you at night from the other side of the wadi. What are you writing? A thesis? A novel? What's it about? You should write about insomnia, a subject that hasn't been enough studied. The insomnia of a fifteen-year-old girl, for example, a student in the sixth grade, who lies awake every fourth night."

Tears in my eyes—

I get dressed in a hurry, changing into a thick pair of woolen trousers, putting a big scarf over the pajama top, taking an overcoat and Daddy's fur hat. I put out the lights in the house and open the front door, holding the key in my clenched fist, going down the dark steps into the street. A little night stroll, I won't go far. A hundred meters down the hill to the roundabout where Yigal was killed and back again. If Mommy and Daddy knew about this going for walks at night they'd kill me. It's two-thirty. I'm in bedroom slippers, my feet are cold and shivering. I walk down a street that's dead and damp, looking at the stars. Suddenly a car with lights full on comes racing down the slope, passes me and stops about five meters from me. I freeze. The car jerks backward. A powerful torch flashes on, searching for me. Maybe they think I'm a little hooker. I'm seized by panic, the key drops into a puddle, someone jumps out of the car, a tall smiling figure. I pick up the key and run, hurrying up the steps, into the house, panting, I lock the door, undress in a hurry, get into bed and pull the blanket over my head.

How will it end, this night life? What's eating me? Everything's fine, after all. Good friends, comforts at home, boys starting to love me in secret, I know, they don't say anything but they can't hide it, those furtive glances in the classroom, those eyes following my legs. Someone from the eighth grade even tried to get off with me. A big boy with a dark face and pimples on his forehead grabbed me once by the school fence and kept me there for a whole hour, and talked. I don't know about what. Crazy. Until I got away from him.

So why is it that I can't sleep, even now at half-past three in the morning after I've gone through the whole program of night activities and I'm exhausted, and tomorrow I've got seven hours in school and a test in history and math that I haven't prepared for.

I throw the blanket off again, getting out of bed heavily and clumsily, putting on the light, stumbling over the furniture, meaning to make a noise. I go to the bathroom for a drink of water, looking bleary-eyed at the man who types. He isn't typing now, he's sitting there resting his head on the typewriter. Even he's asleep. I go to their bedroom, stand in the doorway. They're fast asleep, like little children. I begin to wail softly, "Mommy, Daddy," and then I go away.

At first, when I started having sleepless nights, I used to wake them up, Mommy or Daddy, whichever one I chose, sometimes both of them. Not really knowing why, in despair, wanting them to stop sleeping and to think about me. Mommy used to answer me at once, as if she'd been awake the whole time waiting for me. But it wasn't like that. She'd just finish the sentence and fall straight back to sleep.

It takes time to wake Daddy up. At first he grunts and mumbles nonsense, he just can't understand who is talking to him, you'd think he had a dozen children, I have to shake him to wake him up. But once he wakes up, he's wide awake. He gets out of bed and goes to the bathroom and then he comes into my room, sits down beside me on the chair and starts asking questions. "What's up? What's the trouble? I'll sit with you now until you go to sleep. He covers me up, puts out the light, puts a small pillow behind his head and slowly drops off to sleep. I feel sorry for him. After a quarter of an hour he wakes up and whispers "Are you asleep, Dafi?" I'm wide awake but I don't say anything. Then he waits a little longer and goes back to his bed, stumbling like a sleepwalker.

I don't wake them up anymore. What's the point? Once when I went in to wake him, he said, "Go away, I told you to get out of here." It was in such a clear voice. I was startled and hurt. "What?" I said, but then I realized he was talking in his sleep. I whispered, "Daddy?" but he didn't answer.

Tears. Good morning. The tears again. Under the blanket I cry, out of self-pity, weary, bitter tears. It's four o'clock in the morning. What's going to happen?

I raise the blind, opening the window a little. The night lies cruel and endless on the world. The sky clears a bit, heavy clouds shift slowly, piling up on the horizon. Morning breeze. But I'm getting hotter and hotter. I throw off the blanket completely, undo the buttons of my pajama top, baring my aching chest to the cool wind. I throw the pillow down on the floor and lie there like a corpse, arms outstretched, legs spread-eagled, and slowly, with the smell of the rain as the sky grows pale, I start to doze. Not really asleep, just feeling myself grow lighter. My limbs disappear one by one. Leg, arm, back, the other arm, hair, head, I shrink into a tiny crystal, into my essence. What refuses to disappear is that cruel flame, no bigger than a dry little coin.

And when Mommy wakes me in the morning her voice is vigorous, she draws the blanket from my face (Daddy must have covered me up before he left the house) saying, "Dafi, Dafi, get up now. You'll be late."

I search for my eyes. Where are they? Where did my eyes disappear to? I roll about in a cauldron of lead, searching for my eyes to open them. I hear Mommy in the shower and the hiss of the kettle.

When at last they are wrenched open, cracks in white-hot steel, the window is open to the light, to the high gray winter sky. Between the sky and the earth, hovering like a hit space ship, is the little purple cloud, the hateful cloud that robbed me of my sleep.

Mommy comes in, dressed, her bag in her hand.
"Dafi, are you crazy? How much more can you sleep?"

ASYA

What sort of a trip? A school trip but more than that in a camp near a big mountain city, a mixture of Safad and Jerusalem, a big lake visible in the distance. And a crowd of young people, gray tents full of schoolchildren not only from our school but from others too, former pupils from the senior grades of my old school dressed in khaki, eternal youth training with sticks, standing and beating in long lines. For it seems there was a war and there were soldiers on the hills around us. Midday and I'm walking through this crowded camp looking for the teachers' room, stepping over tent ropes, among thorns and rocks and smoke-blackened camp cauldrons till I see the faces of children from Dafi's class and I see Sarah as well and Yemimah and Vardah in long broad khaki skirts and the janitor and Yochi and the secretaries; the entire staff of the school has moved here complete with typewriters and filing systems. And there's Shwartzy dressed in a khaki British uniform looking young and sunburned and impressive with a stick in his hand.

"Well, what's the matter? The bell is ringing."

Yes, it really is the bell, as if from the sky, like the ringing of cowbells. And I have no books and no notes and I don't know what I'm supposed to be teaching or which classroom I'm supposed to be in. I say to him, "This is a real revolution . . ." and as always he echoes my words:

"A revolution . . . precisely, a revolution . . ." He laughs. "People don't understand that . . . come and see. . . ."

And suddenly he has time to spare despite the bell, leading me to a little cave, a crevice really, and there under a pile of stones is a bundle of page proofs for a book. There the true revolution is written. But the text itself I recognize as the text of his old handbook for the matriculation exams in Bible studies. Simplified explanations of passages set for the exams.

And meanwhile there is silence all around. The great camp is still, students sitting in tight circles and the teachers knitting in the center and someone reading from a book. I feel tense and excited. The word "revolution" will not leave me alone. I want to find my class. I want desperately to teach. Such a pain in my chest from wanting to be with my pupils. I know that they are beside the little acorn tree. I go in search of them but now I can't remember what an acorn tree looks like, I'm staring at the ground searching for acorns. Going down a hill slope to a big wadi. It seems the enemy lines are not far away. Not children patrolling here but grown men, soldiers. Gray-haired men with helmets and firearms. Advance positions among the rocks. The sky clouding over toward evening.

I ask about the little acorn and they show me a little acorn on the ground, light brown. "We are your class." They laugh. I don't mind talking to adults. On the contrary. And the faces are familiar, fathers of children in the seventh and eighth grades who come to parents' meetings. And they are sitting on the ground but not looking at me, their backs are turned and their eyes are on the wadi. They are so uneasy. And I want to say something of general significance about the importance of studying history. Someone stands up and points to the wadi. A suspicious movement there. It's an old man wearing a hat and he's walking down the wadi with such determination, receding in the distance toward the enemy lines. My heart stands still. He looks like my father. Is he here too? Does he belong here or not? Walking erect and excitedly down the rock-strewn ravine. What sort of a revolution is this, I wonder, what are they talking about? It's a war, it's only a war.

VEDUCHA

A stone laid on a white sheet. A big stone. They turn the stone wash the stone feed the stone and the stone urinates slowly. Turn the stone clean the stone water the stone and again the stone urinates. The sun disappears. Darkness. Quiet. A stone weeping why am I only a stone weeping stone. She has no peace begins to stir rolls without sound hovers over a dirty gray floor a great desert there is nothing a giant swamp a dead burned land. Wanders till she stumbles on tight ropes cables in a dark tent touching a spade. A stone halting a stone sinking. A root stirs in the stone, embracing crumbling entwining within. A stone not a stone dying and sprouting a stone sprouting a stone a plant among plants among stillness burrowing in the dust rising from darkness a strong branch and more branches. Strong growth a plant clad in leaves among leaves. A great sun outside. Day. A great old plant on a bed. They turn the plant clean the plant give tea to the plant and the plant still lives.

ADAM

Actually it was we who sent him to the army, he received no orders, nor could he have. Two hours after the alarm was sounded he was already with us. Apparently we didn't hear his knock and instead of waiting he opened the door with a key that Asya had given him. So he's already got a key to the house, I thought, but I said nothing, just watched him as he came into the room, confused, agitated, talking in a loud voice. As if the war that was breaking out was directed personally against him. He asked for explanations, and when it became clear that we had nothing to tell him he seized the radio and began frantically searching for news, for information, going from station to station, French, English, even pausing for a while over a Greek or a Turkish broadcast in his attempt to put some facts together.

He was growing pale, his hands shaking, he couldn't relax.

For a moment I thought, he's going to faint, like that time in the garage.

But there was also the freedom with which he behaved in the house. The way he touched things, going to the kitchen and helping himself to food, raiding the fridge. He knew exactly where to find the big atlas when he wanted to look at a map. And there was the way he behaved toward Asya, interrupting her in midsentence, touching her.

In recent months pictures of that evening have come into my mind again and again. The last pictures of him before his disappearance. The twilight hour, him standing in the middle of the big room, his white shirt straggling out of his black trousers, his thin delicate back a little exposed. The big atlas open in his hands and him standing there explaining something to us, and she, her face flushed with embarrassment and fear, nervously watching, following his movements as if afraid that he'll break something. This is a real lover, I thought, she's really fallen for him.

And in the middle of all this, the war breaking out with such force. The certainty of a new reality overtaking us, there would be no going back. The evening came down quickly and we put no lights on in the house so we could leave the windows open. Every plane flying overhead sent him rushing out to the balcony. Was it one of ours or one of theirs, he had to know. He even gave me a piece of paper and asked me to draw a MiG and a Mirage and a Phantom, and he would take the miserable sketch outside with him, his eyes fixed on the sky.

"What do you mean one of theirs?" growled Dafi, who was sitting all the time in a corner, scowling, not taking her eyes off him.

"But their air force hasn't been destroyed," he explained with a grim smile. "This time it will be a different story."

A defeatist? Not exactly. But there was something strange about him. He was interested only in peculiar practical questions. What was the range of their missiles, could they blow up the ports from sea, would there be food rationing, how soon would he be able to leave the country. He had been abroad for more than ten years, he had no idea what goes on here in wartime. He had old-fashioned, European ideas.

I was patient toward him. I answered his questions, tried to reassure him. Watching Asya, who sat on the edge of the sofa under the lamp, which had an old straw hat for a shade, a stack of exercise books on her lap, a red pencil in her hand, trying to calm herself, I know, but not succeeding, a gray woman with white streaks in her hair, wearing an old dressing gown and flat slippers, her face drawn and the tension filling it with light and power. In love despite herself, against her will, confused by her love, ashamed perhaps. Saying hardly a word, just getting up from time to time and fetching something to eat or drink, coffee for me, fruit juice for Dafi, a sandwich for Gabriel, and all the time the endless stream of garbled information—reports from correspondents, television interviews, foreign stations, news pouring out from all directions but obstinately repeating itself. The phone rings. It's the garage foreman, telling me he's been called up. I myself phone several of the mechanics at home, it turns out they've all been called up, some of them as long ago as yesterday afternoon.

I return from the study and find him sitting in the kitchen. The blinds are closed, he's drinking soup, she sits beside him, watching him.

Establishing himself among us—

He smiles at me apologetically, fear makes him hungry, he admits. He's always been that way, and he scoops up the rest of the soup into his mouth.

It seems that he's decided to spend the night here, if we don't object. He's prepared to sleep on the floor, or on the sofa, wherever we put him. It's just that in his grandmother's house there's no radio, and the house is directly opposite the port, the classic target for a first attack. In the First World War they always attacked the ports first. . . .

He turns to Asya, as if asking for confirmation. But she doesn't respond, she looks anxiously at me.

There was something laughable about him, but something pathetic as well, like a lost child. He will spend the whole war in this house, I thought, without anger but with a kind of excitement, a feeling that anything was possible now. I kept my distance.

Nearly midnight. A phone call from Erlich, the old cashier at the garage. He's in high spirits, informs me that he's been called up. He starts to explain to me where the accounts are kept, what our bank balance is, how much is owed to us, what to do about the wages, you'd think he was going away to fight on the other side of the world. A fussy, tiresome old *yeke,* though not without humor. "It doesn't matter, it doesn't matter," I try to reassure him but he isn't reassured. In financial matters he doesn't trust me. Finally he announces that he'll come into the garage himself tomorrow morning, he's being posted not far away, near the refineries.

"They're drafting the entire population . . . really . . ." I announced. They were sitting in the dark. "And what about you?" I turned to him, not meaning to imply anything.

But he started to mumble, he doesn't know, obviously he has no unit to go to, it's true that at the airport they gave him a certificate to take to an army depot within two weeks, but he had no intention of staying for two weeks, he hadn't known then that his grandmother wasn't dead but had only lost consciousness. He hopes there'll be no problems about leaving the country . . .

"There will be," snapped Dafi. She had been strangely silent since he came into the house. "Why shouldn't there be? They'll think you're a deserter . . ."

And he burst out laughing, in the dark, I couldn't see his face, he laughed and laughed, but when he realized that we weren't laughing he stopped, got up from his chair, lit a cigarette and started pacing about.

"Wait a few more days," said Asya, "maybe it'll all be over."

I say nothing. Something in the tone of her voice fascinates me.

The midnight news. Nothing new. Reports we've already heard. At ten to one the music starts, marching songs. "Let's go to bed," I say, but it's a crazy night, how can anyone sleep? Dafi goes and shuts herself in her room. Asya draws the curtains in the study, switches on the light, makes up a bed for Gabriel. I take the transistor, undress, get into bed with the radio. The window is open. The door to the balcony is open. Radios whisper from all the dark houses. Asya is taking her time, I get up and go out into the passage. I see him standing half naked beside the door to the study and she's talking to him in a whisper, excitedly. She sees me and breaks off at once. A few minutes later she comes into the bedroom, undresses quickly, lies down beside me.

"What's going to happen?" I ask suddenly, referring to the war.

"For the time being he can stay here . . . do you mind?"

I look at her, she closes her eyes. I do the same. The radio whispers beside me, from time to time I wake, turn up the volume, put it to my ear, listen, and go back to sleep. In the house there's a constant movement of bare feet. Dafi is the first to start pacing about, then there's the sound of his footsteps, Asya gets out of bed and I hear her moving about, there are whispers, a mixture of fear and stifled desire. Sweetness mixed with distant blood and fire.

Suddenly weakness overcomes me—

I rise at first light. Asya and Dafi are asleep. From the study comes the sound of lively singing. Another last picture of him, engraved deep in my memory. He's half sitting, half lying, a sheet over his head, the transistor under the sheet playing marching songs. Has he gone mad?

I touched him lightly. He pulled the sheet away, revealing his face, no sign of surprise, but his eyes still closed.

"Are they advancing? Eh? What's happening there?"

He was wearing my old pajama trousers. I stood beside him in the heavy silence that is mine, that I know, that I control, the silence that calms the people around me.

"You'd better go," I said quietly, almost gently.

"Where?"

"To clarify your position . . . you may have problems leaving the country."

Deep anxiety in his eyes. He's cute, I thought, this lover, this poor shaken lover.

"Do you think they really need me . . . haven't they got enough men to be going on with?"

"They won't send you to the front . . . don't worry, but you must get your documentation sorted out, show yourself willing."

"Perhaps in a few more days . . . tomorrow . . ."

"No, go right now. This war may end suddenly and it'll be too late, you'll be in trouble . . ."

"The war may end suddenly?" He was amazed.

"Why not?"

Asya was standing behind me, listening to our conversation, barefooted, her hair in a mess, her nightdress unbuttoned, forgetting herself completely.

I touched his bare shoulder. "Come and have something to eat, and make an early start, there'll be crowds of people there today."

He looked stunned, but he got up at once and dressed, and I went and dressed too. I lent him my shaving kit, he washed and came into the kitchen, I made breakfast for him and for Asya, who was pacing about nervously. The three of us ate in silence, bread and cheese, coffee and more coffee. It was six o'clock. The radio began to broadcast a morning prayer, and then the day's chapter from the Bible.

He was most surprised, listening with close attention, with fear almost. He didn't know that this is how the day's broadcasting starts here.

"Is this because of the war?"

"No, it's like this every day." I smiled. He smiled back at me, sometimes he could be quite charming.

I went outside with him. The blue Morris was parked close behind my car, like a puppy clinging to its mother. I asked him to open the hood, I checked the oil, the fan belt, examined the battery. I told him to start the engine. The sound of the little old engine, vintage 1947, which over the years had developed an odd little whine. The heartbeat of a child, but a healthy child.

"It's O.K." I closed the hood carefully, smiled at him. He suddenly seemed more cheerful. There was a lot of traffic in the street for such an early hour.

"Have you got any money?"

He hesitated for a moment, then said, "Yes, it's O.K."

"If you return today, come here. You can still stay with us. If they detain you for any reason, don't forget us. Keep in touch."

He nodded, absently.

And a last picture engraved on my memory–his cheerful wave through the window as the car drew away down the slope.

I went back to the house. Dafi was sitting in an armchair, dozing, her hair disheveled, Asya was already dressed and sitting in the study marking exam papers. "He'll be back this evening, I'm sure, what could they do with him?" She smiled at me, a relaxed smile, and went on with her work.

He didn't come back that evening. We sat up late waiting for the phone to ring, in vain. For several days his sheets lay folded on the pillow in the study, we were still convinced he'd be coming back. More days passed, not even a postcard. It seemed that they'd called him up after all. The war grew and he was gone.

There was no sign of him at his grandmother's house, evidently he'd passed that way before going to the depot and had closed the shutters. The days of madness pass slowly. The first cease-fire, the second. Peace returning. But he has disappeared, and those last hours with him become so important. Another week goes by. Still no sign. It's as if he's playing games with us. I went to the local office of the army, but there was such a crowd there that I left at once. More days pass. The first reservists are discharged. The first rain falls. I went again to the army office, waited patiently for my turn to speak to the receptionist. She listened to me in astonishment, thinking I'd come to cause trouble. She refused even to write down his name. Without an army number, a military address or the name of his unit she wasn't prepared to start a search.

"Anyway, how do you know that he was drafted?"

How, indeed–

"Who is he? Your cousin? A relative?"

"A friend . . ."

"A friend? Then approach his family. We deal only with relatives."

More days pass. Asya says nothing, but I become deeply uneasy, as if I'm to blame, as if his disappearance is aimed at me. How little we really know about him, we have the name of no other person to whom we can turn. Erlich had a friend in the border police. I passed the name on to him, to find out if he had left the country, perhaps he just went off. Two days later I received an official reply, which was negative. I went to the hospitals to check the lists of casualties. The lists were long and confusing, there was no distinction between wounded and sick. One evening I went to one of the big hospitals, began walking up and down the corridors, glancing into the wards, sometimes wandering among the beds, watching the young men playing chess or eating chocolate. Finding myself sometimes in unexpected places, a big operating room or a dark X-ray room. Going from ward to ward. There was so much confusion in the hospitals in those days that nobody challenged me, in my overalls I passed for a resident technician.

I spent a whole evening checking the floors, combing the place thoroughly. Sometimes I thought that I heard his voice, or saw someone resembling him. In one of the corridors they were carrying a wounded man on a stretcher, he was completely covered with bandages, his face too. He was taken into a room. I hesitated for a moment and then followed. It was a small room, full of instruments, with only one bed. The wounded man, his whole body burned it seemed, lay unconscious, like an ancient wrapped mummy. There was just one small table lamp alight in the room.

Perhaps this is him, I thought, and took up a position by the wall. A nurse came into the room and connected him to a machine.

"Who is he?" I whispered.

She didn't know either, he had been brought in from the Golan just a few hours before. There had been an exchange of fire there at noon.

I asked for permission to remain, I had been looking for some time for a man who had disappeared, perhaps this was him. She gave me a puzzled look, shrugged her shoulders wearily, she had no objection, in the last few weeks they had gotten used to all kinds of lunacy here.

I sat near the door, staring at the shape of the body blurred beneath the sheets, watching the bandaged face. There wasn't a sign, but anything was possible.

I stayed in that darkened room for an hour, perhaps two hours. The hospital grew quieter, from time to time someone opened the door, looked at me and went away again.

Suddenly there was a groan from the injured man. Had he regained consciousness? I stood up, went close to him: "Gabriel?" He turned his bandaged face toward me, trying to locate the voice, but his groans grew louder. It seemed that he was dying in this lonely place, writhing, trying to tear the bandages from his chest. I went out into the corridor and found a nurse. She came, went out again hurriedly and returned with two doctors and another nurse. They put an oxygen mask on his face and tore the bandages from his chest. I was still unable to identify anything. I stood among them, watching. The injured man continued to die. I touched one of the doctors lightly on the shoulder, asked them to remove the bandages from his face. They did as I asked, sure that I was a relative. I saw a fearful sight. His eyes blinked at the light, or at me. It wasn't him. I knew it.

A few minutes later his breathing stopped.

Someone covered his face, pressed my hand and left the room.

I went out, looked through the big windows into the gloom of the day. I still hadn't searched the top floor. I hesitated for a moment, then turned and left the building.

DAFI

We of class six G of Central Carmel High School lost our math teacher in the last war. Who would have guessed that he'd be the one to be killed? We didn't think of him as a great fighter. He was a little man, thin and quiet, starting to go bald. In the winter he always had a huge scarf trailing behind him. He had delicate hands and fingers that were always stained with chalk. Still he was killed. We worried rather about our P.E. teacher, who used to visit the school from time to time during the war in uniform and with his captain's insignia, a real film star, with a real revolver that drove all the boys mad with envy. We thought it was marvelous that even during the war he found the time to come to the school, to reassure us and the lady teachers, who were wild about him. He used to stand in the playground surrounded by children and tell stories. We were really proud of him and we forgot all about our math teacher. On the first day of the war he had ceased to exist for us, and it was days after the cease-fire that Shwartzy suddenly came into the classroom, called us all to our feet and said solemnly, "Children, I have terrible news for you. Our dear friend, your teacher Hayyim Nidbeh, was killed on the Golan on the second day of the war, the twelfth of Tishri. Let us stand in his memory." And we all put on mournful faces and he kept us on our feet for maybe three full minutes, and then he motioned with a weary gesture that we shouldn't stand, glared at us as if we were to blame and went off to call another class to its feet. I can't say that we were all that sorry at once because when a teacher dies it's impossible to be only sorry, but we really were stunned and shocked, because we remembered him living and standing beside the blackboard not so long ago, writing out the exercises with endless patience, explaining the same things a thousand times. Really it was thanks to him that I got a pretty good report last year because he never lost his temper but went over the same material again and again. For me someone only has to raise his voice or speak fast when explaining something in math to me and I go completely stupid, I can't even add two and two. He used to make me relax, which was boring, it's true, deadly boring. Sometimes we actually went to sleep during his lessons, but in the middle of all this drowsiness, in the cloud of chalk dust flying around the blackboard, the formulas used to penetrate.

And now he was himself a flying cloud—

Naturally, Shwartzy used his death for educational purposes. He forced us to write essays about him, to be put into a book which was presented to his wife at a memorial ceremony that he organized one evening. The students that he'd taught in the fifth and sixth grades sat in the back rows, in the middle the seats were left empty and in the front rows sat all the teachers and his family and friends, even the gym teacher came especially, still in his uniform and with his revolver, although the fighting had ended long ago. And I sat on the stage where I recited, with great feeling and by heart, the poems that are usual on these occasions, and between the poems Shwartzy preached a fawning and flowery sermon, talking about him as if he was some really extraordinary personage that he'd secretly admired.

And then they all went and stood beside a bronze plaque that had been put up by the entrance to the Physics Department. And there, too, somebody said a few words. But those we didn't hear because we slipped away down the back steps.

Shwartzy was a quick worker. In Israel they hadn't yet finished counting the dead, and he'd already got the memorials out of the way.

Meanwhile we not only forgot the math teacher, we forgot the math as well, because for two months we studied Bible instead of math. We had eight hours of extra Bible studies every week and we went at such a pace that we did ten out of the twelve Prophets. The joke went around that there'd be nothing left of the Bible for us to study in the seventh and eighth grades, and we'd have to study the New Testament.

At last the replacement arrived. A young man, a student from the Technion, a bit fat, very nervous, a doubtful genius who decided to try the new math on us. Right away I felt that what little I knew was fading fast because of him.

At first we tried to annoy him, at least until he came to know our names. I dubbed him Baby Face and everybody called him that because he really was a baby face, he hardly shaved at all. But he soon made a record of names and he used to put down marks all the time. We weren't much impressed by this record, because usually the teachers themselves get tired of this stupid system long before they broke us. But for some reason he picked on me from the first moment. For almost every second lesson he called me up to the blackboard, and when I didn't know the answers he kept me there and went on being cruel to me. I wasn't particularly bothered, I have no great pretensions in math, but suddenly he began being rude to me as well. He took my name right at the start but he didn't seem to know my surname and he certainly didn't realize that my mother taught history in the senior classes of the same school. Not that I expect any special treatment but I just like it to be known. Just that it be known. But he was determined not to grasp it, although I tried various hints at it.

Only toward the end of the year, when we were really at war with each other, when I said to him in front of the whole class "It's a pity you weren't killed instead of the last teacher" and he went running to the headmaster, only then did he grasp the fact, and then it was too late. Both for him, and for me.

ADAM

Where did I not wander in my quiet persistent search for him. One morning I even went to the Bureau of Missing Army Personnel. It was a bright morning, a spring-like winter's day. Something about the garage was getting on my nerves. All those Arab workers sitting under the shade for their breakfast with their flat loaves of bread, joking, singing to the Arab music from the car radios. And in the morning paper I found an announcement about the bureau, how it functioned, the means at its disposal, its achievements. And before long I was there, sitting in the waiting room beside a silent old couple. I thought, it'll take only a few minutes, to give his name, just to try.

This was after all the great confusion, the return of the prisoners, the notorious scandals. Lessons had been learned and a whole new machinery set up. Three large offices in a secluded suburb of Tel Aviv. Most of the clerks were officers. There was a first-aid room with a doctor and nurses. There were telephones on the desks and outside on the square there were at least a dozen army vehicles. I hadn't waited long when an officer led me into a room that was furnished not like an office but like a room in a private house. Behind the desk sat a very attractive woman, a charming major. Beside her sat a young lieutenant. The entire team listened attentively to my story.

And my story was a little odd.

Of course, I couldn't tell them that I was looking for my wife's lover. I said, "A friend."

"A friend?" They were a bit surprised, but it was as if it made it easier for them. "Just a friend?"

"A friend. A good friend."

They didn't ask me what the hell I was doing looking for a friend here. By what right. The second lieutenant took out a fresh form and handed it to the major, there were already a number of forms there ready for use. Efficiency and sympathy and much patience.

I gave his name and address, told them how he'd come to Israel a few months ago, I mentioned the problem of the legacy and the grandmother lying in a coma in the hospital. They wrote down every word. But only ten lines were filled by the round, feminine handwriting. What more could I tell them, I had no photograph, I didn't know his army number, nor his passport number, nor his father's name, and of course I had no idea to which unit he'd been sent. I said again, "Perhaps he didn't get to the front, perhaps he wasn't even called up. It was we, actually, who sent him to the army. But since the second day of the war he's disappeared. Can it be coincidence? Perhaps I'm wasting your time."

"Oh no," they protested. "We must investigate."

The young officer was sent away with the details to the computer building, and the other two took out a special form for recording physical details and characteristics. Color of hair, height, weight, color of eyes, distinguishing marks. I began to describe him. Of course I'd never seen him naked. I was only a friend. I said something about his smile, his gestures, his manner of speech.

They listened. The major's hair fell over her face, she was always brushing it away from her eyes with a delicate movement, she was radiant, very beautiful. Talking in a quiet voice, little computer cards in her hands, asking me strange questions. Did he have a scar on his right cheek perhaps, or a gold tooth in his lower jaw? Conferring in a whisper with the lieutenant, who supplied her with more computer cards. Suddenly I understood, they had particulars of unidentified corpses, they wanted to give me a corpse in his place.

But nothing fit.

I wanted to leave. It seemed madness to search for him here. But the process had been started, and there was no way of stopping it. Meanwhile the officer who had been sent to the computer returned with a long list of all the Arditis recorded by the computer as having served in the army in recent years. There was only one Gabriel Arditi, fifty-one years old, a citizen of Dimona, discharged from the army five years ago for health reasons.

Obviously they didn't think he was the man I was looking for, but if I wanted to see him a vehicle and a driver would be immediately at my disposal to take me to Dimona.

I must get out of here–

Perhaps I should make inquiries at the hospital, perhaps his grandmother could tell me something.

They wouldn't let me go.

Heavy rain falling outside. The brightness of the morning turned to heavy gloom. I sat sprawled in a comfortable armchair, three girl-officers listening to me attentively. Every word I said, every thought, was taken and written down. The empty file was not so empty now.

Voices rose from the next room. A man's voice shook the partition between us. He was protesting, in a clear voice, with stubborn logic. He couldn't accept the explanation, of course he had no illusions, but he knew for a fact that his son was never in sector (he gave a long number) nor in tank number (another number with a lot of figures). He repeated the numbers with speed, it seemed he'd been studying them for weeks, he knew them by heart. He'd spoken to his friends, he'd spoken to the officers, he had no illusions, he only wanted another sector and another tank number, that was all he wanted to know. He broke down and wept, and slowly, in the silence, embarrassed voices began to console him.

Listening in silence in the next room, we exchanged glances. I stood up, determined to leave, but I was asked to fill out another half page with my own personal details, leaving an address, taking a document bearing the address of the bureau, the phone number, the major's name, promising to get in touch if I heard anything new.

The strange thing is that I did visit the bureau again, not once but twice. When I was in Tel Aviv to buy spare parts I passed that way.

The bureau had shrunk in the meantime. Two of the shacks had been taken over for other purposes and the vehicles had gone, but the girl-officers were still there. The second lieutenant had become a lieutenant, the lieutenant was a captain and the major was in civilian clothes and several months pregnant. She was even more beautiful than before. She had cut her hair and what I saw of her soft bare neck was a most alluring sight. They smiled at me and took out the file, to which nothing much had been added except the name of another Arditi who'd come to light. We discussed him briefly, to make sure that he wasn't the man we were looking for. Then they offered me one or two unidentified corpses, but forcefully I turned them down.

At the beginning of spring I passed that way again. The bureau had gone, there was just one room left in a wing that was now used as a recruiting center. The major had given birth and been discharged, the captain had gone too, there was just the lieutenant left with the files. She was reading a magazine. She remembered me at once.

"Still looking for him?"

"Sometimes . . ."

I sat down. We chatted a little about her work. She too was due to be discharged in a few days. Before I left she took out the familiar file, just as a formality, and we were both amazed to find a new document in it, an armory receipt for a bazooka and two containers of bombs, signed by Gabriel Arditi on the seventh of October.

She herself didn't know how this document had gotten there. It was possible that the clerk had filed it in her absence.

But I shuddered suddenly. If, then, he had gone somewhere after all, if he had been issued a bazooka and ammunition, if all this was so, was it possible then that he had been killed?

But this was another blind alley. Where could I go with this document? The lieutenant had already been discharged, the bureau was closed, the files had been transferred to the archives, and I, searching for him again on the road, said not a word to Asya.

ASYA

I was going around and locking door after door, pulling down the blinds. Adam was in the bathroom, screwing a large bolt on the door to the balcony. It was dark in this house to which two rooms from our previous home had been added, furniture that we had sold or thrown away had come back to us. We switched on the lights. A fine clear day outside, blue sky, and through the cracks in the blinds I saw a double view, the views from both our houses, the open sea, the wadi, the harbor with its cranes, and the houses of the lower city. I was uneasy, waiting for Dafi to come home from school. There was a wave of murders in the city. See, there on the table is a newspaper, banner headlines, underlined for emphasis, printed in an antiquated script. A wave of murders in the city, a gang of murderers settling private scores, pursuing one another. And even law-abiding citizens who are not involved and have nothing to fear must take precautions, lock their houses. The people have imposed a curfew upon themselves, of their own free will. And I am waiting for Dafi, furious with myself that on a day like this we sent her to school, on a day when murderers are roaming the streets, settling their private feuds in our neighborhood. I look out into the street, it's empty, no man, no child. But there she is, at last, walking alone in the empty sun-drenched street, the satchel slung over her shoulder, wearing the yellow uniform of the primary school, and she really does look smaller, as if she's shrunk, and now she's standing at the street corner with a man, a short man with reddish hair. She's talking to him intimately, calmly, smiling, without fear. And again I fall into a dreadful panic, I want to shout but I hold back. The man looks dangerous to me, though there's nothing special about his appearance. He's wearing a broad summer suit. I run to another window to get a better view of them and they've disappeared, both of them. But I hear her footsteps, she comes into the house. Running to her, bending over her, she really has grown smaller, unfastening the broad straps of her satchel, giving her a drink, taking her to her room, undressing her, putting her in her pajamas, treating her like a little child. She protests, "I can't sleep." "Just for a few minutes," I plead with her, putting her to bed, covering her up, and she sleeps. I feel relieved, I close the door of her room, go out into the hallway and see Adam standing looking at the front door, which has been left open. Dafi forgot to close the door after her. Suddenly I understand. He has come in after her, that man, he has gotten inside, he is here. I don't see him, but I know. He is here. Adam knows it too and he starts searching for him. I run back to Dafi's room, she's fast asleep, breathing deeply. Again she seems to me very young, seven years old perhaps, and growing smaller, the bed with its big blanket is half empty. I hear Adam's footsteps in the hallway. "It's all over," he whispers, smiling.

"What is?"

And I follow him, stumbling, to the other, extra rooms, the rooms of the old house, the old nursery, the toys, the cars, the big teddy bear on the blue dresser, and under the old cradle with its peeling paint, with its bird pictures and broken beads, someone is lying, a body under a blanket. The head is visible. I recognize the reddish hair cropped short on the thick neck. A white hair here and there. Adam has killed him, as you kill a bug. For this was one of the murderers roaming the streets. Adam identified him at once. Killed him with a single blow, there is not a sign on his body. For a moment I feel a stirring of pity for the man who lies there, dead. Why? Who asked Adam to get involved? Without asking questions, without consulting me, why did he kill him in such haste, how did he do it? And now we too have joined in the chain of murders. Oh God what has he done? The great distress, my heart stops beating. Who asked him to do it? A fearful mistake, our lives are ruined. How shall we explain it, justify it, we shall never be free of the weight of that heavy corpse. What an idiot you are, I want to shout as I look at him, the smile has faded from his face, he's become serious, horrified, beginning to grasp what he has done. Trying to hide the big screwdriver among the toys. Oh what have you done to us.

DAFI

Does she dream sometimes? Does she allow herself to waste good sleeping and resting time just on some silly, meaningless dream?

At night I quietly go into their bedroom, to look at the sleepers. My parents! My good bearers! Daddy lies on his back, his beard spread on the pillow, his hand stretched out feebly over the edge of the bed, the fist lightly clenched. And Mommy with her back to him, curled up like a fetus, her face pressed into the pillow, as if she's hiding from something.

Is she dreaming? What does she dream about? Not about me, that's for sure, such a busy woman, laden with obligations.

Mommy isn't here, I've begun to realize over the last year, Mommy isn't here even when she's at home, and if you really want a quiet, heart-to-heart conversation with her, you have to book a week in advance. Between 3:00 and 3:45 in the afternoon or between 8:10 and 8:42 in the evening. Mommy is chasing time.

She works full-time in my school, teaching history in the upper grades, preparing three senior classes for the matriculation exam. On her worktable there are always piles of homework and test papers. All day she's correcting papers. I don't envy her pupils. She gets a real kick out of writing "Not good enough" in red pencil at eleven o'clock at night.

But she doesn't spare herself either, she too is always writing tests and projects. She hasn't finished studying yet, and she never intends to finish. She's always running off to the university, to seminars, public lectures, teachers' conventions. She's registered for a doctorate, writing essays, being tested.

A woman forty-five years old, with a bird's face, sharp but delicate, lovely eyes. No make-up on principle, there are streaks of gray in her tied-back hair, but she won't dye it on principle. She likes clothes that are out of fashion, broad and absurdly long skirts, dark woolen dresses with a monastic look about them, flat-heeled shoes. With her lovely long legs she could make herself look really attractive, but she's not interested in distracting people from their important business just for the pleasure of looking at her. That's a principle too.

We live here according to a number of principles.

For example, not to employ a maid, because it isn't reasonable that outsiders should clean our house and cook our meals, even in return for wages. So Mommy does the housework as well, energetically and aggressively.

Is there any house where the floor is washed at nine o'clock in the evening? Yes, ours. Daddy and I are sitting in front of the TV relaxing in armchairs and enjoying this bald man Kojak after the depressing news and she suddenly appears, wearing an apron, with a rag and a bucket, and orders us to lift up our feet so she can wash the floor beneath us. Working quietly but with a sort of restrained ferocity, not asking for help and not getting it either, bending down to scrub the floor.

"A revolutionary woman," Daddy once said with a laugh, and I laughed too, even if I wasn't sure exactly what he meant.

When she cooks it's for several days at a time. At ten o'clock at night she comes home from a teachers' meeting, goes into the kitchen, takes a big saucepan, slices up two chickens and cooks them.

Two weeks' food for the family. Lucky for her she's only got one daughter who doesn't much like the food she cooks.

In the morning, when I go into the kitchen for breakfast, I have to pick my way between test papers of pupils of the eighth grade (which of course I'm forbidden to touch or to look at) and headless fish dipped in flour and stuffed with onion, ready to be fried for supper. Such efficiency.

No wonder she suddenly stops working and falls fast asleep at eight o'clock, most of all she likes to sleep in front of the TV screen. In the armchair, all curled up. On the TV there's a gun fight and she sleeps peacefully for an hour, two hours. Until Daddy wakes her, to get up and go to bed. She opens her eyes, rouses herself a bit and goes to correct exam papers. Sometimes we try to help her with the housework, even I make an effort, but by the time I've picked up a cup, or washed a spoon, the work's all done. We simply have different rhythms, the two of us.

So in principle I'm on his side, even though there's something a bit reserved and primitive about him. He hardly ever talks. Wanders about in overalls and with dirty hands. At least that beard of his is something remarkable, growing wild, making him look like an ancient prophet or an artist. Something special, not like all the others, not like a laborer anyway. When I was at the primary school I was ashamed because he didn't look like all the others. When they asked me "What does your Daddy do?" I used to say innocently "Daddy works in a garage," and at once I felt that they were a bit disappointed. Then I started saying "My Daddy has a factory." "What kind of a factory?" they'd ask. "A garage" I said and then they'd explain that a garage isn't a factory. Then I used to say "My Daddy has a big garage" because it really was a very big garage. Once during vacation I went down there with Tali and Osnat and they were amazed to see all the cars standing there, and the dozens of workers rushing about. A hive of activity.

But then I thought, oh, to hell with it, why should I need to apologize, why add "big," as if I'm defending him. And I used to say simply "Daddy has a garage," and when somebody particularly irritated me with this question I used to say "My Daddy is a garage hand" and look him full in the eyes, enjoying his astonishment. Because in our class most of the pupils' parents are professors at the Technion or the university, architects, scientists, executives in major companies, army officers.

And what's wrong with a garage? Not only are we never without a car, we're the only family with two cars, some of the children in the class don't even have one car at home. And Daddy has a lot of money too, though you don't see much evidence of it at home. This is something that I've realized in the last few months. I don't think even Mommy realizes how much money Daddy's got. For all her education it seems there are some things that just aren't clear to her.

A strange couple. I wonder why they ever got together. What do they want? I don't remember ever seeing them embracing or kissing. They hardly talk to each other.

But they don't quarrel either–

Like two strangers–

Is this what they call love?

Again and again I used to ask them, together and separately, how it was that they met, and it was always the same story from both of them. They were in the same class at school for many years. But surely that's no reason to stay joined until death, to have children.

In their school they weren't particularly friendly. Daddy finished studying in the sixth grade, as he makes a point of reminding me whenever I ask him for help with my homework. Mommy of course went on studying. After a few years they met again and got married.

As if someone forced them–

When do they make love, for example, if they make love at all?

On this side of the wall I don't hear so much as a whisper–

And at night I walk around the house a little–

Strange thoughts, maybe, sad thoughts.

Sometimes I'm terrified they might split up and leave me all alone, like Tali, whose father disappeared years ago, leaving her with her mother, who can't stand her.

I hear their breathing. Daddy moans softly. At the window faint signs of dawn. Accustomed to the darkness, my eyes pick out every detail. My legs feel weak. Sometimes I wish I could go and crawl in between them under the blanket, like when I was a child.

But it's no longer possible–

The faint, early chirping of an early bird in the wadi–

PART TWO

ADAM

How to describe her? Where do I start? Simple, the color of her eyes, her hair, her style of dress, her habits, her manner of speech, her feet. Where do I start? My wife. So familiar, not only from twenty-five years of marriage but also from the years before that, childhood, youth, from the days that I remember in the first class of the little school near the harbor, the green and stuffy huts with their smell of milk and rotten bananas, the red-painted swings, the big sand pit, a derelict car with a giant steering wheel, the broken fence. Days of endless summer even in winter. Like in a blurred picture, no distinction between me and the world around me. She is there among the children, sometimes I have to search for her, there are times when she disappears and then returns, a thin girl with plaits sitting in front of me or behind me or beside me and sucking her thumb.

Until now, when I see her engrossed in reading or writing with her clenched fist to her mouth and the thumb moves restlessly with a slow movement, a relic of the days when she used to suck her thumb. She didn't believe it when I told her once that I remembered her sucking her thumb.

"But I don't remember you at all from that time."

"I was in the class the whole time."

The strange and funny stories about the many years when we sat as children in the same class, told mainly to satisfy the curiosity of Dafi, who sometimes asks us how we met, why we became involved, what our feelings were. She thinks it strange that we sat for so many years in the same class and didn't know that in the end we would marry.

None of the mystery of a woman who springs suddenly out of the darkness and you remember the first time that you saw her, the first words that you exchanged. Asya was beside me always, like the trees in the yard, like the sea that was visible from the windows.

In the seventh or eighth grade when the boys began to fall in love, I fell in love too, not with her but with the two or three girls that everyone fell in love with. Falling in love not because you wanted to be in love but to be freed of some burden, as if it was a duty. Falling in love so as to be free for the really important things—trips, games, the events going on outside. The Second World War was at its height and there was a great army all around us, soldiers, artillery, battleships—all this demanded deep concentration. She wasn't among those chosen for love. A quiet girl, not pretty, a serious and distinguished pupil whose homework it was sometimes necessary to copy. In the morning before school they used to wait for her, to have a look at her exercise books, which she handed over without protest but with such a scowl, watching them copy from her all the good ideas and the correct answers, sometimes having to explain impatiently what they meant. I didn't copy from her, I copied from those who copied from her. Even then, at the end of primary school, my work was beginning to deteriorate, not because I was incompetent but because at home they were already telling me that I shouldn't continue with my studies, that I'd have to work with my father in the garage. Already in the afternoons I was required to come and help him, to fetch tools, wash cars, change wheels. What point was there in making an effort in studies that were beginning to seem more and more irrelevant to whatever was real.

But I completed the fifth grade nevertheless. It was then that the children began to pair off in the classroom but it didn't worry me that I was in love with somebody who already had a boy friend. On the contrary, it was a relief, it freed me from the obligation to court her, to demean myself with excessive compliments during recess. I could love from a distance without any effort, only at times when the friendship was dissolved and the girl became open to new proposals did I become uneasy, feverish almost, as if it was now my duty to try, but I used to hesitate, delay, wait, maybe someone else . . .

It was then that an immigrant joined the class, one of the children from Teheran, an orphan, his name was Yitzhak. The teachers gave Asya the task of making him feel at home, helping him with his studies, with his homework. He fell in love with her immediately, openly, always following her, admiring her. For us there was something perplexing about so obvious a display of love, in an old-fashioned, European style. She treated him with patience, rumor said that she "pitied" him, but she sure devoted a lot of attention to him. Standing with him during recess and having long conversations with him. I had no contact with her but in the class there was a feeling that this love gave her strength, improved her position. I remember that during the girls' gym class we boys used to sit on the fence and watch them playing volley ball. We were already looking at them differently, studying them closely, constantly. It was then that I noticed for the first time that her legs were long and attractive, but she didn't yet wear a bra, and we were interested only in breasts, they were what mattered most, sometimes in class we used to move our chairs around to catch a glimpse through an open sleeve of this desired piece of flesh.

At the end of the fifth grade we went to a camp in the mountains of Galilee, with the teachers and the headmaster. It was a big camp and children from all the fifth grade classes in the city were there. The official purpose was to familiarize us with nature, with our surroundings, but they took the opportunity to bother us with some premilitary training. Most important was sentry duty at night. And since the girls insisted on standing guard too, it was decided that we should guard in pairs, and this understandably caused some excitement, particularly regarding the choice of partners. In the evening of the second day I saw that I'd been selected to go on guard with her, and then that boy, the immigrant, came to me and asked me to change places with him. Naturally I agreed at once. In the evening she came to me to show me her sleeping place in the tent. She asked me to wake her because she was a heavy sleeper and she might not be up when it was time to stand guard. I told her straightaway that I wasn't on guard duty with her, that Yitzhak had asked me to change.

She blushed, angry.

"What do you mean? Did you agree?"

I mumbled, "I thought you'd want . . ."

"Why should you have to think for me? If you don't want to go on guard with me that's a different matter."

There was something bold in her manner of speech, something not quite fitting this thin, quiet girl. It seemed to me that until then I'd never spoken to her as an individual, face to face. I was confused, scared of getting involved in the love affairs of this orphan immigrant.

"But he asked . . ." I added hesitantly.

"Tell him I'm not his wife yet."

I laughed. Something in her proud and resolute stand appealed to me.

I told him. He looked miserable. I despised him for this open and self-torturing love.

At 1 A.M. they woke me to go on duty. I went outside the tent and waited for her. About ten minutes passed and she didn't come. I went into the girls' tent to wake her. Perhaps it was at that moment that the idea of falling in love with her first occurred to me. In the dark tent, among the girls lying huddled together, the smell of their femininity mingled with a light odor of perfume, touching the girl who lay there curled up, lifting away the blanket, seeing in the moonlight her legs in short trousers, the hair scattered about her, bending down to touch her face, perhaps now for the first time touching her intentionally, freely and simply, shaking her, whispering her name. Then it occurred to me that she was dreaming, that I was waking her from a dream. At last she opened her eyes and smiled at me. Then she switched on a big army flashlight that lay beside her. I stood there as if hypnotized, watching her put on trousers and a sweater, and she asked me if it was cold outside. The girls around me began to stir, mumbling. Someone suddenly woke up and saw me. "Who's that?" she cried and I hurried out of the tent. A few seconds later Asya came out, wearing an army combat smock that impressed me. She had all kinds of genuine army equipment that her father had apparently given her. I had a vague idea that her father had something to do with the authorities, with matters of security. We began walking about among the big tents, now and then hitting at the grass and the bushes with the hard smooth sticks that they'd given us. Eventually we sat down on a rock at the edge of the camp, looking down into a dark wadi, she with the big army flashlight in her hand, from time to time shining it down into the wadi, playing with the strong beam of light.

We fell immediately into conversation, as if we'd planned it from the beginning. I was watching her all the time, studying her, trying to decide if it was worthwhile falling in love with her and beginning to fall in love with her even as I thought about it. She talked about the teachers, about teaching methods, asked my opinion. She had firm, clear, very critical ideas. About the system of teaching, against the material taught and especially against the teachers themselves. I was surprised, because in class she was very quiet and obedient, and very respectful toward the teachers. I had no idea that deep down in her heart she despised them. I told her that I was leaving the school, that I was starting to work with my father in the garage, and she responded to the idea with enthusiasm, jealous that I was going out into the world where great changes were taking place, when now, with the end of the war, total revolution was imminent. If only she could, she would leave school as well.

There was something obscure about her, ideas that were confused but daring, something strange to me, very intellectual, almost a chatterbox, but very interesting. We talked and talked and half of the next watch had gone by when suddenly we were attacked by the gym teacher who was in charge of the guard. He snatched the flashlight from her hand and threw it to the ground, told us to shut up, to lie on the ground, to move farther apart and to keep watch quietly for the enemy.

When he had gone and we were still lying on the ground, a little amused and a little annoyed, I said to her, "Did I wake you from a dream?" and she was amazed. "How did you know?" She insisted, she was determined to know how in the darkness of the tent I could tell that she was dreaming. And then she told me her dream, something about her father.

The watch was over and we returned to our separate tents. I took her flashlight to try and repair it. The next day, during the training and the excursions, we didn't exchange a word. I still have time to decide whether to fall in love with her, I thought. In the afternoon I gave her the mended flashlight. She thanked me, touched my hand lightly, intentionally, wanting to start a conversation, but I slipped away, uneasy, still hesitant, afraid of making a fool of myself.

That evening Yitzhak disappeared. Apparently he'd been gone since midday, but it was only in the evening that he was missed. All the training and the activities were suspended and all of us, including the children from the other schools, went out to search for him. Walking over the hills in long lines, searching every bush and every crevice and all the time calling his name. The headmaster supervised the search, shouting excitedly, walking among us pale and desperate. Suddenly she was in the center. They all looked at her accusingly, curiously. Even the children from the other schools came to see her, they all knew by now the reason for the disappearance. Again and again she was called to the headmaster to give more information about him. He stood and shouted at her as if she were to blame for not returning Yitzhak's love.

In the morning two British policemen arrived with a dog. They were very much amused, inspecting the camp and taking advantage of the opportunity to search for weapons. After a few minutes he was found. He'd simply hidden in a little cave about a hundred meters from the camp. The dog flushed him out. He emerged weeping bitterly, shouting in his foreign accent, "Don't kill me." Down on his knees before the headmaster and before her. It was impossible even to scold him, he was so miserable. She was told to sit with him, to comfort him. I couldn't get close to her now, until camp was over.

But it seems that his hopeless love infected me. In the holidays I thought about her constantly, walking by her house in the evenings, searching for some contact. I was already working full-time in the garage, I didn't register for the new school year. My father was growing weaker, already there were screws that he was unable to turn. He used to sit on a chair beside the car and tell me what to do. Now and then when I had time to spare I would go to the school, just as I was, in my dirty overalls, sit on the fence and wait for recess, to see my friends, to try to keep in touch with them. Searching for her, sometimes seeing her suddenly, hardly managing to hold a proper conversation with her at all, especially as Yitzhak was still at her heels and she was cautious because of him. It seemed that in spite of everything they were friends. After a while I stopped going to the school, I broke off, the work in the garage kept me more and more busy. My friends suddenly seemed childish to me, with their books and their note pads and their little stories about the teachers.

In the middle of the sixth grade she disappeared. Her family moved to Tel Aviv. Her father's name sometimes appeared in the papers as one of the leaders behind the scenes, a security chief. The months leading up to the establishment of the state were upon us, there was turmoil in the land. I tried to study in the evenings, to prepare at least superficially for the matriculation exam, but I gave it up.

At the beginning of the War of Independence my father died and I joined the army as a mechanic, maintaining armored vehicles. It was years since I'd seen her.

It wasn't until after the war that we met again, at a school reunion. It was impossible to invite only those who had completed their schooling, many like me had left halfway through, had taken up employment, had joined the army or the Palmach. Some had fallen in the war.

It was supposed to be a big occasion. An assembly, parties, speeches, an all-night barbecue. At first I didn't recognize the girl who approached me. In the years since we'd last met I'd grown taller, and she suddenly seemed small to me.

"How's the revolution?" I asked with a smile.

She was surprised, then she smiled.

"It'll come . . . it'll come."

And from that moment she didn't leave me. We both felt a bit out of place there. We'd both left the school in the sixth grade. Many of the people there were strangers to us. Some of them were married and had brought wives and husbands with them. We sat apart from the others at the back of the hall and listened to the long speeches, she was whispering in my ear all the time, telling me about herself, about her studies in the teachers' seminary. When we stood up to remember the dead, listening with bowed heads to the long list, and Yitzhak's name was mentioned, I glanced at her. She stood there, her head bowed, not batting an eyelid. I didn't know what to do, she stayed at my side all evening, going with me from place to place, unwilling to enter into long conversation with other friends. Her father's name was in the news at the time, something to do with some obscure episode, a hasty decision taken with unpleasant consequences. Her father had been dismissed from office and there had been demands that he be brought to trial, but in the end they let him alone on account of his past service.

Perhaps this was the reason for her oversensitivity with the others, for her decision to leave in the middle of the party and return home to Tel Aviv. She asked me to accompany her to the bus station and I took her there in my car, my father's old Morris, the back seat full of tools, automobile parts, oil cans. We stood and waited for a bus in the deserted bus station in the lower city. She grew closer and closer to me, talking about herself, asking me about my work. She remembered the night watch that we'd shared, and what I'd said then. The bus was late in coming. I decided to drive her to her home in Tel Aviv. We arrived there after midnight. A small, modest house with a neglected garden in south Tel Aviv. She insisted that I spend the night there. I agreed, I was a little curious to see her father. It was dark inside the house, huge piles of newspapers lay in every corner. Her father came out to meet us, a hairy man, older and smaller than he looked in the newspaper photographs, with a hard face. She told him a little about me, he nodded distractedly and disappeared into another room. I thought that we'd sit for a while and continue our conversation, but she made up a bed for me on the sofa in the living room, lent me some of her father's old pajamas and left me. At first I had difficulty getting to sleep, still thrown by the sharp transition from the noise of the party, the speeches, the meetings with old friends to this dark and quiet house among the sparse orchards of Tel Aviv. But finally I slept. At three in the morning I heard somebody moving about beside my bed. It was her father, in khaki trousers and a torn pajama top. He was bending over the radio and fiddling with it, going from station to station, the B.B.C., broadcasts in Russian,

Hungarian, Rumanian, languages that I couldn't even identify. All the stations of the awakening east. Listening for a while and then passing on to another station, his eyes tightly closed, perhaps it was a habit that he couldn't shake off from the period when he was in charge of the Ministry of Information, or perhaps he was searching for something affecting him, some commentary on his case from a foreign and distant source. He ignored me, as if I didn't exist. He didn't care that he'd roused me from sleep, that I was exhausted, sitting beside him in silence, listening with him.

At last he switched off the radio. His face looked serious, severe. "Do you study in a seminary too?"

I told him what I did.

"What is your father's name?"

I told him.

He knew at once that he had died about a year and a half before, even though we hadn't published an obituary in the newspapers because of the war. He added some dry, precise details about my father.

"Did you know him personally?" I was amazed.

No, they had never met, but he knew all about him, as if he had a personal file in front of him.

And he left me to myself—

I couldn't sleep anymore. At five in the morning I got up, folded the sheets, I had to return to Haifa to open the garage at seven. It was only a few months since I'd reopened the garage, which had been closed during the war. Competition was tough at the time and one had to work very hard not to lose customers.

I went outside. A hazy summer morning. I strolled about the neglected garden, hungry, drowsy after my uncomfortable night, watching the newspaper delivery boys arriving one after another and throwing at the doorstep all the morning papers, in all the languages. I wanted to leave, but not without saying good-by, and I didn't know which was her room. In the end I tapped lightly on one of the windows.

It wasn't long before she came out to me, her hair combed, wearing a light morning dress, her face radiant. She came close to me and said seriously, almost solemnly, "I dreamed about you." And she described a dream that was clear, orderly, logical, almost impossibly so. A dream that could be taken to mean that she was telling me directly —"I am willing to marry you."

ASYA

The old cabin of the movement, but a little larger. The time early evening, winter twilight. They seemed to be preparing for a play, some of them were wandering about in patchwork costumes, straw hats, coats made from blankets, rope belts. Someone paced about with make-up on his face. One of the young men was writing the music for the play, and the girls crowded around him as he sat on the floor in an oriental position, bent over an exercise book, writing the words at great speed. They hummed a tune and he wrote words that were not just words, but words in which music was hidden. From the corner where I stood I could see above the heads of the girls the melodious words that were written at such haste. But they were still waiting for somebody to arrive. The star? The producer? Somebody important, somebody precious, without whom the play could not go ahead. Listen, the sound of a train approaching, stopping for a moment and continuing on its way. We rushed outside to meet him. And he really had arrived. The train that had stopped for a moment and disappeared again, leaving only the shining tracks behind it, had put down a big hospital bed on the platform. Somebody was lying in it. We crowded around him, he was sick, not actually sick, exhausted rather. Something had really exhausted him. Postnatal exhaustion, he had sired sons, but he was happy as well, proud of himself, a weak smile of triumph on his pale face, a combination of Zaki and somebody else, lying there in khaki clothes, under an army blanket.

And the group began to fuss around him, carrying the bed into the cabin, happy all, a collective happiness, because the babies were there too, like a pile of sacks. Piled to one side, quiet and smiling. They were little people already, not newborn infants, they had hair and teeth, and were dressed in little romper suits with buttons and buckles. They put them up on a wooden stage, under a baggage canopy, and there was general confusion and happiness, and only this solitary, independent childbearer was perplexed, sad even. And I stood to one side, feeling deserted. Did he not love me once? Lying now supported on a pillow, watching the crowd dance around the children born of no mother, the children borne by him for the sake of all, that was the point. I approach him cautiously, without looking at him, watching instead the children, who lie there immobile, their lower limbs tied tight. I know that they have some terrible, hidden defect. The people pick them up and put them back, choosing them, urging me too to take one of them, and I see there lying in the corner a child almost fully grown, an aged fetus, a cataract in his eye, stretching out his little hands to me.

"Quickly, quickly," I hear around me—

ADAM

So at least I understood. Disturbed and excited, standing there in the withered, neglected garden, on a crisp summer morning, leaning on the wing of my little car, watching the girl who stood there in front of me, both strange and familiar, watching her serious face, the sharp face of a bird, the thick lock of hair falling on her breast, studying her body, her sandaled feet, the shape of her legs, while listening to a clear and vivid dream, which for a moment I was sure that she'd invented as a means of declaring her love. I didn't know then what became clear to me after I married her, that such are her dreams, clear and lucid, that she always remembers them, to the smallest detail. So different from my dreams, which are rare and unfathomable.

We agreed to keep in touch—

But I returned to her that same evening, this time bringing pajamas, shaving gear, a toothbrush and a change of shirt. Already in love with her, as if by secret orders, my love required no effort. It was enough for me to remember the girl whom I roused that night in the tent, who seemed to me infinitely more beautiful than this girl. In love not with her, nor with the other, but with something between the two.

She was a little surprised to see me returning that same day. Her father, who was pacing about like a caged lion, stopped for a moment and looked at me, then resumed his pacing. (He paced around the house like this for many years, hardly ever stepping outside, not wanting to see his friends. He was proud and angry with the world, sure that he was right, that an injustice had been done to him.) Only her mother, a gentle, delicate old woman with weak eyes, came to me and shook my hand lightly. Most of that evening we spent in her room. She talked about her studies and her plans and what was going on in the world. She was interested in politics, in equality, in socialist policies, she mentioned the names of leaders and events, in possession of all kinds of secret, unknown information which seemed to her of the highest importance. Then I realized how those long years of hard and solitary work in the garage had diminished my curiosity. At last I touched her, took her in my arms, kissing her lips and her breasts, tasting the bitter taste of soap.

That night once again a bed was made up for me on the old sofa in the living room. At two or three in the morning again the deposed leader came in, in his torn pajamas, his face on fire, bending over the old radio set and turning the knobs, passing from station to station, searching for the mention of Israel or his own name in the distant void. I curled up silently, pulling the sheet over my head, asking myself if I really loved her. When he finished and went back to his room I couldn't sleep anymore. In the end I got up, dressed quietly, shaved and went to her room to wake her, but she was in a deep sleep, curled up, probably dreaming. Do I really love her, I never stopped wondering, wouldn't it be better to escape from here before it's too late? I left a brief note and drove with the first light back to Haifa.

At noon she arrived at the garage. Her father must have given her the address. I was lying under a car changing the exhaust pipe and suddenly I saw her standing nervously in the doorway. I got up at once and went to her, oily and dark, but without speaking she signaled to me to carry on with my work. She looked at me with a scared look that pleased me and put me at my ease. It seemed appropriate. I lay down again under the car, working quickly and with concentration, to be rid of the owner of the car, who was watching her now as she paced around among the heaps of junk, glancing at the tools that were scattered about, examining a picture of a nude girl that I'd cut out from a newspaper and put up on the wall. She examined everything carefully, with great interest, even putting her head inside an old engine that lay on the workbench. At last I succeeded in fixing the exhaust pipe and the customer disappeared with his car. I went to her. She didn't explain why she'd come so suddenly, nor did she ask why I ran away in the morning without saying goodby. She just wanted to know how an engine works. I explained it to her. She listened gravely, her eyes sad, her voice shaking a little, on the verge of tears. But she asked intelligent questions and let me talk of nothing else. And I talked, I even dismantled an old carburetor to show her its parts, explaining and explaining. I never thought it possible to say so much about the workings of a simple gasoline engine.

Three months later we were married—

She transferred her studies to Haifa and we lived for the first few years in my mother's house.

I didn't know if it would last long, sometimes I was sure that in a while she would leave me, would regret it, find someone else to take her in. I wouldn't have been at all surprised if she'd betrayed me within a short time. But our life went smoothly from the start. She was engrossed in her studies and we lived an orderly life. In the mornings she went to college, then to the library. And when my day's work was done I went there to pick her up. With my old invalid mother she got on splendidly, attentive to her endless chattering, going shopping with her, sympathetic to all her silly ideas, heedful of her advice. When my mother and I realized that she was a very poor cook we gave her other chores around the house, the washing of the dishes or the scrubbing of the floor, tasks she performed with great efficiency, not turning up her nose at any work. Even then I noticed her strange liking for older women. She had several elderly aunts in Haifa to whom she was devoted and frequently visited.

And studying, studying. Always with books, note pads and files. While at the seminary she also enrolled for evening classes at the university. She seemed to be taking an exam almost every fortnight, preparing for it with her fellow students. She would leave me an address where I could pick her up at the end of the day: a library, a private house, a cafe, sometimes even a public park. And I would arrive there after work, grimy, my clothes dirty, walking heavily through the reading rooms of the library, between the tables, drawing the attention of the readers, finding her and touching her lightly on the shoulder. She would nod her head and whisper, "Just let me finish this page." I would sit down beside her and leaf through a book lying open on one of the tables, reading and understanding nothing. Once I said to her with a smile, "Perhaps I ought to study something too, change my profession, it isn't too late." She was astonished. "Why you?" Why me, indeed. Nothing in her world attracts me particularly.

Although she suggested we abandon these meetings, that she was quite prepared to make her own way home, I insisted on always going to meet her. I wanted to know where she was, who she was seeing, what her daily routine was. Sometimes I was gripped by a strange jealousy, hurrying to close the garage before my work was done, leaving early, deliberately arriving an hour or two before the time we'd agreed on, lying in wait for her on the stairs, or spying on her from a corner of the library. But all in vain. She had no intention of leaving me, it never occurred to her to fall in love with anyone else. Now that she'd found herself a husband and a home, she could be free for the things that really interested her, she could even take a mild interest in public affairs. She was a member of the Students' Committee and once she organized a successful strike.

In the second year of her studies she'd already found herself a part-time job, teaching in a primary school. At first she had a difficult time there. The children drove her mad, although she never said exactly what the trouble was. She used to come home a little dazed in the evenings. But she tried very hard, preparing for her lessons with care, sometimes even shutting herself up in the bathroom and reciting the lesson aloud, asking questions and answering them. She used to draw illustrations and charts as well, painting big sheets of cardboard, sticking them with dried flowers and making cheerful patterns. As in all practical matters, she had two left hands, and I used to help her a little with these preparations.

All in all, as I saw at once, a complacent and agreeable woman. At pains not to argue with me, treating me with respect, even with a trace of fear. Perhaps a little too talkative, but since I had a habit of subsiding into prolonged silences it was only natural that she should sometimes talk on my behalf as well. We used to make love almost every day or every other day, but for some reason I was usually the only one who was satisfied. Mother was with us all the time, and since we were both out all day, she used to look forward very much to the evenings when she could talk to us. She never left us alone. She used to come into the room without knocking, while we were undressing. If I tried to lock her out she hammered on the door, calling to me in panic. At night she left the lights on in the house, she was a light sleeper and we were sometimes visited in the middle of the night. Sometimes I was forced to wait until the early hours of the morning before waking Asya.

She obeyed me. Sometimes she would whisper in her sleep, her eyes still closed, "One minute, just let me finish this dream," and I would sit on the end of the bed waiting for her to wake up by herself, and she would smile a final smile, open her eyes and help me to undress her. In the second year, when she started working, it became harder and harder for me to wake her early in the morning before I went out to work. I made love to her while she was still asleep, interfering with her dreams. Then I hired my first Arab worker, Hamid, and I gave him the key to the garage so that he could open up in the morning and receive the first customers. He was the first worker I ever employed, on a temporary basis of course. I paid him a daily wage and could dismiss him if I found him too expensive, but business began to prosper and it wasn't long before I took on another worker. So we could take our time in the mornings, and listen to her dreams, which were becoming for me increasingly strange. Sometimes we talked about ourselves, how and why we had got married, if we regretted it. She was shocked. "Do you regret it?"

No, of course not, why should I regret it. But sometimes when it seemed to me that I no longer loved her I became terribly depressed. Still, as I say, she was an agreeable woman, she did what I wanted, but I wanted nothing special. That's it—she aroused in me no special wants. I worked very hard in those days, difficult physical work, but it wasn't for that reason alone that I was so tired in the evenings.

Something in her fatigued me, something unclear. I'm not talking about the little speeches that she used to make to me, it wasn't that, I was quite willing to listen to them, though there did seem to be something unreal about them, not because she inhabited a reality different from mine, no, it wasn't that . . . something else . . . something that I didn't know how to express, and so I said nothing. More and more it seemed to me that she was missing the real world, drifting away from it, but what the real world was of course I couldn't say. And clearly she was no dreamer. She organized, worked, studied, rushed about, had contacts with all kinds of people. She tended to walk quickly, decisively, with a slight hunching of her shoulders. Elderly movements. No, not elderly, grayish, not grayish, something else, these aren't the right words. But how to describe her? I want to describe her. Where to begin? It seems to me that I still haven't begun.

DAFI

But do I complain? Lately they've both been leaving me alone, in their different ways. Osnat's always telling me "They leave you alone, your aging parents."

Your old parents?

I was a bit surprised, but I didn't say anything. Is it true? Poor Osnat, she gets no peace. Her ten-year-old sister shares a room with her, she's exactly like her, only uglier, and apparently more intelligent. She gets on Osnat's nerves, prying in her drawers, trying on her clothes, butting into every conversation. There's no getting away from her. Then there's the little baby, who was born a year and a half ago, causing a lot of excitement in the class because we were all invited to the circumcision to see what they'd do to him. Such a sweet little baby, already starting to walk on his twisted little legs, getting everywhere, Osnat calls him a moving disaster. Always catching colds, wiping his runny nose on blankets, on sheets, on the clothes of guests. His hands covered in black ink, and if they try to get it off him he shrieks so loud you'd think someone was murdering him. He scribbles on the walls, on books and note pads. And always howls and tears and confusion. Bedlam, this house. In addition to all this they have guests from all over the world coming to stay with them, and Osnat has to give up her bed and sleep on a mattress in the living room.

"It's so quiet in your house. Dafi, let's switch places."

True, it is quiet in our house. In the afternoon when Mommy's not at home and Daddy's still at work, it's so quiet in the dark, tidy house you can hear the ticking of the thermostat. It's not natural. It's lucky that I've got a room of my own, my kingdom, where I can be as untidy as I like. My bed's always in a mess, my clothes scattered about, books and note pads on the floor and posters on the walls. There was a time when they tried to force me to keep my room in order but they gave up in the end. This is my order, I said, my rhythm, and I took to shutting myself in, so they wouldn't come in and look for disturbed things.

In general this trick that I've adopted over the last year of shutting myself in my room has proved a great success. When guests arrive I can ignore them. But we don't have many guests visiting us. Sometimes when the bachelor uncle from Tel Aviv is passing through Haifa he stays to eat supper and then goes. Now and then, on a Sabbath eve, four or five couples come to eat with us, dull people usually, with fixed expressions, their childhood friends or teachers from the school, sometimes even the ones who teach me. Once they even invited Shwartzy to the house on a Sabbath eve. I came out to see how he behaved in his natural surroundings, and I saw that there wasn't much difference—pompous and bossy as usual. These evenings are so boring, they never really talk about themselves or discuss personal things, they argue about politics or the price of apartments or the trouble caused by children. There's always one of them who dominates the others, who bears down on everyone. Daddy's very quiet, passing around the plates of biscuits and nuts and sitting there not saying a word. Working in the garage dulls him a bit. Sometimes I used to go in quietly and sit down among them, making sure to eat a cake that I'd had my eye on since lunchtime, before everything got eaten. But lately I've decided that I see enough of the teachers in the morning at school, I don't have to meet them in the evening at my home as well. So I've taken to shutting myself away in my room and showing no sign of life. Sometimes a guest opens the door cautiously, thinking it's the bathroom, and he's surprised to see me sitting there quietly, thinking thoughts. He smiles at me ingratiatingly, starts talking to me, asking questions. They're always amazed at how much I've grown, listening to them you'd think I'd grown right there in front of them.

Then I took to locking the door, sometimes even in the daytime. But there are times in the afternoon when Mommy knocks loudly on the door, Aunt Stella, Grandfather's sister, has come to visit us with one of her friends, she wants to see me. So I go out to meet them, kissing her, sometimes kissing the other old woman, who I don't always know. Sitting with them and answering questions. Aunt Stella, erect and tall, with a long mane of white hair and a wrinkled face, beside her another old woman, a dried-up midget, with dark sunglasses and a thick, short cane. And the interrogation begins. She knows a lot about me, she even nursed me when I was a baby, when Mommy was studying. She asks me about my marks in school, she knows I have problems in math, she remembers the names of Tali and Osnat, she even knows something about Tali's father, who left home. I answer her quietly, smiling. I listen as she interrogates Mommy as well, asking her what she's been doing over the last month, scolding her for being involved in so many activities, she's interested in the back pains that Daddy had years ago, she passes on the good wishes of friends of hers who've had their cars repaired in his garage. Hardly saying anything about herself, interested only in us, or in others. Mommy sits all tensed up on the edge of the armchair, blushing like a little girl, laughing an unnatural laugh, running to show them a new dress that she's bought, all the time fetching biscuits, sandwiches and salads from the kitchen, but Stella doesn't touch anything, only the other old woman sits there, munching away. She really admires these old women, waiting on them humbly and eagerly, and when at last they get up to leave, she pleads with them to let her drive them home.

At last they go. Mommy drives them to the center of town. I open the little box of chocolates that Stella brought, very superior chocolates. Mommy comes back half an hour later in an agitated mood, sits down in the chair that Aunt Stella sat in, dazed from the experience, incapable of doing anything. I take a good look at her, her hair that's going gray, the wrinkles in her face, the slight hunching of her shoulders, she's aging happily, soon she'll get herself a cane.

ADAM

But how to describe her? Where to begin? With her feet, the graceful legs of a girl set in solid, low-heeled shoes that hide most of the foot, comfortable shoes perhaps but lacking style, even a bit shabby.

She had strange taste in clothes. A taste that became depressing. In the Carmel Center she found a shop belonging to a pair of fussy little old women who dressed her in gray woolen dresses with white poloneck collars and half-length sleeves. Pretty masculine-looking clothes with padded shoulders. They used to give her a discount and this delighted her, even though sometimes she had to take a dress with some slight fault in the material. When Dafi was little the old ladies used to bring her little dresses of the same design and the same material, and Dafi looked like a little old woman.

I don't know much about these things but it always seemed to me there was something wrong with the match of the colors in the clothes she wore, apart from the fact that she had a number of old dresses that she was fond of, that she was always lengthening or shortening, according to her notion of what fashion demanded. She would even set to work on the new dresses that she would buy, trimming and adjusting, and all this with hands that weren't all that skillful.

For some reason it was important to her to save money. She had an obsession with money. Her tightness amused me, she was almost miserly, and especially hard on herself.

I'd noticed this years ago in her house, seeing them dividing up the food at meals into exactly equal portions, eating up the leftovers, frying them up a second time. Seeing the way they used old envelopes, the way her father filled up notebooks with his memoirs, writing on both sides of the page, filling up the margins, even writing on the cover. But in that house there was perhaps a good reason for such an obsession, because since the establishment of the state her father hadn't worked and they lived on a small pension from the Ministry of Defense. Such was his pride that he refused to accept any employment after his dismissal.

But in recent years we've had money, more and more each year. It's true that in the early years we went short of things, it was a struggle to keep the little garage going. And to make things worse my father's partner, Erlich, decided to leave and I had to buy out his share and so I was plunged into debt. When the first profits began to come in I invested every cent in new equipment, in enlarging the site. She didn't understand the business, she was content with what I gave her. She never asked for more and when she started working her salary went straight into the bank and became mixed up in the garage's assets. I doubt if she herself knew how much she was earning. It's strange, but the topic of money didn't generally interest her, she just continued with her frugalities as if it was her duty. After a few years she began supporting her parents a little. I of course said nothing and she was so grateful she went even further with her frugality and her self-denial.

We never had any professional help in the house. In the first years after the boy was born and before he went to the nursery her mother used to help us, she came over especially from Tel Aviv at the beginning of the week to help us, and an old aunt who lived in Haifa used to help her at the end of the week. Sometimes she even took the child to her own house. And Asya was rushing about between the school and classes at the university, studying and teaching. When something went wrong in the house, the fridge or the electric oven, I used to repair it myself, then I got tired of this and without consulting her I'd replace them with new ones. She was shocked, astonished by my extravagance. "Can you afford it? Are you sure?" When we changed houses and incurred new debts she decided on her own account to take on another part-time job in a night school, although we could pay off our debts without difficulty. But I said nothing, I was used to letting her do what she wanted. At that time the garage began to prosper, the profits began pouring in in increasing volume. Erlich, the former partner, returned to the garage, this time as an employee, as chief cashier, and though he'd been a poor mechanic, he proved to be a financial wizard. He had a special way of playing with payments, of manipulating bills. If a new customer came along with a problem that wasn't too complicated we'd charge him very little, and sometimes we even did the repair for nothing, and naturally he'd come back, and after a few times we'd clobber him, not too excessively but at least twenty per cent above the tariff. And he'd pay up quietly, without thinking twice. Erlich also devised a system of sending bills through the mail. We didn't demand immediate payment but gave the car back as soon as the repair was done, giving people the impression that the question of payment was a side issue, that the important thing was the repair of the car, the service. We didn't mention the bill. And after a week or two, when the customer had forgotten all about it, the bill would arrive in the mail. And people paid up without protest, as if settling an electric or a telephone bill. More and more of the bills were paid by insurance companies and industrial concerns, which of course didn't protest, but only demanded receipts. Erlich knew how to make the most of this as well. Although he was no longer a partner he still thought of the garage as his own and he fought over every cent of mine, learned all sorts of complicated practices, studied the tax system in detail, consulted lawyers. We began to expand, to employ more and more workers, opening new departments, selling spare parts. We began to make clear a profit of ten thousand, fifteen thousand pounds a month. In my wallet alone I used to carry some five thousand pounds all the time, just like that, for no special reason.

But she didn't exactly understand what was going on, or rather she didn't want to understand, and I made no particular effort to explain. She still saw the garage as some sort of co-operative, unaware that all the profits ultimately accrued to me. She didn't often visit the garage, as if she was afraid to wander about there. I doubt if she knew where it began and where it ended. But she was full of respect for my work, seeing me get up at dawn and return in the evening. True, I no longer came home black and oily like in the early years.

"Do you need more money?" I used to ask her from time to time.

"No," she'd reply quickly, without even thinking, advising me to put money aside for the garage, in case something happens. Precisely what could happen I can't say, perhaps they'll stop using cars and take to horses.

She didn't want a car for herself under any circumstances. For what? She was perfectly happy to use the buses. But sometimes when I had to collect her from the school or the university, and I saw how the teachers or the students looked at me, walking beside her in my dirty working clothes, lightly touching her arm–she didn't care, but I did. I bought a small second-hand car and parked it outside the house and I insisted that she learn to drive. She failed her test the first time but after that she mastered the thing, even began to enjoy it. Now she could rush about even more, could take on extra obligations. She understood nothing about the engine, nor did she need to understand it, I always made sure that everything was in order. Once she arrived at the garage in the middle of the day. The fan belt had broken and she'd almost burned out the engine, and was scared out of her wits. I wasn't there and the workers didn't recognize her and ignored her. She sat there in the driver's seat, at the end of the line, marking exam papers as she waited. Eventually Erlich saw her, ran to her, took her into his office and ordered the workers to repair the car immediately. I remember, when I arrived and she was standing beside the mended car, the curious glances of the workers, studying her critically, with a sort of smile of disappointment, now that they knew she was my wife. "Is that the old lady?" one of them asked his friend in a whisper.

To hang around the shops looking for things to buy always seemed to her a waste of time, an unnecessary effort. Sometimes she postponed essential purchases, making do with articles that were completely worn out, a purse, gloves or an umbrella. For a long time she went around wearing a shapeless straw hat of which she was very fond. Whenever I commented on it, she'd promise to buy a new one, but postpone it from day to day. Eventually I just took it and threw it away, without telling her. She'd been looking for it for a day or two before I told her.

"But why?" She was amazed. "You're just throwing away money."

And then I decided to go shopping with her. We met in town after work and walked around the shops looking for what she wanted. As a customer she wasn't hard to please, she liked everything she saw. All the time studying the price tags, torn between a purse costing a hundred pounds and one costing a hundred and forty, and I stood beside her with three thousand pounds in my pocket.

"Not too expensive?" She asked my advice.

"No, not at all. That's all right."

In the end she bought the cheaper one after all.

I said nothing, but I was livid.

I deliberately took her from there to a fashionable and expensive restaurant and ordered coffee, cakes and sandwiches, a light meal. She refused to eat anything and just drank coffee. "I'm not hungry, not hungry," she insisted, but she watched me hungrily as I ate sandwich after sandwich.

"Sure you're not hungry?"

"Quite sure." She smiled, looking at the purse that she'd bought, trying to convince herself that she'd gotten a bargain. "It's bigger than the more expensive one," she explained, and I said nothing, smiling to myself, paying the waitress with a hundred-pound note and leaving a generous tip. But she ignored the fat wallet lying there on the table, she didn't care how much money I carried about with me.

"Is that the old lady?" I remembered what the Arab worker had said and my heart missed a beat. But she smiled at me good-naturedly, picking up the crumbs from my plate and putting them in her mouth, finishing her coffee, glancing at the clock, always in a hurry, always thinking about something else, history, exams, teachers' meetings. Am I getting her right?

ASYA

Driving Adam's car and driving it well, though I've never driven it before. I feel the dreadful weight of the car, I never imagined it would be so heavy, the engine roars like a tractor, even so I make progress, changing gears smoothly. It's hard for me to see the road, my seat's so low, through the front window I see only the roofs of houses and the sky. I drive by instinct, feeling all the time that parts of the car are outside my control, slightly misjudging the turns, hearing the dull thuds as the car collides with the corners of the houses, but the car goes on, like a tank, no obstacle can stop it. I arrive home and it's already evening. I park the car under a streetlamp, get out to inspect the damage. Nothing too serious, vague dents here and there but the paint hasn't been chipped off, the metal has just sunk in, little pools forming in the surface. He'll repair it himself, I think, and I run up the stairs. The door is open, there are people in the house, in armchairs, on the sofa, some of them sitting on the floor. Plates of cakes and nuts, dishes of olives and pickled cucumber. Who's prepared it all? Perhaps they themselves. Sitting and whispering, not yet touching the food, waiting for me. But I go looking for Adam. Where is he? I go into the bedroom, he's sitting there on the bed in his overalls, alone, as if he's hiding. He looks strange, pale, younger, something's upsetting him.

"What have you done to the car?"

"What have I done? Nothing . . ."

But he moves the curtain aside and shows me the car, lying capsized under the streetlamp, wheels in the air, turning slowly, like an insect pinned down on its back, flailing its legs, hissing softly. I'm really surprised, a little amused, from the next room the voices of the guests grow louder, they're losing their patience.

"Hurry now, get dressed and go out to them, you can straighten the car out later . . . what's the trouble?"

And he goes to the bed, stripping off his shirt, such pain in his face, and all the time I'm asking myself, how has he changed? How is he different? And suddenly I realize–he's got no beard, he's pulled off his beard, torn it out by the roots, scalped himself. It lies there on the pillow, lies there intact, I can't bear to look.

ADAM

So how to describe her? Where to begin? With her smooth little feet at which I fell one night after the disaster, gripping them hard, hurting her, covering them with kisses, pleading in a confusion of lust and terror that we have another child, that we do not lose hope. This was perhaps the only time that I lost control.

It was about three months after the disaster, from which it seemed she was recovering rapidly. After only a week she went back to work full-time, to all her activities, but at night she didn't sleep, didn't even undress, sitting down instead to correct her pupils' work, or reading, or dozing a little in her chair, or getting up to wash the floor, to wash dishes, sometimes even cooking at midnight. And she never put out the light until dawn. Quiet, businesslike, behaving sensibly but wary of me, recoiling slightly when she saw me approaching, as if I was to blame, or she was to blame, as if there was any question of blame.

For I refuse to attach any significance to a disaster that was nothing more than an accident. I'm not capable of listening to the arcane explanations–a deliberate accident, he sought his own death, subconscious intentions. I have some experience with car accidents. Every week cars are brought into the garage after accidents on the road and I'm forced to listen to explanations, even though I never ask questions, how it happened, what happened, who was to blame. It's not my job to judge people, just to assess the damage and repair it. But the drivers are excited and they can't restrain themselves, they must tell me what happened, thinking that I'm blaming them as I walk around and around the wrecked car with paper and pencil in my hand. As if I cared. They start describing the accident, detail by detail, in complicated language, sometimes even drawing a little sketch, ready to admit responsibility too but only in a very partial way, a very limited responsibility. The other man was driving too fast, the traffic lights were defective, or they start unfolding strange theories about blind spots in the field of vision of this type of car. The road, the sun, the government, explanations upon explanations, anything but–I drove like a lunatic, stupidly, carelessly, I am to blame. There are bloodstains on the car and still they continue to describe their expert maneuvering–at the last moment they turned right, left, reversed, it could have been much worse, there could have been another death. Only occasionally is anyone prepared to say–A miserable accident, without meaning.

And that's how it was–

After five years we had a son. He was deaf. We called him Yigal. His deafness was detected very soon. In the maternity hospital they gave us a special letter for the children's doctor at the clinic. They explained it to us: "There's something a little defective in his hearing, you'll have to be careful, he can't hear." I won't start going into detail, there'd be no end to it, a man gets to be an expert on his grief, learns the terminology, becomes acquainted with mechanical aids, compares notes with others in a similar plight, makes friends with other parents who have deaf children. Nor is it really such a terrible catastrophe. There are worse disabilities: blindness, severe blood diseases, brain damage. In general he was a healthy child, with a handicap that he could overcome. They were always giving us hope for the future. In the first year there were even certain advantages. He slept a lot, noise didn't disturb him, it was possible to switch on the radio beside his bed, the sound of the vacuum didn't worry him, in the street he slept peacefully through the roar of the traffic.

It was a full-time occupation. Asya spent a lot of time with him, and I, at that time working from morning till night, made an effort at least not to miss his bedtime. Standing in front of him and speaking in a loud voice, my mouth wide open, moving my tongue slowly and teaching him to say "daddy" or "head," and he watching me with deep concentration, repeating the words after me with a strangely fluctuating volume of sound, very quiet or very loud, producing other words: "gally," "sed." You begin to grasp another language, indistinct expressions, strange sounds, your own hearing gets sharper, you begin to take in nuances. He used to talk with broad gestures, and when a child does this he has great charm. It's interesting that I understood him better than Asya did. I developed a special sense for understanding his words, which, peculiar as they were, still had a logic of their own.

When he was two years old they gave him his first hearing aid. When guests come to the house and see him, you immediately start to explain, even when they ask no questions. It's the first topic of conversation and sometimes the last as well. Just don't let them think he's mentally deficient or backward or abnormal because of the way he expresses himself. You begin to get used to the handicap, it seems natural. There are some educational and social problems, but with good will they can be overcome. The crucial thing is to treat him as if he's normal, even to hit him from time to time, which I did, sometimes without really sufficient reason.

For he was an intelligent child and at the age of two he was already chattering constantly, looking at your face all the time, at the movement of your lips. If you forget and turn away from him when you're talking, he touches you to remind you, to make you turn and face him, or he shakes his head with an endearing gesture so sweet it would melt the devil's heart. All in all, a happy child. Minor problems–like calling him back home when he's playing outside. No use just shouting, you have to go down and touch him. What exactly did he hear? Even this we were able to discover, thanks to the clever instruments in the clinic. They think of everything there, even educating the parents. They gave us headphones and played us the sounds that they reckoned he heard, so we could understand better, identify with him.

At the age of three we sent him to a nursery near our home. A charming old nurse took care of him. There were maybe five children there altogether and he got along fine. She didn't really understand him very well, because she was a bit deaf herself, but she gave him warmth and love. She used to put him on her lap and kiss him, carrying him around from place to place as if he were crippled, not deaf. He loved her very much, and always talked about her with love, with enthusiasm. From time to time I found an opportunity to leave the garage for a while during the day and go to the nursery, to try to explain to her and the other children what he was saying, training the children to stand directly in front of him, to open their mouths wide and to speak slowly and distinctly. The children were a little scared of me, but basically they were friendly and helped out.

Perhaps I overdid things a bit. Asya told me to abandon these visits, she herself had gone back to full-time work, a little too early perhaps, but it's hard to judge.

At first we were interested in special schools, Asya even thought of trying to find a job in a school of this kind, but we soon saw there was no need. He showed independence and was capable of normal relationships with other children. His ability to express himself was improving all the time. In the evenings I used to remove his hearing aid and talk to him face to face, through lip movements only. There was a time when the hearing aid made him self-conscious, we let his hair grow and he was able to hide it. I made him a smaller earpiece on the lathe in the garage. The business of the hearing aid brought me particularly close to him at that time. Together we dismantled it, I explained to him how it worked, he examined the little microphone, the battery, he seemed to have inherited a technical sense from me.

It was essential not to take him too seriously, essential to joke with him even about his deafness, to expect him to help with the chores, to take out the garbage or dry the dishes. We were already planning another child.

When he was five years old we moved to another house. To his sorrow he was forced to part from the old nurse, he was so at home there. He found it hard to get used to the kindergarten. There were tears in the mornings. But it seemed that things were working out. The Passover seder before his death we celebrated in our new home. Asya's parents came and various other elderly relations of hers and he sang his part without a single mistake, rolling out the tune in a strong, jaunty voice. We clapped our hands and applauded him. The gloomy, taciturn old grandfather looked at him with great interest, with astonishment, then wiped away a tear and smiled.

Sometimes he used to take out the hearing aid when he wanted to read a book or when he was building something, a tractor or a crane. We used to call him and he wouldn't hear, buried deep in his own silence. I envied him this ability to break off contact with the world, to enjoy his own personal silence in his own way. There can be no doubt that the handicap speeded up his development. He also knew how to exploit the advantages of his situation. Sometimes he complained of pains in his ears because of loud noises from the hearing aid. We consulted the doctors and they saw this as a good sign, some of the nerves were showing signs of life, but the doctors were able to predict his condition only for the next few years. There was no way of knowing if the noise really disturbed him or if he just enjoyed having silence around him. I agreed to make him a little cut-off switch, to wear under his shirt, beside his heart, so he could now and then switch off the hearing aid without removing it. Of course this was intended only for use in the house.

In the meantime we bought him a little bicycle to ride on the pavement outside the house. We found him new friends in the neighborhood. He settled down well with them, but sometimes when they got on his nerves he simply switched off the hearing aid. One of the children even came to me once to complain that "Yigal makes himself deaf on purpose when he doesn't want to give something or join in a game."

I mentioned it to him, though I was pleased with this evidence of independence.

Why not?

On that Sabbath afternoon, a week before the beginning of the school term, he went to visit a friend of his who lived just four blocks away from us, on the same street. His friend wasn't at home so he decided to come back, and it seems that he switched off his hearing aid on the way, though I can't be sure. Suddenly he saw his friend on the other side of the road playing with some children. They beckoned to him to join them, and so he crossed the road, still in total silence. The car coming down the hill, not all that fast (the skid marks were checked), sounded its horn, confident that he'd have time to stop, but Yigal went on crossing the road, in his silence, not running, but at a slow walk directly into the path of the car.

It all happened for him very slowly and in total silence.

The children woke me from my sleep, a dozen little fists hammering at the door. I ran out into the street barefoot and half naked. The ambulance was already there. The children shouted wildly, "Wait, wait, here's his daddy." He was still breathing, his eyes were full of blood, the hearing aid was broken, he could no longer hear me.

The two of us are realistic, rational people, we tried to behave reasonably, not to lay blame, not to make accusations. I thought she might say something about the cut-off switch that I'd made for him, but it didn't occur to her. I hinted at it, and she didn't understand what I was talking about.

The strange thing is that for a long time, for two or three months after the disaster, we were hardly ever alone. Her parents came immediately from Tel Aviv and at our request they stayed on with us. The father was himself very ill and had to be cared for. Elderly aunts came to help, to cook, to clean the house. It was all taken out of our hands, as if we'd both gone back in time and were children again. I slept in the study, Asya apparently on the sofa in the living room, and all the time there were people moving about the house. Practical matters took on great importance, they absorbed the grief, diverted it. Concern with her father's medicines, special diets, above all with the constant stream of guests passing through the house who came not to visit us but Asya's father.

I remember it well, the last days of summer, mild and clear, the house full of silent people, most of them old. All the time the door opening and someone arriving on a visit of condolence. All his friends, former officers in the secret service, labor leaders, all those who had shunned him after his disgrace, those with whom he had most of all lost touch, decided now to come and be reconciled with the dismissed former leader whose grandson had been killed in a road accident and who was himself slowly dying. They arrived diffidently, nervous about seeing him, and he received them in groups of two or three, sitting in a big armchair on the shaded balcony, in the light of the approaching sunset, all white, a light woolen blanket covering his knees. His face calm, his eyes uplifted, staring out to sea, hearing words of self-justification, of loyalty, words of consolation, even secret information. And to one side, at a distance, sat the old ladies, drinking tea and whispering in Russian. The days of mourning were for him the days of great reconciliation with his enemies.

I walked about the house like a stranger. Afraid even to go into the kitchen. Coming home from work and after a while they call me to eat a meal cooked by one of the old ladies. Erlich, my father's former business partner, arrived on a visit of condolence and offered to help out in the garage. He began to work with me on the accounts and he gave me some good ideas. After a while I suggested that he return to the garage as an employee and to my surprise he agreed. I used to sit with him after work, waiting until dark, going home late in the evening and finding the house full of people and Asya sitting in a corner, and they bringing her a meal, and scolding her for something.

After months her parents left, though we implored them to stay. Her father was now in a critical state.

Only then did we realize how empty the house was. The nursery was bare. We went back to sleeping in our bedroom, though in fact I slept alone, she continued in her insomnia, her night wandering. I had no thought of touching her, but it was a little strange that she didn't want to sleep in her own bed. A week went by, two weeks, she was growing very thin, her face was pale, but she went out to work, organizing herself as usual, only continuing to doze in armchairs, fully clothed. Perhaps now is the time to part, I thought, perhaps the time has come to leave her, but my longings for a son were painful, I wanted another son, even another deaf son, I didn't care, I wanted to start again from the beginning, to bring him back. But there was to be no touching her, none at all. She said, "I don't have the strength to start again."

I was unshaven and untidy, she looked pale and neglected, we were in no fit state for love. I gripped her forcibly, without desire. She resisted: "What is it that you want?" Then I fell on my knees, kissed her feet, trying to arouse my desire for I had no desire.

DAFI

Sabbath eve. No movement in the air. They've gone out to visit friends. When they're at home you hardly notice them, but when they go out you know that they aren't there. I walk around the house, alone. It's very unusual for me to be alone on a Sabbath eve. But there's no chance of getting together with Osnat, because they're having a big party at her house. Her brother has suddenly gotten leave from the army. I phoned her at nine o'clock to arrange something but she said, "We're in the middle of a meal, my brother's home and he's got a lot of stories to tell and I'll phone you later," and she hung up, and she hasn't rung yet. Tali's gone with her mom to visit her grandma in Tel Aviv. Every two months her mom takes her to see her grandma, to show her how well Tali's growing up and how well she's being looked after, and perhaps she'll increase the maintenance that she pays in place of her son, Tali's dad, who ran away. I've got so used to spending all my time with those two that when they aren't there I'm completely lost. I shouldn't have quit the Scouts so soon, they're always good for dead evenings like this.

Ten o'clock. I phone Osnat. They're on the last course. A real feast. She sounds impatient, doesn't think she'll be able to come over tonight. I hinted that I could go around to her house but she pretended not to understand, guarding her brother so jealously, not wanting anyone else to have a share in him.

Such heat. From the balconies of nearby houses come voices and laughter. The students who are renting the house opposite have turned the lights out, they're dancing now to some sexy melody. There's one couple hugging and kissing out on the balcony. I walk around the stifling house from room to room, turning out the lights, maybe that'll make it a bit cooler. Stopping at the kitchen door so as not to see the pile of dishes in the sink. After supper there was an argument over the washing up. Daddy decided to interfere, insisted that I do the washing up, he snatched the sponge out of Mommy's hand, even though for her it's a two-minute job. In the end I promised to rinse them and I shall rinse them, but not yet, the night is long, the job requires a bit of inspiration. It's so awful having to work on my own, if only I had a little brother or sister that I could talk to when I'm working, someone who could help me, drying the dishes beside me. These silences, this stillness, it's all so depressing. To think that I could have had a brother too, he'd be nineteen now, in the army too. And they just let him get killed in the street. A boy of five, you can tell from the old photograph how sweet, very solemn, they couldn't get a smile out of him, as if he knew he didn't have long to live.

When I was ten they told me about him for the first time, and they said he'd died of an illness. It was only a year ago that Daddy told me about him for the first time, that he was killed in a road accident, he even showed me exactly where it happened. How is it that they kept no trace of him in the house, how have they managed to forget him all these years? Lately I've been more and more interested in him, my life could have been so different. I grieve for this brother. I talk to him in my imagination, sometimes he's a youth of nineteen, sometimes he's just five years old. Sometimes I help him to undress, make his supper and wash him, and sometimes he comes into my room, a tall smiling youth, to talk to me.

Ten-thirty. Not a breath of air, everything's white-hot. The sky's standing still, the moon and stars are covered with a milky mist. I move slowly from chair to chair. I'd take a shower and go to bed and set the alarm for seven o'clock in the morning and get up early to wash the dishes, but Daddy'll go crazy if he sees the sink full. Why should he care who washes them? I glance at the newspaper. Life is all so intense, and around me are the music, the voices and the laughter. And I'm alone here, where am I in the middle of all this?

I get up and go hurriedly to the kitchen. How can such a small family use so many dishes? First I move aside the two saucepans and the burned frying pan. They aren't my responsibility. On the rest of the dishes, without touching them, I pour out a lot of washing-up liquid, turn on the tap, a gentle stream of water, must soften them up first. What kind of a job is this for Sabbath eve? I go out of the kitchen, putting out the light, sitting down at the big table, listening to the water running in the kitchen, perhaps the dishes will wash themselves. Sitting and watching the flames of the two Sabbath candles. I'm the one who's insisted on them lighting Sabbath candles this last year, they wouldn't have thought of it by themselves, neither of them believes in God.

The heat gets stronger, I strip off my clothes, in my underwear, in the dark, I sit watching the flames, hypnotized. I could sit for hours watching them being consumed, wondering which one will burn longest. The siren of an ambulance in the distance. Long thin insects with delicate wings walking on the walls, on the table. I start to doze, the light dances in my closed eyes. The lapping of water at my feet wakes me. Water? Where'd all this water come from? Oh God, the floor's flooded. The tap.

You didn't want to wash the dishes and now you'll have to wash the floor as well. It's nearly midnight. They're not home yet. I run to fetch rags, start to mop up, cleaning, bending down and scrubbing. Chasing the water as it runs under the cupboard, wetting a little old suitcase that's hidden behind it. I clean, mop and scrub, streaming with sweat. Going to the kitchen and washing the damn dishes, scraping the saucepans and the frying pan as well, polishing them. Working like a demon, washing, drying, putting things away in the cupboard. At last I go and take a shower, putting on a dressing gown and sitting down to look inside that old suitcase that I never noticed before. Some moth-eaten old children's clothes, mine or his? Who can tell? They can't have thrown everything away. I put them back in the case, put the case back where I found it, dead tired but waiting up for them. What's happened to them? Outside the voices are fainter. The music stops. A cool breeze passes through the house, the air stirs.

I only remember that suddenly they were beside me. I didn't hear them open the door or come in. Daddy lifts me up, supports me, leads me to my bed. Through my sleep I hear Mommy say, "She's gone mad, she's washed the whole house." And Daddy laughs suddenly: "Poor Dafi, she took me seriously."

ADAM

So really, is that the way to describe her? Starting with her smooth little feet, so wonderfully preserved, the fleshy, smooth and silky curve, the feet of a pampered child, not belonging at all to this gloomy woman with wrinkles in her face, who seems to insist on growing old before her time.

If only someone was to touch me, quietly, out of genuine friendship, good will, interest, let's say on a Sabbath eve at one of those social gatherings at a friend's house, teachers from Asya's school or friends from our school days, former neighbors with whom we've kept in touch. At one of those gatherings that we get invited to every few weeks, where most of the faces are familiar and after a while the conversation breaks down and the one who's dominated the proceedings falls rather silent and starts to eat his cake, or gets up to go to the bathroom, and the great discussion of political problems, of the meanness of contractors or a visit to Europe is broken off and the minor conversations begin, echoes of whispers, the women discussing obscure feminine disorders, the men getting up to stretch their legs, going out to the main balcony, someone even switches on the television at low volume, and I'm still marooned in my chair, picking at the shells in an empty dish of nuts, silent as always, already thinking of moving homeward, if only someone, a good friend, a childhood friend, was to turn to me, put a hand on my shoulder, touch me gently, with a good-natured smile, seeking a genuine connection, and whisper for example, "Adam, you're always so quiet, what are you thinking about all the time?"

I'd tell him the truth at once. Why not? I don't mind.

"You'll be surprised, but I think about her, I can't think about anyone else."

"About whom?"

"About my wife . . ."

"About your wife? Very good . . . why not? Sometimes it seems that your thoughts are far away and all the time you're thinking about her."

"I'm busy with her constantly . . ."

"Has something happened?"

"No, nothing's happened."

"Because you seem so good together, I mean a steady sort of couple without bickering or strains. We were a bit surprised at the time when she married you . . . she's such an intellectual type, sitting over her books all the time, and we thought it was strange that you, out of all her friends . . . you understand? No offense . . . you understand?"

"I understand, I understand, go on."

If only one of our friends, and we don't have many, one of the three or four that we see regularly, who've been close to us for years, was to touch me once with friendship, with sincerity, even with all the noise, even in a small room, there's always an opportunity for a little private, personal conversation.

"We lost track of you in the middle of the school course, you went away to work, the years went by and suddenly–the two of you. It was a surprise."

"For me too."

"Ha ha, and we were sure that all the time you were secretly in love."

"I . . ."

"Yes, you. We remember that affair of hers. But now the bond between you seems so natural, when we talk about you it's always with good will, believe me, it's always good to see you among us, even when you sit there without saying anything. No, don't think it's annoying, the opposite, really, I don't know how to say it, Adam . . ."

"Thanks very much. Thanks very much. I understand."

"So what do you think about all the time?"

"About her, I've already told you."

"No, I mean what are you thinking about her, if you don't mind my asking."

"Not at all. I think about her feet."

"Pardon? I didn't hear you. All this noise . . . about what?"

"About her little feet."

"Is something the matter with them?"

"No, nothing in particular, I just wonder, incidentally, if you've ever seen them. The sweet girlish curve, the legs of a pampered child, she isn't quite . . . as she seems."

If someone was to lay his hand on my shoulder, taking me aside in a friendly way, with affection, with a whisper, with arrogance even, with curiosity, but still talking to me with genuine affection, looking me straight in the eye.

"But of course . . . how could I have known, forgive me. Her feet, you said? But how could anyone know . . . except for you of course . . . forgive me . . . she wears . . . forgive me . . . such heavy shoes with flat heels . . . I mean . . . I don't know much about these things but I'm surprised . . . my wife mentioned it . . . that dress . . . something a bit shabby about it . . . I don't think she does herself justice . . . when she was young she was so charming, not pretty but quite attractive and now she's aging so quickly, that is, not aging, far from it, but she's deteriorating a bit, perhaps because of that tragic business with the boy. I understand, but people mustn't be allowed to age like that, we all have a responsibility, we must look after one another, warn one another, we still have a long life ahead of us . . ."

"I know . . . I'm sorry."

"Oh, Adam, forgive me. But I spoke as a friend. We've known each other for such a long time, right? You understand?"

"That's quite all right, go on."

If only someone was to approach me, casually, when it's nearly midnight, even a little drunk, when they're all getting up and moving about the house, because a young couple has to go and relieve their baby-sitter, and the rest are wondering whether to stay a little longer or to leave, starting to wander about the house, going into other rooms, weighing themselves in the bathroom, pacing about on the balcony, and the hosts run around after the guests, urging the undecided to stay, running to the kitchen and fetching hot rich soup and slices of bread, the leftovers from the Sabbath-eve supper, or what they've prepared for the Sabbath lunch, gathering the guests together, handing the plates around, pouring out the strong reddish soup, putting on a record of Greek songs, then the drowsy conversations begin, and if anyone comes to me it's only to discuss car prices or to hear my opinion of a new model that's just arrived on the market, or to consult me about how tires should be crossed, they stand there holding plates and cups and listening with respect, on such subjects I'm the supreme authority.

Some of my friends were also my customers, though I never encouraged them to come to me, even in the days when the garage was small and I had to fight for customers. I wasn't interested in them, but they were interested in me.

In the early days there weren't many of them who could afford cars. Teachers in primary schools, minor officials, students, former kibbutzniks, just weren't in a position to possess their own cars. But after a few years the majority of our friends began buying cars, second-hand ones of course, which they used to bring to me for inspection, consulting me before buying. I had to be careful not to foster illusions, above all not to take any responsibility. Otherwise they'd have been at my door constantly, imposing the most awful obligations on me. I was forced to take a detached view of their cars.

Naturally I did some jobs for them.

For the headmaster, Mr. Shwartzy, I did an entire overhaul. For some old school friends I changed the shock absorbers and tuned the engines. For a charming couple that we met at a party, a middle-aged university lecturer and his young artist wife, I cleaned the temperature control and replaced the clutch. For the school secretary and her husband I rebuilt their car after an accident and fitted a new generator. For the gym instructor, a bachelor of thirty-five, I relined the generator and charged the battery.

I expect they all felt they'd gotten a bargain out of me, and in fact they hadn't really gotten a bargain at all, their only advantage in coming to me was that I didn't do unnecessary work and I didn't keep their cars in the garage for longer than was necessary.

There were a few who came back to me, especially when they needed a quick job, but the garage grew larger, I was often absent for long periods and the foreman wasn't prepared to give them preferential treatment. Erlich made a point of not giving discounts to anyone and they themselves got to understand their cars better, changed them for newer ones, found cheaper or more convenient garages.

There was one friend of ours, a woman whose husband had deserted her. At one time she was always turning up at the garage. She was scared out of her wits, she was always hearing strange noises from the engine, she was afraid there was going to be an explosion. She used to stand aside waiting until I was free to go out with her for a drive, to hear and to feel the vibrations and the mysterious noises. I used to drive with her to the main road by the sea, breathing in the smell of cheap perfume, stealing a glance at the short fat legs beside me, while she sat there looking at me with longing and talking about her husband and weeping, all this to the accompaniment of my technical comments. She was really hooked on me. Finally I decided to get rid of her and I sent Hamid to deal with her. He went out to test the car, drove once around the block, came back and said scornfully, "There's nothing wrong, lady, everything's quite all right." After that she left me alone.

So among our friends I really was only a friend. They had no ulterior motive for inviting us to their homes. I used to arrive, sit down and say nothing. In some houses they already knew about my passion for nuts and they used to put a big plate in front of me, as if I were a dog, and I'd sit there in silence all evening, nibbling slowly. I had a special method of cracking the shells quietly in my hands. After the boy was killed they were wary of us. For a long time they didn't dare invite us but eventually they made cautious advances and we responded. But my silences became deeper. Asya on the contrary talked more and more, she was especially active in political discussions, getting into arguments, always coming up with little-known facts, going into detail. Her knowledge never ceased to amaze me. Was it just the professional ability of a history and geography teacher, or a quality inherited from her father? She knew, for example, the population of Vietnam, the exact location of the Mekong River, the names of all the ministers of France, the principal clauses of the Geneva Convention, when the troubles began in Ireland and how the Protestants came to be there, the date of the persecution of the Huguenots in France, and who the Huguenots were, and she knew that there were Dutch units in the Wehrmacht. In fact it wasn't always clear exactly what she was trying to say, but she was always putting others right, or clarifying some point. Not that anyone was prepared to change his mind because of the information that she poured out in such a constant stream, but I saw that the men were a little nervous around her, as she sat there in the middle, a cigarette between her fingers, not touching the food but only drinking coffee and more coffee, at an hour when all the others were prevented from drinking coffee by fear of insomnia.

And I listened to her and also to the other women, who, weary of these arguments, whispered about their own concerns. One of them had a lover and everybody knew about it, it was a source of great interest although the details weren't clear. Only her husband knew nothing, sitting there proudly in a corner, a contentious bastard, every time a view was expressed he said the opposite.

But Asya, how to describe her, I'm still trying to describe her, in the early hours of the morning, when we're still among our friends, time for us to go but we've not yet found the right moment. And I watch her, thinking only of her, noticing the bitter, combative tone in her voice, the strange self-confidence. Just occasionally, when someone forcibly contradicts her argument, is she at a loss for a moment, putting her fist to her mouth in her old childish sucking movement, the thumb quivers for a moment at her lips, and then she realizes what she's doing, and hurriedly returns her hand to her lap.

Sabbath eves at friends' houses, old friends, pointless, meaningless conversations, but the bond remains and it's genuine and deep. I watch my wife all the time, studying her sidelong, with a stranger's eyes, thinking about her, her mind, her body. Is it still possible to fall in love with her, some stranger who would see her just as she is, in these clothes, in the gray dress with the faded embroidery, someone who would fall in love with her for my sake too?

DAFI

One day at supper he said suddenly, right out of the blue, "I'm going to shave this beard off tomorrow, I'm sick of it." He looked at Mommy.

She shrugged her shoulders. "It's up to you."

But I leaped in at once. "Don't you dare, it suits you so well."

He smiled. "What are you shouting about?"

"Don't shave it off," I pleaded with him.

"What are you getting so excited about? What does it matter . . . ?"

But how could I explain to him why his beard was important to me, how could I tell him that without it he'd be feeble, he'd lose all his vigor, he'd just be a simple mechanic, a dull garage boss.

I mumbled something about his nose that would look too long, about his ears that would stick out, about his short neck, I ran and fetched a piece of paper and drew a picture to show him how ugly he'd look without a beard.

They were both amused, smiling at me, not understanding my agitation. But how could I explain that for me the beard was a symbol, a flag . . .

"Eat your supper."

"Do you promise then?"

"I shall shave it off and grow another."

"You won't grow another one, I know."

I couldn't eat any more. They gathered up the plates, silent again. Why didn't Mommy say something? Daddy sat down in front of the TV with his paper. Was it really that important? Mommy was washing the dishes but I paced around uneasily. After a while I went to him.

"Well, what have you decided?"

"What?"

"About your beard."

"My beard? What about my beard?"

He'd forgotten, or maybe he was just teasing me and he never intended to shave it off.

"You must be mad. Haven't you got anything else to worry about?"

"Then tell me."

"You've never known me without a beard."

"I don't want to either."

He laughed.

"So what have you decided?"

"Well, let's wait and see."

ADAM

What was my beard? A flag or a symbol, a way of telling the world that it can't classify me that simply, or pigeonhole me, that I too have dreams, a different horizon, eccentricities, mysteries perhaps. Anyway, a complex man.

And in recent years the beard has grown long and wild.

There were certain distinct advantages in it. In the garage it helped me to keep my distance. People would hesitate a little before approaching me. Also, I was told, the beard made a great impression on the Arabs, they were very respectful toward it.

At first people think I'm religious–

And in fact that's how it started. After the boy was killed an unknown relative of mine appeared at our house, not a young man, he came to supervise the religious formalities. He insisted that we sit *shiva* at home for a week, not leaving the house, I was forbidden to shave for thirty days, and every day for a year he arrived at the house at dawn to take me to the synagogue to pray. Asya thought he was crazy, couldn't understand why I let myself be swayed by him, but the death of a child puts you into such a state of depression, bewilderment and fear that it's comforting to have someone around who knows exactly what to do. In a month the beard grew very quickly, it already had a shape to it, and as I had to get up early in the morning for the journey to the synagogue, it was a relief not having to shave.

Then Dafi was born and she was fascinated by the beard, all the time running her little hand through it. Perhaps one of the first words she learned to say as a baby was "beard."

At work I was careful not to put my head inside a running engine in case my beard got caught in one of the moving parts.

They were forced to take bits of the engine out to show them to me.

Sometimes I thought, I've had enough, time to shave it off, but at the last moment I'd think better of it, Dafi used to plead with me not to shave it off. Sometimes I went to the barber shop to have it cut and trimmed, but before long it was unruly again. White hairs began to appear in it, the golden color faded and turned brown, there were several different shades in it. The barber once offered to dye it but of course I refused. I didn't touch it a lot, I wasn't in the habit of smoothing it down unnecessarily as bearded men tend to do, but sometimes I used to catch myself chewing it between my teeth.

Sometimes I even forgot about it, and at night in bed, when I folded the newspaper and tried to sleep, I'd catch sight of my face in the big mirror and think for a moment that a stranger was staring at me.

DAFI

In the silence of the room, in the afternoon, the three of us each reading a different chapter of the history book, to brief the other two on the contents, preparing for the exam tomorrow, and Osnat's kid brother lying on the floor in a T-shirt and underpants, quietly spreading cake on the carpet. Through the wall I hear a sort of moan, whispers and the creaking of a bed. "My love, oh, my love, oh my darling." So clear. My heart stops, I feel like I'm going to faint. And Osnat looks up from her book, blushing bright red, starts shuffling papers to cover the sound of the whispering, terribly embarrassed, cuffing the child, who starts to howl, and jumping up from her seat, not daring to look at me or at Tali, who's still staring at her book, reading or daydreaming, there's no way of telling if she too has heard the sound of Osnat's parents making afternoon love in the next room. It seems this is their favorite time, this isn't the first occasion, apparently it was in the afternoon one day many years ago that Osnat was conceived.

And now I can't help it, I just have to smile, Osnat looks at me angrily and then, slowly, she begins to smile too. What's she got to be embarrassed about anyway?

Because she sure has really nice parents. A cheerful, noisy loud-mouthed mom, a larger version of Osnat, tall and thin with glasses, always sitting down to gossip with us in her American accent, helping us with our English homework, she knows everything that goes on in the school and the names of all the children in the class. They've got a lovely house with a little garden, inside it's always chaotic, but it's a nice place to be, they always invite Tali and me to stay for supper. They're used to children. Besides Osnat there's an older brother in the army, a younger sister and the little boy, who was born a year and a half ago, causing a lot of excitement in the class because we were all invited to the circumcision. Perhaps Osnat's the only one who isn't charmed by him, though he's a sweet kid, awfully fat, with a round tummy and still no hair, reminds you of Osnat's dad, who looks a lot older than her mom, he's a professor at the Technion, plump and bald but full of life, madly in love with his ugly wife. He comes home from the Technion in the afternoon, opens the door and heads straight for the kitchen, kissing his wife quite shamelessly, in front of us, they stand there hugging for so long you'd think they hadn't seen each other for ten years. Then he bursts into Osnat's room, starts cracking jokes and taking an interest in her work, he's really sweet.

And after a while her mom comes in, bringing in the baby and a plate of cookies, our reward for looking after him while they go to "rest." And Osnat starts to protest, we've got our homework to do and an exam to prepare for, then her mom winks at us and says "Dafi and Tali will look after him then, O.K.?" And she hurries away to their bedroom on the other side of the wall. They don't sleep, we hear them whispering, laughing, the deep voice of Osnat's dad—"Oh, oh, oh"—and then silence, and suddenly it hits me, like a sharp stab in the heart, I hear her moaning softly "Oh, my love, my darling. . . ."

And Osnat hits the baby and her mom calls out "Osnat, what's the matter with Gidi? Let us have a little peace." I pick the baby up, trying to calm him, kissing him, he claws at my face with his grubby hands, pulling my hair, yelling triumphantly "Tafi, Tafi."

After a while they finish resting and they go to take a shower. Her mom comes in to fetch the baby wearing a long flowery dressing gown, smelling nice and with her hair wet, and her dad comes in too, in short trousers and a vest, carrying a big tray loaded with different flavors of ice cream. And they're both relaxed and happy, smiling brightly, sitting with us and licking the ice cream, wanting us to share in their happiness, playing with the baby, kissing him hard, with what's left of their passion. And Osnat shows him her math homework and he solves a problem or two for us, making us laugh with his funny explanations.

They've just been making love, I think to myself, watching them from the side, unable to forget that deep powerful groan, something comes over me, a sort of sweet pain, I don't know why. How could she call this fat little man "my love, my love, my darling"?

Why should I care anyway–

"Are you staying for supper?" says Osnat's mom. Tali's always eager to stay, but I jump up from my seat. "I can't stay, must go home, they're waiting for me." It's a lie. I pick up my books and run home. Of course nobody's waiting for me. Mommy's not at home. Daddy's sitting in a chair in his working clothes, reading the paper. When do they make love? When does he get kissed? Who says to him "my darling"?

I go into the living room, look at him. A heavy, serious man, leafing through a newspaper wearily, without interest. I go to him, kiss him lightly on the cheek, feeling the thickness of his big beard. He's surprised, he smiles, touches my head lightly.

"Has something happened?"

ADAM

But why not describe her detail by detail, clearly, precisely, why do I hesitate to consider everything? But what do I really want, I'm changing too, it's impossible to preserve eternal youth, nor is that what you're looking for. In the garage the workers stick pictures of nude girls on the walls. I say nothing, it's not my business and if it helps them to work, fine. But Erlich's annoyed by it, he interferes and imposes his own censorship, declares what's permitted and what isn't, going and taking down a picture that he thinks is too daring, protesting in his angry, pedantic voice, "Please, nothing tasteless, nothing pornographic, only what's aesthetic," and the workers laugh, sneer at him, start to argue, try to snatch the picture out of his hand, a gale of laughter sweeps the garage, work stops, the boys stand and stare, open-mouthed. I go to see what all the fuss is about, not interfering of course, the workers smile at me and gradually they drift back to their work. I look at the pictures, the smooth young bodies, endless variations on the same theme. There are some pictures that have been hanging here for perhaps ten or fifteen years, girls who have changed in the meantime into dull, middle-aged women, growing old, perhaps even dying and becoming dust and ashes and here they are on the grimy walls of the garage in their eternal youth and Erlich stands beside me blushing, is he angry or is he smiling, looking at the torn picture in his hand, the dirty old man, he still gets turned on, he winks at me—"The bastards, they want to turn the garage into a whorehouse."

But I don't care, it's as if I've lost my desire. Soon after Dafi was born I felt the first signs, a deep sense of disappointment overcame me, I regretted that I'd been so persistent. We couldn't bring the boy back. We really should have parted.

And I see Asya returning to her daily routine, as if she's forgotten everything, and a new, unfamiliar lust takes hold of her. She wants to make love to me, at every opportunity. Sometimes she sits naked on the bed, reading a newspaper and quietly waiting for me and when I touch her she goes wild, comes quickly, as if by herself, ignoring me.

I begin treating her crudely, though she doesn't seem to mind, delaying her on purpose, sometimes leaving her halfway through, a violence I never knew taking hold of me. Sometimes I'm afraid I may be going too far, but she still clings to me, the violence doesn't scare her, perhaps the opposite.

I grow distant, changing my habits, going to sleep early, putting out the light, pulling the blanket over my head, playing dead, getting up with the dawn and going out. She tries to follow me, afraid to say plainly what's on her mind, in the end she gives up. She's grown thin again lately, has shrunk a little, there are signs that her bony frame is beginning to stoop, she walks briskly.

She's beginning to despair of me, she comes into the bedroom at night without putting on the light so as not to rouse me but there are times when I wake up, suddenly, take her in my arms and try to make love to her. She whispers "You don't need to struggle so" but I reply "I'm not struggling." I'm looking around for the bedroom mirror, to see what I don't feel.

VEDUCHA

A row of plants a vineyard an orchard a wheat field among them a big old growth. Banana? Watermelon? Dark eggplant? A dry dense little bush planted in a bed under pajamas and a gown. Little twisted roots beneath the sheet like hard thumbs. A thick stem, a ball soft and damp, two sinewy branches a thin coat of resin. Thin moss covers a branch of white leaves. Thoughts of an ancient plant will she grow to the ceiling or break out through a window into the sunlight give flowers and fruit.

They come and pour gruel on the obstinate plant give it yellow tea to drink. The plant drinks in silence feeling only the sun revolving from window to window disappearing. Night. A plant in the darkness. But a door opens and a piercing draught stirs the waking plant the breeze passes through her branches penetrates to the roots. A door closes, a wind trapped in the plant, stirring free. Her bark peels off grows soft moss turns to hair resin to blood the stem grows weak and hollow, a whistling begins deep inside a wind comes in a wind goes out and a wind comes in again. A plant self-nourished spreading thin moisture a noisy plant the wind choking in her. Two acorns bursting out of the branch, growing fine, frosted glass absorbing light, soft hairy leaves hear voices. A plant sniffing herself tasting the bitter taste of a split leaf in her mouth. Hunger, thirst, feeling. Starting to groan–oh . . . ohhhh . . . ooo . . . the groan of a creature that once was a plant.

DAFI

It's always dark there because the flat's on the ground floor of a house on the hillside, but also because of the curtains that shut out the light and the weak light bulbs that her mom uses to save electricity. She doesn't believe in ventilation, either, even though she gets the air free. The place always reeks of scent but such a nasty scent. When Osnat and I arrive we feel depressed even before we go inside. We wouldn't be visiting Tali at all, only she's sick today.

Always wearing the same dressing gown with the button missing right there in the middle, so you can see her gigantic tits. A big, untidy woman with pale blond hair scattered over her shoulders, maybe she was pretty once but now she's all dried up, so unnerving, opening the door and giving us a mean look, saying, "Ah, at last you've remembered that you've got a friend," although Tali's only been sick since this morning.

We go into Tali's room and find her as pretty as ever, with a high temperature, we sit down beside the bed waiting for her mom to go and then we start to gossip with her, telling her what's been going on in the school, giving her the test paper that was handed back today and consoling her that half the class failed it, and Tali isn't a great talker, she just smiles that dreamy smile of hers, takes the test paper and puts it under her pillow. After a while her mom comes in, moving a chair into the doorway, half in and half out, sitting there with a book in Hungarian, a cigarette in her mouth, glancing angrily at us, wanting to join in, as if we've come to visit her as well.

Osnat once told me that Tali's mom is only half Jewish and didn't want to come to Israel at all, except that Tali's dad forced her to come here and then ran away and left her. We never said anything about this to Tali, maybe she doesn't know that she's quarter not Jewish, but it helped to explain all sorts of things, most of all her mother's awful bitterness.

She sits there, not far from us, pretending to read her book, in a cloud of smoke, so solemn, staring at us as if we're some kind of merchandise, not smiling even when we tell jokes. Every now and then she suddenly interrupts Osnat in midsentence with the most unexpected questions.

"Tell me, Osnat, how much does your father earn?"

Osnat's taken aback.

"I don't know."

"Roughly?"

"I've no idea."

"Three thousand a month?"

"I don't know."

"Four thousand?"

"I don't know," Osnat almost shouts. But Tali's mom is quite unperturbed.

"Then ask him sometime."

"What for?"

"So you'll know."

"All right."

And then there's an uneasy silence, and we're trying to pick up the threads of the interrupted conversation when suddenly—

"I'll tell you then. In the Technion they give them a raise every month. He's bringing home at least four thousand clear."

"Clear of what?" asks Osnat angrily.

"Clear of tax."

"Oh . . ."

And again that uncomfortable silence. Why the hell should she care how much Osnat's dad earns?

"As for Dafi's father"—suddenly she turns to me with a scornful smile—"I don't ask you because you really don't know, he doesn't know himself. He'll be a millionaire soon with that garage of his, though your mother does her best to keep it a secret."

It's my turn to be startled and struck dumb. The witch, sitting there in that chair with her bare legs, smooth as pats of butter, her toenails painted with bright red nail polish. When I see her sitting like that I know which half of her isn't Jewish, the lower half for sure.

The odd thing is that Tali never interrupts her mom when she starts to prattle, pays no attention to her, just sits there quietly in bed, staring out the window, not caring that her mom's getting on our nerves. We start groping for another subject, we start telling Tali something and suddenly there's another blast from the corner of the room.

"Tell me, girls, do you need a new dress every week, like Tali?"

We look at Tali but she's so calm you'd think she doesn't understand what we're talking about.

"Tell me, tell me . . . I get only twelve hundred pounds a month and I pay out three hundred in rent. Please tell her she shouldn't ask for a new dress each week, once every two weeks is enough. Maybe you have some influence over her."

We want to escape from here right away, like Tali's dad, but that would be hard on Tali. Osnat starts cleaning her glasses, her hands shaking. I see that she's getting into her usual state of panic, but she's not saying anything, neither am I. Knowing that any reply will get a scornful comment. We ignore her, going back to our conversation, whispering, muttering in low voices, sneaking a sidelong glance at the woman sitting there in the doorway, her hard face, the blond hair scattered over her shoulders. Perhaps after all her un-Jewish half is the top half, I think. A quarter of an hour passes, we've almost forgotten her, and then—

"What do you think, should I keep Tali at the school? Is it worth it?"

"Why not?" we both start up.

"But she's a very poor pupil."

"Not true," we protest, giving her the names of children in the class who are worse than Tali.

But her mom isn't impressed.

"Is she really going to get a living out of all this? Maybe she should leave and just get a job . . ."

But we're scared of losing Tali, we start to explain the importance of going to school, education, the future . . . and her mom stares at us angrily, intently, listening with interest but sticking firmly to her opinion.

"In another two or three years Tali can get married, Tali's very pretty, everyone knows that, she's prettier than either of you, she's sure to get snapped up . . . so why should she stay at school?"

Now I begin to see the funny side. But Osnat goes pale, stands up, ready to go, whenever people talk about physical appearance she gets awfully up-tight.

"But maybe you're right, Osnat," she continues in her calm, irritating voice with the Hungarian accent. "It's good she should have some qualifications, I've got no qualifications and I've paid dearly, I thought love was enough . . ."

And her face twists as if she wants to curse or to cry, she runs out of the room. We look at Tali. Her mom's worn us out completely, but her it didn't touch. She's not normal, smiling a thin smile to herself, dreaming, playing with the edge of the blanket, nothing matters to her.

Osnat wants to go but Tali says softly, "Just a moment, what was the homework?" and we sit down again, this after all is what we came here for. Her mom suddenly appears again, but this time with cream cakes and coffee, she sits down in the chair again, chain-smoking, we wait for the next blow but she says nothing. At last we say good-by to Tali, her mom goes with us to the door in silence, then at the door she suddenly catches hold of us, violently, whispering, her face full of pain: "But what does she say? She never talks to me . . . what does she say?"

And we're still groping for words and she hugs us tightly. "Don't abandon Tali, girls."

And she lets us go.

We're stunned, we can't say a word, walking in silence down the street, stopping outside Osnat's house, unable to speak but also unable to part company without saying something. It's as if Tali's silence has stuck to us as well. At last Osnat confesses, "If my parents split up I'd kill myself."

"Me too," I say at once, but with a stab of pain in my heart. She can say things like that because in her house there's love and kissing and cuddling and "my darling" every afternoon. But in our house—it's so quiet. I look up, she's staring at me, as if she's testing me.

"Ciao," I mutter and quickly walk away.

ADAM

Maybe we should part. It's the beginning of summer. Oppressive heat, I wake up covered in sweat, it's nearly midnight. Where's Asya? I get up. The light's on in Dafi's room, but Dafi's asleep, a book lying open on her face. I pick up the book, put out the light, but there's still a light on in the house. I go into the study. She's sitting there, small and thin beside the big table, her hair still wet from the shower, wearing a tatty old bathrobe, her little bare feet swinging. The room is full of big shadows, the table lamp hardly lights the papers and the books in front of her. She's startled by my sudden appearance. Is she still afraid of me?

She's decided to try to write over the long vacation a source book for the teacher of the French Revolution, collecting new material, with explanatory notes for teachers and systematic questions. She goes around to the libraries collecting books, thick and heavy dictionaries filled with the old French terminology.

I sink down on the bed beside her and smile at her, she smiles back at me and then goes back to her books. It doesn't bother her at all that I'm sitting beside her watching her. She's so sure of the bond between us that she doesn't even need to lay down her pen and say something to me. Could anyone want to take her from me?

It's a long time now since I've touched her. She says nothing. I watch her with squinting eyes. Her pale breasts show through the open bathrobe. If I was to go to her now and hold her she wouldn't resist, she might even be glad, surely she hasn't lost her desire as well.

"Do you still dream?"

She lays down her pen, surprised.

"Sometimes."

Silence. Perhaps she'll tell me a dream, like in the early days, it's years now since she's told me one of her dreams. She seems troubled, staring at me intently, then she picks up her pen, reads what she's just written and crosses it out.

"Aren't you tired?"

"Yes, but I just want to finish this page."

"Making progress?"

"Slowly. This old French is very complicated."

"You're always having to study something new."

She blushes slightly, a gleam in her eye.

"Do you want me to stop?"

"No, why? If it's important to you . . ."

"No . . . I shall stop now."

"No, there's no need. If you're not tired."

I stretch out on the bed, put a cushion under my head, feeling heavy and drowsy. I didn't say that I don't love her, I haven't said that yet, only I'm sure this can't go on much longer. To the sound of the scratching of her pen and the rustling of her papers I begin to doze, until I hear her whispering, "Adam, Adam." The room is in darkness and she's standing over me trying to wake me. I don't move, I want to see if she'll touch me, but she doesn't touch me, she hesitates for a moment and leaves the room.

ASYA

I'm in a classroom, some bricks left over from the building are still on the floor, a pile of sand still in the corner. Most of the pupils aren't in the classroom, though the bell has rung and a sort of echo is still ringing in my ears. I ask one of the pupils where the rest of the class is and he says, "They're having a gym session, they'll be here soon," but they don't come and I'm getting nervous, because I want to start on the lesson, the books and the notes are open in front of me. The subject is something to do with the Second World War, a subject that I'm not sure of, it's always so difficult to explain it to the children.

The pupil who has spoken to me is sitting in the front row, an immigrant from Eastern Europe, with a sickly face and a heavy accent, sitting there all wrapped up in a heavy coat, a funny Siberian cap and a scarf, looking at me with such crafty eyes, testing me. In fact he's the only one in the class, what I took to be the other pupils were just the shadows of chairs.

Angrily I ask him, "Are you that cold?"

"A little," he replies.

"Then please take off your coat, you can't sit like that in the classroom."

He stands up, removes his hat, his coat, unwraps the scarf, takes off his gloves, pulls off his sweater, unfastens the buttons of his shirt, strips it off, sits down and takes off his shoes, his socks, he goes and stands in the corner, beside the little pile of sand, and takes down his trousers, his T-shirt and his underpants, quite calmly, without even blushing. Now he stands there in the corner, naked, a little plump, his body white as marble, he makes no attempt to hide his paltry member, the member of a growing boy. I catch my breath, feeling a mixture of repulsion and fierce desire. But I say not a word, flicking constantly through the notes in front of me. He walks past me and out of the room, walking slowly, his shoulders bent, his ass wagging. I want to say to him "Come here" but I'm left alone in the classroom that's now completely empty, in the light of a strange twilight.

PART THREE

VEDUCHA

But which animal is it, a rabbit a frog an old bird? Perhaps something big a cow or a gorilla. They haven't decided yet. A universal animal an animal of animals a sad monster lying beneath a blanket warming herself in a big bed rubbing her body on a crumpled sheet her soft tongue constantly licking the nose the pillow her eyes flitting about. Thinking animal thoughts about food and water that she will eat and drink about food and water that she has eaten and drunk whining a soft whine. They come and raise the blanket urging the animal to rise sitting her on a chair washing her skin with a sponge bringing a plate of gruel taking a spoon and feeding her.

Night. Darkness. An animal sniffing the world a sweet smell of rotting flesh. A big moon comes to the window and cries to the animal. The animal cries to the moon—ho . . . ho . . . oy . . . trying to remember something that she does not know that she only thinks she knows scratching at the wall tasting the peeling plaster. They come to silence the animal stroking her head quietly comforting her—sh . . . sh . . . sh . . . the animal grows quiet. Wants to weep and does not know how.

Strong light around and voices. Sun. The cattle shed the stable the hen coop rustle. The face of a creature before her a creature not an animal, a creature talking to the animal. She wants what does she want? She wants how does she want? Why? A creature that once was. A little pain waking within. Deep down inside the animal something stirs such a soft wind a breath without air without movement bride to the creature her soul her soul. She is here she has not vanished. She always was. The man talks. From a familiar distance. But what is he saying his speech is dark. Gives up and leaves. The animal begins to understand with surprise that she is also human.

ADAM

In fact it was I who found him, who brought him home to Asya. People put themselves in my hands sometimes, I've noticed, they throw themselves at me as if saying—"Take me," and sometimes I take them—

At the beginning of last summer, in the quiet months before the war, I detached myself more and more from the general work of the garage, arriving in the morning, seeing everything working at a high pitch and after two or three hours getting into my car and driving around the shops looking for spare parts, driving to Tel Aviv, touring the automobile agencies, looking through catalogues, visiting other garages to pick up new ideas, driving back to Haifa by side roads leading up to the Carmel range, walking in the woods to pass the time, arriving at the garage before the end of working hours, chasing back into the workshops the men who thought they'd get away early, telling one of the boys to unpack the equipment that I'd bought, hearing reports from the foreman, glancing at an engine or two, deciding the fate of a car smashed up in a road accident and going into the office to sit with Erlich over the accounts, to sign checks, to receive the keys of the safe and to hear the last of his explanations before he goes.

I used to enjoy counting on my fingers the bank notes accumulated during the day, but over the last year this has all changed into a pen and paper business, all calculations, studying bank balances, making decisions about shares, estimating future profits, a quiet assessment of the financial assets accruing to me, and all this while around me there's silence, the garage empty, the work benches clean, the floor swept, the winches released, the generators switched off. My considerable kingdom into which the old night watchman now comes with his funny little lame dog, his big bundle jingling, locking the side entrances and leaving just the main gate open for me. He takes a kettle and fills it with water to make coffee, all the time staring intently toward the office, to catch my eye before bowing to me humbly, and then through the main gate a little car enters slowly, a very old Morris painted bright blue, rolling slowly into the garage without a driver, without a sound, like something out of a nightmare.

I straightened up in my seat.

And then I saw him for the first time, still through the window of the office, wearing a white shirt and sunglasses, a beret on his head, walking behind the car and pushing it like a baby carriage. The watchman in the corner by the tap hadn't noticed him, but the dog started barking hoarsely, ran slowly toward the man and attacked him. The man stepped back from the car, which rolled on a few more meters and then stopped. The watchman dropped the kettle and ran after his dog shouting, "The garage is closed, get that car out of here."

I looked at the car with great interest. A very old model, dating from the early fifties, perhaps even earlier. It was many years since I'd seen this little rectangular box, with the windows like lattices, on the roads. It seems they still exist, I thought to myself, but I didn't go out of the office.

Meanwhile the dog had fallen silent. He'd found the strange old running board on the side of the car and was amusing himself jumping on and off it, but the watchman went on shouting at the man, who made no attempt to argue. He'd gone around to the front of the car and was trying to push it back, but he couldn't do it, the car had settled into a dip in the garage floor.

The watchman went on shouting, acting as if he owned the place. I went out into the garage. The dog wagged his tail, the watchman turned to me and started to explain.

"What's the trouble?" I asked the man. He began to explain—"Nothing serious, the engine won't start, there's a screw missing," and he went and opened the hood.

He looked rather pale, as if he hadn't been out in the sun for a long time, there was also something odd about his way of speaking, about his style, his manners were a little strange. For a moment I thought he was religious, a yeshiva student, but his head was already uncovered, the beret crumpled in his hand.

The little car fascinated me, it had been kept in good condition, it seemed incredible but it was possible that this was the original paintwork, the chassis was clean, without rust, there were spokes in the old-fashioned wheels, the windshield wipers shone. Drops of water fell from it. My hands instantly began to stroke it.

"What's missing?"

"Just one screw . . . I think."

"One screw?" I'm always scornful of such assurance. "Which screw?"

He doesn't know what it's called . . . it should be here . . . in this part . . . and he bent over the engine to find the place . . . there was always one screw that used to fall out here . . .

I looked at the engine, in contrast to the bodywork it was in a hideous state, all dry and dusty and parts of it were even gummed up with spiders' webs.

"Look, I don't understand, when did you last drive this car?"

"About twelve years ago."

"What? And hasn't it been touched since then?"

He smiled, a gentle, pleasant smile, no, it's been used, he thinks it's been used, perhaps not a lot . . . but not by him, because he hasn't been here, in Israel that is . . . he only came back a few days ago . . . it had been left in storage at a garage not far away, he pushed it from there after cleaning it up a bit . . .

"Then why didn't you look for the screw there?"

They didn't want to have anything to do with the car . . . they don't know . . . they don't have spare parts . . . they sent him here . . . they told him this was a big garage with a stock of spare parts . . .

"For a 1950 Morris?"

"1947 . . . I think . . ." he corrected me cautiously.

"1947? Even better . . . do you think I run a museum here?"

He was embarrassed at first, then he laughed, taking off his sunglasses for a moment to see me better. He had bright eyes and a pleasant face, his body was thin with a bit of a stoop, and he had a slight accent that I couldn't place.

"So there's no chance of finding just one little screw so the engine will start?"

Either he's a simpleton or he's mocking me.

"It's got nothing to do with a screw." I began to feel irritable. "This engine, can't you see, it's ruined and rusted. Do you want to sell it?"

"Do you want to buy it?"

"Me?" I was astonished by his frankness. "What would I want with it. Twenty-five years ago I used to have a car exactly like it, it really wasn't at all bad, but I don't feel any great nostalgia for it. You might find some nut, some antique collector, who'd give you something for it . . ."

Right from the start I noticed that I was talking to him in the manner I usually reserve for customers, with him it was as if I was trying to establish a bond, and refusing to desist. Something about that old blue box fascinated me, as if I was looking at something from a distant dream.

"Anyway I can't sell it now . . . it isn't mine yet."

"Well then, do you want me to restore it?"

As if I was short of work in the garage–

He thought for a moment, hesitated.

"O.K., but . . ."

But I cut him short, afraid he might change his mind, and at that very moment an idea occurred to me, I thought of starting a new line in restoring old cars, in the general climate of affluence there'd surely be nuts interested in a new hobby.

"Come back in three days and collect it, it'll be fit to drive again. Leave the keys inside and push it into a corner so it won't be in the way. Help him," I ordered the surprised watchman and went back to the office, wondering for a moment if I should say something about the cost of repairs, but I decided against it in case he would change his mind.

I sat down at the table, going over the last accounts, through the window I saw him and the watchman pushing the car into a corner. He paced around the car for a while, deep in thought, looked toward the office and disappeared.

Five minutes later I finished my work, stuffed a few thousand pounds in my wallet, locked away the rest in the safe and prepared to drive home. Before getting into my car I went again to the Morris, opened the hood and looked inside. Again I was astonished to see the tangle of spiders' webs entwined around the engine. I took off the oil-filler cap and a big black spider crawled out of the dry rusty sump. Just one screw missing . . . I grinned to myself, squashing the spider with my fist. I closed the hood, got inside the car. I sat down at the wheel, which was completely loose, playing with it like a child, studying the primitive dashboard. The interior of the car was very clean, the seats were covered with hand-sewn flowered upholstery, on the back seat lay an old traveling hat with a long scarf attached to it, an old-fashioned lady's hat. I looked in the mirror and saw the old watchman standing behind the car, watching me curiously.

I got out hurriedly, smiled at him, climbed into my own car, started the engine and left the garage, a hundred meters farther on I saw him standing at a bus stop, he couldn't have known that the last bus had gone. This entire commercial district was deserted at that hour. I stopped. He didn't recognize me at first.

"You'll have to wait till tomorrow for a bus."

He didn't understand, turning his head with the winter cap toward me.

"Come on, get in, I'm driving to the city."

He took off his cap and sat down beside me, thanked me politely, asked permission to pull down the sun shade.

"This awful sun, how can you stand it? I'd forgotten what it was like . . ."

"How long have you been abroad?"

"Twelve years, perhaps more, I've already lost count . . ."

"Where have you been?"

"In Paris."

"And you suddenly decided to return?"

"No . . . why should I? I haven't returned . . . I only came to pick up an inheritance from my grandmother . . ."

"The Morris . . . is that what you inherit?"

He blushed, embarrassed.

"No, I wouldn't have come back for that load of junk, but there's a house as well . . . an apartment actually . . . an apartment in an old Arab house in the lower city . . . and a few other things . . . old furniture . . ."

He spoke sincerely, with a pleasing candor, without apologies, without guilt for having left the country, without excuses, admitting that he'd come to collect a legacy and leave.

"You'll be surprised, but that Morris isn't a heap of junk at all . . . it's basically quite sound . . ."

Yes, yes, he knows . . . he and his grandmother used to drive around in it in the fifties, they got a lot of good use out of it.

We drove slowly, joining a long line of traffic at the approaches to the city. He sat there beside me, with his big sunglasses, busily adjusting the shade, as if the sunlight might sting him. I couldn't make him out, his Hebrew was good, admittedly, but he used all kinds of old-fashioned expressions. I carried on with the idle conversation.

"And your . . . your grandmother . . . she used to drive the Morris all the time . . . who used to look after the car for her?"

He didn't know, to tell the truth he hadn't been particularly close to her . . . he'd been ill . . . out of touch . . . for a few years he'd been in an institution in Paris.

"An institution?"

"For the mentally ill . . . that was several years ago . . . but now everything's all right . . ."

He hastened to reassure me, looking at me with a smile. Suddenly it all became clear to me, the way he came into the garage, pushing the car, his search for one screw, the oddity of his speech, his hasty confessions. A lunatic who suddenly remembered an ancient legacy.

"When did she die, this old lady . . . your grandmother?"

An idle conversation in the heavy, slow, burning traffic.

"But she isn't dead . . ."

"What?"

He started to explain to me the "mishap" that had befallen him, with that same reckless sincerity. Two weeks ago he heard that his grandmother had died, he made arrangements, scraped together the money for the ticket and arrived here a few days ago to collect the inheritance, as he was the sole heir, her only grandson. But it turned out that the old lady was still dying, she'd lost consciousness and was in the hospital; but she was still alive . . . and in the meantime he was stuck here, waiting for her to die . . . that was why he'd tried to move the car, otherwise it wouldn't have occurred to him to have anything to do with it . . . he knew as well as I did what it was worth . . . but if he had to wait a few more days perhaps he'd tour the country a little . . . see the new territories . . . Jerusalem . . . before going back to France . . .

Cynicism or just eccentricity, I wondered. But for some reason there was something charming, open, agreeable in his manner of speech. Meanwhile we were entering the center of the town, going up toward Carmel, he still didn't ask to be put down. As we climbed the hill, with the sun beating down on the windshield, dazzling me too, he really seemed to shrink, curling up in his seat as if he were being shot at.

"This Israeli sun . . . it's impossible . . ." he complained. "How can you stand it?"

"We get used to it," I replied solemnly. "Now you'll have to do the same . . ."

"Not for long." He hoped with a smile.

Conversations about the sun–

I was approaching central Carmel. He still showed no sign of wanting to get out.

"Where do you want to go?"

"To Haifa . . . I mean to the lower city."

"You should've gotten out long ago."

He didn't know where we were.

I stopped at a corner, he thanked me, put on his cap, looked around him, not recognizing the place. "Everything here has changed," he said very mildly.

Next morning I asked Hamid to dismantle the engine to see what could be done with it. It took him five hours just to shift the rusty screws, and they were ruined by the time he'd managed to free them.

"Is it really worth it, working on this heap of junk?" From the start Erlich had taken a violent dislike to the little car, which perhaps reminded him of the days of his unsuccessful partnership in the garage. To make matters worse he couldn't even make out a work sheet because I'd forgotten to take the owner's name and address and there were no documents in the car.

"Why should you care?" I said, but I knew he was right, was it really worth the effort of removing the engine, dismantling it to its smallest components, looking through old catalogues to find replacements for the rusted parts, testing the pressure of the pistons, drilling, cutting out new parts, welding, and all the while improvising with odd spares. Only an old lady could have put a vehicle into such a state. If instead of sewing covers for the seats she had once changed the oil . . .

We worked on that car for three full days, building it up from scratch, Hamid and I. Because for all his abilities, Hamid couldn't manage the work on his own, he didn't have enough imagination. Sometimes I used to find him standing motionless for half an hour with two little screws in his hand, trying to figure out where they belonged. Erlich paced around beside us like a restless dog, noting down the hours that we worked and the spare parts that we used, afraid that the owner of the car wouldn't come back at all. "The repair will cost more than the car's worth," he grumbled, but it may be that deep down that's what I intended. I wanted to get control of it.

On the third day we reassembled the engine and it worked. We discovered that the brakes were in a hopeless state and Hamid had to dismantle them too. At noon he appeared. I saw his funny hat bobbing about in the crowd, among the moving cars and the whispering workers. I hid from him. He stood beside the car, unable to imagine the amount of work that had been put into it. Erlich pounced on him, wrote down his name and address, but as was his way made no mention of the bill. He was told to come back when the job was finished, the car had yet to be tested on the road, there were final adjustments to be made.

A few hours later he returned. I myself took him for a test drive, listening to the engine, which throbbed delicately but steadily, testing the brakes, the gears, explaining to him all the time the meaning of the various noises. He sat beside me, silent, with a strange weakness that was somehow endearing, worried about something, pale, unshaven, occasionally closing his eyes, without appreciating the miraculous resurrection of the ancient car. For a moment it occurred to me that he might already be in mourning.

"Well then, has your grandmother passed away?" I said softly.

He turned to me hurriedly.

"No, not yet, there's no change in her condition . . . she's still unconscious."

"If she recovers she'll enjoy riding in the car with you again . . ."

He looked at me in terror.

We returned to the garage, I gave him the keys and went out to talk to one of the mechanics. Erlich had been lying in wait for us and he came out at once with the bill, demanding payment immediately and in cash. The man looked dubious to him, not to be trusted with a bill sent through the mail. The cost of the repair amounted to four thousand pounds. A bit steep, but still reasonable in view of the amount of work put in. Erlich had decided to impose an especially high rate on work in which I was personally involved.

The man took the bill, glanced at it, he couldn't understand the writing, Erlich explained it to him and he shook his head. Then Erlich left him. I stood to one side, deep in conversation but watching him with a sidelong glance, watching him go to the car, starting to pace around it, glancing at the bill, his face growing dark, looking around for me, seeing me deep in conversation and drawing back. Erlich returned, he retreated, muttering something, came to me. I finished my conversation and turned toward the office, he began to walk beside me, his face very pale, I noticed white hairs at his temples, although he couldn't have been more than thirty years old. At the door of the office he began to speak, he didn't understand, he was sorry, but he didn't have the money to pay now, he was sure that a lot of work had been put into it, he didn't deny it, but such a price . . .

I stood watching him, listening in silence, cheerfully, smiling to myself, I knew just how it would be, that I was involving him in a repair job beyond his means. I was calm. But Erlich, who came and stood beside me and also listened, was furious.

"Then why did you leave it here to be repaired?"

"I thought it was something trivial . . . a screw . . ."

That screw again—

He was very pale, confused, but nevertheless retaining something of his civilized manners, taking care in phrasing his answers.

"Then kindly borrow some money," Erlich interrupted him.

"But from whom?"

"From relations, your family, anyone. Haven't you any relations?"

Perhaps, but he didn't know anything about them . . . he had no contact with them . . .

"Friends . . ." I suggested.

He had none . . . he'd been away for more than ten years . . . but he was prepared to sign a promissory note . . . he'd sign . . . and as soon as . . .

I was inclined to leave him alone, but Erlich was getting more and more angry.

"Of course, we can't let you take the car. Give me the keys, please."

And he almost snatched them away from him, went into the office and put them down on the table. My first thought was, the car is staying with me.

We both went into the office.

"If you don't pay within a month we shall have to sell it," Erlich announced triumphantly.

"We can't, Erlich," I explained quietly. "The car doesn't belong to him."

"Doesn't belong to him? What is this?"

The man began to tell his story again, the grandmother whose death he was awaiting . . .

To Erlich the whole business was a scandal, all this talk about an old woman dying. He stood there stiffly by the table, with his short khaki trousers and his army-style close-cropped hair, staring at him with disgust.

"How is she now?" I asked, taking an interest, retaining my composure. Suddenly I too depended on his grandmother's death.

"She's unconscious . . . no change . . . I don't understand . . . the doctors can't say how long it will go on like this . . ." He was desperately unhappy.

"But where the hell do you work?" yelled Erlich, losing his temper. "Don't you work?"

"What for . . . ?" The man was very pale, trembling, his hands shaking, Erlich had terrified him, and suddenly, I could hardly believe my eyes, he collapsed at our feet on the floor.

"He's only acting," hissed Erlich.

But at once I felt concerned for him and picked him up in my arms, a light warm body, sat him down on a chair, cleared space around him, opened his shirt buttons. He recovered immediately.

"It's only hunger." He covered his eyes. "I've eaten nothing for two days . . . I've got no money left . . . yes, I'm in a mess, I know."

DAFI

Supper isn't really over yet. Daddy's drinking his coffee, Mommy's already washing the dishes, in a hurry to get back to the study, and I'm standing in front of the big mirror with a little mirror in my hand examining my back and behind my legs, carefully touching the sunburned places, tasting the taste of salt. A week ago the long vacation began and because the Girl Scout camp was canceled Tali and Osnat and I began going down to the beach every day, sitting there till evening, we want to be real Negresses when school starts again, and suddenly Daddy says:

"I must phone Shwartzy . . ."

"What's happened?"

"To ask him if he wants a French teacher at the school."

"What on earth?"

And he starts to tell a strange story, to which I listen with half an ear, about a customer who fainted in the garage because he couldn't pay a repair bill, someone who arrived in the country without a cent, a crank, an immigrant who'd lived many years in Paris and came here to pick up an inheritance and found that there wasn't any . . .

"And you want them to give him a job as a teacher in our school," I interrupt. "Aren't there enough idiots there already?"

"That's enough, Dafi!"

It's very unusual for Daddy to tell stories about what goes on in the garage, sometimes you forget there are people there as well as cars.

But Mommy thinks it's a strange idea too, asking Shwartzy to give a teacher's job to some guy who left the country.

"All right then, not a real teacher . . . a temporary appointment . . . an assistant teacher . . . he needs help . . . he hasn't got a job . . . he fainted of hunger in the garage."

"Hunger? Is there still anyone who's hungry in this country?"

"You'd be surprised, Dafi. What do you know about this country?" says Mommy coming out of the kitchen, her hands wet, taking off her apron.

"How much does he owe you?"

"More than four thousand pounds . . ."

"Four thousand?" We're both astonished. "What did you do for him that cost four thousand pounds?"

He smiles, surprised at our excitement, he does repairs that cost much more than that.

"So what will you do?"

"What can I do? Erlich has confiscated the car, but that doesn't help because the car isn't his anyway . . . it can't even be sold . . ."

"So what will you do?"

"I shall have to cancel the debt . . ."

Oh, I see, Daddy's a public charity—

"A debt of four thousand pounds?" I feel really bitter. Just think what I could do with four thousand pounds.

"It's none of your business, Dafi," says Mommy.

But she too looks baffled, standing there in the doorway of the study, wondering how Daddy can throw away so much money so easily.

"Perhaps you could find him work in the garage . . ."

"What could he do there? It isn't his kind of work . . . well, it doesn't matter . . ." And Daddy turns to go.

"Bring him here," I say.

"Here?"

"Yes, why not? He can wash the dishes and scrub the floor and that way he can gradually pay off the debt."

Daddy bursts out laughing. "It's an idea."

"Why not? He can do the ironing, the laundry, tidy the rooms for us"—I'm getting carried away, as usual—"he can take out the garbage . . ."

"That's enough, Dafi," says Mommy, but she's smiling too. A strange family conference this, I in front of the mirror, half naked, Mommy with her hands wet at the study door, Daddy in the kitchen door with a coffee cup in his hand.

"When a man's suddenly down on his luck"—Daddy tries to explain—"you feel sorry for him, and he really is a nice fellow, pleasant, educated, he even studied for a while at the university in Paris . . . perhaps you need somebody to copy, to translate for you . . . I know . . ."

"What on earth for?"

"I just thought . . . oh, it doesn't matter . . ."

"But I could use a secretary"—I'm all excited again, trying to make them laugh—"someone to copy, to translate . . . to do my homework for me . . . I shall find work for him."

Mommy laughed, at last, and perhaps this laughter meant that the idea didn't seem so odd to her, or perhaps she really was upset over the loss of the money, because next day when I came back from the beach in the evening, suntanned and stained with oil and my hair in a mess, I found someone sitting in the living room with Mommy and Daddy. Maybe this was the first time they ever succeeded in surprising me. At first I thought he was just a guest, I didn't realize he was the man they'd been talking about, they too were a bit confused and embarrassed, sitting there in the dark room, in the twilight, staring at the thin, pale man with the big bright eyes. He looked as if he'd once suffered from a severe illness, no wonder he fainted in the garage when he heard the price. He blushed when he saw me come in, jumped up from his seat and held out his hand. "Gabriel Arditi," he said and shook hands with me. Why on earth did he want to shake hands with me, what kind of manners are these? Right from the start I didn't like him, so I didn't tell him my name, I fled to my room and undressed, hearing Mommy ask him about his studies, Daddy murmuring something and he talking about himself in a low voice, talking about Paris.

I went to have a shower, washed off the oil stains. When I came out he wasn't in the living room, Mommy had disappeared too, only Daddy was still there, deep in thought.

"Is he still here?"

Daddy nods, pointing to the study door.

"When are we going to eat?"

He doesn't answer.

I go back to my room, put on a blouse and shorts, return to the living room, find Daddy still sitting there motionless, as if he's been turned to stone.

"What's going on?"

"What do you want?"

"Has he gone?"

"Not yet."

"What's happening?"

"Nothing."

"Do you really mean to employ him here?"

"Perhaps."

I go into the kitchen, everything's tidy and clean, no sign of supper. I take a slice of bread, go back to him, pick up the paper and glance through it, go to the study door and listen, but Daddy looks up and angrily signals to me to move away.

"What's she doing in there? How long's he going to stay?"

"What business is it of yours?"

"I'm starving."

"Then eat."

"No, I'll wait."

It's a bit strange to see him sitting there in the dark, without a paper, without anything, his back to the sea.

"Shall I put the light on for you?"

"There's no need."

I eat another slice of bread, which only increases my appetite. At the beach we hardly had anything to eat. It's eight o'clock now, I'm frantic with hunger.

"But what's happening?"

"Why are you making such a fuss? If you want to eat, eat," he snaps. "Who's stopping you . . . anyone would think Mommy still had to feed you . . ."

"You know I don't like eating alone . . . come and sit with me."

He looks at me angrily, groans, gets up from his seat, scowling, comes into the kitchen and sits down beside me, helping me to slice the bread, bringing out cheese and olives and salad and eggs and after a while he too begins to nibble, digging around in the dishes with a fork. The study door is still closed, she's gone quite crazy, taken my idea seriously, made him her slave.

Suddenly the door opens, Mommy comes out to us, her face tense, she's very alert.

"Well?" I say, jumping up.

"O.K." She smiles at Daddy. "He can help me with translating at least . . . he's translating something already . . ."

"Now?"

"He's got time to spare . . . why not?"

"Come and eat with us," I suggest.

"I can't leave him on his own, I'll make sandwiches and coffee, you carry on without me."

Hurriedly she prepares sandwiches, makes coffee, puts some olives in a dish, lays it all out on a big tray and disappears again into the study. We finish our supper, Daddy insists that I clear the table and wash the dishes and then he goes and sits down in front of the TV.

Nine o'clock. Ten. They still don't come out, now and then I hear their voices. Daddy goes to his room, but I can't relax, I don't know why, this strange and sudden invasion has upset my balance, made me nervous. I undress slowly, put on my pajamas, feeling the pain of my sunburned limbs. I sit in the living room and watch the closed door. At a quarter to eleven he leaves the house, I leap up and rush into the study. Mommy sits there in a chair, the room's full of cigarette smoke, she's flushed, papers and books scattered about her in a chaos that reminds me of my own room, a light smell of sweat in the air, in her hands a bundle of papers covered with a strange, rather ornate handwriting.

ADAM

Erlich of course wasn't impressed, wasn't mollified, a hard-boiled *yeke,* standing erect at my side, his turnip head tilted back, glaring at the pale man with the stumbling speech. To him, all this fainting was just an act, an attempt to escape payment.

"That's all, Erlich," I said pleasantly. "It's O.K. . . . you can go home now . . . I'll see you tomorrow."

Erlich was taken aback, blushed a bright red, mortally offended, never had he heard such an explicit order from me. He snatched up his old briefcase, tucked it under his arm and stormed out of the office, slamming the door.

By this time the garage was empty. I'm always struck by the sudden silence that falls within a few minutes of the workers leaving. The old watchman came in through the gate, Erlich stumbled against him, the dog barked at Erlich, Erlich kicked the dog and walked out.

I knew I'd offended Erlich, but I wanted to be left alone here with the pale young man who sat there with his head in his hands. Did I already know what my intention was? Is it possible? I knew very little about him, but enough to feel that unconsciously I'd cast a net and a man was caught in it, and was writhing in my hand. The sense of warmth that I'd felt when I helped him up from the floor, it certainly wasn't regret at having involved him in such an expensive repair job, because I was already prepared to cancel the debt, but . . .

I smiled at him, he looked at me gloomily, but then a light flicker of a smile appeared on his face. My slow, relaxed, assured movements can instill calm all around me, this I know. I bent down and picked up the bill, which still lay on the floor. I read it through, folded it and put it in my shirt pocket. I left the office, called the watchman and sent him to buy coffee and cake from a nearby cafe, I switched on the electric kettle and made coffee for him and for myself.

Again, the story about his grandmother, which sounded to me more and more like a hallucination. A very old woman who had brought him up after his mother died. A few months ago she fell into a coma and was taken to a hospital, but only two weeks ago he received a letter in Paris, a neighbor found his name and address and wrote to him, telling him that she was dying. He wasn't sure whether to come, but since he knew he was the only heir he decided to come and claim whatever there was. There wasn't much, he had no illusions, but there was after all an apartment in an old Arab house, this car, a few bits and pieces, perhaps some jewelery that he didn't know about. What did he have to lose? He spent most of his money on the plane ticket . . . he didn't intend to stay here long . . . he thought he'd just sign some papers, take the money and go . . . but in the meantime . . . from an official point of view there was nothing he could do . . . the small amount of money that he'd brought with him was running out fast . . . it seemed prices had risen a lot . . . and his grandmother wasn't yet . . . almost . . . today he was at the hospital again . . . she was like a vegetable . . . worse than that . . . a stone . . . but, alive . . .

What did he do in Paris?

All kinds of work . . . in recent years he even taught Hebrew . . . private lessons . . . the Jewish Agency even sent him three priests who wanted to learn Hebrew, enthusiastic and reliable pupils . . . and friendly, not like the Jewish businessmen . . . aside from this he taught French to foreigners, to other Israeli immigrants, Arabs, Africans, students especially, helping them to write their papers . . . recently the agency had sent him some Zionist publicity to translate . . . he hadn't been short of work and his needs had been few.

Had he studied there?

Yes . . . no . . . a little . . . years ago he attended lectures on history and philosophy but because of his illness he'd been forced to give them up . . . he used to feel faint in crowded rooms . . . not enough air . . . but this last year he'd started going to lectures again . . . not for a degree . . . for pleasure . . . now if he was going to have money he'd be able to spend more time studying . . .

Meanwhile he finished off the sandwiches, eating delicately, picking up the crumbs around him. A hungry man in Israel in 1973.

"Do you intend to work now?"

If there's no alternative . . . if he has to wait much longer for his grandmother to die . . . but not work in the sun . . . he'll go to the Jewish Agency . . . perhaps I know somebody there . . .

Such an alien passivity amid the chaos of life all around, but no particular worries either.

The watchman came in, took away the empty cups, the man put his hand to the keys lying on the table and played with them.

"Excuse me, I don't know your name."

"Gabriel Arditi."

"You won't be able to take the car."

"Not even for a few days?"

"I'm sorry."

He put the keys back on the table, I took them and hid them away in my pocket. "Don't worry," I said, "we'll take care of it here, nobody will touch it, until you're able to pay the bill . . ."

He was disappointed but he bowed his head with a captivating gesture, thanked me for the meal, put on his cap and left. A few seconds later he came back, asked me to lend him five pounds. I gave him ten.

He left the garage, the dog no longer barked at him but followed him for a few paces. I hurriedly finished my work with the bills, went out of the office and climbed into the Morris, which stood there in the middle of the floor. I was going to move it into a corner but I changed my mind and decided to take it home with me, to see how it climbed the steep slope of the hill. It went up slowly but surely, the engine throbbing steadily. Everyone overtaking me turned to look, some with astonishment, some with a smile.

At noon the next day someone touched me lightly. He stood there beside me, a pleasant smile on his face. He held out ten pounds.

"Has your grandmother passed away?" I smiled.

No, not yet, but at the airline office they'd agreed to buy back his return ticket at half price. He now had a thousand pounds. Could he take the car? I thought carefully, for a moment I considered taking the thousand pounds and canceling the rest of the debt, letting the car go, but suddenly I didn't want to let it go.

"No I'm sorry . . . you'll have to bring the rest of the money . . .

anyway it's better you should keep the money for the time being . . . have you started looking for work yet?"

He was disappointed but he didn't insist. He murmured something about Jerusalem . . . he'd go there and look for work . . . there were no opportunities in this town . . .

Somebody's going to get control of him, I thought.

At supper I found myself thinking about him again, seeing him pace slowly about the garage, his back slightly bent, moving cautiously among the cars, avoiding the Arab workers. The faded French beret, the professional vagrant. I remembered him fainting on the garage floor, his opened shirt, his thin white chest, his history of mental illness, his fixation about a dying grandmother. He doesn't stand a chance in Israel. He must be taken in hand. I asked Asya, I thought perhaps there might be something at the school. Of course she didn't understand what I meant, washing the dishes, in a hurry to get back to the study, surprised at my concern over a customer, not understanding the interest I took in him. But when I told her about the lost money she stopped short at the study door, and of course Dafi interrupted every other sentence. To my surprise I realized that it really was the loss of the money that bothered them. Dafi in her usual way started being facetious, suggesting ways of employing him in the house, her imagination running wild, he could wash the dishes, scrub the floor, help her with her homework. I looked at Asya, she smiled.

Of course I didn't decide anything. But the next day I found the phone number that Erlich had written on the bill, which was still in my pocket. I phoned him. I got him out of bed, he was half asleep and confused, I told him to come around and see me in the afternoon. He asked, "Are you going to give me back the car?" I said, "We'll see . . . in the meantime I may have found you a job."

Five minutes before he was due to arrive I told Asya, she was surprised at first, then she laughed. He arrived with that perpetual cap of his, but in a clean shirt, sat down in the living room and began to talk. She liked him, as I knew she would, slowly the conversation developed, she asked him about Paris, about his studies there. And he, a confirmed lover of the city, started talking about places that she knew only from maps or books, describing ways of life, mentioning historical events, all this in a light, colorful style of speech, sometimes getting quite carried away.

Dafi came back from the beach, came straight into the room, just as she was, her hair untidy, all stained with oil. He leaped up at once, took her hand, told her his name, he had strange, funny manners, he even bowed slightly. The girl blushed, fled from the room. I whispered to Asya, "Why don't you see if he can help you, he's done a lot of translating and copying work."

She took him into the study to show him her papers.

Dafi started pacing about restlessly, standing listening at the closed door of the study. But I felt suddenly weak, I couldn't get up from my seat, couldn't even switch on the light. Wondering if I should have told her something about his time in an asylum in Paris, or if it was better to let her find out for herself.

DAFI

It began just with going down to the beach at the beginning of the vacation, because Osnat and Tali and I had nothing to do after the Girl Scout camp was canceled and it grew into a full ritual. Since I was born I've seen the sea every day from my bedroom window, but it was only in this last vacation that I came to know it, really discovered it. The sea fascinated us, made its way into our souls and our bones, I didn't know it could be so wonderful. At first, in the first week, we were still taking books with us, newspapers, our holiday assignments, rackets, a transistor, afraid we might be bored, but after a while we realized it was another world and we began going just as we were. At nine o'clock in the morning we'd meet at the bus station wearing only swimsuits, no hats, no blouses, barefoot, like savages, clutching only some folded money, going down to the beach, finding a place in a corner a long way from the lifeguard's booth, collapsing on the warm sand, the sun on our backs, talking lazily, telling one another about our dreams, beginning to enter the slow rhythm of sea, sun and sky, losing our sense of time, roasting in the heat, diving into the cold water, swimming, sinking, floating, finding a little island of rock, rising and falling on the surf, coming out and lying on the water line, wallowing in the muddy sand, digging holes, then going to buy *falafel* or ice cream, drinking water from the big tap, moving away from the crowd, finding a quieter place, sinking into drowsiness, a kind of Nirvana, a quiet listless reverie, like corpses on the beach, to the sound of the waves, not caring that the sun's in our eyes. Slowly waking and starting to run, a light run, a gentle long run, the whole length of the deserted beach, farther and farther from any sign of human life, stripping naked and plunging again into the sea, where it's shallow, among the rocks, looking at one another no longer with curiosity or with embarrassment but studying the parts that the sun hasn't reached, needing to be brown all over, on our nipples and our asses. Putting on our swimsuits again and walking slowly back, hunting for shells, bending over a yellow crab, motionless in its crevice. Sometimes one of us dives into the surf again and the others wait till she comes back, all the time our eyes fixed on the blue horizon shimmering in the heat, feeling the sands shift beneath our bare feet. When we reach the lifeguard's hut the last of the people are packing up to go, with their baskets, chairs and children, we stand and watch the setting sun, not wanting to move, until the lifeguard comes to us, tells us to go.

Day after day it's the same and we never tire of it, that's the amazing thing, we're never bored, we find less and less need to talk among ourselves, we could lie there side by side for hours, or walk together in silence. Even Osnat relaxes, begins to realize that she doesn't always have to be making remarks about everything, she's even a bit prettier, she takes off her glasses sometimes, tucks them away between her tits and starts wandering about dreamily, like Tali.

On the bus going home, in the evening, we're like foreigners among the smelly people, the pale, sweaty, noisy people who take care not to touch us. We sit on the back seat, ignoring the crude looks that we get, they stare at us so hard you'd think we were still naked, turning around and looking again at the sea as it recedes.

On the steps of the house it's already twilight. Barefoot and saturated with sun and salt, hair wet and bedraggled, I go into the dark house that's full of the smells of cooking, the stench of people. Mommy's in the study, in the pale electric light, papers and books scattered about her, dirty coffee cups, plates and scraps of food, the bed unmade, pillows squashed, the ashtray overflowing, the traces of that man, the assistant, the secretary, the translator, the devil knows what, all around her.

ADAM

He used to arrive in the morning and leave early in the afternoon, I didn't meet him but I knew that he came almost every day to translate, to copy, to consult dictionaries. Asya really made him work, because he had time and he very much wanted to redeem the car that still stood there in the garage covered in dust, from time to time it had to be moved so as not to interfere with the work until finally Erlich told them to lift it and push it into the storeroom, they found room for it there between two boxes, it was that small.

"You're in pretty deep with that car," Erlich couldn't resist saying. "You won't see a single cent from that crazy bastard."

But I just smiled.

Heavy summer days, the long vacation at its height. Dafi goes down to the sea every day, she wants to get as sunburned as she possibly can, she says she wants "to be a Negress." And I'm in the garage, which is working at only half capacity because of the workers going away in turn on their holidays. Erlich has gone abroad too, and I have to look after the accounts on my own, staying on to a late hour. When I arrive home in the evening I find Aysa in her room, in a new, unfamiliar kind of chaos. Books and papers on the floor, dirty coffee cups, pips and nut shells on the plates, full ashtrays. And she sits in the middle of all this, silent, milder than she used to be, thinking her thoughts. A quiet woman, detached perhaps, refusing to look me in the eyes.

"So, you've been working," I say softly, a statement, not a question.

"Yes . . . I haven't been outside the house."

"How's he doing?"

She smiles.

"He's odd . . . a strange man . . . but easy to get on with."

I ask no more questions, afraid of alarming her, of upsetting her confidence, of showing surprise, even when I find some strange-looking stew, reddish-brown, in a bowl in the fridge, she's never cooked food like that before.

She blushes, stammering.

"I tried something new today . . . he gave me the idea for it."

"He?"

"Gabriel."

They're cooking together now—

I smile amiably, not saying a word, eat some of the stew, it has a strange sweet taste, I compliment her on it, mustn't give her a sense of guilt, crush her hope, show her a sign of the jealousy that isn't there. Give her strength, give her time, we're no longer young, both in our forties, and the man is strange, unstable, he may disappear at any moment, the long vacation will be over soon.

I remember a particularly hot summer, heavy on the limbs, and I'm up to my eyes in work in the half-empty garage, among the few workers, hardly managing to cope, walking around among the cars and thinking about him, how to hold on to him, maybe I should give him some sign. One day I come home early, waiting in my car at the corner of the street, watching them as they both come out of the house, climbing into her Fiat, she drives and I follow, my heart beating fast. She drives him to his house in the lower city, in the market area, he gets out, she says something to him, leaning out of the window, talking earnestly, he listens with a faint smile, glancing around him. They part. I park my car, run after him to catch him before he disappears in the crowd. I see him standing in the doorway of a vegetable shop buying tomatoes. I touch him lightly, he blushes when he recognizes me.

"How are you?"

"Fine."

"Your grandmother?"

"No change . . . I don't know what to think."

So, he's still trapped here–

"Where do you live?"

He points to a house on the corner, his grandmother's house.

"How's the work that I found for you?"

He smiles, taking off his sunglasses as if he wants to see me better.

"From my point of view it's fine . . . perhaps I really can help her . . . she's trying to do something very difficult . . . but . . ."

"The car?" I interrupt him, I don't want to let him talk too much.

"The car . . ." He's puzzled. "What about it?"

Has he forgotten it?

I study him closely, the dirty shirt, the crumpled clothes, the bag of tomatoes going soft in his hands.

"I'm sorry, I can't let you have it yet, my partner's a stubborn type . . . he isn't prepared . . . but if you're short of money I can always give you a small loan . . ."

And before he can reply I take a bundle of bills out of my pocket, a thousand pounds, and lay them carefully on top of his tomatoes.

He's confused, touching the bills, wanting to count them. He asks if he ought to sign something.

"No need . . . you'll be coming back to us, of course."

"Yes, yes, of course."

"By the way, I ate some of that food that you cooked . . . it was excellent."

He laughs.

"Really?"

Just be careful not to scare him–

I lay a hand on his shoulder.

"Well then, have you gotten used to the sun? You don't want to run away from us . . . ?"

"Not yet."

I shake his hand affectionately and he quickly disappears into the crowded market.

ASYA

Wooden steps, flowery paper on the walls, the stairs up to the village dentist, a tall old woman comes out of the office, putting on an overcoat. She glows–A wonderful dentist, you won't feel a thing.

And through the open door I see a big dentist's chair facing me, and the dentist, with clean-shaven rosy round cheeks, a bow tie straggling over his white coat, sitting in the chair, his head leaning back on the rest, his hands folded in his lap, and the pure reddish light, the rural light, the otherworldly light, oh, such a clear light, shining on his sleepy face, full of glowing contentment at the painless treatment he has just performed.

I enter. In the corner of the room, beside the big primitive washbasin stands Gabriel, in a short white gown, dressed as an assistant, offering me a cup half full of a whitish liquid, like milk mixed with water. A soporific. Apparently this is the revolutionary innovation of this rustic office, this primitive place. They no longer give anesthetic injections, they give you a drink to soothe the pain.

I take the cup from his hand and drink. The liquid's tasteless but it's heavy. Like drinking mercury. It slips down my throat and plunges into my stomach like a clear and smooth weight. A festive feeling, I've drunk something full of meaning. And I've already mounted a second chair, like the armchair in the study except that one arm is missing, to make it easier for the dentist to approach the patient. Such a pleasant silence. At the window that wonderful light. I wait for the drug to take effect, for the light paralysis within, Gabriel lays out instruments on the tray, thin wooden rulers, not threatening, not dangerous, and the dentist still doesn't move from his seat, he really is asleep.

"It's taking effect," I say. I feel nothing but I know that it's taking effect, I want it to take effect, it must take effect. And he takes a thin ruler and with a light touch opens my mouth, his face tense with concentration, sliding gently into the hollow of my mouth, as if trying to make certain where it is, to see if I really have a mouth. I'm overwhelmed by the sweetness of his light touch.

"Where does it hurt?" Indeed, where does it hurt, why did I come to this dentist's office anyway? I must concentrate and find the pain in this delight, so I won't disappoint him, so he won't leave me, I must say something to him.

ADAM

And suddenly her voice in the silence, in the morning light, mumbling something, just as I'm beginning to wake up. Breaking out of a dream, she's excited, groping about her, clutching at my shoulder, I freeze, again she says something, a short sentence, her hand is weak, caressing, and suddenly she realizes that she's touching me, her hand drops, she's midway between dreams and waking, her eyes open.

"What's the time?"

"Quarter to six."

"It's already so light outside." And she turns over, trying to go back to sleep, curling up.

"You were talking in your sleep," I say quietly.

She turns over again quickly, looking up at me.

"What did I say?"

"Just nonsense . . . it wasn't clear . . . a short sentence . . . what did you dream about?"

"A confused dream . . . just . . ."

I get out of bed, go to the bathroom, wash my face, return to the bedroom. She's awake, leaning on the pillow, smiling to herself.

"A strange dream, funny, something about a dentist . . ."

I say nothing, slowly removing my pajama top, sitting down on the bed. It's a long time since she's told me one of her dreams.

"A strange dentist . . . a sort of yokel . . . in a wooden house. A rustic, primitive office. The chair was like the armchair in the study but without one of the arms, they took it off on purpose . . . I remember the afternoon light, a reddish light . . ."

She breaks off, smiling. Is that all? I don't understand why she's telling me. She wraps herself in the thin blanket, closing her eyes, asking me to pull down the blinds. She'll try to sleep a little longer. To carry on with her dream? I put on shirt and trousers, folding my pajamas and putting them under the pillow, pulling down the blinds and darkening the room. I'm on my way out when she suddenly throws the blanket aside, there can't be any doubt, something's exciting her.

"What did I say? Can't you remember?"

"Words that didn't add up to anything . . . I don't remember . . . you were just excited . . . was it a nightmare?"

"No, the opposite, it was supposed to be treatment without pain, instead of an injection they gave me a transparent liquid to drink, it was supposed to be a soporific, a tasteless drink . . . I can still taste it . . . it was the specialty of the dentist's office, before I went in the door a woman came out, all radiant from the wonderful, painless treatment, a really strange dream . . ."

And she laughs. She's hiding something, she's excited, lately there's been something about her that isn't right, she can't relax, she's always watching me. I wait in the doorway.

"What did I say? What did you hear?"

"Just confused things, I wasn't awake either."

"What, for example?"

"I can't remember. Does it matter?"

She doesn't answer, lies back slowly, as if at peace. I turn and leave the room, glance at the sleeping girl, the wet swimsuit still lying there beside the bed, passing through the study and seeing the chaos there, a Dafi sort of chaos. I go into the kitchen, switch the kettle on, slice the bread, bringing out butter, cheese and olives, starting to nibble as I stand there. The water boils, I make coffee, take the cup and the slices of bread out to the balcony, sitting on a chair wet with dew, slowly sipping the coffee and looking down at an ugly sea covered with a yellow mist. What does Dafi do there all day? From the bay comes the sound of explosions from the munitions factory, firing shells out to sea to test them. The cup of coffee in my hand, strong, bitter coffee, bringing me swiftly and firmly to wakefulness, no thoughts in my head, just waiting for the time to pass so I can go out to work. And suddenly Asya's beside me, in an old dressing gown, pursued by her dreams, her face unwashed, unable to go on sleeping, leaning on the rail, breaking the heavy drops of dew with her finger.

"Still thinking about that dream of yours?"

She blushes. "Yes, how did you know?" She pulls out a crushed pack of cigarettes and a box of matches from the pocket of her dressing gown, lights a cigarette, inhaling the smoke deeply.

"It's strange, I keep remembering more details, the dream's getting clearer. There was someone there in a white coat, sort of in disguise, assisting the dentist, because the dentist was asleep. He gave me the drink and started the treatment, with wooden instruments, a narrow ruler, and it really didn't hurt, he treated me so gently, so pleasantly . . . a real experience . . ."

"Who was it?"

"A stranger . . . I didn't know him . . . just a young man."

I look at my watch. She goes inside, switches on the kettle, goes to wash, the air grows warmer, the sounds of the awakening city. Looks like a heavy day of *hamsin.* She comes out to join me with a cup of coffee and a plate of biscuits, it's a long time since we've sat together like this in the morning. She sits down in the corner of the balcony, in the worn wicker chair that they brought here especially for her father in the days of mourning, the cigarette between her fingers, her face reminding me of her old father, who sat there in the last months before his death, a blanket on his knees, solemnly receiving the people who came to console him, to ask his forgiveness.

We sit in silence, sipping our coffee, our faces to the sea.

"Is he coming today?"

"Yes."

"Are you making progress?"

"Slowly."

"We shall have to start making a note of the hours he works." I smile, but she takes me seriously.

"How much does he owe you?"

"I can't remember, I shall have to look at the bill . . . soon we'll be owing him money."

She doesn't answer, she stares at the ground, can she still fall in love?

"We shall have to think about it . . . perhaps I should give him back the car."

"Already?" Softly it slips from her mouth.

"But if he's really making himself useful of course we can continue . . . is he helping you?"

"Yes . . . he's helping me . . . do you mind?"

This fear of me, that frightened look my way.

Pity stirs in me for the little woman gripped by desire. I smile at her, but she's still serious.

"What else was there in your dream?"

"The dream?" She's forgotten it already. "That's all."

I drink the rest of my coffee, bring my boots out to the balcony to put them on. She watches me uneasily. I stand up, comb my hair, smooth my beard, put my keys and wallet in my pocket, she gets up and follows me, accompanying me to the door like a faithful dog, not knowing what to do with herself, as if suddenly she can't bear to be parted from me.

At the door I say, "Now I remember . . . you said something like . . . 'my love, my love' . . ."

"What? 'My love'?" She laughs, astonished. "I said 'my love'? That's impossible."

DAFI

I just didn't understand, I didn't realize at first that the door was locked on the inside, because I'm the only one who locks doors in this house. I pressed the handle hard and started to turn it, trying to force the door open thinking someone was trapped in there, I don't really know why I tried so hard. I was a bit giddy, the sudden change from the sunlight to the darkness in the house confused me. Because today I left the beach at midday and came home, suddenly I got tired of that Nirvana by the sea, and myself too. Osnat stopped coming with us last week and just Tali and I have been going down there. The last days of the vacation and there's a change in the air, a mixture of *hamsin* and autumn, the sky clouding over. And I see that Tali doesn't want to go into the water, doesn't even want to run, just lying there in the sand, studying her brown, shapely body, which attracts more and more furtive glances from passers-by. She hardly talks, just smiles her weary, enigmatic smile. The beach is getting empty and I look across at the houses of the city, at the road and the speeding cars, feeling suddenly alone, seeing that if I go on just being with her I'll begin to be as bored as she is. Today I jumped up and said, "I'm going, I've had enough of this, I'm bored." But she didn't want to come with me, I left her, took the bus and went home, I had to talk to someone, I went straight to the study, because Mommy's always there, and suddenly the door was closed.

I went and fetched my own key and tried to fit it in the lock, then I saw a key in the lock on the other side.

"Mommy?" I shouted. "Mommy?"

But there was no answer, not even a whisper, and suddenly, what a fool I am, I was sure something had happened to her, she'd been murdered, I don't know why the idea of murder suddenly came into my head, perhaps it was all the movies I'd seen in the vacation, I couldn't think of anything less than murder, and I started to wail, thumping the door fiercely—"Mommy! Mommy!"

And suddenly I heard her voice, clear and soft, not the voice of somebody who's just woken up.

"Yes, Dafi, what is it?"

"Mommy? Is that you? What's happened?"

"Nothing, I'm working."

"Then open the door."

"In a moment, I'm just finishing something, don't bother me now."

I still suspected nothing, I was so confused, all hot from the sun. I went to the kitchen for a drink of cold water, came back to the living room, waiting, I don't know what for. After a few minutes the door opened, and Mommy came out, closing the door behind her, she was barefoot, wearing a thin dressing gown, her hair in a bit of a mess, she came and sat down beside me, there was something odd about her but I couldn't think what, she was all attention.

"What's the matter?"

"I just didn't know if you were in the house . . ."

"Have you been down at the beach?"

"Yes."

"Why did you come back so early?"

"I just got tired of it, I suddenly got bored with the sea."

"Perhaps you should go and rest for a while, the vacation will be over soon and you haven't had any rest at all, you've been rushing about everywhere. Are you going to the movies again today?"

"Maybe."

"Come on then"—and she lifted me up—"go and rest, you look really worn out."

She was gentle, inscrutable, her eyes darting about anxiously, and I still didn't understand, I let her lead me to my room, watched her as she tidied up the bed that was still in a mess from the night before, straightening the sheets and the pillows, helping me to unfasten the buckle of my swimsuit, stripping me naked, gently brushing the sand from my shoulders.

"Should I take a shower?"

"Take a shower later . . . you'll be all right . . . you're really burning."

And I didn't understand, hell, I didn't understand anything, letting her put me to bed, covering me up, pulling down the blinds, making the room dark for me, her movements brisk and agile.

She smiled at me, closing the door behind her, and I lay there under the blankets, at midday, shutting my eyes, as if really trying to sleep, as if she'd hypnotized me, and suddenly I jumped out of bed, put on my clothes in a hurry, and barefoot, without a sound, I went to the study, stood by the closed door. It was quiet in there, just the faint rustle of papers. Then I heard her say in a low voice, "I've put her to bed"—a soft chuckle—"she doesn't suspect anything." I shuddered, I thought I was going to faint, and just as I was I fled, going out again into the sunlight, running to Osnat's house, I had to talk to somebody, but there was nobody at her house, I ran to Tali's house, perhaps she'd come back. Her mom opened the door, in her dirty stained dressing gown, a cigarette in the corner of her mouth, a big knife in her hand.

"Tali's not at home," she said and she was about to close the door but I clutched the handle, pleading with her.

"Can I wait for her here?"

She looked at me with surprise, but she let me come in, I went to Tali's room to wait there, but I was in such a state of nerves, pacing about the room, stumbling against the walls, in the end I went into the kitchen. Tali's mom was busy cooking, all the burners of the stove were alight, she was slicing onions, meat, vegetables—great confusion.

"Could I sit here for a while . . . just to watch . . ." I asked, my voice shaking.

She was surprised, but she found a little stool and put it in the corner, I sat there huddled up, watching her, a big woman, sure in her movements, banging the saucepans about angrily, impatiently, impulsively, rushing about the kitchen with a wet cigarette in her mouth, among the piles of vegetables and headless fish streaming blood, the smell and the smoke made my head spin. Tears rose to my eyes, I started to cry a bit. If she'd asked me about Mommy and Daddy I'd have told her everything, but she said nothing. Finally she went out and changed her dressing gown for a broad embroidered skirt with a little white apron, hastily she set the table, looking at me again, a huge woman, her hair combed, a strange, beautiful goy, the knife still in her hand. She touched me gently, raised my head.

"What is it, Dafi?"

My eyes full of tears, I started to tell her but there was a ring at the door and people were arriving, local tradesmen, a tailor, a grocer, I didn't know she was having a lunch party. Conversations began in Hungarian, in Polish, there was laughter. She sat them around the table, scolding them, ran out to bring in the first course, some of them followed her into the kitchen, full of high spirits, sniffing at the saucepans, winking at me. Some of them I knew and I never realized they could be so friendly and cheerful. Tali's mom gave me a plate of meat and potatoes, and I sat there on the stool in the corner, the plate in my lap, my eyes dry now, eating among the crowd, the stampede, the clatter of knives and forks, leaving the empty plate in the sink and slipping away, without saying a word.

In the street I met Tali, walking slowly, she passed me by without seeing me, I went on home. There was nobody there, the study was empty, they'd gone. In the afternoon I went to the movies, and then home in the evening, Mommy and Daddy were there but Mommy didn't look at me, nor I at her, instead a conversation about technical matters, you'd think we were in the garage. I take a shower, watch TV, go to bed with a book, the letters start to go dim, I doze off, and suddenly, with a shock, as if someone's shaking me from inside, I wake up. I go on reading, taking nothing in. Daddy's already asleep, Mommy's pacing around the house, she stops at my door, not looking at me. "Shall I put the light out?" I nod my head. She puts it out. I close my eyes, sure that I'll sleep but I don't sleep. I get up, start to roam around the house, going from room to room, drinking water. The magic of a night at the end of the summer. The dark sea far away. Two more days and it'll be back to school and for the first time I have no desire to study, nor any desire for the vacation to go on, I have no desire for anything. I go back to bed, try to sleep, get up again, the tension's like electricity in my veins. Nothing like this has ever happened to me. I call softly to Daddy and Mommy but they don't wake up. I go to the bathroom, wondering if I should take another shower. I sit on the edge of the bath, exhausted, I've never felt so lonely in my life. Through the window I see in the distance, on the slope across the wadi, an open lighted window. For years now they've been building a house there, and now at last the occupants have moved in. A man sitting in a room almost bare of furniture, in a T-shirt, his hair tousled, a pipe in his mouth, typing feverishly, every now and then he stands up, paces about the room and sits down again, attacking the typewriter with deep concentration. I watch him for a long time. I somehow feel relieved by watching him. I'm not as alone as I thought.

ADAM

Everything's upside down. The long vacation's over, the house full of Dafi's books and note pads, wrapping paper, new writing materials, and Dafi herself is an unhappy "Negress" wandering about distracted, going from room to room, baffled by the masses of homework that she has to get through. In her room the light stays on after we're asleep. Asya has gone back to work, and on Sunday, without consulting me, she cut off her hair, standing in front of the mirror, an aging child looking at herself in despair. It looks like Gabriel has disappeared, but he hasn't really, occasionally I find traces of him in the house, the beret, sunglasses, a cigarette stub in the bathroom, the imprint of his head in a cushion, a French magazine. Once I phoned home during working hours and he lifted the receiver. I didn't say who I was, I just asked for her, he said, "She's not at home, she's at the school, she'll be back soon."

"Who is that, if I may ask . . . ?"

"I'm just a friend of the family."

Is he already a lover, how can I tell, it's all a mystery, nothing is said openly, nor do I want things to be said, I know that I must make myself scarce, not show any special interest. I told them to move the Morris out of the storeroom, to clean it, to fit a new battery and fill the fuel tank. Erlich protested, "What about the bill?" "Tear it up," I said. He didn't tear it up. I found it in a new file, marked in red ink "Not paid, consult the tax people."

I brought the car home, gave the keys to Asya and told her to hand it back to him, and I added a thousand pounds as payment for his work. She took the keys and the money and said nothing. The car stood outside the house for a few days and then disappeared.

Are they meeting all the while in secret? I still don't know, the very idea rouses a sweet pain within, but those days were confused and moved quickly. The festivals were beginning, no, not exactly the festivals, just Yom Kippur. Nineteen hundred and seventy-three.

VEDUCHA

And if this is a human lying in the bed and humans passing by looking at him then why should he be silent? Let him say something he should speak and indeed he has begun to speak without pause hearing his voice a soft voice a broken voice the babbling of an old woman talking and talking perhaps she will grasp some thought. For in her is deep sorrow she has lost much perhaps she will find a little. Smiles all around but no understanding moving the pillow adjusting the blanket turning from side to side saying it'll be all right. Soon. Sleep a little. But if she must sleep better to die and who is this walking about? Dear, familiar, important, going and coming, standing and disappearing. Where is this? Bring me this! Show me I want so much. This, this, crying from the pillow, the mouth hurts from the shrieks.

And this suddenly comes. Suddenly goes. Suddenly stands. Suddenly disappears. Staring darkly always in a hurry hands in pockets and it's night.

He had one word to transform the world but the world is in hands in pockets pacing indifferently, forgetting everything, ready for nothing.

Stars at the window. This, she whispers a word, spits a word, throws off a blanket kicks the pillow rolls to the floor rises and falls crawls rises walks rolls, pushes a door and another door into the sky field orchard. Thorns in the feet and a chill in the head, pushing branches sinking to the ground digging to find a word that will open it all.

PART FOUR

NA'IM

They're getting themselves killed again and when they get themselves killed we have to shrink and lower our voices and mind not to laugh even at some joke that's got nothing to do with them. This morning on the bus when the news was coming over the radio Issam was talking in a loud voice and laughing and the Jews in the front of the bus turned around and gave us a dry sort of look, and at once Hamid, who's always so serious, who reckons he's responsible for us even though he's not our boss officially, touched Issam, nudged him with his finger, and Issam shut up right away.

Knowing where to draw the line, that's what matters, and whoever doesn't want to know had better stay in the village and laugh alone in the fields or sit in the orchard and curse the Jews as long as he likes. Those of us who are with them all day have to be careful. No, they don't hate us. Anyone who thinks they hate us is completely wrong. We're beyond hatred, for them we're like shadows. Take, fetch, hold, clean, lift, sweep, unload, move. That's the way they think of us, but when they start getting killed they get tired and they slow down and they can't concentrate and they suddenly get all worked up about nothing, just before the news or just after, news that we don't exactly hear, for us it's a kind of rustle but not exactly, we hear the words but we don't want to understand. Not lies, exactly, but not the truth either, just like on Radio Damascus, Amman or Cairo. Half-truths and half-lies and a lot of bullshit. The cheerful music from Beirut is much better, lively modern Arab music that makes your heart pound, as if your blood's flowing faster. When we're working on the cars that they leave with us the first thing we do is switch off Radio Israel or the army wave bands and look for a decent station, not a lot of talking, just songs, new and attractive songs about love. A subject that never tires. The main thing is to have none of that endless chattering about the rotten conflict that'll go on forever. When I lie under a car tightening brakes the music in the car sounds like somebody walking over my head. I tell you, sometimes my eyes are a bit wet.

I don't exactly hate the work. The garage isn't such a bad one, big enough not to be always tripping over one another and getting on everybody's nerves. My cousin Hamid isn't far away, he pretends to ignore me but he makes sure they don't pester me too much. But how can I tell them, I wanted to go on studying, not work in a garage. I finished in primary school with very good marks. The young student teacher was very pleased with me. In Hebrew classes I even used to think in Hebrew. And I knew by heart maybe a dozen poems by Bialik, though nobody ever told me to learn them, something catchy about their rhythm. Once a party of Jewish teachers came to the school to check up on what we were doing and the teacher called me up in front of the class and I stood there and recited by heart two verses from *In the City of Slaughter,* they nearly dropped dead on the spot, they were that impressed and maybe that's what the teacher intended, he wasn't exactly a great lover of Jews. Anyway, I could have stayed on at school, the teacher even went to my father to try to persuade him, "It's a pity about the boy, he's got a good brain." But my father was stubborn, "Two studious sons in the family are enough for me," as if we're tied together with a rope and if one goes to college it makes the others educated too. Faiz will be finishing medical school in England soon, he's been studying there for ten years already, and Adnan's going to the university next year, he'll be studying medicine too, or electronics. And I'm the youngest so I have to work. Somebody's got to earn a bit of money. Father's decided to make me a master mechanic like Hamid, who earns lots of money.

Of course I wept and cried and pleaded but it didn't do any good. My mother kept quiet, she didn't want to get into a quarrel on my account, she couldn't tell me why it was Adnan and Faiz and not Na'im, she couldn't say it was because they were the children of another woman, an old woman who died years ago and Father gave her his word before she died.

It was so hard at first getting up in the morning. Father used to wake me up at half-past four, afraid I might not wake up by myself, and I really didn't want to wake up. Darkness all around and Father touching me, pulling me gently out of bed, sitting there and watching me getting dressed and eating breakfast. Leading me to the bus stop through the village that's just beginning to wake up between electric lights and firelights through side streets full of mud and puddles among donkeys and sacks. He turns me over to Hamid like a prisoner. They put me on the cold bus with all the other workers, Mother's homemade bread in a plastic bag in my hand. Slowly the bus fills up and Muhammad, the driver, takes his seat and starts running the engine and shouting at late comers. And I look out through the steamed-up window and see Father sitting there hunched up under the awning. A wrinkled old man wrapped in a black cloak raising his hand to everyone who goes past, starting to talk to somebody but all the time watching me sidelong. And I used to get really angry with him, laying my head on the rail in front of me and pretending to be asleep and when the bus started moving and Father tapped on the window to say good-by I'd pretend not to notice. At first I really did sleep the whole journey and I used to arrive at work dead tired. Yawning all the time and dropping things. Always asking the time. But after a while I began to get used to it. In the mornings I woke up on my own and I'd be one of the first to arrive at the bus stop, sitting down not far from the driver, no longer feeling sleepy. At first I tried taking a book with me to read on the way but they all laughed at me, they couldn't understand it, me going to work in a garage with a book, and a book in Hebrew at that. They thought I was crazy. So I gave it up. I couldn't concentrate anyway. Reading the same page over and over again but not taking it in. So I just look out at the road, seeing the darkness disappear, the flowers on the mountains. I never tire of this route, the same route day after day, an hour and a half there and an hour and a half back.

At four o'clock in the afternoon we're already standing at the bus stop waiting for Muhammad's bus and from all over the city the people of our village and villages nearby are assembling, construction workers, gardeners, garbage men, kitchen workers, manual laborers, domestic help and garage hands. All of them with plastic bags and identity cards ready at hand in shirt pockets. Jews get on the bus too, Jews of all kinds with heavy baskets, most of them get off at the Acre Road. And in Acre more Arabs get on and some Jews as well, a different kind, immigrants from Russia, and Moroccans too. They hardly understand Hebrew. And on the way the Jews thin out and the Arabs too and in Carmel the last of the Jews leave the bus and only Arabs are left. The sun on our backs is nice and the road flies. Haifa disappears from the horizon, Carmel is swallowed by the mountains, the electricity pylons thin out. No smell of Jews now. Muhammad tunes the radio to a Baghdad station that broadcasts verses from the Koran, to entertain us. We go deeper into the mountains, driving among orchards on a narrow road twisting among the fields and there's nothing to remind us of the Jews, not even an army jeep. Only Arabs, barefooted shepherds in the fields with their sheep. Like there never was a Balfour Declaration, no Herzl, no wars. Quiet little villages, everything like they say it used to be many years ago, and even better. And the bus fills with the warbling of that *imam* from Baghdad, a soft voice lovingly chanting the *suras*. We sit there hypnotized, silent at first and then crooning softly along with him.

ADAM

One of those Friday night debates, fruitless conversations among the plates of nuts and the dripping olive oil, when they start on that political crap about the Arabs, the Arab character, the Arab mentality and all the rest of it, I get irritable, start grumbling, lately I've lost patience with these debates. "What do you really know about them? I employ perhaps thirty Arabs in my garage and believe me, every day I become less of an expert on Arabs."

"But those Arabs are different."

"Different from whom?" Getting up from my seat angrily, not knowing why I'm so agitated. Asya blushes, watching me tensely.

"They depend on you . . . they're afraid of you."

"What? What are you talking about?"

But how can I explain? All entangled in my ideas. I sit down again, saying nothing.

Hamid, for example–

My own age perhaps but with the body of a youth, very thin. Only his face is wrinkled. The first worker I ever had, he's worked with me nearly twenty years. Silent, proud, a lone wolf. He never looks at you straight, but if you catch his eye you'll see that the pupils are very black, like coffee grounds in an empty cup.

What's he thinking to himself? What does he think about me, for example? He hardly ever says a word, if he does speak it's always to do with work, engines, cars. Whenever I try to draw him out on other subjects he refuses to talk. But his loyalty is really unique, or maybe it isn't loyalty. In all these years he hasn't been absent a single day, and not through fear of getting sacked. He's a permanent employee with full rights. On the first of the month Erlich gives him four thousand pounds in cash, which Hamid stuffs into his shirt pocket, without counting it, saying nothing. What he spends this money on I can't imagine, he always appears in scruffy clothes and worn shoes.

An expert and senior mechanic. These last few years he's worked in a small shop that he built for himself in a corner of the garage, and that's his kingdom. He restores old cars. A complicated professional job requiring precision, imagination, golden hands and infinite patience. He dismantles old engines, some of them completely wrecked, drills and cuts out new parts and breathes life into them. He works without rest, no radio beside him, no casual conversation or joking with the other workers, no teasing the customers. He's the first to return to work after meal breaks but he also stops working the moment it's time to go, he's never been prepared to work overtime, he washes his hands, picks up his empty plastic bag and goes.

Two or three years ago he suddenly became religious. He brought from his home a dirty little prayer mat and every now and then he'd stop work for a few minutes, strip off his shoes, go down on his knees and bow toward the south, toward the lathe and the tool racks on the wall. Reciting passionate verses to himself, to the Prophet, who knows? Then putting on his shoes and going back to work. A strange kind of piety, grim somehow. Even the other Arabs in the garage used to stare at him darkly.

Because in spite of his solitariness he is a kind of leader to them, even if he doesn't try to have too much to do with them. He walks among them aloof and silent. But when I need a new worker he brings me a boy or a youth within two or three days, as if he's the chief of a whole tribe. Eventually I realized that most of the Arabs in the garage are in fact his relations, close or distant cousins.

I asked him once, "How many cousins have you got?"

A lot, he'd never bothered to count them.

"And how many of them work here?"

"How many?" He tried to evade the question. "There are a few . . ."

In the end he admitted to at least ten, in addition to his two sons. This surprised me very much because I never imagined that those were his sons, he didn't seem to have any special tie to them.

"How many children have you got altogether?"

"Why do you want to know?"

"Just . . . curious."

"Fourteen."

"How many wives?"

"Two."

He was really upset by questions like these, fidgeting nervously all the time with a screwdriver, turning his back to me, impatient to get rid of me and go back to his work.

To his credit, although he used to provide me with new workers, he never interfered later on and if I was forced to sack them he didn't say a word, only bringing me a few days later some new cousin or relative from his endless supply.

On the first day of the war he arrived of course, but only a few others came with him. They were afraid to leave their villages, they didn't know what was going to happen. I grabbed him at once.

"Where are the others?"

He said nothing, not even looking at me, what did I want from him? But I wasn't letting him off that easily.

"Hamid, you tell them all to come to work. What is this? This war of ours isn't a holiday for you. There are cars here that need repairing, people will come back from the front and expect to find their cars repaired. Do you hear?"

But he didn't reply, looking at me with hatred, his hands in his pockets, as if all this had nothing to do with him.

"You should really be fighting with us, you should've been called up too. Anyone who doesn't come in tomorrow will be fired. Tell all your relations."

He shrugged his shoulders, as if he didn't care.

But for the whole of that day I didn't let him work on his engines, I gave him dirty, menial jobs, tightening brakes, changing flats, charging batteries. He said nothing but it was obvious that his pride was hurt. The next day all the Arabs came in and he went back to his workshop. During the entire war not a single worker was absent. Hamid even made it his business to bring in workers to take the place of Jews who'd been called up.

But beyond this I don't get involved with him, nor with the others. I've always refrained from visiting their villages and being a guest in their homes, as some of the employers in the neighborhood do. It always ends in trouble, it gets out of hand sooner or later. In general I've rather kept my distance in recent years, convinced that the business runs itself quite smoothly without me. Already there are many workers whose names I don't know, what with such a turnover. The garage has become full of boys over the last few years, sometimes even children. The Arabs bring small boys with them, brothers, cousins, or just waifs from the villages. They are quiet and obedient, dragging the boxes of tools around, fetching keys, opening hoods, tightening brakes, wiping black handprints from the doors, changing stations on the radio. The Arabs love little personal servants like these, they like having somebody they can shout at, give orders to. It gives them a sense of importance and security. The more the garage grew in size, the more little boys ran about in it.

Once I asked Erlich, "Tell me, is this kindergarten costing me money?"

But he smiled, shook his head. "Don't worry, they're saving you tax, you're profiting from them."

Some of the boys were given the job of cleaning the garage, sweeping up, scrubbing the floor. The garage began to look clean and respectable. One day I was standing by myself in the yard, deep in thought, and suddenly somebody pushed a broom between my feet and said rudely, "Do you mind moving?" I looked down, a little Arab boy with a big broom, looking at me steadily and insolently. I felt a little stab of pain in my heart. I was reminded of Yigal, I don't know why, something about those dark eyes.

"Who brought you here?" I asked him, wondering if he knew I was the boss.

"My cousin, Hamid."

Hamid, of course. Every other man here is his cousin. It won't be long before I discover that I'm related to him too. These Arabs, they don't spare their children. They'd be better off at school than sweeping up the garbage and picking up screws here.

"How old are you, boy?"

"Fourteen years and three months."

"How is this? Didn't you want to stay on at school?"

He blushed, in a panic, afraid I was going to throw him out. He started to mumble something about his father, who wouldn't let him . . . little liar.

And he went on sweeping around me. And suddenly I was moved, I put out my hand and lightly touched his tousled head, covered with dust from his work with the broom. This little Arab, my employee, what's he thinking about? What's his business? Where's he from? What's happening to him here? I'll never know. He told me his name a moment ago and already I've forgotten it.

NA'IM

In the early days it was very interesting in the big garage. New faces all around me, coming and going, all kinds of Jews bringing their cars in, laughing and shouting. Some of the mechanics were Jewish bastards, some were local Arabs, corrupt as hell with their complicated jokes. Noise and confusion. On the walls in every corner there were pictures of naked girls, showing nearly everything, maddening, breath-taking, Jewish and non-Jewish blondes and brunettes, Negresses and redheads. Amazing. Unbelievable. Lying with eyes closed on new tires, opening the doors of smart cars, resting tits and asses and long legs on engines or screws or sets of spark plugs. On the ass of one of these gorgeous chicks they'd drawn the whole year's calendar, it was that big. These pictures drove me crazy. I was afraid to look at them and I couldn't keep my eyes off them. Sometimes I got so hard it hurt. In the noise and the dirt among the cars and the workers I used to wander about in the first few weeks daydreaming. Several times my underpants got wet. In bed at night I was squeezed by desire, remembering the girls and not letting them go. Coming all over the place, a fountain of come I was. Leaping from one to the next, unwilling to do without any of them, kissing and burning and coming and getting horny again. In the morning I used to get up exhausted and pale and Mother and Father were worried about me. But then slowly I began to get used to the pictures and after a month I could stare at them indifferently, like at the other pictures on the wall, the two presidents, the live one and the dead one, and that old woman who's the prime minister, all hanging there among the girls. I stopped getting excited.

At first I wasn't really doing anything. Fetching tools for the mechanics and taking them back to the toolboxes, cleaning dirty fingermarks off the cars. I tried to keep close to Hamid but of course he didn't need an assistant because he didn't work on the actual cars, he stood at a workbench taking engines apart.

After a week they gave me a broom and a rag and a bucket and I spent all my time sweeping the floor, picking up old screws, spreading sawdust on patches of oil, it was my job to keep the garage clean. An impossible job and terribly boring. Everybody ordered me around, Arabs, Jews, anybody who felt like it. Even strangers who just happened to be passing. Fetch, boy, lift, boy, grab this, boy, clean that, boy. Anybody who felt like giving orders used to catch me and order me around. And they called me "boy" on purpose to annoy me. But I kept quiet, not wanting to argue. I was really fed up. I hated the work. I had no enthusiasm for anything, even the cars didn't interest me. When will I get to be a mechanic, when will I learn something and what's it all for anyway? Luckily the garage was so big I could disappear sometimes without being missed. I'd take the broom and looking at the floor I'd sweep and sweep toward the back exit until I was right outside the garage, go into the backyard of some empty house and sit down on a box watching the street, seeing children in school uniform going home with their school bags. So miserable. Thinking about the poems and stories they read and how I'm going to end up really dumb with this broom and these rusty screws. I'd cheer myself up a bit whispering a few lines from Bialik, once I knew so much of it by heart and now every day I remember less and less. In the end I'd get up and take the broom and start sweeping around me and slowly go back to the garage, still sweeping, going inside and mixing with the people, who hadn't noticed that I'd gone or that I'd come back.

Who's our boss anyway?

It was a long time before I figured out who the boss of the garage was. At first I thought it was the old clerk who sits there all day in the little office, the only place where there's no pictures of naked women. But they told me he was only the cashier, just a clerk.

Then I had my eye on one of the Jewish mechanics who was in charge of the work and gave out orders, he was the one who dealt with the customers, testing their cars for them. But they told me he was the foreman. In the end they pointed him out to me, the real boss, the one that everything belongs to, his name's Adam, about forty-five years old, maybe more than that, with a big beard. Maybe it was because of the beard I didn't realize he was the boss. I didn't think he belonged to the garage at all, I thought he was some kind of artist or professor. What's the beard for? How should I know? I never guessed that everything belonged to him.

He wears partly working clothes and partly not working clothes. A white shirt or a nice clean sweater and blue working trousers. Most of the time he isn't in the garage but driving around in a big American car, an old car but very quiet. Uses the car to fetch a new engine or some complicated bit of equipment for the garage. When he arrives he's surrounded straightaway by a bunch of mechanics, they follow him, talking to him, asking him questions, consulting him. And he looks all the time like he's about to drop, he always looks tired, thinking about something else that's got nothing to do with the garage. But in the end the circle closes around him and he stands there in the middle, listening and not listening. Standing there patiently, looks like all he wants is not to touch them and not to be touched. If he talks at all it's quietly, with his head a bit bent, chewing the end of his beard like he's ashamed of something. He's not even interested in women and sometimes we get some really attractive high-class chicks coming into the garage with neat little cars and they spend half the day wandering about and getting in the way. We're so busy watching them we start dropping tools. Even the ones lying underneath the cars watch them. And they run after Adam as well, trying to talk to him, trying to make him laugh, but he isn't the type that laughs easily. He hardly notices them. He looks through us ordinary workers like we're air. He doesn't really care about the work in the garage anyway. But when he walks around the place we all start to move faster and we even turn the radios down, though he's never said anything against Arab music. Sometimes when there's a difficult problem they ask him to look at an engine or listen to it or bring him some part that they've taken out, showing it to him and asking if it's any good or if it should be changed. He looks and listens, his hands in his pockets. And then, so sure of himself, without hesitation, he tells them what to do.

But sometimes he can spend the whole morning standing at the lathe cutting out some missing part. Consulting Hamid, who seems to be the only one he really respects.

He doesn't concern himself with the accounts. He goes into the office only when an argument starts there, when some customer gets a nasty shock because of the price they're asking. He checks the bill again but he's as stubborn as a mule and he doesn't knock off a single cent. I sometimes sweep the office at the end of the day and I overhear the arguments. They say to him "You're the most expensive in town." And he answers "It's up to you. Nobody's forcing you to come back. Do you want me to show you the price list?" And he smiles, partly at them but mostly to himself.

Once, just before work was over, when I was sweeping the garage for the second time I came to a place where he was standing talking to somebody and I waited quietly for him to move. The workers were already changing their clothes and washing their hands and the garage was nearly empty. He stood there talking and just didn't notice me standing there with the broom. I'm sure he didn't know who I was, or that I'd been working in his garage for more than a month.

I stood there leaning on the broom and he stood on a pile of dirt listening to some important-looking guy who talked and talked. It'd been a crazy day and I'd already cleaned the garage maybe five times. All the time they'd been bringing in cars that wouldn't start, cars that had been driven too fast and had skidded in the rain. There was no end to it. At last the important-looking guy in the suit who'd been talking about politics went away, but Adam stayed where he was, thinking hard. I was afraid to say anything to him. Suddenly he noticed me standing just a few feet away from him waiting with the broom. "What do you want?" I got all confused. He scared me staring at me like that.

"Would you mind moving a bit? I must sweep under you . . ."

And he smiled and moved a bit and I started sweeping where he'd been standing in a hurry so he could move back there if he wanted to. But now he was watching me, staring at me like I was some kind of freak. Suddenly he asked:

"Who brought you here?"

"My cousin, Hamid," I said at once, trembling and blushing and not knowing why. What could he do to me anyway? After all he gives me only a tiny wage that one way or another goes straight to my father. And he doesn't really scare me that much, it's just that big bushy beard of his.

"How old are you, boy?"

Him too—"boy"—damn him.

"Fourteen years and three months."

"How is this? Didn't you want to stay on at school?"

I couldn't believe it. How was it he knew about the school? I started to mumble "Yes, of course . . . but my father didn't want . . ."

He was about to say something but he kept quiet, still staring at me. And I started carefully moving the broom and cleaning around him, piling up the dirt in a hurry. And suddenly I felt him touching me, laying his hand lightly on my head.

"What's your name?"

I told him. My voice was shaky. No Jew had ever touched my head before. I could've recited a poem for him. Just like that. If he'd asked me to. He really hypnotized me. But he didn't know such a thing was possible.

And since then he's smiled at me every time he sees me. Like he remembers me. And a week later they took me off sweeping and taught me another job, tightening brakes. Not too difficult. I started tightening brakes for them.

DAFI

So tired. What do you think? At night I lie awake, snatching maybe one hour of sleep in the morning when Mommy's already dragging me out of bed. And until she sees me sitting at the table drinking my coffee she doesn't leave the house. It's odd, but at first the tiredness isn't so bad and I'm not even late for school. In the first class I'm fairly lucid, anyway most of them are asleep, including the teacher. But the crunch always comes in the third class, just then, at around quarter past ten, I feel all empty inside, my heart sinks, my breathing gets heavy, I feel dead. At first I used to go outside by myself, to wash my face and try to sleep on a bench somewhere. Near the outhouse I found a sort of alcove and I tried to catch some sleep there, but it wasn't safe because Shwartzy's always snooping around (what the hell does he think he's doing patrolling the girls' toilets?) and once he caught me there, the sneaky bastard, and sent me back into class on the double. I started looking for other places to sleep but it wasn't any use, the school wasn't designed to furnish sleep for its pupils. It really was depressing, after all I needed only a quick doze, quarter of an hour maybe, to bring me back to life. At last I had a wonderful idea, I'd sleep in the class during the lesson, and I even found a suitable place, at the end of the fourth row a pillar sticks out and this makes an ideal hiding place, especially if you push the desk right up against the wall. That way you can escape the teacher's notice, present but not present.

Once during recess when the classroom was empty I sat down there and Tali and Osnat came in looking for me and went out again without seeing me.

Then I had to work on Yigal Rabinovitch to get him to change places with me, without telling him the real reason. But he didn't want to change, it seemed he'd discovered the advantages of his place too. So I started buttering him up, smiling at him, chatting with him during recess, walking home with him after school and even touching him as if by accident. He found all this a bit confusing, the dumb cluck, I saw it wouldn't be long before he started falling in love with me. He took to waiting for me outside the house in the morning to walk with me to school, even skipping basketball practice before class. I didn't want to overdo it, just enough to persuade him to change places. He refused and refused but in the end he gave in. Poor devil, his marks are so bad he could be in real trouble, he's got a good reason too for not wanting to be too conspicuous. I really wanted to kiss him but I had to be careful not to give him the wrong idea. We went to the teacher and told her we were changing places and I brought in a cushion that I'd prepared especially, it fit into the corner nicely, in just the right position for keeping me out of sight, putting the cushion against the wall, laying my head on it and going to sleep, yes, really going to sleep. It's winter now, the sky's gray and it's dark in the classroom, to save energy we're not allowed to switch on the lights, and we sit there in our overcoats because Shwartzy's taken the heaters away, he's taking the energy crisis seriously and he thinks we must save fuel in the national interest.

And this way I snatch some sleep. In Bible or Talmud or Citizenship. Of course not in math, because I'm too scared of Baby Face, who stalks around like a fat cat, always picking on me. But in the subjects in which I'm strong I don't care.

Best are Arzi's Talmud classes. For one thing, he's short-sighted, and then, he hardly ever moves from his chair, he comes in and sits down and doesn't get up until the bell rings, one of these days the chair will catch fire underneath him and he won't budge, also, he talks in a sort of quiet drone that's just great for sending you to sleep. Finally, and most important, in his lessons I don't miss much by sleeping. Even if I sleep right through till the bell goes the class has only learned two lines in the meantime.

The others in the class have gotten used to the idea of me catching up on my sleep like this, and Tali, who sits in front of me, is always having to wake me up if anyone comes near. But today there was bright sunlight and I was dead tired. I got into my corner, put the pillow in place and leaned against the wall (where the plaster had already peeled right off) and went to sleep straightaway. Suddenly Arzi stood up, something made him excited or maybe the sun went to his head, and he started walking about among the benches. He saw me at once and when Tali tried to warn me he said, "Sh . . . sh . . ." and the others all held their breath, grinning as they watched the little old man creeping toward me. He stood there beside me for a few seconds (so I was told later) and suddenly he began to sing, "Sleep, sleep little girl," and the class started laughing. But I still didn't wake up, I think I was actually dreaming, I was that tired. In the end he touched me, thinking maybe I'd fainted or something, and I opened my eyes and saw his kindly, smiling face. Lucky that it was him. And he began to intone like a proper Talmudist, "And what do we learn from this?" And his answer: "That they are repairing the beds at your house!" The old man had a sense of humor. And everyone roared with laughter. What could I say? I just smiled back at him. Then he said, "Perhaps you should go home and sleep, Dafna." And I really should have refused and told him I wanted to learn Talmud, but the idea of more sleep appealed to me so much that I stood up, shoved my books and note pads into my school bag and left, slipping away through the empty corridors before Shwartzy could get on my track. I walked home quickly.

At first I was so bleary I thought I'd come to the wrong house, because when I opened the door I saw a boy I didn't recognize standing in the kitchen trying to drink something. But it really was our house and the boy was just one of Daddy's workers who'd come to collect a briefcase that Daddy had forgotten. I startled him, he picked up the briefcase and left in a hurry. I undressed, in midmorning, put on my pajamas, pulled down the blinds and got into bed. Bless Arzi, a real teacher, so considerate. But this damn bed of mine. I just lay down, and closed my eyes and again sleep fled.

NA'IM

And one morning they pulled me out from under a car and said, "Go to him, he wants you." So I went to this Adam. He looked at me and said, "What's your name?" I told him again, "Na'im."

"Good, take this key and go to my house and on the little cabinet on the right in the foyer you'll find a black briefcase. Bring it here. Do you know Carmel?"

"Yes," I said, I didn't really know it at all but I just felt like wandering around the city for a while. He wrote the address on a piece of paper, told me which bus to take, took out a fat wallet full of notes, gave me ten pounds and sent me off.

And I found his house on my own without asking anyone. A three-story house in a nice quiet neighborhood, full of trees and gardens. And from everywhere you could see the sea, really beautiful, a slice of blue between the houses. I kept on stopping to take another look at it. I'd never seen the sea from so high up. Not many people in the streets, just a few old women with baby carriages, feeding the fat babies. These Jews spoil their children like hell and then send them off to war.

I went into the building. The staircase was brightly polished, I went up to the second floor like he told me and found the name on the door. I rang the bell first so if there happened to be anyone at home I wouldn't be accused of breaking in.

I waited a moment and then opened the door myself. The apartment was a bit dark but very tidy. Chaos in the garage and here everything's tidy, everything in its place except for his briefcase, which wasn't on the cabinet on the right or on the cabinet on the left but was on the dining table. I picked it up and was about to go because this was all he'd asked me to do but suddenly I didn't want to go, I liked the look of this dark apartment. I went into the living room, treading on the soft carpets. I looked out through the window and saw the sea again. I even sat down to rest for a moment in an armchair beside a green potted plant. I looked at some of the pictures on the wall. Beside the radio, in a black frame, there was a picture of a boy, about five I'd say, I could tell right away it was his son. I really ought to have gone, it isn't nice to walk around like this, touching things, but suddenly I wanted to have a look inside their kitchen. What do the Jews eat? I'd never looked inside a Jewish fridge. The kitchen was very clean. The table sparkled. In the sink there was just one unwashed cup. I opened the fridge. There wasn't much food in it. Some cheese, a few eggs, some yogurt, a bottle of fruit juice, a piece of cold chicken on a plate, a few medicines and about a dozen different kinds of chocolate. I guess they eat chocolate for lunch.

That's enough, I thought, I'd better go. But a big jug with a thick red drink in it looked interesting. I'd never seen a drink like that before. I decided to have a taste of it, though I wasn't at all thirsty. I found a cup and poured out a little bit, and I was drinking it, it had a funny taste like turnips, when I heard a key turning in the lock. Quickly I emptied the cup into the sink, turned on the tap and washed the cup. A girl about the same age as me in school uniform came into the apartment and threw down her school bag inside the doorway. Suddenly she noticed me and stood there looking confused, like she thought she'd come into the wrong house. I walked a few steps toward her, feeling myself blushing, waving the black briefcase and before she could scream or anything like that I said, "Your father sent me to pick up this briefcase that he forgot and he gave me the key as well." She didn't answer but she gave me such a sweet smile. I knew straightaway that she was his daughter, she was very pretty with big black eyes and fair hair. A bit short but very pretty, a bit fat but very pretty. It's a pity I've seen her because I won't ever be able to forget her. She's one of those girls that I only have to see and I know I loved them even before I saw them. And she said, "Would you like something to drink?" and I said, "No," and walked past her taking care not to touch her, holding the briefcase tightly under my arm, and I fled.

Half an hour later I was already downtown on the way to the garage. But suddenly I had an idea. I went into a hardware shop and got a copy of the key to the flat. I went back to the garage and personally gave him the briefcase and the key and the change from the ten pounds. And in my shoe I could feel the duplicate key against the sole of my foot.

But of course he didn't suspect anything, smiling at me like his daughter.

"Thank you. That's fine. And very quick."

And he let me keep the change.

That was all.

ADAM

The end of December already. More than two months have passed since the end of the war. Every day I still hope for some sign of him, but there's no sign. Did he just get tired of us? But where is he? Asya hardly ever mentions him but it seems to me that she thinks I should be out looking for him. I spend a lot of time driving around the streets, searching for the little Morris at least. How can a car disappear without a trace? Once I caught sight of a blue Morris and followed it through the streets until finally it stopped outside the Technion and a tall old man, smartly dressed, got out of it, looking at me angrily. Naturally hardly a day passes without my going down to the old house in the lower city to see if a shutter or a window has been opened there. But the apartment on the second floor is just as he left it on the first day of the war. Sometimes I'm not content with looking from the outside but I go inside and up the stairs to knock on the door itself. On the first floor there's a clothing store. It's always closed. And on the second floor, aside from the grandmother's flat, there's another apartment and an old widow living alone. She's watched my investigations with great suspicion. I had only to walk up the stairs and the door of her flat would open a crack and she'd peer out at me, watching in silence as I knocked on the door, waited for a while and then went down again. At first I used to ignore her, after a while I decided to try getting some information out of her.

She was very suspicious of me–

Had she seen Gabriel Arditi? No. Did she know of any change in the old lady's condition? She didn't. Which hospital was she in, by the way? Why did I want to know? I explained that I was a friend of Gabriel and since the war I'd had no news of him.

She thought for a moment, then gave me the name of the institution to which the old lady had been taken. A geriatric hospital not far from Hadera.

She was a heavily built woman, with bright eyes, a little mustache sprouting from her lip. Still she looked at me dubiously.

"Do you happen to have a key to the flat?"

No, she had no key, she gave hers to Gabriel.

"I suppose I shall have to break down the door," I whispered to myself, thinking aloud.

"In that case I think I'd better call the police at once," she said without a moment's hesitation.

"Who?" I smiled.

"The police."

"What do you mean?"

"What do you mean coming here and breaking the door down? It's not even your friend's house."

She stood in her doorway immovable as a rock. There was no doubt she would call the police.

I went away.

A few days later I arrived there late at night. Slowly I climbed the stairs and in the dark I began quietly trying to open the door with a bundle of keys I'd brought from the garage. But after only a few minutes the other door opened and the old neighbor appeared in a nightdress and with a kerchief on her head. She looked at me angrily.

"You again."

I decided not to answer, to ignore her, continuing my vain attempt to open the door with my keys.

"I shall call the police."

I didn't reply. She watched my unsuccessful efforts.

"Why don't you go and see the old lady herself, perhaps she'll let you have the key."

I said nothing, didn't respond. But the idea seemed to me a good one. Why not, after all? I went on trying the keys. In the end I went away slowly in the dark.

Two days later I was at the geriatric hospital. An old building but painted green, between the orchards, on the edge of one of the older settlements. I went into the office and told them I was a relative of Mrs. Ermozo and I'd come to visit her. They sent for the matron, an energetic, vivacious woman about my age. She greeted me with enthusiasm.

"At last somebody has come. We were afraid she'd been completely forgotten. Are you her grandson too?"

Strange, thinking I was her grandson.

"No . . . I'm a more distant relation . . . has Gabriel Arditi been visiting here?"

"Yes, but for a few months now there's been no sign of him. Come and see her."

"How is she? Still unconscious?"

"Still unconscious but in my opinion there's been some improvement. Come with me, watch them feeding her."

And she took my arm and led me into one of the wards. She pointed to the bed where the old woman lay.

So this grandmother really does exist. Wrapped in a white smock, like a big ball. Sitting up in bed and looking around her wildly. Her long hair, still dark, scattered over her shoulders, a big napkin tied around her neck and a dark-skinned little nurse, probably a Mexican from the immigrants' settlement, feeding her with endless patience, with a wooden spoon, giving her a gray porridge that looked like soft mud. It wasn't easy to feed her because she seemed quite unaware of the fact that she was being fed, and every now and then she'd suddenly turn her head to one side, looking for something on the ceiling or at the window. Sometimes she spat out the food and the gray liquid trickled down her face. The nurse took a sponge and wiped her carefully. There was something very sad in the empty eyes moving backward and forward about the room, sometimes pausing on some random object.

There were several old women in the ward, they got up from their beds and approached us with great curiosity, standing around us in a little circle.

"Every meal takes nearly an hour," the matron said with a smile.

I was staring at her as if hypnotized.

"How old is she?" I asked suddenly, forgetting that I'd introduced myself as a relative.

"I'm sure you don't know . . . even though you are one of the family . . . guess . . ."

I mumbled something.

"Well then, you won't believe it . . . but we've seen her Ottoman birth certificate. She was born in 1881. '81. You can do the arithmetic yourself. She's ninety-three years old. Isn't it wonderful? 1881 . . . Do you know any history? That was when the first Bilu settlers arrived in the country . . . *Hibbat Zion* . . . the beginnings of Zionism . . . to say nothing of world history. Isn't it amazing? She was alive then . . . a lady of history . . . a real treasure . . . perhaps she concealed her age from you? And her hair is still black . . . her skin is smooth . . . only a few wrinkles . . . it's a wonder . . . and that's the truth, although we're used to old people here, that's what the place is for, after all. We've never had such an old lady before."

And the matron went to her, took out from the old lady's hair a little comb that was hidden there and started to comb her hair, smoothing it over her cheeks, pinching them gently. The old lady didn't look at her, feeling nothing, staring at the window.

"I tell you, if she hadn't gone into a coma she could have carried on for years . . . or perhaps it's the opposite . . . it's because she's gone into a coma that she will carry on for years . . . come and see . . . come closer . . . don't be afraid . . . perhaps she'll recognize you . . . perhaps something in you will revive her . . ."

"You still have hopes for her?"

"Why not? She's changing all the time. You don't know, but I've been watching her, and seeing her progress. A year ago they brought her here and she was like a vegetable. A vegetable? Worse than that . . . a stone . . . a big silent stone. And very slowly she began to change. She began to move like a plant, like some primitive creature, do I know. But these last few months there's been a dramatic change. You're smiling? Of course you can't know. But she's a human being again, her eyes are alive, her movements are human. She doesn't speak of course but she's already thinking, speaking her first syllables. One night she even tried to get away, they found her outside in the orchard. Of course we have hopes. Have you given up hope, in the family? That Mr. Arditi, her grandson, he seems to have disappeared."

Hesitantly I went closer to the bed, and suddenly the old woman turned her head and looked at me, screwing up her eyes as if trying to remember something. From the corners of her mouth, still full of porridge, two thin streams began to ooze.

"No, she doesn't recognize me . . . I'm a distant relation . . . it's many years since she's seen me . . ."

"But even so you came to see her . . . that was very nice of you."

The old woman was staring at me, simply staring, she couldn't take her eyes off me, she even began to murmur. Strange sounds came from her mouth.

"The beard . . . the beard . . ." the old women around us began calling out excitedly. "The beard reminds her of something."

The old woman's hands were shaking, something was troubling her, she was fascinated by my beard, as if she wanted to grab it.

I felt a stab of panic, I started to retreat, afraid she might wake up and I'd get involved here. The dark-skinned nurse wiped away the streams of porridge.

"You're doing a wonderful job here."

"I'm glad you think so." The matron's face lit up. "Perhaps you'd like to have a look around . . . see the other wards . . . do you have time?"

She, at any rate, seemed to have plenty of time. For the sake of public relations she led me from ward to ward, to see the old men and women lying there, playing cards, eating a second breakfast. She stopped to talk to them, touching them as if they were pieces of furniture, adjusting their clothing, even combing the hair of some of them. And they smiled at her, a little frightened. Meanwhile she explained to me some of the problems of the institution, the rising cost of laundry, the cut in the government subsidy, fruitless attempts to interest benefactors. Nobody's prepared to invest in a geriatric hospital.

"I'm prepared to," I said suddenly, already at the door.

"What do you mean?"

"I'm prepared to make a small donation to the hospital."

She was stunned, and blushing she clutched my hand.

"Perhaps we should go to my office . . ."

"No need . . . I'm in a hurry . . . but . . ." And standing there at the door I took out my wallet and gave her five thousand pounds.

She took the notes hesitantly, unable to disguise her joy, amazed at the size of the gift.

"Sir . . . sir . . ." she mumbled. "But what is to be done with the money? I mean, do you have any special requests?"

"The money is in your hands . . . you can buy games for the old people . . . or some piece of equipment . . . the only thing I ask is that you look after that old lady, don't let her die . . ."

"Of course . . . naturally . . . you've seen for yourself . . ."

"I'll be in touch again to find out how she is . . . and if anyone else comes here . . . Mr. Arditi . . ."

"You're always welcome, we shall do all we can . . . even without the money."

She was holding the notes in both her hands, confused, and very grateful.

"Perhaps after all some kind of receipt . . . I don't even know your name . . ."

But I didn't want to give her my name, didn't want him to know I'd been there, looking for him. I shook the matron's hand and said with a smile:

"Write in your books—an anonymous gift."

VEDUCHA

The black hand wants to feed the eyes, to move the head and give ear. Caress of soft little white worms trickling down. Bitter milk that once was sweet. Sounds of orchards and smell of people. Wet below, a secret pool, a gushing fountain. And sunlight at all the windows. Count the people. Four six one three. But why has a walking broom come in a confusing man, an upturned broom moving about the room walking alone anxious and now approaching the radiant laughing woman wants to sweep her face. Wants too to sweep an old woman in her bed. Oh, oh, oh, come heavy broom, bearded face. I know this broom, there were many such brooms walking the narrow streets full of black brooms there there in the old place in these ruins. Suddenly not orchards but thorns, little bushes rocks and strong sunlight houses upon houses and slopes. What is this called? What is the name? Oh, oh, an unknown woman, a woman without a name, oh, oh, what is the name of the place? Must know the name quickly must think the name. A blank wall has fallen here, gray stones with little clumps of moss. How did they say? How did they say it? How did they say it?–Usalem. Oh, I have it–Usalem, that's it, Usalam. No, not that, something else–Rusalem. Yes, Rusalem. An important place, a hard place–Rusalem.

But that's not the name. Something very close. Find it find it. Oh, oh, inside all is shaking but find it, it's important, think, oh, oh, find it inside, inside is a little light, a distant light. Oh, oh, little light.

Usalem? Usalam? But not so heavy, not lam, lighter, humbler–Usalim. Oh, Usalim. I have it. No, not that again? Rusalim. Rusalim. I'm sure they called it Rusalim. That's the place, the rocks, the thorns, quiet now.

The broom has gone. What? The sun at another window. What? Yes, Usalem, Usalem again. What does Usalam want. Usalam has returned. A mistake, sorry, Rusalem. Now it's clear. Where was she born?–Rusalem. Where are they from?–Rusalem. Next year where? –in Rusalem. But did they really say–Rusalem? Not that. Just like it, but a little different. I've forgotten. Must rest.

Black hands turning me. Pulling a sheet spreading a sheet. Light has gone, no sun. Dark at the windows. That place with wall and towers, with brooms, that place with a desert at the end. Suddenly a desert. What's its name? Not Usalem–Rusalim. But there was something at the beginning. Gerusalem, Sherusalem, Merusalem, Jerusalem. Oh, oh, oh, Jerusalem. Jerusalem, Jerusalem. Exactly, but no. I weep. Great pain. Jerusalem. Simple. Ah, that's it. Jerusalem.

NA'IM

And since then I had my eye on him all the time. Even without looking I could tell when he was in the garage and when he wasn't. Like a dog almost I could sniff him out. I could tell the sound of his American car apart from all the other cars. Even though now I spent most of the time on the floor under a car tightening the brake cables and I saw the world mostly between the legs moving about beside my head. I carried the key to his house around with me all the time, passing it from pocket to pocket, at night putting it under the pillow. I was very aware of this key, it was like carrying a gun without a license. I watched him a long way off standing in a crowd of people and I was underneath a car thinking about his house, the dark rooms and the blue sea through the big window. The clean and tidy kitchen and the chocolate in the fridge, the door opening suddenly and the pretty girl coming in from the sunlight, throwing down her school bag and smiling at me.

I smile back, to myself, feeling the key in my shirt pocket. Whenever I want I can get in there again, I go there in the mornings for reasons of my own, quietly opening the door and wandering about the rooms, eating chocolate or taking something as a souvenir, money even, and if she comes back from school and opens the door again she'll stand there and stare at me and I'll say quietly, "Your father sent me to take you to the garage, he needs you." And she's surprised at first. "To the garage? What's up? Maybe I ought to phone him first." "No," I'll say, "the phone there's out of order, that's why he sent me here." And then she'll obey me and follow me going down the stairs with me and I lead her to the bus station, pay for her ticket, sit her down beside me and proud and serious I talk to her, asking her what she's studying in school, and she's impressed seeing I'm not just a thick laborer but a guy with a bit of education, I can even recite her a whole poem by heart. She takes a real fancy to me. And then we get off the bus and walk side by side through the street to the garage. Going in through the gate and straight to her father, who's standing there with a bunch of people, he's surprised to see me bringing him his daughter in the middle of the day. And before he has time to think I take out the duplicate key and give it to him, saying softly, "You see I could've raped her but I took pity on you." And before he can catch me I flee the garage forever, leaving the city and going back to the village, become a shepherd, let them send the cops after me, we'll show them.

And I'll weep in front of Father and say, "I can't stand it anymore. Send me back to school or I'll bring you even greater shame."

I was so busy dreaming that instead of sealing the brake cable I let go of it and it flew out of my hand, springing back and cutting my face and hand open. I felt a burning pain and blood started to flow. Slowly I dragged myself out from under the car and the fat Jew who owned the car and was standing there waiting for me to finish the job got quite a shock seeing me crawling out all black with oil and grease and my face covered in blood.

Seems like I was pretty well cut and the blood was pouring all over the place. Adam was talking to somebody but he stopped and came running to me in such a panic you'd think he'd never seen anyone bleeding before. He took me into the office, sat me down on the chair and shouted at the old man to bandage me. I didn't know the old man was the garage medic as well. He opened a little first-aid box and took out all kinds of dirty little bottles and started pouring stinging stuff all over my cuts. He took out absorbent cotton and bandages as well and started to bandage me with his hard dry fingers. It hurt like hell. And Adam didn't move from there. His face was pale. They finished patching me up and left me to rest for a while in the office, but the bandages began to go red and blood was dripping on the bills on the table. And then they decided maybe they'd better take me to the Red Cross after all. A car that was just going out on a test drive was called in to take me there. And Adam led me to the car himself. And again he took out that famous wallet of his, stuffed full of notes, and gave me twenty pounds so I could come back by taxi. The man's just loaded with money. They took me to the Red Cross and sent me in to the nurse. And she unwrapped the bandages lightly and laughed. "Who put these bandages on you?" and then she started to clean the cuts and put on ointments and all kinds of stuff that didn't sting at all. And they gave me an injection too and put my arm in a sling. They weren't at all stingy with their materials. Then they sent me away.

It was eleven o'clock in the morning. And I was alone in the big city wandering about with twenty pounds in my pocket. I didn't feel like going back to the garage right away. I wouldn't be able to work anyway. So I looked around the shops a bit, bought some chocolate. Then I got on a bus heading for Carmel, not knowing why, maybe I wanted to look at the sea again. But of course I went to his house, maybe I wanted to check if he was still living there. I went in and up the stairs, just to look at the door and then go away. In the end I knocked on the door softly and rang the bell too, though I knew there wasn't anybody there. Silence. I took the key out of my shoe and put it in the lock. The door creaked a bit but it opened smoothly. And there I was in the apartment again, like in my dream, trembling a bit, suddenly seeing myself in the mirror beside the door, covered in bandages, bloodstains on my face and shirt like some war hero in the movies.

This time it might be dangerous but I couldn't stop myself. The apartment was still dark and tidy, like it hadn't been used in the weeks since I'd been there. I didn't go into the living room but headed straight to the bedrooms to see the places I hadn't seen before. First his and his wife's room, very tidy. Again I saw that picture of the little boy. Their son? No sign of him anywhere, maybe he's dead or he disappeared. I left the room in a hurry, meaning to go away, but I couldn't stop myself and I went into the other room. I knew right away it was the girl's bedroom. No doubt about it. I really trembled, I was that curious. Because this was the only room that wasn't tidy, like it didn't belong with the other rooms. A room full of light, blinds open and all kinds of posters on the walls. Lots of bright colors. And books and papers scattered around on the table. And the bed, the bed all messed up, a pillow here and a pillow there and some thin pajamas lying there in the middle. I felt all weak and I sat down on the bed for a moment, lying back and leaning my head on the dip in the middle, kissing the sheet.

I must be crazy.

It's like I'm really in love with her–

God, got to get out of here before they really call the cops. But I'm not going till I've taken something. A book maybe. Nobody ever reckons on thieves if a book is missing. I started looking through her books. I opened one–Bialik. Bialik again, the same textbook we had in school. I opened another book–arithmetic. The next one was by some guy called Nathan Alterman. Never heard of him, let's give him a try. I put the book inside the big sling on my arm and left the apartment in a hurry, feeling faint and very weak. The key was still in the lock on the outside. I'd make a lousy burglar. Quietly I started down the stairs but on the first floor a door opened and an old woman with a face like a witch was standing there like she was waiting for me.

"Who are you looking for, boy?"

"Er . . . the Alterman family . . ."

"Alterman? There's no Alterman here . . . who sent you here?"

I didn't say anything. She stood in my way, if I pushed past her she'd scream. I know these witches. We've got a few in the village.

"Who sent you, boy?"

I still didn't say anything. I had no idea what to say.

"Are you from the supermarket?"

"Yes . . ." I whispered.

"Then come and take some empty bottles."

I went into her kitchen and took a dozen empty bottles and some jars and gave her ten pounds. She was delighted. She didn't seem to notice I was all bandaged up.

"Come back again next week."

"O.K."

And I went away in a hurry. They're quick enough when it comes to taking money back, these Jews.

Three blocks farther on I threw everything into a garbage can. I went back to the garage. My cuts were starting to hurt again, the bandages were dirty. In the garage they were worried about me. They'd even sent a car to the Red Cross station to find out what'd happened to me.

"Where have you been? Where did you disappear to? How are the cuts?"

"Fine . . . just fine . . ."

I was careful not to look him in the eye. If he knew where I'd been he wouldn't stroke my head again. I could've given him his neighbor's compliments.

In the bus when we'd got past Carmel and there was just us Arabs left I took the book out of the sling. I opened it at the first page. *Stars Outside.* And in round handwriting–Dafna. I put the name to my lips. Like I said before I must've been a bit crazy. I turned another page.

The tune you idly forsook still remains and the roads still open lie and a cloud in the sky and a tree in the rain still await you passer-by.

Not bad. I can understand it–

I had three days holiday in the village while the cuts healed. Quiet days full of sun. I lay in bed the whole time and Father and Mother looked after me. I read the book through maybe a dozen times. Though there was a lot I didn't understand, I could learn some of it by heart. But I said to myself–what for? Who for?

ADAM

You're sure now that the garage can get along without you, and all you have to do is call in the afternoon and collect the money. Over the years you've built a machine that works perfectly, you've trained a staff of capable and experienced mechanics, some of whom hardly touch a screwdriver now but take care that others work, giving good advice and carefully checking every car when the repairs are done. Not to mention Erlich, who works wonders with the accounts. And you walk about the garage in the morning and see the foreman taking charge of the cars as they're brought in, directing them to the different workshops according to the different problems—cooling systems, batteries, brakes, engine tuning, electrical transmission, body work and painting. And we have our own expert on vehicle licensing who renews customers' licenses, and Hamid is there too in his dark little corner renovating his engines. So you wander about in the middle of all this activity, beginning to feel you're not needed, and even if they are always coming and asking you to listen to an engine or look at some component or other they don't really need your advice, they're just informing you of decisions that they've already taken.

Until suddenly something happens and you see how helpless everyone is. One of the workers gets hurt. One of the boys. You see a boy crawling out from under one of the cars covered in blood. His face and hands dirty with soot and grease, and a lot of blood. And he stands there quietly, nobody taking any notice of him, they walk past him without a word or even joking among themselves and if you don't do something nobody will move a muscle. Erlich seems surprised when you lead him into the office. "He can wait outside," he says, "I'll come right away, I just want to finish sorting out this bill." You have to scream your head off before Erlich makes a move.

It may be I'm exaggerating. The cuts aren't deep, but all that blood scares me. And after all this is the boy who a week ago was sweeping up here, already he's being allowed to lie under cars and fix brakes. What do you know about him? Suppose he gets killed—no matter, tomorrow Hamid will bring you a replacement. They're a bit surprised at your sensitivity but this isn't the first time you've seen a boy lying in a pool of blood.

Now I watch Erlich bandaging him, bringing out little old bottles of iodine and pouring it over the cuts. The boy's as white as a sheet, eyes popping out of their sockets, groaning with pain but not saying a word. And Erlich brings out narrow bandages and starts to fold them in a strange manner.

Meanwhile I examine the first-aid box. Completely inadequate. It's been here since the days when my father and I worked alone in the garage. I take five hundred pounds from my pocket and tell Erlich to buy a new box and equipment tomorrow. He waves the money aside brusquely, he'll get the stuff for next to nothing from a customer who manages a firm that produces surgical equipment and he'll claim the rest from taxes.

Now the boy's all bandaged up, sitting there beside the cash register, looking at me with those dark eyes of his, not realizing that the blood's escaping through the badly tied bandages and dripping on the papers.

Of course Erlich yells at him—

I send him to the Red Cross station, giving him money so he can come back by taxi.

And I stay behind in the garage, wandering uneasily around the various workshops, starting to get involved in all kinds of things. Suddenly all sorts of minor scandals come to my notice. One of the workers who doesn't have a driver's license is moving cars around and collides with one that was just standing there. Another tries to start the engine of a car that's got a broken fan belt and he ruins the pistons. Another nearly sets fire to an engine putting in the wrong kind of oil. They're all angry and on edge. They're used to being without me. They don't know why I'm hanging around here and taking charge.

But I'm waiting for the boy to come back and there's no sign of him. I send a car to the Red Cross station and it doesn't return.

I have an argument with the foreman, who's been rude to a customer, I even have a go at Hamid when I find him taking parts for the car that he's renovating from an old car parked at the side. At last when it's almost time to go home the boy comes quietly into the garage, all covered in bandages. The little bastard's been wandering around the town. And I was worried about him. I touch him.

"Where have you been? How are the cuts?"

"Fine . . . just fine . . ."

Hell, why am I so worked up? I get into my car and drive off in a hurry.

NA'IM

He applied to study medicine in Tel Aviv and was turned down, he applied to study medicine in Haifa and wasn't accepted, he tried Jerusalem and got rejected, he went to the Technion and failed the entrance exam, he wrote to Bar-Ilan and got a negative answer. He had a chance of getting into Beer-Sheba but was late with his application. All the time we thought of nothing but him and his studies. The whole house revolved around him. Father couldn't sleep at night from worry. People came and advised him to apply here, to write there. Somebody knew so-and-so and so-and-so knew somebody else.

They began working on their connections. They even wrote a letter to the Citizen's Advice Bureau. They sent an old sheik to the Registration Department. Father even went to the Ministry of Defense and said, "For twenty-five years I've informed on whoever I'm supposed to and when my son wants to study medicine they slam all the doors in his face." And they really did try to help. They told him they'd found him a place to study Arabic language and literature and Adnan turned it down, he didn't want to be a teacher, everybody's a teacher. They found him a place to study the Bible, he said, "I must be crazy." They offered him a course in Hebrew literature, he said, "You want to bore me to death?" He was so stubborn and proud. It had to be medicine or electronics or something like that. He drove us all crazy. In the mornings he got up late and did nothing. Father didn't want him to tire himself with work, just to study and prepare for the entrance exams. They gave him the best room in the house and made sure he wasn't disturbed. They bought books and note pads and spared no expense. But he shut himself up in his room and paced around nervously all the time, he went whole days without eating. He was desperate right from the start. On nights before exams Father sat and prayed outside his door. In the morning Adnan left the house as white as a sheet, trembling all over. Wearing a new suit that they'd made for him and a little red tie, Father's old tie from Ottoman times, but with dirty old shoes, going to some university or other to fail, and coming back in the evening exhausted and hardly saying a word. He'd sleep for two or three days and then start wandering around the village in the same suit but without the tie, sitting in a cafe with the other young men of the village and waiting for the results to arrive by post. And meanwhile his hatred grew and grew. He hated them all and the Jews especially. He was sure they were failing him on purpose. One evening at the supper table after he'd got another rejection slip he started to curse and went on and on. They sat there eating and drinking and hearing him curse the whole country. Suddenly I got fed up with listening to him and said quietly, "Could it be that you're just not smart enough and it isn't Zionism that's to blame?" and before I'd finished the sentence Father hit me across the face with all his strength. The old man nearly tore me apart. And Adnan jumped up, knocking over the dishes. I fled and he fled and Father was yelling and howling. For a whole week I slept at Hamid's house. I was afraid he was going to kill me, even then I got the feeling he was dangerous.

In the end, after we hadn't spoken to each other for maybe a month, Father forced me to make up with him. I went and asked his forgiveness because I was younger. I kissed his thin hand and he patted my shoulder like patting a dog and he just said, "You . . . Bialik, you." And he smiled a bit.

Nuts–

But when the university term started and he still hadn't found a place I too began to hurt. Faiz sent papers from England to try to enroll him at some university there but Adnan had no strength left. He really began to think that maybe he wasn't college material. He thought maybe he had a talent for something else. Now when I left the house in the morning I sometimes met him in the alleyway beside the house. He looked very thin, his clothes were crumpled, returning from nights spent prowling around Acre and the other villages. He'd found himself new friends. We'd stand and talk for a while, I in my working clothes and he still wearing his suit and the white shirt with the black collar. I already felt more friendly toward him. I didn't know that he'd decided to leave us, that at night he was already checking out the roads and the gaps in the border fences. Some time later he disappeared. Somebody said he'd been seen in Beirut. Although we were sorry he'd gone and Father was terribly worried about him we thought maybe it was a good thing for him to get away for a while from the Jews, who bothered him so much.

We never imagined that suddenly he'd want to return.

ADAM

It's a real art, you don't appreciate it, to live this kind of double life among us, to live our world and to live its opposite. And when you're talking again in your Friday-night armchairs, unable to keep off the subject, quibbling about elite groups and voluntary suicides and frustrated fanatics, I want to laugh or cry (but in the end I say nothing, just angrily stuffing another handful of nuts into my mouth). What are you talking about? Today he's a worker in my garage, humble and patient, smiling and reliable. And tomorrow–a savage beast, and it's the same man, or his brother, or his cousin, the same education, the same village, the same parents.

There, for example, was this ghastly terrorist attack starting at the university, and I watch my workers closely. I employ thirty Arabs and I have time to watch them, because I no longer concern myself with cars, only people. You ask yourself, what are they thinking? Does anything matter to them? Do they have any idea what's happening?

They know. The news spreads fast. In the garage there's a fussy old *yeke,* Erlich, the cashier, who hates music during working hours. He thinks it's barbaric. And Arab music irritates him most of all. He's already started coming to work with cotton stuffed in his ears, because sometimes there're as many as twenty radio sets in the garage blaring Arab music at full blast. And when this nasty business starts he takes a little transistor out of his briefcase and, trembling with irritation and tension, shouts "Turn that music off, bloody murderers" and within a few minutes all Arab music is gone from the garage. They know where to draw the line, they tune their sets back to Radio Israel or the army wave bands. They're on our side after all, you say to yourself. But after a while you see that something in the tone of the newscasters and commentators makes them nervous, they switch the radios off, preferring not to hear the news, working quietly, a little closer together perhaps, in no hurry to take the cars out on road tests. The boys are uneasy. They stop laughing. And someone working by himself in a dark corner quietly tunes in to a foreign Arab station, and a few others go over to him to hear the story, a sort of thin smile on their faces.

So, then, they're on the other side.

But during the lunch break they sit in a corner eating their bread, starting to laugh a little, and this at a time when we're crazy with suspense, they talk among themselves about trivial things, it doesn't concern them at all. And as the gunfire of the shoot-out comes over the radio they come to me with practical questions, do the tires of the Volvo need changing or just repairing?

They're in a different world, they don't even ask how it's ended.

But when it's time to go, after they've put away the tools and washed their hands, they wait for one another, which is unusual for them, and they leave the garage and go to the bus stop in a tightly knit group.

And next day I understand why. A first cousin of Hamid, a brother of one of the workers, related to most of them, led the terrorists there. And it seems they knew this from the start, they sensed it. And yet they gave no sign, didn't bat an eye. Perhaps at home, when they're alone, they'll weep for themselves.

NA'IM

And suddenly the nervous voice of a newscaster breaks into the music and the singing. Something's happened. The Jews start to huddle around the radio. Hamid gives us a look and all the Arab music is switched off. We too begin to hear the details. Something at the university. An attack on the registrar's office at the university. They've taken hostages.

My heart stands still. That's him. Adnan has returned.

The whispered curses of the Jews. The bright ideas. Everybody has ideas about what should be done. And we make ourselves small. Walk about quietly, we have nothing to do with all this. Trying to behave naturally, only working feverishly.

At ten past twelve they threw the body of a clerk out the window. Such cruelty. One of the Arabs smiles to himself, a thin, faraway smile. I slip down under one of the cars and try a thousand times to tighten a screw that keeps slipping out of my hand. I'm not here.

All around the usual talk about the death penalty and revenge. Our brother. What's he doing? Where does he get the guts? This cursed pride. And why don't the damn Jews take better care of themselves?

A cabinet meeting. The army. The Ministry of Defense. The same old story. Time for our lunch break. Drying our hands, taking our bags and sitting down on the floor to one side. I sit beside Hamid and keep close to him. He doesn't say anything. As silent as usual. The others talk in low voices about other things, arguing about the new Volvo, about automatic gear boxes. I have no appetite, I want to cry but my eyes are dry.

Negotiations begin. Declarations. Conversations through a bullhorn. The arrogance. The usual descriptions. Just one novelty. One of the *fedayeen* is walking about in a suit and tie like he's at a party.

I throw my bread to a stray dog that's always wandering around the garage. Go back to work with the others. Everything's as usual. The Jews come to take away the repaired cars, arguing over the price, but with anxious eyes, listening to the songs on the radio in great agitation. One of the Arabs quietly tunes in to Radio Damascus. It's a different story there. A great battle, the university in flames. The lies. The fantasy.

And all the time I'm thinking only of Adnan.

We start closing the toolboxes and changing our clothes. And suddenly everything's happening at once. The newscaster starts shouting like a commentator at a football game. They're attacking. The sounds of gunfire come over on the radio like the rattle of a broken drill. They understand nothing. They're killing him. Right now, they're killing my brother. His eyes are seeing the light for the last time. Good-by. Madman. Curse him. What he is doing to us. The shame. The cursed pride. My poor brother.

The Jews start to breathe more easily, even though a few of their own people have been killed. Suddenly they stop answering our questions, they've remembered to be angry with us. And we walk to the bus stop a bit closer together than usual, there are cops on the street to stop anyone having a go at us. But nobody wants to touch us, they don't even look at us. On Radio Damascus the battle's still raging. They've brought in tanks and fighter planes. We get on the bus. I sit beside Hamid on the back seat. Nobody says a word. Now Hamid takes out his transistor and puts it to his ear. And I look up at the hill, at the university sitting there like a flat white stone, like a tombstone. God, how long will this go on? Suddenly Hamid bows his head. On Radio Damascus they're reading out the names. Hamid nudges me gently. It's him. But I knew already, right from the start I knew it. Attacking the registrar's office at the university in a suit and a tie and with a Kalashnikov. That could only be his idea. Only his.

In the village they know already. News travels fast. We don't need the radio to tell us. A crowd of people outside the house. Women crying. I go inside the house and it's full of chairs. They've brought in chairs from all the other houses, brought them here for the mourners. And Father has shut himself up in his room and isn't speaking to anyone. And relations arriving all the time from other villages. And the women all in one room, their eyes red. What good is crying? To hell with it all.

And the house fills up with people. All sitting quietly and waiting. What for? In the evening somebody switches on the television, no sound, just to see if they'll show the corpses. But they show only the room where the hostages were kept, the files scattered on the floor, the mess and the wreckage. They sit there in silence. Nobody speaks. Just now and then somebody groans "O God." And at midnight the security forces arrive. In their innocent-looking Escorts. *Welcome back sweet little bird.* More like dogs than birds. Fat, with black mustaches. They're tired and unhappy too. No blame, no threats. Wishing peace on everybody. They know all of us by name, hell. Shaking hands. The strange Iraqi Arabic they speak. People make space for them in the middle of the room but they decline and go stand in a corner. Drinking coffee. In the end Father's brought out to meet them, he looks a hundred years older. Bit by bit they start telling the true story of what happened. Silence in the room, they're all holding their breath. And the village outside is hushed as well, like the whole village is listening to the story in the dark. They tell us the facts we don't want to hear but must. Hearts beating fast, eyes closed. We hear of the cruelty, the heroism, the madness. Already the bombers are roaring overhead.

Father listens and listens. His eyes closed like he's asleep. And when they finish he starts to speak. Softly, going around and around in circles. First about the fields, about the rain and what the Koran says about brotherhood and peace. And then he starts to curse. Weeping and cursing. Better that the boy had never been born.

And they listen to the curses, the words of loyalty and abuse. Nodding their heads but not believing. Not believing that we believe in what we say, but not wanting to hear other things from us.

Nobody goes to bed. All night we sit there in the big room and people come and go and in the morning the journalists arrive. With cameras and microphones. There's no getting rid of them. They corner us and ask questions, they want photographs of him. Where did he go to school? Who were his teachers? How did he behave? Who were his friends? And Father with his Hebrew full of mistakes sits like a baby in a highchair, a microphone tied around his neck as they focus the lights on him, trying to smile. Again and again they ask him the same questions. And he says, "He was just mad, that's all. Look at his little brother, he's a good boy." And he hugs me hard, hurting me. All this in front of the cameras. The shame. Adnan's no longer his son. We've forgotten him. And that's what we say, over and over again. The relations, the cousins, they all smile into the cameras. He was just crazy, off his rocker, even though we know he wasn't.

ADAM

Rainy days. A heavy winter. I wake up as usual at five o'clock in the morning, a habit that I can't change now. Lately I've been the first to go to sleep and I find a different house when I wake up in the morning. The leftovers of supper in the dining room. Pillows and blankets on the chairs. Dafi's night struggles. Asya curled up beside me like a fetus. Her gray hair on the pillow. Wrinkles at the corners of her eyes. Behind the lids her eyes are moving. Dreaming again. Dreaming all the time.

"Asya," I whisper, as if trying to penetrate her dream.

She moans, turns over quickly.

I drink coffee, eat a slice of bread, then drive through the empty streets, sometimes stopping by the seashore, parking the car and starting to walk along the wet beach. Very cold. The sky clouding over. A strong wind rising from the sea. But there's always somebody there. An elderly couple in swimsuits running slowly hand in hand along the water line, chattering happily. A woman, not young, emerges from the stormy breakers and slowly walks toward me. She picks up a towel that was lying almost at my feet and covers herself with it. Taking off her bathing cap, shaking out her hair and spraying cold drops of water on my face. She smiles at me, perhaps she wants to start a conversation. Not a pretty face, but a superb figure. I stand beside her, wrapped in my big fur coat, watching her change her bathing suit for a dress, watching her white breasts in the freezing wind. Without interest. Deep in thought. Somebody touches my shoulder.

My heart stops–Gabriel.

But it's Erlich, the old *yeke,* in swimming trunks, laughing, thin and strong, his silver body hair reeking of salt and sand.

"Erlich! Do you still swim in the sea in the morning, even on days like this?"

"For thirty years now. I used to swim with your father. Every day before work. Come on now, strip off and get into the water."

"I'm an old man . . ." I reply with a smile. We talk for a while, Erlich running on the spot to keep warm. Then he leaves me and goes running away to climb on some horizontal bars. A light rain falling. All kinds of weird people turning up. Friendly fishermen. It's nearly seven o'clock. Time to go. Driving out toward the main road I see the woman who came out of the water, whose breasts I caught sight of for a moment, walking on the left-hand side, in a short coat, stopping and turning to look at me, slowly raising her hand. For a moment I think of stopping and picking her up, I hesitate, slow down, but then drive on, feeling defeated, a light nausea rising in me.

On the way to the garage once again I pass by the old house. Although I know I won't find anything I can't resist stopping there, getting out of the car to look up at the closed shutters. It's four months now since he disappeared.

If only I could break into this house—

I examine the pipes on the outside of the building. A long drain pipe leads up to the second floor, uneven bricks protrude on the outer wall, the shutter up there is still a tiny bit open.

Whistles behind me. A girl traffic cop comes walking up to see what's happening. I move, drive to the garage. Erlich's already sitting over the accounts, looking fresh and invigorated. If he had been in my shoes he could have climbed that wall long ago. At night that alleyway's deserted. Perhaps I could ask Hamid to find me somebody to break in there. If he had a terrorist among his relations, surely he could find me a professional housebreaker, but afterward it might be tricky.

No, I need to find a boy, some boy who can climb quickly, somebody who wouldn't understand exactly what he was doing, a stranger, but not a complete stranger, somebody who trusts me a little, perhaps somebody employed temporarily in the garage.

I watch the workers closely, moving about among them, they pretend not to notice me but I'm conscious that the chattering stops when I approach, the music is turned down slightly. I know very few names here. But there's one fellow who looks up, staring back at me. It's that boy again, the one who was hurt and has recovered now. Smiling a sincere understanding smile at me. He picks up a big screwdriver and swaggering like a veteran mechanic he walks over to a large plump woman standing beside a little Fiat with a raised hood. He says boldly, "Get in, lady, and start the engine. Keep your foot on the throttle and do exactly as I tell you."

And she smiles, looking around her with embarrassment, gets into the car and starts the engine. The boy climbs onto the fender and starts tuning. Scandalous. Only two months ago he was sweeping the floor and now he's got the nerve to tune engines. But I say nothing, I just stand there watching him, and he knows that I'm watching him and he carries on tuning, raising and lowering the revolutions of the engine, with no idea what he's doing. In the end one of the Jewish mechanics comes along and shouts at him, pushing him aside. But the boy isn't offended, watching me from a distance, with a smile as if to spite me.

This, it comes to me in a flash, is the boy who'll climb that wall, and perhaps he'll keep quiet about it too.

It was like a dream that Friday. A sweet dream. Because I slept in her house and ate breakfast and supper with her, and even if I had maybe done something criminal still I was happy.

As soon as I arrived at the garage that morning he grabbed me like he'd been waiting for me. He took me into a quiet corner and told me he needed me for a small job that night, if it was all right for me not going home to the village. I said that was all right, no problem, I didn't mind sleeping at the garage. He said, "No, you don't need to sleep at the garage, you can sleep at my house. I'll look after you." I was so happy I thought I was going to faint. My head went fuzzy. But I just smiled at him. And he said, "Only don't talk about it, can you keep a secret?" "Of course I can," I said. "I'll keep as quiet about it as you like." He looked at me like he was checking some bit of machinery. "Can you climb?" "Climb on what?" I asked. "It's not important." He was embarrassed. "You'll see. What have you got in that bag?" He didn't give me a chance to reply but snatched it out of my hand and looked inside it, seeing the bread and the book of poems by Alterman. I thought I was going to die. He took out the book and asked me what it was. "It's a book," I said. "But whose is it?" "It's mine, I'm reading it." "You're reading this?" He was surprised, he laughed and he put his hand on my head again like he did the first time. In the distance I saw the other workers watching us curiously. He flicked through the book but he didn't look at the first page. He just asked, "Do you understand this stuff?" "Sometimes," I said, and snatched it back in a hurry. He was thrilled, really impressed, and he touched me again, he was always so careful not to touch the other workers but it was like with me it was O.K. Then he took out his wallet again, the one that was always stuffed full of money like it was weighing him down and he wanted to get rid of it. He took out a hundred-pound note and said, "Go and buy yourself some pajamas and a toothbrush and come back here at four o'clock after the others have gone and I'll pick you up. I'll tell Hamid you won't be going back to the village tonight." "But I can go straight to your house," I said. He was surprised. "Do you know where it is?" I reminded him that he'd once sent me to his house to fetch a briefcase, he didn't remember but he said, "All right, come straight to the house at four o'clock." "O.K.," I said, "but what kind of pajamas do you want me to buy?" He laughed. "The pajamas are for you, not for me." I knew that but I only asked him because I was getting all mixed up I was so happy. How happy I was suddenly.

And I went straight out into the city with the hundred pounds. At first I wandered around the streets, walking in the middle of the road and nearly getting run over. All the time feeling the hundred pounds in my pocket, stopping in the middle of the road and fingering it. I'd never had so much money all at once. And though it was a cold and rainy day I was free, like in holidays from school. And I walked among the people aimlessly, looking in the gloomy faces of the Jews, always so worried about their Jewish destiny. And though the sky was dark I was already sniffing the smell of spring. I wanted to shout out loud I was so happy. Because all the time I was thinking I'd be seeing that girl in a little while and I'd be able to fall in love properly and not just in my imagination. I walked and walked and nearly came out the other side of the city and turned back and this time started looking in the shops. Going in here and there to look at things, because aside from the pajamas I wanted to buy a whole lot of things for myself. This time I wasn't giving any change back. And they realized I was an Arab right away and they started looking in my bag, feeling the loaves of bread to check if there were bombs hidden inside them. So I ate some of the bread in a hurry and threw the rest away with the bag so they'd leave me alone and I just kept the book, tucking it under my arm. I felt lighter that way.

In the end, after I'd looked in the windows of toy shops, bookshops, radio and TV shops, I began to look for a pajama shop, but there weren't any pajamas in the windows and I didn't know exactly which shop to enter. Anyway, why did he insist on pajamas? I could sleep in my underwear and buy something more important with the money. Suddenly I saw a high-class clothes shop that had pajamas in the window but didn't show any prices. I went inside and wanted to go straight out again because it was dark in there and there was nobody about. But as soon as I turned to go a thin old man came out from a dark corner. "What do you want, boy?" I said, "Pajamas." He asked, "Have you got any money?" and I took out the blue bill and showed it to him.

Then he grabbed my hand, he didn't seem to mind that I was wearing dirty working clothes. He didn't even realize I was an Arab. All he wanted was to get his hands on that little blue bill that I'd been stupid enough to show him and he did take it off me in the end.

He started taking all kinds of pajamas out of boxes, fine silk pajamas with tassels and fancy embroidery. He showed me pair after pair, spreading them out in front of me. And I stood there and couldn't say a word because they really were nice. In the end he came over to me, took my measurements and told me to undress. I took off my shirt and sweater and he put a pajama top on me and turned me toward the mirror to see if it suited me. Then he took it off and tried another on me, and every set of pajamas was crazier than the last one, gold buttons and colored tassels. When he saw I was struck dumb he chose some red pajamas for me and said, "Look, these suit you best," and folded them up and packed them in a box and wrapped the box in soft paper and put it in a new plastic bag and then gently but firmly he took the blue bill that I still held in my fingers and said softly, "That's it." I saw he didn't mean to give me any change and I asked him in a feeble voice, "Do these cost a hundred pounds?" He said, "More than that, I've given you a discount." I didn't move, I felt stunned. And he smiled at me and said, "Where are you from, boy?"

And suddenly I was afraid he might be angry if he knew he'd been dealing with an Arab.

"From here . . . from this neighborhood."

"And your parents? Where are they from?"

"From Poland," I replied, without even thinking, because they'd told us in school that all the Zionists came from Poland.

And I still didn't move, weeping in my heart for the hundred pounds that had gone on just one pair of pajamas. And still I didn't touch my pajamas, which were lying there before me in a bag. At last I said, "But I've still got to buy a toothbrush, I need a toothbrush as well, I can't take such expensive pajamas." And then he went through a door into a back room and came back a few seconds later with a toothbrush, which was red and not exactly new. He put it into the bag and said, "There you are, boy, I've given you a toothbrush as well, I've made a deal with you." But when he saw I was still rooted there, in a panic over the money I'd lost, he put the bag in my hand, took my arm and led me out into the street, closing the door behind him.

And so I was left without a cent, just with a set of crazy pajamas wrapped in a plastic bag. Heavy rain started falling. I still had five hours to go till four o'clock and I didn't even have the money for the bus. I walked up to Carmel and arrived at his house, still with three hours to go before four o'clock. I didn't want to wait on the stairs so I found a little shelter opposite and sat down there to wait, until somebody came along who didn't even live there and said, "Move, get out of here."

So I moved. I circled the streets of the neighborhood, which was nice even in the rain, and went back and sat under the shelter opposite the house and waited for the time to pass. And again two men came along and said, "What are you doing here? What are you waiting for?" I didn't answer, just got up and started walking around again. I've noticed before that as long as we're moving, working or walking they don't take any notice of us, it's only when we stand still in some place that they start getting suspicious. And so I walked about, very tired and completely wet and even though the sun came out now and then it couldn't dry me because I was as wet as a rain cloud. And I went back again to my shelter and it was already half-past two and the children were coming home from school, first the younger ones and then the older ones. And I saw her arriving, the last of all maybe, running along without a raincoat, without galoshes, just in a short coat, soaking wet. I watched her disappear into the house. The sun came out again.

I threw *Stars Outside,* that Alterman book, into a garbage can, it was like dough it had gotten so wet. Then his wife arrived. I recognized her right away by her green Fiat 600. Once I'd tightened the brakes and changed the oil for her. And she took out a whole lot of baskets and then stood and fumbled for a long time in the letter box, though I'd already checked it out and I knew there wasn't any mail for them. Ten minutes later she came out again and drove away and came back with some milk and after half an hour she drove away again and came back with bread.

Slowly the street emptied and there was a strange sort of silence. People were arriving in their cars and disappearing into their houses with baskets, closing the shutters. And I was still sitting there opposite the house waiting for him to come. I was already sick of the whole thing. The door to the balcony was open and the girl came out to look at the sky. I tried to huddle up small so she wouldn't see me, but she stared down at me like she was trying to remember something. And the rain started again. Her mother shouted something and she went back inside. And now it started raining really hard and I thought I was going to be swept away, off the pavement, down the hill and into the sea that you couldn't see because of the mist.

Already I was feeling miserable as hell, the rain was getting inside my head, driving me crazy. I was regretting the whole thing now, even love. Sitting alone in the street watching the sealed shutters, it was already after four o'clock and he hadn't arrived yet and I was afraid I'd be stuck there all night in the street with the pajamas. Perhaps he'd forgotten me and the job he wanted me for. But at last I heard his American car coming down the hill. Before he'd even had time to turn off the engine I'd opened the door for him. He smiled at me like we'd only just parted, and he asked, "Have you just arrived?" "Just now," I lied. He said, "Good, come and give me a hand," and he started unloading flowers and cakes and bread and nuts. Looks like everybody here cooks and eats his own food.

We climbed the steps to his house, he rang the bell and the girl opened the door and he said:

"This is . . ."

"Na'im," I said, just moving my lips. The girl looked at me in surprise. And again I was stunned by her beauty. And the woman came out straightaway to meet us and when she saw me she took the flowers and the bread from me and said, "Why didn't you come in before? Why did you wait outside all the time?" Adam was amazed. "You waited outside? In all this rain? You must be crazy." I didn't say anything, just wiping my feet all the time on the brown mat beside the door. And they said, "It doesn't matter, it doesn't matter, come inside," but I went on wiping my feet, staring at the floor. In the end Adam took hold of my arm and pushed me into the house like he'd only just realized how wet I was. And I went inside and maybe they were sorry they'd said it didn't matter because straightaway I made their carpet all dirty with mud. Then I took my shoes off and that made things worse because my socks were wet and torn and my feet were black, there was a black puddle under my feet and wherever I went in the house the puddle went with me. It was only then they began to realize how much water I'd absorbed during the day. And so frozen and trembling before the girl's stares, I started messing up their nice clean house.

There was nothing to do but shove me into the bathroom. It was the woman who realized the state I was in. She went and filled the bath with hot water and insisted on me getting in. The three of them started fussing around me, fetching towels, shifting the laundry out of the way. The woman was the most friendly, more than him, he was horrified at the dirt I'd brought into the house and maybe he was even sorry he'd asked me to help him with his job.

Before long I was alone, lying there in the hot bath with scented bubbles. In the hot water I slowly warmed up. It was nice lying in the Jews' bath, in a little room full of colored towels and all kinds of bottles. I don't think anybody from the village has ever had a bubble bath like this in a Jewish house. Meanwhile they were looking around for clothes for me in place of the wet things that I'd taken off, but they didn't find anything because they'd never had a son of my age, only a daughter, and they didn't want to put me in a dress. In the end the woman, who was standing all the time on the other side of the door talking to me, suggested I put my pajamas on while my clothes were drying on the radiator. I said, "Fine," what else could I say, but I was so ashamed I could have drowned myself in the bath and to hell with this night job. I went on lying in the water, washing and scrubbing myself, at last I pulled out the plug and started cleaning the bath that I'd made very dirty. I dried it with a towel and I cleaned the floor as well and I even polished the sink, and I cleaned other things that I hadn't made dirty but I didn't know if they'd remember it wasn't me. Already it was dark and I couldn't find the light switch and so in the dark I put on the pajamas, which were really crazy, and I thought of escaping through the window but there wasn't a proper window there. I was scared to go out and I just sat there quietly in the dark. But they were getting worried about me and Adam opened the door and saw me in my pajamas and burst out laughing, and the girl came running in to see me and she burst out laughing and the woman started laughing too, even though she came and took me by the hand and led me out of the bathroom. And I tried to laugh too so they wouldn't be embarrassed because they were laughing but somehow the laughing changed to tears. This was the end. I broke out sobbing. It was awful. It was all the weariness, all the excitement, I cried bitterly, it was years since I'd wept like that, not even when they buried Adnan. I couldn't stop, like a baby, like an idiot, tears pouring out like the rain was still inside me, weeping and weeping before three strange Jews, before the girl I love who'll never be my love.

DAFI

Mommy and Daddy both said at once, "It doesn't matter, it doesn't matter, come inside," but he was scared and confused, so serious, all the time wiping his feet on the door mat. A little Arab, one of Daddy's workers, just think, Daddy's got thirty workers like this and they're all afraid of him. The poor kid had been waiting outside in the rain. But suddenly I recognized him, I'd seen him before, the boy who came here once to fetch Daddy's briefcase. A nice kid. At last they got him inside, almost by force, they suggested he take his shoes off and he took them off, standing there in his torn black socks, still spreading dirt all around him. Such a silly boy, why did he have to wait outside in the rain? It isn't a very nice thing to say but I was reminded suddenly of something that happened a few years ago. One day Daddy brought me a puppy that had been wandering around in the rain near the garage, it came rushing inside in high spirits (it didn't think of wiping its feet outside) and immediately dirtied the floor and the carpet. And we washed it and combed it and fed it chopped meat, and we even bought it a leash and took it to the vet for injections, and the puppy was in the house for a month maybe until we saw he was growing fast and getting hard to control and somebody who knew about dogs told us "You're rearing a donkey here, not a dog" and Mommy got scared and decided to give him away, even though I wanted to see how big he'd grow in the end.

And this time—it's a boy, that is, a young man. Daddy's brought him here to supper because he needs him tonight to break into the house of that man who disappeared.

Mommy took charge of him straightaway, took him under her wing, because Daddy didn't know what to do with him. Helpless ones like this are right up her alley, she waves a red flag and charges into battle. She took him by the hand and led him to the bathroom, he took off his wet clothes, she put them on the radiator to dry and sent him straight in to have a bath.

It seemed so strange having a guest in the house on a Sabbath eve in winter. It's always so quiet here. We hardly ever have guests. Sometimes in the summer there's some distant relative from Jerusalem who stays overnight but these last few years there hasn't even been that.

Meanwhile, Mommy started looking around for clothes for him. But where do we have clothes for a boy of that age? You could put three of him in Daddy's clothes. But Mommy went on looking, she even came into my room and started rummaging about in the wardrobe. I said to her, "Why don't you give him a skirt? Why not, in Scotland they wear skirts." But she got really angry, didn't think it was funny at all. She began yelling at me, "You be quiet now, how dare you laugh at an unfortunate Arab? Keep your jokes to yourself."

So what if he was an Arab, and why was he unfortunate all of a sudden? Not because he was an Arab. Just like that . . . even if he was a Jew, and what's the difference? Hell . . . she really offended me. Meanwhile, Daddy found a solution, he could put on the pajamas that he brought with him, because Daddy gave him money this morning to buy pajamas (what a weird idea!) and they didn't even ask him if he was ready to put pajamas on in the late afternoon, they just threw the pajamas into the bathroom and now we were all waiting for him to come out. But he didn't come out, five minutes passed, ten minutes, a quarter of an hour and he still didn't come out. He must be preening himself like some grand duchess. It seems he didn't realize we have only one bathroom and Daddy would need a shower before supper. At last Daddy opened the door and we saw him sitting there in the dark on the edge of the bath like a frightened animal, wearing pajamas like I never saw before in my life. The bastard, to think Mommy was worried about him. He went and chose something really special, and expensive too I'll bet, elegantly trimmed, with wide sleeves and a sash and shining buttons.

We were stunned, and looked at one another in amazement. And then I began to smile, and such a silly embarrassed grin appeared on Daddy's face I felt I was starting to shake inside, for some reason it struck me as awfully funny. My famous laugh that breaks out like a clap of thunder followed by a trail of hee . . . hee . . . hee . . . and it's always infectious because anyone who's nearby, whether he likes it or not, starts laughing and can't stop, he's carried along by it. And Daddy started laughing and Mommy with a solemn face started to cackle and I broke out with another thunderclap, not laughing at the pajamas any longer but at their silly laughter. And the little Arab was blushing bright red, he tried to smile but suddenly, all at once, without warning, he began to cry. So bitterly, so deeply, an ancient Arab moan. Suddenly I stopped laughing. Honestly, I felt heartbroken. I knew how he felt. How could he stand it? In his place I'd have been wailing long ago.

NA'IM

But in the end I stopped crying because they were so embarrassed. And I let them take me into the living room and sit me down in an armchair and so there I was talking to them quietly, actually only to the woman, who began talking to me and asking questions right away to take my mind off what had just happened. And I'd never spoken to a woman like her. Not young at all, with a sharp face, chain-smoking but very friendly and clever too, knowing how to get on with people. Sitting facing me, her legs crossed, and behind her the sunset through the window, the sea spread out and the rain falling on the horizon like a rosy fan. It was nice and warm in the room, all around it was clean and tidy. And they didn't know that I'd been there before, I knew all the little objects on the shelves. My bare feet on the carpet, sitting on the edge of the chair and answering questions. She asked me so many questions you'd think she worked for the Secret Service. What does my father do and what does my mother do and what exactly is Faiz doing in England and what do we think about it, and what did we learn in school, how many hours of Arabic, how many hours of Hebrew, how many hours of math, how many hours of history and what kind of history. How long has my family lived in this country, for how many generations that is, how many people live in the village, how many go outside to work and how many work in the village. And what do I know about Jews, have I heard of Zionism and what do I think it means. All the time she's so serious and friendly like it's really important to her. Looks like this is the first time she's spoken to an Arab about things like this because till now she's talked only to Arabs bringing her things from the supermarket or cleaning the steps.

And I answer her quietly, the tears are already dry. Making a great effort. Not moving from my seat, afraid of breaking something. I've done enough damage already. I tell her everything I know, everything I haven't forgotten, careful not to annoy her. Looking only at the woman, not daring to look at the girl, who now I know is called Dafi not Dafna. She sits beside me all the time, staring at me hard, her eyes covering me like a hot wind, sitting and listening and smiling a bit. And so the conversation goes on and on and I see they really know nothing about us, they don't know that we learn a lot of things about them. They don't realize that we really are taught Bialik and Tchernikhovski and other saints and we know all about the Bet Midrash and the destiny of the Jews and the burning *shtetl* and all that.

"Poor things," said the girl suddenly, "what have they done to deserve that?"

But the woman told her to shut up and laughed and I didn't know if I was allowed to laugh as well so I just smiled a little twisted smile and kept my eyes on the floor. And suddenly it was quiet and I was afraid there'd be nothing more to talk about so I went on in a low voice without even being asked.

"We learned poetry by heart as well and I can remember . . . would you like to hear?"

And quietly I began to recite—"No pride of young lions shall hide there the eye of the desert nor the glory of Bashan and his choicest oaks fallen in splendor by the somber tents sprawl angry giants amid the golden desert sands."

And they were so impressed they nearly fell off their chairs. I knew they'd be surprised, I don't know myself why I suddenly had to start reciting. I just felt like it. I wanted them to know that I'm really not stupid. And Dafi jumped up out of her seat and ran to call her father to come and hear and he came straight out of the bathroom in a dressing gown with his beard wet and stood there staring with his mouth open like I'd grown another head.

Because I carried on, all excited—"We are heroes! The last generation to bondage and the first to deliverance our hand alone our mighty hand did cast off from our neck the heavy yoke and we raised our heads to the heavens and they were narrowed in our eyes . . . and who shall be our master?"

And the girl Dafi shook with laughter, running to her room to fetch the book to check if I'd got it right. Then in a cracked voice I went on a bit further—"In spite of heaven and its wrath see we have risen in the storm."

Already it was dark outside, and in the room it was warm and quiet. I saw now how quietly they lived. And they played with me like I was a toy. And I can tell when people like me just by the way they look at me. I'm not exactly ugly and the girls in the village sometimes look at me for no special reason, thinking that I don't see them looking. But in those red pajamas with the tassels and the imitation gold buttons I didn't know if I was just weird or a bit cute as well.

The girl fetched her slippers and put them down beside my bare feet. And they all smiled at me happily.

"What did you say your name was?" the girl asked suddenly. She hadn't caught it the first time.

"Na'im," I said.

DAFI

Mommy of course could've killed me even though she was laughing herself but she quickly turned serious and took him into the living room, the tears still streaming down his face, made him sit in a chair and started asking him questions to distract him, an old trick from the days when I used to cry. Asking him about his village and his family, about his school and what he'd learned there and he answered seriously, his head bent, sitting on the edge of the chair.

I sat behind him and didn't take my eyes off him. This little Arab really took my fancy. Daddy had brought us some entertainment for the Sabbath, Friday nights in our house are usually so boring with all the heaps of newspapers. Sitting there in his pajamas, combed and clean and fragrant, his cheeks rosy. Suddenly he looked small, reminding me of someone, not ugly, there's lots of boys uglier than him.

Mommy frowned at me, because when she saw me staring at his face like that she was afraid I might be trying to annoy him or make fun of him, like sometimes when I sit and stare at one of the old women who come to visit us. But I didn't mean to do anything like that, this Arab really interested me. He soon recovered himself and started giving clear answers, talking about himself, about his village, his family, about what he'd learned in school, they'd taught him Bialik and Tchernikhovski and all that boring stuff of ours, how strange, the swine, inflicting that crap on them as well.

Then I said quietly, "Poor things . . . what have they done to deserve it?"

And Mommy scolded me and the Arab was a bit puzzled too, because it seemed he really enjoyed Bialik, and straightaway, without anyone asking him, he began to recite some lines from Bialik's *Dead of the Desert*. I nearly fell off my chair. A young Arab, an assistant in Daddy's garage, reciting Bialik, unbelievable. If that's the general standard in the garage no wonder business is booming.

I ran to my room to fetch the poems of Bialik to see if he was reciting it properly or just making it up. I called to Daddy too to come out from the bathroom and listen, maybe he'll give him a raise. And Mommy was impressed too. All three of us stared at him. And he decided to impress us some more and quietly and without a mistake he began reciting that bit that Shwartzy's crazy about and sneaks in at every opportunity whether it's appropriate or not. "We are heroes, the last generation to bondage and the first to deliverance, our hand alone . . ." sitting on the edge of the chair with head bowed, still not looking at us straight, in a low voice. And I watched Mommy and Daddy seeing how they stared at him open-mouthed and suddenly it hit me, it came to me in a flash. Of course. This boy looks a bit like Yigal, there's something about him, some similarity, and they don't realize it, they don't understand. They don't see what it is that draws them to him. Daddy doesn't know why of all his workers he decided to send this boy here to fetch the briefcase, or why he chose him for the job tonight. And if I tell them they'll say, "Nonsense, what do you know about Yigal, you never saw him."

And so in the stillness and the darkness of early evening I watched the quiet little Arab, his eyes bright with happiness. Now we were the ones who bowed our heads, seeing his swarthy bare feet on the carpet. And suddenly I felt like giving him something and I went and fetched my bedroom slippers and put them down beside him. Just for one evening let him wear a girl's slippers. Then I realized that I didn't actually know his name and I asked him and he looked at me straight, no longer evasive, and told me.

I didn't know they have such simple names.

NA'IM

At last we sat down to eat. Since morning I hadn't eaten anything and I was weak with hunger and maybe that was why I got a bit mixed up in the poem as well. And there was a white cloth on the table and two candles and a bottle of wine. I didn't know they were religious. But they didn't even pray, just started eating right away. I sat beside the girl, being very careful not to touch her, and the woman brought in the food. To start with it was sort of gray meatballs, so sweet they made me feel sick. Looks like this woman doesn't know how to cook, she puts in sugar instead of salt, but nobody else noticed or maybe they thought it wasn't polite to mention it. And I forced myself to eat it too so she wouldn't be offended like my mother, who's offended if you don't eat everything. I just ate a lot of bread with it to try and kill the sweetness. And that Adam ate so fast, I hadn't had time to look at the food and he'd already finished it all. They brought him some more and he gobbled that up too. And I was eating slowly because I had to be careful to eat with my mouth closed and luckily the girl was eating slowly too so the grownups didn't have to wait only for me.

At last I finished those disgusting meatballs. I've never eaten anything like them before and I hope I never will again. I asked them what they were called so I could avoid them if ever I fell into a Jewish house again. They smiled and said, "It's called *gefilte fish.* Would you like some more?" I said, "No thank you," in a hurry. And the woman said, "Don't be shy, there's plenty more," but again I said quickly, "No thank you, I've had enough," but she'd already gotten up and gone to the kitchen and fetched a full plate and again I said, as firmly as I could without offending her, "No, really, I'm full, no more, please."

And she gave up and took away all the plates and I thought that was the end of the meal but since I was still hungry I quietly ate more and more slices of bread, too damn sweet also. And the woman was in the kitchen busy with the dishes and the girl was watching television, it was an Egyptian film with belly dancers, she was interested but she didn't understand what they were saying, and Adam was reading a paper and I was eating slice after slice of bread and suddenly I saw that I'd eaten all their bread.

And then the woman came in with new plates and a dish of meat and potatoes. So the meal wasn't finished after all, but what a mixed-up way, every man for himself. And I'd noticed that Adam and his wife, who now I knew was called Asya, never really looked at each other when they were talking.

So we sat down to eat again and this time the food was better, there weren't enough spices in it but at least it wasn't sweet, and there was brown bread as well. The girl ate only a little bit and her mother said something to her. Adam filled his plate and started eating in such a hurry you'd think he hadn't eaten anything all week, taking a look every now and then at the newspaper that was folded on the table. This silence at meals. Such loneliness.

Suddenly he remembered something and turned to me.

"Tell me, somebody was saying in the garage that one of the terrorists in the attack on the university was your brother, or something like that . . ."

The woman and Dafi put down their knives and forks looking like they were really shocked. I blushed bright red, trembled, now everything was going to be ruined.

"What terrorist?" I pretended I didn't quite understand. "The one who killed himself at the university?"

And they smiled a bit at the idea that Adnan might really have gone to the university just to do away with himself quietly.

"He was a distant cousin of mine," I lied. "I hardly knew him, he was a bit sick, crazy I mean." I smiled at them but they didn't smile.

I picked up my knife and fork again and began to eat, staring down at the plate, suddenly seeing Adnan lying under the ground with his eyes closed in the rain. The other three looked at one another and went back to their food. The meal went on. Dafi said something about a friend of hers and her parents and what the math teacher said to her today. And again the plates were changed and they brought in little dishes of ice cream, left over from the summer maybe. I ate this too, what the hell, with a slice of bread.

And then the meal was over and Dafi sat down in front of the television and they sat me down too in one of the armchairs in my pajamas and the girl's slippers. I'd already forgotten to be shy. I felt like one of the family. I even went to the bathroom and came back on my own. Now it was Jewish programs on the television, first they sang songs and after that there was a discussion and then more songs, songs for old people this time. And still I didn't know anything about the job tonight, you could say I'd forgotten about it, maybe he'd forgotten about it too. That's the way it seemed. Adam was watching television and reading the paper, actually he wasn't doing either, he was dozing a bit. And the girl was talking on the phone, she'd already been there half an hour and the woman was in the kitchen washing dishes and so there was just me sitting by myself in my pajamas in front of the television that was playing old songs from the Second Aliyah, there was one of them I knew the words to.

I could hardly keep my eyes open, in the end I dropped off to sleep, I was so tired after this strange and wonderful day. At eleven o'clock I saw their smiling faces in front of me and the television was already dark and the lights in the house had been turned down. They helped me up and led me like in a dream to a room full of books, put me in a soft white bed and Adam said, "Soon I shall wake you and we'll be off," and he covered me with a blanket.

So there is a job tonight after all, I thought, and went back to sleep.

At about two o'clock he woke me. The house was all dark. At first I was so confused I spoke to him in Arabic. He laughed and said, "Wake up, wake up," and he gave me my clothes, which were dry and stiff. And I got dressed in the dark while he watched me. He wasn't wearing his working clothes but clean clothes and he had a woolly hat on his head and a big fur coat, he looked just like a bear. We left the dark house where there were just the two candles still there on the empty table and even then I began to suspect there was going to be something criminal about the job.

The street was empty and it was a cold night, a light rain was falling and I didn't know where he was driving to but I guessed we were going down all the time toward the lower city. In the end he pulled up in a little side street, stopped the engine and got out of the car telling me to wait inside, he disappeared for a moment and then came back and told me to get out. I followed him and he seemed tense now, looking from side to side like a thief or something, I didn't know he went breaking into houses at night, I thought he made enough profit from the garage, and then we went into a little dead-end street and he stopped opposite an old Arab house that was all dark, then he grabbed hold of me, pointed to a window on the second floor and whispered, "Climb up there and open the shutter and get inside the apartment, don't put a light on, go to the outside door and open it for me."

So this is what it was all for, the meal and the pajamas and all the nice talk. I could have wept from misery, if my father could see me now. One son abroad, the other a terrorist and the youngest a housebreaker. A fine family. But I didn't say anything, what could I say? Too late now. He gave me a big screwdriver to bend back the bolt of the shutter and said, "If anyone comes I'll whistle and you must try to escape."

"What will you whistle?"

"Some little tune . . . what do you know?"

" 'Jerusalem of Gold.' "

He laughed. But I was serious, standing there rooted to the spot and not saying anything, watching him nervously. Then he said, "Don't be afraid, there's nobody here, this is the house of a friend of a friend of mine who went to fight in the war and I must find some papers of his . . ."

Still I didn't say anything because the lie was so stupid I felt really embarrassed. Then he said sternly, "Go on . . ."

And I went. He stood on the other side of the street watching. I started searching the wall for crevices for my hands and feet. The wall was wet and slimy. A crumbling old Arab house. After I'd gone a little way I caught hold of a rusty old drain pipe and began to climb it, slipping back a bit but making progress. It wasn't easy at all, I could have slipped and fallen and broken something and the rain was getting heavier but after yesterday rain won't ever scare me again. And so at last I reached the window and stood up on a little ledge. I looked down at him and he was watching me. I thought maybe he'd call it off at the last moment but he signaled to me to carry on. I tried to open the shutter that was the same kind as the ones in our house. I pushed in the screwdriver and easily lifted the bolt but as soon as I started moving the shutter there was a loud creaking noise, like an alarm going off, maybe it was a thousand years since they'd oiled the hinges. Slowly the shutter opened. The window was closed but not locked, looked like they'd closed it in a hurry. Another second and I was inside the dark apartment. I looked down into the street but there was no sign of him.

The stink of a place that hasn't been aired for years, spiders' webs tickled my face. Slowly my eyes got used to the dark. A man's clothes were scattered on the bed, there was a heap of old socks in a corner. The door of the room was closed. I opened it and found myself in a little corridor. I opened another door and went into a kitchen that was big but dirty, full of pans and sacks. Something was cooking on a low flame. I began to panic. There was somebody here. I went out of the kitchen in a hurry and opened another door, it was a storeroom, I opened another door that was the toilet, another door that was the bathroom, another door led onto the balcony, bringing me out again into the night, the sea was close by, quite a different view.

I was baffled. Everything looked old and neglected. There wouldn't be much loot here. I tried another door and it was a big room with a bed in the middle and on the bed there was something wrapped in a blanket, like an old woman lying there. I went out of there and at last I found the main door. The lock was broken. Somebody had beaten us to it. The bolts were fastened. I pulled them back. Adam was waiting outside, smiling, he came in quickly, closed the door behind him and switched on the lights.

"The bolts were fastened."

"The bolts?" He couldn't believe his ears.

"It looks like your friend has come back."

"What?"

But at that moment one of the doors opened and an old lady, small and plump and wearing a nightdress even crazier than my pajamas, came out, looking at us. She stood there not saying anything, not a bit frightened. I saw right away that she could tell I was an Arab.

Now I really wanted to run away. I'd had enough of this night job that still might end in murder. I'm only a kid, I wanted to shout, even if I have finished school, he just doesn't see that.

But the strange thing is that neither of them was a bit scared. The opposite, they smiled pleasantly.

"I see you have begun collaborating in housebreaking."

He bowed.

"Mrs. Ermozo . . . grandmother of Gabriel Arditi . . . correct?"

"That being so, are you the bearded man?"

"The bearded man?" He was so surprised you'd think he'd never had a beard.

"Where is Gabriel?"

"I am always looking for him."

"Then he really has come back."

"Certainly."

"Where is he?"

"That's the question I ask myself all the time."

They talked quietly, without fear. There was a silence. They were both excited. Suddenly they both spoke at once.

She said, "But why on earth should you be looking for him?"

He said, "When did you come back from the hospital?"

"I came home yesterday."

"But I thought you had lost consciousness."

"I found it again."

VEDUCHA

And how did this begin? With the smell of a market. Yes, with the smell of a market. A long time now I have been saying, what do you smell? What is it? And then I understand, the smell of the market in the Old City. Smell of Arabs, smell of tomatoes, green onions and eggplants, smell of roast meat spluttering over the fire and smell of baskets, fresh hay, smell of rain too. And after the smells come the voices, little sounds, muffled, but I'm dragging myself up out of the well, clutching at Grandma's skirt, Grandma Veducha, wrapped in a black scarf, erect and tall, walking about the dim alleys tapping with a long cane, her face white and mist floating among the domes. I jump from puddle to puddle looking up into the faces of the Arabs with their brown cloaks. On the churches, mosques and synagogues is a layer of white wool, a fall of snow, and I want to show myself to Grandma but she takes no notice, her face very pale, looking for something all the time, her basket still empty, but not stopping. I tug at her cane, wanting to stop her beside a candy vendor, but she pushes me away, walks on, from alley to alley, passing by the Western Wall as it used to be, old and small, the houses closing it in, climbing up to the Jewish quarter by steep and twisting steps, this must be before the War of Independence and I am full of wonder, for even when I was small I had the mind of an old woman. Everything isn't in ruins yet. But Grandma pays no attention to me, it's as if by chance that I come to be clinging at her skirt. From time to time she goes to one of the stalls, to finger a small tomato, to sniff an eggplant, grumbling in Arabic to the traders who laugh. Asking questions but buying nothing. Suddenly I understand, it's not vegetables she's looking for but a person. Arab? Jew? Armenian? And then I start to cry, from weariness, from the cold, from the mist, I'm very thirsty but Grandma doesn't hear me, or if she hears me she doesn't care, it's like walking with a corpse. I've irritated her with my crying. And the bells start to ring and there's a light rain falling, the sound of gunfire, people running, Grandma is hurrying too, laying about her with the cane to clear a path, striking at the heads of the Arabs who run before her shouting, and in the confusion she slips away from me, her dress slips out of my hand, and I'm still whimpering, not in the alley but in the corridor of a house, weeping softly, not the weeping of a child but the stifled weeping of an old woman, melting in tears. But I'm not unhappy, on the contrary, such pleasure, through my tears I am free of something from which I should have parted long ago, the world becomes lighter. Then I open my eyes, seeing the window beside the bed a little open, a black night and rain falling outside, heavy rain but very quiet, as if it doesn't reach the ground but just hovers. And it's cold but the mist has gone, I notice this at once, the mist that all the time has covered everything–gone.

I rose from the bed and drank a cup of water.

Still weeping–

Later they told me that for a day and a half I had wept without pause and the people around me were most concerned, they held my hand, caressed me, did not understand. This is how it began, this how consciousness returned. Only consciousness? More. The light itself. More light than I thought existed. Still consciousness without knowledge. Illumined consciousness, slowly breaking out, opening up. At noon on the second day I stopped crying as if the crying machine had broken. And when the nurse brought my lunch I knew already what they did not yet know. I have returned. I am here. I can remember it all. Everything is ready. All that is missing is my name. Someone has only to remind me of my name and the rest will fall into place. I smiled at the dusky nurse and she smiled back, a little scared and a little astonished to find me smiling now and no longer weeping.

I said to her, "What is your name, my child?" and she told me. "And what is my name?" I asked. "Your name?" She was utterly bewildered, thought I was playing games with her. "Your name . . . ?" and she came closer to the bed, searching for a piece of paper down there among the latticework, glancing at it and saying in a shy whisper, "It says here Veducha Ermozo."

That was all that was missing, I heard the name and at once my head opened. The card with my name had been hanging there on the bed all the time and I, foolish woman, had not seen it. Now I knew who I was and I remembered other things too. All at once I understood everything. I felt dizzy with all the knowledge returning to me. Mother, Father, Hemdah and Gabriel, the State of Israel, Golda, the house, the bay, Galilee, Nixon. My neighbor Mrs. Goldberg, *Yediot Aheronot*, my little Morris, the Jewish people. It all flooded over me. One thing only I did not know, what is this lovely place in which I am lying, the white room and the beds, the orchard outside, and who are these charming girls who walk around me? Surely I'm not dead, this isn't the world to come.

Quickly I got out of bed and asked for my clothes and a little nurse brought them. And two old women in gowns came into the room and when they saw me dressing they almost screamed. I frightened them. They realized that something had happened to me. Later they described the change—the light had returned to my eyes. Every look of mine was different.

How happy I was! Freedom and joy, I was dressing myself and singing. And everything around me interested me. The names of the old ladies who introduced themselves. An old copy of *Ma'ariv* lying on the chair. I wanted to devour it. At once I began to read. For I am well known as an avid reader of newspapers. I saw new and wonderful things, the world has not been slumbering in the meantime.

My head was spinning—

The news of my awakening had spread quickly. The matron and the secretary came hurrying into the room, very excited, they hugged me, led me straight to the matron's office. They called the doctor to come and examine me. They were laughing and I laughed too. "That's it, I've woken up," I said. "Now tell me everything."

And they told me, a frightening story. How they brought me here nearly a year ago, unconscious, they lost all hope for me. For ten months perhaps I had been lying there like a stone, like a vegetable, like a mindless animal, not knowing anyone, not even myself. Talking like a baby, nonsense, dreams, all meaningless.

On the table there was a pack of cigarettes and I remembered that I used to smoke and that I used to enjoy it very much and I asked permission to take a cigarette and so I sat facing them in the armchair, smoking cigarette after cigarette, a real resurrection from the dead. Hearing the confused stories about myself and the country. First of all—the war. I did not know that there had been another war and that the bastards surprised us on Yom Kippur. And they enjoyed telling me about the war, one interrupting the other and the doctor too adding his bit. Describing the suffering, terrible things, the treacherous government too, to think that all this happened while I lay senseless in bed. More stories, more sorrows, more deaths, I take them all in. Not yet satisfied, and the smell of cigarettes blending with the smell of gunpowder. The news that I had come to life had taken wing. Nurses, cleaners and clerks peered at me through the door, smiling at me pleasantly, some of them introducing themselves, shaking hands like old friends. People who had known me all the time, who had washed me, who had fed me, I knew nothing about them. Friendly and devoted people. And I all the time discovering more facts, even though they were beginning to tire of me. Now I was asking them about prices. How much had prices risen. How much did a pound of tomatoes cost, for example, how much must you pay for good eggplants. What the war did to the market.

And so passed two days of happiness and awakening. I embraced the whole world in the joy of my second birth. Walking about the wards, making new friends, old men and old women, doctors and nurses. Asking questions and getting answers. Gossiping all the time, as if I have an empty sack to fill. And at night too I used to wander about, chatting to the attendants and the night nurses. I hardly slept, just dozing for a while and waking with a start, for I was afraid of losing consciousness again.

The doctors scolded me, but smiled–

And already they were hinting that I might go home–

Then they took out my file and hesitantly, cautiously began to tell me about him. My grandson–Gabriel. I did not know that he had suddenly returned to Israel. A month after they brought me here he apeared. Oh, God, for what?

My head felt weak. It seems I went pale as well. They gave me a sedative, even wanted to put me to bed.

Gabriel has returned! For ten years now he's been wandering around the world not wanting to return, and suddenly he is back. I just lose consciousness and here he is. Even bringing a doctor, an expert on comas, to examine me, bringing a lawyer to take instructions from me. Conferring beside my bed. A consultation. It seems he's interested in the legacy, my poor bewildered grandson.

Now I am going crazy. The details aren't clear, it's as if they have all lost consciousness. Everything is so confused. At first he used to come here every week. Sitting beside my bed, trying hard to talk to me, waiting for the doctor's visit, glancing at the medical reports and going. Then he came seldom and for short visits, he did not even come to my bed but used to go straight to the office, take out the file himself, look at it grimly and disappear. But since the war he has not been here at all, he has disappeared. He got scared and fled.

There had been a phone call to check if there had been any change in my condition, but they didn't know if it was him or someone else. Just a few weeks ago another man appeared, older, with a big beard, they all remembered his beard. (But who was it? Who was it?) He said he was related to me, he spoke hesitantly, he stood beside my bed and looked at me for a long time, he wanted to know if Gabriel had been here. More than caring about me he was looking for Gabriel.

A detective story–

They'll make a film of it yet–

Suddenly I'm sad. No longer the joy of awakening of the first few days but worry and depression. The newspapers full of dark news. Now I realize how hard the war was. Gabriel came back from Paris and I didn't know him and it seems he lost hope and went away. Now I must think about returning home, paying my bills, going out into the world again, I must vacate my bed, there are other old people going into comas all the time, and not only old people. I phone my house but the line's been disconnected. Phone my lawyer but he's away on army service. I order a taxi and drive home, a terrible fog outside, rain and mud and darkness. I arrive at my house and the heavy door is closed. My neighbor Mrs. Goldberg, the Ashkenazi bitch, comes out to see who it is, almost faints when she sees me.

I go into her apartment and hear her story. It was she who found me unconscious, sitting at the table, a plate in front of me, motionless as a stone. She called a doctor who took me to the hospital. She looked through my papers and found Gabriel's address in Paris and wrote to him telling him about my illness, told him that I was dying. And a few weeks later the young man actually appeared, and stayed in the house until the war. But on the first day he disappeared and hadn't been seen since. Some time later a man with a beard came, that beard chasing me again, he came looking for Gabriel, wanted to get inside the apartment, to break down the door, but she threatened to call the police, she stood on guard, she even moved her bed closer to the door, to hear him if he came.

I had to call a locksmith to break down the door of my apartment. For I had no key, neither did Mrs. Goldberg, Gabriel took them all. He worked for a quarter of an hour and charged a hundred pounds, thief. But at least I was able to get inside. A neglected house, full of spiders, in the kitchen dirty dishes and filthy scraps of moldy food. Tins of preserves everywhere. And a lot of pans. He's taken all the cutlery out of the cupboards so as not to have to wash up every day. Beetles scuttled about under my feet, as if I'm the intruder. And a little mouse that was born in the rubbish there stares at me insolently from a corner, making no attempt to run away.

Signs of my grandson everywhere. He always was an untidy boy but now he's lost control. His shirts hanging on top of my dresses, dirty linen on the chairs, socks in the bathroom. French newspapers and magazines from before the war. An open suitcase on one of the beds. Everything laid out as if he's just gone out for a short walk.

Well, then, where is he?

Mrs. Goldberg brings me something to eat, *gefilte fish* that she cooked for the Sabbath. It's Sabbath eve, I forgot. For a whole year I have been outside time. She looks in silence at the chaos in the room, dying of curiosity, she would have liked to stay for a while but I get rid of her politely. The evening falls quickly and I'm still looking for a piece of paper, some message, to help me understand. The light bulbs are all burned out and I have to light a candle to find my way from room to room.

And suddenly I feel again the loneliness of the last years. Now I understand how I lost consciousness. I wish I could lose it again. I should never have left Jerusalem, even though there was not a single member of my family left. It was wrong to break away. Sin and iniquity. I tried to taste the *gefilte fish* and it's so sweet it makes me sick. When will the Ashkenazim learn to cook? Sitting there in the kitchen among the dirty dishes, among the moldy scraps of food, forcing myself to eat, not to weaken, eating and tears falling on the plate. And outside–storm, destruction.

So, he was here. What did he look like? Oh, Lord of the Universe. Where did he go? Perhaps he is dead, perhaps he too is lying somewhere unconscious. And how am I to find the man with the beard? I must start searching every corner of the house. Perhaps I will find some trace. I leave the dirty dish in the sink, I don't have the strength to wash it. How dirty he's made the house, he's learned dirty habits from the French. I take the candle and roam around the half-lit house, examining the cupboards and the beds, searching under the sheets, he's slept in all of them.

In the end I feel tired, put on a nightdress and get into my bed. He's slept in this one too. The sheets are soiled, but I don't have the energy to change them.

The first night at home after a year. Who would believe that it would be like this? Better I had died. The rain lashes the windows. A hard winter. The doors in the house creak and a draught blows in, from where I don't know. I lie there with my eyes open. I have never been afraid of loneliness, people know me as a solitary person, but never have I felt so uneasy in my bed. And then I hear a rustle from the shutter in the next room, as if someone is climbing in through the window. At first I thought it was just the wind, but then I hear light footsteps. He's come back, I say to myself. And the door of my room really does open and a boy appears in the doorway, looking in. What is this, has Gabriel turned into a boy once more, and is he wandering about the house as he used to twenty years ago, when he was having a bad dream and walked about the house making noises on purpose to wake me up?

Oh, help, I'm sinking back again. Farewell old lady. This time there'll be no awakening. But the boy is real, standing there in the doorway, in the light of the candle that I left in the passage, not a dream, he closes the door and goes away, opening more doors and closing them again. Finally drawing back the bolts of the front door.

Hurriedly I get out of bed, and just as I am in my nightdress I go out into the passage, seeing there a middle-aged man, a total stranger, wrapped in a big fur coat, with a big blond beard, the bearded man has descended from heaven again, talking to the boy who opened the door of my room, I know right away that he's an Arab, I can sniff them out. Smell of eggplants, green garlic and fresh straw, the very smell that returned me to consciousness.

ASYA

I really trembled. For so many years I hadn't seen him. And there he was, riding a bicycle outside the house. I must not lose him again. I clung fast to the dream. Yigal. He was riding back and forth on the broad pavement, so serious, on a big bicycle, he was tall and thin and I thought, he is alive, what happiness. I didn't dare say a word. And he was riding around and around in a circle, very serious, concentrating on his riding, so intense, I couldn't see his eyes. The bicycle looked very colorful, shining, loaded with gears, cog wheels and coils of wire. But most of all I was impressed by the brakes. Thin cables led from them directly to his ears, as if he must listen to the brakes. Some kind of safety precaution.

"Do you see?" said Adam, smiling, standing behind me on the steps, I hadn't seen him, he was in the dark. It seemed he had arranged this. But I didn't reply, only looked with longing at the boy on the bicycle. Slowly I began to realize that this wasn't Yigal but some kind of replacement that Adam had brought here for me. But I didn't mind this, it seemed wonderful and right to bring me a substitute. I just waited for him to grow tired of cycling around and around so I could see him close up, touch him, embrace him. But he didn't look, didn't hear, continuing gravely with the endless ride. "Yigal," I said in a whisper, "come here for a moment." And I thought, perhaps he can't hear, perhaps he too can't hear, but he heard and understood, he just took advantage of his deafness to ignore me.

And then we were in a big hall, Adam and I, a big hall flooded with sunlight, it was a party, a bar mitzvah or a wedding, long tables laden with salami sandwiches, and Adam pounced on them in his usual way and started to munch, ravenously hungry, and I was worried about Yigal, whom we had left there on the pavement. I left the party in the middle without touching the food and went back home in the afternoon, Sabbath, the streets deserted, the pavement outside the house empty. I started walking the streets searching for the "replacement," growing more and more dispirited, whimpering to myself. Until beside a half-built house, on the hillside, on a heap of sand I saw the bicycle, slightly damaged, smaller than I had thought, less ornate than it looked before, but still those cables coiling out of the brakes, and at the ends, like little boxes, the earpieces of a transistor. They were quivering, something rustled in them. I picked them up, I heard a man talking, like a newscaster, someone saying, "Life . . . she has come to life."

ADAM

Suddenly I felt so happy I laughed. I had thought I was so clever breaking in here in the middle of the night, and here she was–erect, small and vigorous. The grandmother come to life. And that blank face down which the porridge had trickled was gazing at me, alert and inquisitive. Oh, she's found her lost consciousness all right, every last bit of it.

I wanted to embrace her–

The amazing thing was that she didn't look afraid, didn't try to cry out or call for help, on the contrary, she looked calm, as if she'd been expecting this nighttime intrusion. She looked at me with trust, even held out her dry little hand. I gripped it firmly in both my hands.

"I hear that you are related to me, sir, I would like to know your name."

And she winked at me.

I was puzzled. It seemed she even knew about my visit to the hospital. Her hand was still in mine, what could I tell her—that I had spent months searching for my wife's lover?

First of all I got rid of Na'im, who was still standing there staring open-mouthed, quite baffled. I sent him out to the kitchen and the old lady went with him and gave him sweets. Then I followed her to her bedroom. She moved a heap of clothes from a chair and invited me to sit down. Then she got into her bed. The bedroom was dim, the candle was burned down, only in the passage was there a small light. And so, sitting facing her in the dark, seeing her silhouette like a giant Ping-Pong ball, I heard her say, "I am listening . . ."

And I began to tell her all that I knew. From the moment that the little Morris appeared in the garage to the morning of the second day of the war. About my search for him, about the army authorities who knew nothing about him, and more personal details, how he looked, how he dressed, what he used to say, how he spent his time. And she listened in silence, for a moment I thought she was asleep, I stood up and went closer to her. She was weeping quietly, clawing desperately at her hair, yearning for him, afraid he might be dead.

Meanwhile my eyes were becoming accustomed to the gloom and I saw his possessions scattered about me, his clothes, his shirt and trousers, an open suitcase, illustrated newspapers, the cigarettes he used to smoke, all lying there just as he had left them. Again his presence seemed so poignant.

I said, "He hasn't been killed, that's impossible."

"Then something frightened him. He is hiding. We must search for him. Especially at night."

"At night?"

And then she began telling me about him, how she brought him up after his mother was killed and his father deserted him. A lonely, bewildered child who couldn't sleep, a creature of the night. She remembered the names of some relations on his father's side, an uncle living in Dimona, another uncle in Jerusalem, a friend or two with whom he had been in contact many years ago. It was five o'clock in the morning, my head felt dizzy from all these stories, but there had been a breakthrough in the quest for him.

The telephone in the house had been disconnected, I promised to have it restored. I gave her my phone number, we agreed to meet again.

Outside the rain had stopped, the sky was clearing. Time to leave. Na'im was asleep in the kitchen, I roused him, we said good-by to the old lady and drove back up to Carmel. The streets were wet and deserted. The first signs of daylight. It was quiet in the house. Asya and Dafi were fast asleep. I put Na'im to bed in the study and went to the bedroom. I felt no weariness at all, watching Asya, who went on sleeping, the morning light falling on her face. I touched her lightly. She was dreaming again, I could tell by the movements of her eyes behind the closed lids. Strange, knowing that at that very moment she was engrossed in a dream, evidently a painful dream, because her face was twisted. My aging wife, caught up in her dreams. I bent over her cautiously, almost on my knees, tugging at her gently. But she didn't want to wake up, so strange, clutching at the pillow with a pathetic, almost desperate gesture, whimpering. I caressed her, smiling.

"Asya, wake up, there's news. It's incredible, but the grandmother, the old woman, she has come to life."

NA'IM

And they went into one of the rooms really pleased with themselves and they put me in the kitchen among the tomatoes and the eggplants to wait for them. And the old woman gave me some old sweets, probably left over from the time before she went bananas, and I sat there until they finished chattering, chewing the sweets, half asleep in the chair. And after maybe two hours Adam came in to fetch me and we went back to his house through the empty streets and the sky was clear and the rain had stopped. There wasn't any left, it had all fallen on me.

It was dark in the house and he put me back to bed and went to his bedroom, started talking to his wife, who'd woken up. They talked excitedly but I didn't have the strength to listen. I went to sleep right away. I slept a lot. I was really tired and I didn't mind just sleeping and sleeping. It was so nice in the soft bed in that lovely room with all the books, deep down among the Jews.

It must have been the end of the morning already and I began to wake up, stretching lazily in the bed. Once or twice the door opened and the girl's pretty head peeped in at me. The phone rang and the radio was on at full blast. The girl was walking around the whole time. I heard her footsteps and she peeped into the room again, looks like she wanted me to wake up but I didn't want to. I'd done a professional job that night and I deserved a bit of rest. Through the window I saw blue sky and heard the voices of children. On the radio it was the usual chatter, they never get tired of it, even on the Sabbath. The girl was standing at the door now and tapping softly. I closed my eyes in a hurry and she came in quietly and went to the bookcase pretending to look for a book, making little noises to wake me up. She was wearing jeans and a very tight sweater and I noticed that she had firm little tits, yesterday I was sure she hadn't had any and here they were like they'd grown overnight.

In the end, when she saw I wasn't moving, she came closer and touched my face with her warm hand. I was really pleased that she touched me and didn't only talk. At last I decided to open my eyes so she wouldn't think I was dead.

And she said quickly in her hoarse voice, "You must get up. Mommy and Daddy have gone out. It's eleven o'clock already. I'll make breakfast for you. How do you like your eggs?"

She was all flushed and very serious.

"I don't mind."

"I don't mind either."

"Whatever you make."

"But I don't mind . . . tell me what you want."

"Whatever you're eating." I smiled.

"I've eaten already . . . do you like scrambled eggs?"

I didn't know what scrambled eggs were but I didn't mind trying, then suddenly with an audacity that surprised even me I said, "Fine, but no sugar, please."

"Sugar?"

"I mean, like yesterday," I mumbled. "I thought there was some sugar in the food."

And suddenly she understood and burst out laughing, awfully amused.

And I smiled a bit too.

And she went out, I got dressed quickly and tidied up the bed and went to the bathroom and washed my face and cleaned my teeth and combed my hair with their comb and cleaned the sink. And I went out to the kitchen and found the table covered with all sorts of things. You could see she'd taken everything out of the fridge and put it on the table. Maybe this was the first time she'd ever made breakfast for a guest. And she was wearing an apron and frying something on the stove in a great hurry and then she brought me a very messy half-burned egg and gave me toast and cereal. She sat tensely, opposite, watching me eat and all the time offering me something else. Cheese, salted fish, chocolate. She wanted me to finish off all the food in the house. She buttered the bread for me herself, changing plates the whole time, fussing around me like she was my wife or my mother, playing some part and enjoying it.

And I ate with my mouth closed, slowly. Sometimes refusing what she offered me and sometimes not. And she watching me closely like I was a baby or a puppy being fed. And I just now and then looked at her straight, seeing her all fresh, so different from yesterday, sort of brisk, not dreamy. Her hair tied up on top of her head, her eyes darting about, wide awake. She didn't touch the food.

"Aren't you eating?" I asked.

"No . . . I'm fat enough already."

"Are you fat?"

"A bit."

"I don't think so."

And again she burst out laughing. Really frightening the weird noises she can make, like a mare in heat. Something about me makes her laugh. Laughing and going quiet again. Getting serious. And then again, smiling a bit and without warning and for no reason breaking out into a great shriek of laughter.

And I eat and eat and as I eat I fall deeper and deeper in love, falling in love for real with all my heart and soul, I could kiss that white foot of hers that's swinging there in front of me all the time.

"The food wasn't too sweet for you?"

"No . . . it was fine." I go red all over.

"But you drink coffee with sugar?"

"Coffee, yes."

And she goes out to make coffee for me.

Such a clear day, it's like the winter's over. Music on the radio now, waiting for the new talkers to come and take over from the old talkers who've gone away for a rest. And I'm head over heels in love already. No longer any need even to look at her. She's there in my heart. Drinking coffee. A crazy life. Like it's not me. And she watching me and watching me like she's never seen a man eating before.

"Do you hate us very much?" I suddenly heard her say.

"Hate who?"

Of course I knew what she meant but it was weird, her of all people starting to talk politics.

"Us, the Israelis."

"We are Israelis too."

"No . . . I mean the Jews."

"Not so much now." I tried to give her a straight answer, seeing her pretty face, her fair hair. "Since the war, after they beat you a bit, we don't hate you so much now . . ."

And she laughed, she liked what I said.

"But that cousin of yours . . . that terrorist . . ."

"But he was a little crazy . . ." I interrupted her in a hurry, I just didn't want her to talk about Adnan.

"And do you hate us?"

"Me? No . . . never." It was a lie because sometimes the Jews do get on my nerves, they never pick you up when you're hitchhiking, they pass you by even in the rain when you're alone on the roadside.

And then the phone rang. She ran to answer it. Must have been a friend of hers because she stood there talking for maybe half an hour. Laughing and talking, she suddenly started talking in English so I wouldn't understand, talking dirty maybe. I heard her too, "A sweet little Arab" she said, and she said more things about me that I didn't catch. And I sat still in my chair, not moving. Eating some more salted fish and chocolate, staring at the empty candlesticks, wondering if it was all right to get up. Looking at the furniture, at a newspaper lying on a chair, reading the headlines.

At last she came back, surprised to find me still sitting there.

"Have you finished?"

"A long time ago."

"Then you can go. Daddy said he wouldn't need you anymore. He said you should have a meal and go home. He'll see you at the garage."

So, that's it, all over. Give the laborer a meal and send him home.

I stood up quickly, took my pajamas and went to the door.

"Have you got money for the bus?"

"Yes"–though I hadn't.

"Do you know where the bus station is?"

"Yes. But I'll walk."

I felt so sorry it was all over, even though I had no idea how it could go on.

"Would you like me to walk with you?"

As if she understood, as if she was sorry too.

"If you like," I said casually, though I could've fallen at her feet and kissed them.

"Then wait a moment."

And she went to put her shoes on.

And we set off together, a really strange pair. People turned to look at us, because she was pretty and nicely dressed and I was in my working clothes, all dirty and crumpled by the rain. Walking fast and not talking much. We started going down the hill. She showed me some steps going down the hill in the middle between flowers and trees and bushes and grass like a path in the Garden of Eden. She went down first and I followed. We hardly talked. Just once she stopped me and asked me when we Arabs get married, that is, at what age. And I said, "The same as you," and we carried on walking. But halfway down the hill she met two boys, friends of hers who were really pleased to see her. She told them, "This is Na'im." And they didn't understand who I was but they told me their names, which I didn't catch, and it was like she realized only then how different I was, all dirty, and she said, "You can find your own way from here."

"That's O.K.," I said.

And I left her chatting with her friends, and I remembered I hadn't thanked her for the meal but I didn't go back, just looked up and saw her still talking to them and they turned and she started climbing back with them. They disappeared. The air all around full of scents. A spring Sabbath, people in their best clothes and little children running about.

There was no bus at the bus station. A van from the next village took me to within a few kilometers of my village. I walked the rest of the way, waving to the men working in the fields as usual. Where we live, they work all the time, they never rest. And suddenly I felt a lump in my throat, from happiness or misery I don't know which and I started to cry, out loud, like an engine switched on. So much excitement the last two days. I cried on the empty road, collapsing on the wet earth like I was sorry I was an Arab and even if I'd been a Jew still nothing would have come of it.

DAFI

He's fast asleep and here I am, stuck in the house because of him. A beautiful day outside. I phoned Tali and Osnat in the morning, telling them not to come around, they might have found him entertaining but I didn't want him to be bothered by a lot of girls all at once. Mommy and Daddy got up early and went off somewhere leaving me here, to give him his breakfast and send him home. It's all ready, I've taken everything out of the fridge and put it on the table and I've opened a can of sardines too and a can of beans so he can choose what he wants and not grimace like he did yesterday when they gave him *gefilte fish*. I don't want any trouble with him and I don't want him to think he's being kept without food because he's an Arab. The pan on the stove, oil, matches, two eggs, water in the kettle. He's only got to place his order, I'll light the stove and the meal will be there, like a short-order service. If Mommy saw how good I am at organizing things she'd make me cook breakfast every Sabbath. But he just goes on and on sleeping, does he think this is a hotel? I'm getting all worked up. I've changed my clothes twice. First I put on a dress but I'm never sure if it makes me look fat from behind. Then I put on my long caftan but then I took it off because it really looked a bit much, and I put on the jeans that I wore yesterday with a thin sweater, no point in trying to hide what can't be hidden anyway. I switched on the radio at full volume, maybe the music quiz will wake him up. But he's about as lively as a corpse. I'm not going to sit at home all day. At eleven o'clock I knocked softly on the study door a few times and in the end I decided to go in as if I was looking for a book. There he was, sleeping peacefully, in his wonderful pajamas, dead to the world. He's had quite long enough, I decided. He can catch up on his sleep at his mother's house. I went to him and touched him, right there on the face. Why not? After all he's one of Daddy's workers and I too have a bit of authority here. At last he opened his eyes.

"Mommy and Daddy have gone out and they told me to make breakfast for you. How do you like your eggs?" I said in a hurry.

And he lying there with his head still on the pillow, I was already wishing I hadn't made that offer. In the end I persuaded him to eat a scrambled egg because that's what I cook best. And the little bastard, still lying there in bed, asked me not to put sugar in it, because it seems yesterday the *gefilte fish* was too sweet for him. He made me mad.

What can I say? People get used to anything. He didn't seem a bit impressed when he came out of the bathroom and saw the table covered with good things, all for him. Yesterday he was crying and wailing like a stray dog and now he sits there upright and proud, eating like a gentleman with his mouth closed. Congratulations. Taking this and refusing that. He's got a mind of his own. And I fuss around him, buttering his bread for him, changing the dishes. I don't know why I'm doing all this. I don't know any other person who's had service like this from me and it's not going to happen again either. I feel tense as hell. I've already forgotten the resemblance to Yigal. That really was an absurd idea. Now in his dirty overalls he looks older, there's even the first signs of a mustache and a beard on his face. Eating at great speed, it's all right for him because he's so thin. There's something relaxed about him, even though he blushes every two minutes for no reason. Saying "Very nice, thank you" but really hating us of course, like all of them. Buy why? Hell, what have we done to them? Surely things can't be that bad. So suddenly I asked him, to his face, how much they hate us. He didn't know what to say, started to mumble, explaining that since the war, after they beat us a bit, it wasn't so bad. Beat us a bit? They must be out of their minds.

But I decided I wasn't going to be content with a general answer. It was important to me to know if he personally hated us and what he was really thinking. Then he said he didn't hate us at all, and he looked me straight in the eye, blushing bright red.

Of course I believed him—

The phone rang. It was Osnat. She was worried because I told her she couldn't come around to our house. She started asking questions and in the end she dragged the whole story out of me, and she was really surprised when she heard I had a little Arab in the house, one of Daddy's workers, even though I told her he was really sweet.

In the meantime he'd finished his breakfast and he was sitting there motionless in his chair. I'd noticed before that he always stays wherever you put him until you move him to somewhere else. Now it's about time he started moving by himself and taking on some personal responsibility, as Shwartzy's always telling us. I said to him, "You can go now, Daddy doesn't need you anymore. Go home now and he'll see you in the garage."

He jumped up from his seat in a hurry, grabbed the bag with his pajamas in it and was about to go, I didn't mean for him to rush off so fast. I was sorry I hadn't invited Osnat along to hear him recite poetry. I asked him if he knew where the bus station was but he said he'd walk. Suddenly, I don't know why, I felt sorry for him, he looked so forlorn in his dirty overalls, having to walk alone down Carmel on the Sabbath, on the way back to his village, wherever that is. Suddenly I was sorry he was going and I'd never see him again, he'd turn into a big stupid Arab like all the Arab workers that you see around the place and he'd marry some stupid Arab woman. So I said to him, "Just a moment, I'll come with you," because I wanted to show him how to get down Carmel by the steps in the middle of the hill, where it's nice to walk on a day like this.

A bit strange walking with a laborer on the Sabbath in Carmel Center beside the busy cafes and the people in their best clothes, my luck that he was taller than me. I showed the steps going down and even went a little way with him. Suddenly I got the crazy idea that maybe he was married after all, who knows when they get married. I asked him, indirectly, and I understood that he wasn't. We carried on walking down among the bushes and the flowers till we met Yigal Rabinovitz and Zachi coming up the hill. They were a bit surprised to find me with him. And then I thought, how far am I going to walk with him? To his village? And I parted from him. He could look after himself now. And he disappeared down the slope straightaway, into the wadi. I stood there for a while chatting to them and we went back up the hill. I thought maybe they'd like to come to a cafe with me but they were on their way to a basketball game. Such babies. I went to Tali's house but she wasn't in and her mom as usual didn't know where she was and didn't care. I went from there to Osnat's house but there the whole crowd were just sitting down to their lunch. I wouldn't have minded being invited to eat with them, but they didn't invite me. I went home and the house was suddenly terribly quiet, his sheets and blankets folded in the study, everything still in its place. People just don't realize how depressing it is to be an only daughter. I felt exhausted and miserable. All my energy had gone into that ridiculous breakfast. Outside it was starting to cloud over, the brightness of the day had gone and it was getting darker. I sat down at the table and ate all the chocolate that was left, looking at the huge pile of dirty plates and pans. I went out of the kitchen in a hurry so as not to make my depression worse. I wanted to read something, something real and not the depressing newspapers again. I remembered how yesterday he sat on the edge of the armchair in the dark and quietly recited *Dead of the Desert*. I looked for a poetry book to read. I used to have Alterman's *Stars Outside* always on the desk but for a few weeks now it's been missing. So I picked up the Bialik, what else could I do, the book was open at *Dead of the Desert*, maybe at last I'll understand why it's so important.

I heard Daddy and Mommy coming in, I took off my shoes in a hurry and got into bed with the book, covering myself with the blanket so they wouldn't bother me. They were tired and irritable, they'd found nothing. Mommy saw the mess in the kitchen and came right to my room.

"Why did you leave all those dishes in the kitchen? Couldn't you have washed them?"

"Nothing to do with me. That Arab boy of yours . . ."

"Did he need that many plates for his breakfast?"

"Picture to yourself . . . he's a growing boy, you know, you were there last night."

She looked at me with hatred but I held up the book to cover my face, and went on reading.

And silence returns as before and barren the desert stands.

ADAM

I was full of hope. I felt that I was finding him, that I was now on his trail. I didn't want to lose a moment. Asya got dressed, Na'im was still asleep, when Dafi woke up I told her what to say to him and what to do with him, and the two of us set off for Dimona to look for his uncle. It was a bright Sabbath day, the roads full of traffic. It was five years perhaps since we'd been down in the Negev and it was pleasant to discover new roads, unfamiliar settlements. I had no address in Dimona, just the name–Gabriel Arditi. The same name that the army computer stubbornly kept producing all the time–not without reason, it now appeared. This man was his uncle, perhaps he was hiding in his house. I had always thought of Dimona as a small town and here it was, a booming desert city. We didn't know where to start, we could see no end to the blocks of apartment houses. But the inhabitants turned out to be friendly and co-operative and they took the trouble to help us. This man knew one Arditi and that man knew another. They took us from one to another until at last we found him. He was in the middle of lunch and he opened the door with a fork in his hand. It was a disappointment. I told the story briefly. He looked at us suspiciously. First of all he didn't believe that the grandmother was still alive. "You're mistaken," he insisted, "Gabriel's grandmother, his mother's mother, died just after independence." He was certain of that. Even then she was a very old woman. We must be thinking of another grandmother, or an old aunt. About Gabriel he knew very little. He had heard that he went away to join his father in Paris. He hadn't heard that he'd come back.

"Are you part of the family too? Surely you are Ashkenazim . . ."

In vain. He didn't even invite us into his house. He just gave us the name of another relative, Gabriel's father's cousin, who had kept in touch with that side of the family, perhaps he would know.

It was too late now to drive to Jerusalem. The sky was beginning to cloud over, we returned to Haifa. Na'im had already gone, Dafi was in a foul mood. For some reason I was worried about the old lady so I drove to her house, told her about my visit to Dimona, of course I didn't mention what he'd said about her supposed death, I mentioned the new name that I'd been given, that cousin of Gabriel's father. She remembered him. "Oh, that silly old man. Try him, why not?"

The next day at noon I drove to Jerusalem to look for him. This time I had a clear address. But a different family was living there. They told me that the old man used to live there but he had gone to live with his daughter in Ramat Gan. It wasn't easy to find him because his daughter and her husband had changed houses three times in the last few years, each time moving to a more luxurious apartment. Eventually I found the right address. He wasn't at home, he'd gone out to an old people's club. I waited a long time, in the meantime I talked to his grandchildren. From my conversation with them it soon became clear to me that there'd been no sign of Gabriel here. Even so I wanted to talk to the old man. He arrived at last and he was delighted to find somebody waiting for him. I began to tell him the story, he too insisted that I was wrong about the grandmother being alive. The information that she'd gone into a coma and recovered made no impression on him. He argued with me, I was confused, I was mistaken, he was positive that she'd died back in '48, just a few days before the Declaration of Independence. He even thought he remembered attending her funeral in Jerusalem during the siege. He was convinced, there was no persuading him. I said, "I can take you to her right now," but he laughed hysterically—"No thank you, at my age I don't go visiting corpses at night."

He remembered Gabriel as a boy. Sometimes his father brought him to visit them. But then they went to Venezuela. They may have gotten only as far as Paris, but the intention was to go to Venezuela, to join a wealthy branch of the family that had settled there in the middle of the last century.

Anyway, he was very friendly and didn't want to be parted from me. He insisted on me staying for supper and told me stories about the whole family, about his grandchildren.

It was late at night when I left his house. Although my efforts so far had been fruitless, I was more and more convinced that he hadn't been killed, that he was alive, wandering about the land. The stories that I'd heard about this adventurous family convinced me that perhaps there was some truth in what the old lady had said and that I should try searching for him at night. I turned off the main highway and continued heading north by old side roads, looking around me, surprised to see so much traffic on the roads so late, nearly midnight. At one intersection I saw a little car parked at the roadside, its hood raised. My heart thumped wildly. I was sure it was the little Morris that I was looking for, but it was an Austin, a similar model, 1952. Somebody was pacing about beside it. Something in his profile caught my attention, I stopped at once, got out to have a look. No it wasn't Gabriel, I must have been imagining things, but he was about the same age and something about him really did remind me of Gabriel. Coincidences like this increase my conviction that Gabriel is close by, that he is wandering about this very neighborhood perhaps, that right here, on these little side roads in the night hours I shall find him.

I pulled up beside the parked car. "What's the problem?" The boy explained, some kind of blockage in the engine, he doesn't understand these things. He called for a tow truck and he's been waiting for it three hours. I glanced at the engine. "Start it up," I said. But he looked at me suspiciously, my heavy beard misled him.

"Do you know anything about engines?"

"A little . . . start it up."

He started the engine. A fuel blockage. I took a small screwdriver out of my pocket and dismantled the carburetor, cleaned the cup and released the jammed needle. A ten-minute job. The young man looked on anxiously all the time, afraid I was damaging something.

"Start it up."

The car sprang easily to life. He was amazed. "Is that all it was?" He was so grateful. At least he'd be able to drive to the nearest garage. "No need to drive to a garage," I said. "It's O.K. now."

Midnight. Looking around me all the time. Cars passing by in an endless stream. I had no idea there was so much traffic about at night. He got back into his car, thanked me again and drove off. It seemed strange to me, doing a repair job and not getting paid for it.

I continued on my way, ten kilometers farther on, and then another vehicle parked at the roadside. This time it was a tow truck, presumably the one that went out for the Austin that I'd repaired. It had broken down itself. I was tired but I stopped nevertheless.

The driver was dozing on the seat, under a blanket. I roused him.

"Do you need help?"

He woke up, confused, a heavy, bony man, his hair going white, his face wrinkled.

Oh, it doesn't matter, he'll wait till morning. There's a fuel blockage that he can't shift. One of the gas stations in this area is clogging up everybody's engines selling dirty fuel.

"Let me try."

"You won't do it."

"Let me try, it can't do any harm."

He opened the hood, I probed in the dark at the dirty and neglected engine, unscrewing the fuel pump. It was years since I'd done jobs like this.

Meanwhile we talked. He told me about himself. He came originally from a *moshav* not far from here, after the Six Day War he got tired of working on the land, he sold his land and bought this tow truck, now he did towing jobs at night. But this work too was beginning to bore him. His eyesight wasn't good, and he knew nothing about modern cars, he didn't even try to identify the fault, he just used to hitch up straightaway and start towing. His boss had doubts about him.

"What goes on around here at night? Is there enough work for you?"

"Plenty of it. The Jews are always speeding."

He watched me cleaning the fuel pump and fitting a new screw, giving me strange advice. His knowledge of mechanics was hopelessly vague.

"Have you perhaps in the last few months come across an old Morris, 1947, colored bright blue?"

"You get them all here. Morris, Volvo, BMW, Volkswagen, Ford, Fiat. All the models there are. The more they raise the road tax, the more crowded the roads are."

"But a little Morris, blue . . ."

"Morrises too, the lot."

What a fool the man was.

I got his engine going for him. He was most impressed. He could go home now and sleep. Perhaps I'd like to work for him, he'd give me a percentage.

I smiled, the idea amused me.

"No, but I'd be prepared to buy this tow truck from you."

"Buy it?"

"Yes, why should you be driving around at night at your age?"

He scratched his head.

"How much would you give for it?"

"Bring it around to my garage tomorrow and we'll make a deal."

At noon the next day Erlich said to me, "What's going on, did you invite someone around here to sell you a tow truck?" I went out to meet him. He stood there, squat and heavy, an old farmer beside his tow truck. Something about the way he talked reminded me of my father, the same habits of pronunciation, the same way of putting his sentences together. He looked around him, astonished and impressed by the giant garage and the dozens of workers.

"Is all this yours?"

"Yes."

"And I wanted to employ you . . ." He said, partly in bitterness, partly in amusement.

I examined the vehicle. It was in a thoroughly neglected state. I called Hamid to inspect the engine and told Erlich to check the market price. An hour later they both reported to me. I said to Erlich, "Right now, give him the money and buy the truck."

Erlich wasn't keen on the idea.

"What do you want a tow truck for?"

"We're going to start towing at night, it'll bring in more customers."

"But who's going to do the driving?"

"I am."

"You?" He didn't believe me.

"Yes, why not? I know you think I've forgotten what work is . . ."

NA'IM

The next day he didn't come to the garage. The Arabs didn't ask me any questions, it was like they really didn't care about me sleeping at his house. Only Hamid asked me what job I'd been doing that night and I told him Adam was repairing a rusty old water tank in his house and I was passing him the tools. So I lied quite calmly though he never asked me to lie.

The next day Adam came to work but he didn't say a word to me, another day went by and it was like he didn't see me, and then another day and then another. Once he saw me and smiled and said, "How's the poetry?" but before I could answer he was called away to the phone and disappeared. Maybe two weeks had gone by since that night and it was like he'd forgotten me. Forgotten that I'd slept in his house, washed in his bath. And I don't know why, it made me sad, even though I didn't really expect anything from him.

I didn't feel like reading poetry either. I tried as hard as I could to keep close to him, so he'd say something to me, give me a job to do, but he ignored me. I got to be like a little hound, I could sniff him out anywhere, follow his tracks. But he was busy, running backward and forward all the time. He'd bought a second-hand tow truck and he spent all his time on it, he wasn't interested in the garage. He overhauled it, painted it, fixed all kinds of gadgets on it.

The days are getting longer. It's light when we leave for the garage in the morning and it's light when we go home. I'm bored stiff already. Tightening brakes all the time. Lying underneath the cars and shouting to the Jews "Press, let go, harder, ease off, slowly, press." The Jews do exactly what I tell them.

And the days go by and they're all pretty much the same. Nothing happens. They're talking about war again and the radio's buzzing all the time. We start listening to what the Jews are saying about themselves, all that wailing and cursing themselves, it pleases us no end. It's nice to hear how screwed up and stupid they are and how hard things are for them, though you wouldn't exactly think so seeing them changing their cars all the time and buying newer and bigger ones.

Late one afternoon he brought in his tow truck to have the brakes tightened. He himself got down underneath and I pressed on the brake pedal, it was like he didn't trust me to do the tightening for him. By now we were sick of that machine of his, all of us, he messed around with it all the time, like a kid who's never seen a car before. Then he finished tightening the brakes and crawled out and stood there beside the truck, drooling over it and wondering if there were any more fancy things he could do to it. Just the two of us there. I was afraid of him slipping away from me again and suddenly I came out with:

"How is the grandmother?"

I'd meant to say "How is Dafi?" but it came out as—the grandmother. I blushed.

"Whose grandmother?" He didn't understand.

"The grandmother we visited that night, the one who went into a coma and got better."

"Oh . . . that grandmother? . . ." He roared with laughter. "Grandma . . . ha ha . . . she's fine, she sends you her regards."

And he started working the winch, raising it and lowering it. Suddenly he turned and looked at me, staring at me so hard you could tell he'd just had an idea.

"Listen, I need you for night work with this tow truck. Would your father let you sleep in town?"

"No problem . . ." I got all excited. "My father doesn't care where I spend the night . . ."

"Good, bring your things here tomorrow, your pajamas and the rest . . . you'll be starting to work nights with this tow truck . . . we'll tow cars in . . . tour the roads . . . you and me . . ."

My heart beat fast, I lit up inside.

"Fine . . . but where shall I sleep? At your house again?"

He looked at me a bit surprised.

"We'll find you a place to stay . . . don't worry . . . we'll fix something for you here at the garage . . . or perhaps even at Mrs. Ermozo's . . . grandma's . . ." And he started to laugh again. "Perhaps you should sleep at her house . . . an excellent idea . . . she can look after you and you can look after her a bit."

ADAM

And the next day Na'im came in carrying a big suitcase, wearing a winter coat too big for him. The Arabs watched him from a distance as he came toward me. I'd noticed before that they were very interested in our relationship, the association seemed to them suspicious and strange.

"What did you tell your father?"

"I said you were going to take care of me."

"And what did he say?"

"Nothing." He blushed. "He said you'd look after me as if you were my father."

"That's all?"

"That's all."

They don't seem to care much about giving the boy up.

"Good. Sit here and wait."

And all day he sat there at the side in his big overcoat, the suitcase beside him, waiting quietly, already apart from the other workers, watching me, wherever I went those dark eyes followed me. Suddenly I had a boy at my disposal, as if I'd adopted a son.

At midday I decided to have a word with Hamid.

"I'm taking Na'im with me to help with the night towing, he'll be staying with an old lady. It'll be all right, don't worry."

But he had no intention of worrying, hardly even looked up, went on tightening a nut in the engine in front of him, not understanding what I wanted from him.

After work I took him to the old lady's house, I rang the doorbell, heard her shuffling little footsteps.

"Who's there?"

"It's me, Adam. I've brought the boy." And then she began shifting the bolts, drawing back one after the other. At first I hardly recognized her. Standing there small and upright, in a flowery pink dress, wearing glasses, her face full of life. And this was the old lady who a few weeks before was lying unconscious in the old people's home, a nurse pouring porridge into her mouth. I put my hand on her shoulder.

"How are you, Mrs. Ermozo?"

"Fine, fine . . . as long as my brain is in the right place everything is fine, even though I'm working all the time, cleaning, tidying . . . please don't look, everything's in such a mess . . ."

"What do you mean, a mess . . . I hardly recognize the place . . . it's all so clean . . ."

But she interrupted me.

"Do you call this clean? This is nothing. You should have seen the place forty years ago, you'd have seen what cleanliness is. You could have eaten off the floor."

I pushed Na'im forward.

"I've brought Na'im here. Do you remember him? He came with me that night."

She looked at him closely.

"Yes . . . yes . . . this is the Arab who climbed in through the window. . . . How are you, boy? You can come in through the door from now on."

She addressed him in Arabic and he blushed bright red, looking at her with hatred.

"He can stay here for a while, during the night he'll help me look for Gabriel."

She groaned when she heard Gabriel's name.

"Come on, come inside . . . what's he got in that suitcase?" And, again, to him in Arabic: "Come on, let's have a look. You haven't brought me any bugs, have you?"

He was still speechless and she bent over the suitcase, opened it and began examining the contents. On a heap of folded clothes there were eggs, peppers and eggplants.

"What's this? The Turks left this country long ago."

He was embarrassed, angry.

"I don't know who put them in . . . maybe my mother . . ."

She started taking out the vegetables, examining the eggs by the light from the window.

"Very good. Fine eggs these. Take all these clothes out and hang them up to air. Thank your mother very much but tell her next time not to mix clothes with food, you'll get egg yolks in your pockets. . . . Where did you steal these pajamas from? . . . You won't need the towel, put it in the laundry basket . . . we'll look at these clothes later. In the meantime you go and have a wash. Do you hear? Off you go. The water will go cold. I lit the boiler this morning when I heard that you were coming. He should wash before he eats, not good to bathe on a full stomach. . . . But don't make a mess, this isn't a hotel and I'm not cleaning up three times a day. . . . I've prepared a separate room for him . . . a wardrobe . . . all for him. . . . You'll sleep on your own here, without donkeys and goats and chickens."

And she led the bewildered Na'im into the bathroom, the poor fellow was getting used to being sent into the bathroom every time he entered a Jewish house. She sat me down in the big room and brought in plates full of biscuits, nuts and almonds. She made coffee and brought it to me.

"Don't bother."

"I've already bothered. I'm not going to throw it all away."

The coffee was excellent and she charmed me with her courtesy, with her thin smile. I explained to her my intention of patrolling the roads at night, towing in cars and looking for Gabriel. I told her that of course she could make use of the boy, he could help with the cleaning, go shopping, do minor repairs if necessary. "A good boy," I said. "You'll see."

"When they're young, perhaps, before they join Fatah."

I laughed.

Then she put on her reading glasses and picked up a heap of newspapers, most of them copies of *Ma'ariv* and *Yediot Aheronot* of the last few weeks, and she began leafing through them excitedly. After a while she took off her glasses and turned to me with a question.

"Perhaps you can help me?"

"By all means."

"Tell me, what is this Kissinger?"

"What?"

"What is he? Who is he? Before I went into the hospital I'd never heard of him. Now that I've recovered the papers are full of him, they never mention anyone else. Why?"

I told her about him.

"A Jew?" She was amazed, didn't believe it. "That's impossible! An apostate, perhaps . . . how could they let him? What do you say? Isn't he ashamed to make so much trouble?"

"It's not so bad . . ." I tried to calm her.

"What's not so bad?" she protested. "Read what the papers say about him. Somebody ought to talk to his father."

Na'im came out of the bathroom, scowled at us.

"What's this?" she said, in Arabic. "So quickly? You've just been playing with the water. Come here . . . let's see how well you've washed . . . behind your ears, isn't that part of you? Next time I shall wash you. . . . Don't look so surprised, I've washed bigger boys than you . . . now sit down and eat."

She was a real live wire. Drowning in newspapers and politics, all the time pumping me for information about politics and parties, complaining that she'd missed the election, she'd never missed one before. Even unconscious she would have known how to vote.

"How would you have voted?" I asked with a smile.

"Not for the Communists anyway . . . perhaps for that slut . . . what's her name? The one who sticks up for women . . . perhaps for someone else . . . but that should be a secret, shouldn't it?" And she winked at me.

Na'im sat there in silence, eating biscuits and drinking coffee. I'd noticed before how relaxed he could be, he had an astonishing ability to adapt himself to new surroundings. Watching her suspiciously but calmly, picking up the paper that lay in front of him and starting to read it with deep concentration, trying to ignore us.

She looked at him in astonishment, whispering to me, "What's this? Can he read Hebrew or is he just pretending?"

"He knows Hebrew very well . . . he's been to school . . . he knows poems by Bialik by heart . . ."

She was furious.

"What does he want with Bialik? What use is it to him? Oh, we're ruining these Arabs of ours . . . they'll stop working and write poetry instead . . . but if he can read then he can read to me a little . . . my eyes get tired so quickly. And there are so many interesting things in the newspapers . . ."

She took the paper from him, leafed through it and handed it back to him.

"Leave off the pictures now. Read the article by Rosenblum on the first page. He's a wicked man but he knows the truth."

I stood up from my seat. I was charmed by her.

"You see, Na'im, you'll have interesting work here."

But he didn't smile.

"Are you going already?" She was disappointed, didn't want me to leave. "What's the time? Drink some more coffee . . . eat some supper perhaps . . . your wife won't have cooked anything for you yet . . . when should I put him to bed?"

I laughed again.

"Oh, he'll go to bed by himself. He'll be fifteen soon . . . he can look after himself."

"But all the same . . . will you be coming to fetch him tonight?"

"Perhaps."

And suddenly she clutched at me, unsteady, weeping.

"I wish I could come with you to search for him . . . so kind of you to care about me, not turning your back on me, like all the others."

I put my hand on her shoulder, she smelled of baby soap.

And Na'im was sprawled in his chair, ignoring us, sipping his coffee, turning the pages of the newspaper one after the other.

NA'IM

I told Father and Mother, "He wants me again, the garage boss. I'll be staying with an old woman because he wants me at night for special work, but he can't say when he'll be bringing me back."

"Is his boiler out of order again?" Mother asked, because I'd told them too that I'd helped him repair his boiler that Friday night, not that I'd broken into the house of an old woman who turned out to be at home.

"No, he's starting to tow in broken-down cars, he wants to catch new customers when their cars are smashed up, looks like he's expanding the garage. And I'm helping him with the tools and things like that."

And they were very impressed, really proud. And Father said right away, "You see, Na'im, you wanted to stay on at school, wasting your time, it's not yet five months since you started working for him and already he can't do without you."

"He can do very well without me, he just wants me there."

And Father went straightaway to Aunt Isha's and came back with a big old suitcase, and Mother started folding up my clothes and putting them in, putting in more and more clothes like I was never coming back. But I don't have that many clothes, the suitcase was still only a third full. Then Father looked inside the case and called Mother aside and they went into the room that used to be Adnan's and whispered a bit, then they called me in and I went in and saw Adnan's clothes lying there on the bed and they told me to undress and I undressed, and they tried some of his clothes on me, shirts and trousers and sweaters, and Mother marked with pins the places that needed shortening, and Father looked at me with tears in his eyes and started to moan, "Adnan, Adnan," and Mother said, "Perhaps we shouldn't do this," but he said, "No, who else should we give his clothes to, the security police?" and so they put some of Adnan's clothes into the case too, and they gave me his overcoat, which had once belonged to Faiz as well, and even then the suitcase wasn't full so Mother went out into the fields and came back with peppers, eggplants and garlic and she even put some eggs in at the top—"These are for the old lady that you're going to live with, so she looks after you properly and feeds you."

And they were all excited and confused and anxious but they were pleased as well that I was getting to be a real expert mechanic. And Father took me aside and said solemnly, "Wait two more weeks and then ask for a raise. Promise me." And that night I had a bath. And in the morning they were all awake extra early and Father fetched a wheelbarrow and he put the suitcase on it and we went to the bus stop.

I saw on the bus that morning that the workers were looking at me in a shifty sort of way. The news had already gone around the village that I was going to do a special job and they were all a bit jealous of me because is there anyone who wouldn't like to leave the village and sleep in the town and not be awakened by the cocks crowing in the morning? The only one who didn't care at all was Hamid. He just gave me a dry sort of look, didn't say it was good or bad, just indifferent.

I got to the garage late because I had to carry the suitcase by myself and it really slowed me down. And he saw me and told me to wait on the side. And I sat there with my suitcase the whole day, it seemed strange to me that they were all working and I was sitting there on my own, and all of them watching me from the side. And I looked at the pictures of naked women, not many changes. Only the picture of that old woman who used to be Prime Minister was torn and dirty, someone had drawn glasses on the President's face, only the ex-President was left as he was.

After work he took me to the old woman's house and this time we went up the stairs and she opened the door, at first I thought it was someone else, she was so clean and nicely dressed and the apartment was clean and tidy, but it really was the same woman and right from the start I saw I was going to have problems with her, that, like I heard one of the Jewish workers in the garage say about somebody, she was going to fuck my mind up, and my spirits fell.

First of all, she started talking to me in Arabic and I don't like it when Jews speak Arabic, they make so many mistakes and it always sounds like they're making fun of us. Those are the Jews who think they know us best, damn them. The only things they know about us are the things they can make fun of and they never have any respect even when they're pretending to be good friends.

Straightaway she opened up the suitcase to see what was inside it and she found the eggs and the vegetables on top of the clothes. I almost wished the ground would swallow me up for the shame that

Mother was causing me in front of Adam, who thought I'd brought these things to sell. And then she told me to have a bath, even though I was very clean. Only dirty people need to wash all the time, Adnan used to say. And she seemed to think I might be bringing bugs into the house, though the last time I saw fleas was in her kitchen that night and there'd been a mouse too.

But I didn't say anything and I went to have a wash, I'd had a bath in a Jewish house before and I wasn't afraid but I felt offended all the same. Then I went and saw the room that she'd fixed up for me and it really was a nice room with a bed and a wardrobe and a view of the bay, nothing to complain about. But I knew I wouldn't get any peace here, she's such an old windbag, a real political old lady, every other word she says is something about politics, she's a newspaper nut. Can't understand how she ever went into a coma, her mind is the only part of her that works, the rest of her is like a big ball of fat, she can hardly move.

And Adam liked her, laughing at everything she said, laughing happily. And that irritated me, I didn't see anything special about her. In the meantime she brought in coffee and some cookies that were really good. These Oriental Jews know how to cook, they learned it from us Arabs.

I decided I wasn't going to have too much to do with her, it wasn't for her that I came to live in the city but for Dafi. I want to see her again and get to know her and fall in love with her. And I wasn't going to get too friendly with this old woman so I sat there quietly reading *Ma'ariv* and that surprised her, she thought it was odd an Arab reading a newspaper in Hebrew. Pity she never knew Adnan, he knew the papers by heart and he had answers to everything they said.

I'll have to keep on my guard here, sit quietly and not get into arguments, otherwise things will be unbearable. I'm not here for politics but for love. And so I sat there quietly, pretending I didn't care about anything, like Hamid, looking out the window, thinking maybe I'd go to the movies if only I had some money. And at last Adam got up to go and the old woman went with him to the door and suddenly she started crying. Hanging on to him. Damn her.

So the evening began and she went into the kitchen to get a meal ready and I didn't know if I ought to take the dirty plates off the table or not. I didn't want her to get the idea that I was here to help with the housework, I'm just a mechanic lodging with her, but I saw she really was terribly old, hardly able to walk, and groaning with every movement, and the evening light made her look all white, like a corpse. She must be over seventy, Father is seventy, and I was afraid she might suddenly drop dead so I quickly got up and picked up the dishes and took them to the kitchen and she smiled at me, a dead smile, and said:

"Sit down quietly and read the paper and I'll make you some supper."

I asked, "Do you have any repair job that needs doing?"

She began to think, then she bent down, nearly crawling on the floor, opening cupboards and looking for something, then she got out a small stepladder and started climbing up it. I almost shouted, "Tell me what you want and I'll do it for you."

And she smiled with her toothless mouth.

"You really are a good boy."

But I didn't want her to start talking Arabic again and I said straight out, "You can talk to me in Hebrew, no need for you to make an effort."

She laughed.

"But then you'll end up forgetting your Arabic and your father will be angry with me."

"I won't forget, there're plenty of Arabs even in Haifa."

Then she smiled her dead smile again and told me to climb up the ladder and look in the top cupboards to see if there was a good bulb to put in the socket in the dining room so we'd have more light and we'd be able to see what we were eating. And I went up the ladder right away and looked in the cupboard and there were maybe twenty bulbs there, all of them burned out. I don't know why she kept them, maybe she thought she'd get a refund on them at the supermarket. I had to try them all before I found one that worked.

In the meantime she was cooking supper, mutton with rice and beans, great stuff, really tasty, Arab food. And she fussed around me all the time, not eating herself, going and fetching salt, pepper, pickled cucumber, bread. I kept telling her, "I'll fetch it myself," but she said, "You sit there quietly and eat."

The last course was sweet *sahalab*.

And she was walking slowly, dragging her feet. When the meal was finished I took the dirty dishes off the table and said to her, "All right, I'll wash them." But she wouldn't let me, like she was afraid I'd break something. So I said, "O.K., at least let me take out the garbage."

And I went out to empty the garbage and it was already dark in the street, and I walked along with the empty can to have a look at the street, to see what there was, who the neighbors were, what the shops were like.

When I got back she was sitting in her chair, everything was clean and tidy, she looked at me angrily.

"Where have you been?"

"I was just walking in the street."

"You must always tell me where you're going. I'm responsible for you."

I felt like shouting, What do you mean you're responsible? but I didn't say anything.

And she picked up *Ma'ariv* and I picked up *Yediot Aheronot* because that was all there was, she didn't have a TV or a radio for listening to music, and we sat there opposite each other like a pair of old people, quietly reading. It was really boring. And every five minutes she asked me what the time was. In the end she got tired of reading, took off her glasses and said, "Read me what Rosenblum says on page one."

And I read it to her, I can't remember all of it, the main thing was that all the Arabs want to destroy all the Jews.

She groaned, nodding her head.

Then I couldn't stop myself and I asked, "Do you think I want to destroy you?"

She smiled and muttered, "We'll see, we'll see. What's the time?"

"Seven o'clock," I said.

She said, "Off you go to bed, he may be coming to fetch you tonight, we don't want him to find you tired out." I wasn't a bit tired but I didn't want to argue with her on the first evening so I stood up to go to bed. And I looked at her, she really scared me, with her pale face and red eyes she looked like a witch. Staring at me so hard. I started trembling inside. She was really scary. And then she said something weird, crazy, whatever could have put the idea in her head?

"Come here, give me a kiss."

I thought I was going to faint. What was the big idea? Why? I cursed myself and her but I didn't want to quarrel with her the first evening so I went up to her and quickly brushed my lips against her cheek that was as dry as a tobacco leaf. I made a kissing noise in the air and ran off to my room, wishing I was dead. But then I cheered up a bit because through the window I could see the lights of the harbor coming on, really beautiful. I undressed slowly, put on my pajamas and got into bed, thinking maybe tonight I'd see the girl I love in a dream and I really did see her but not in a dream.

VEDUCHA

At the time of the siege of Old Jerusalem, just two years after the cursed World War, I realized that God had lost consciousness. I didn't dare say he no longer existed, because it's hard for an old woman of sixty-seven whose father was a great Jerusalem rabbi to start fighting against God and those who believe in Him, but when my daughter Hemdah, Gabriel's mother, was killed by a bullet and I went with the child and his strange father to the New City and they put us up a monastery in Rehavia, I used to say to all the people around me, whether they wanted to hear or not, "He is unconscious," and they thought I meant the child, or his father, but I said, "No, up there," and they would look up, searching and not understanding, and I said, "Don't seek Him, He isn't there." And the people cursed me, for to lose Him at such a time was the last thing they wanted. It was then that my love for Jerusalem died. It was a city of madness, and when they offered me a deserted Arab house in Haifa I accepted it at once and moved there with the child Gabriel, whom I had to bring up. And his strange father didn't want to go to Haifa, but he didn't care in the least that I was taking the child, he wasn't much interested in him, he spent all his time wandering about trying to remarry and not succeeding. And the child loved his father greatly, pined for him all the time. And when at last his father went to Paris to try his luck there, because his prospects in Israel were very bleak, Gabriel never stopped thinking about Paris, collecting pictures of it, reading books about it, and the more I tried to make him forget his father, the more he remembered. I bought an old car and after taking the test seven times I learned to drive. I used to take the boy with me on little trips, to Galilee and other parts of the country, but he had only one idea in his head, how to get to Paris to be with his father, he wrote letters, made plans. As soon as he finished his army service he went to Paris. And so for the last ten years I have been alone, no family around me, they're all in Paris, dying off one by one, I can't even get to the funerals. And the world has become strange, but it's still here and it's not so bad, it could be much worse. I said to myself, perhaps it's a good thing that He is still lying there unconscious, if He wakes up then the troubles will begin. Please, good people, speak softly, don't wake Him. But I began to yearn and my yearning was so great that in the end I lost my wits, I don't even remember how it happened. It was in the middle of lunch, because Mrs. Goldberg came in that evening and found me still holding the fork. And I lay unconscious for maybe a year and if I met Him I do not know, for every meeting was unconscious. But in the end I woke up, and still I don't know why. For now I feel no yearning for anyone. Perhaps Gabriel's return did touch me after all. And I go home, an old woman of ninety-three, that's the truth, and this loneliness again. What will become of me? But mercy and grace are still with me. On the first night that I'm alone in the house, a thunderstorm outside, that bearded man breaks into the house–Gabriel's friend, kindred souls they are, he will search for him on my behalf. A wonderful man. He reconnects my telephone, takes care of everything, and one afternoon he even brings along a little Arab boy to stay with me. It's a little sad that it should end like this. The second generation of a great Jerusalem family, every other Sephardi who walked the streets of the Old City at the turn of the century was somehow related, and now at the end of my days I have nobody in my house but an Arab. Better if he had brought me a Jewish orphan and I could have performed a mitzvah before my death, but what can you do, there are no more Jewish orphans on the market, only Arabs, at least *they* do not flee the country. God is having a joke at my expense, that at the age of ninety-three I must look after a little Arab, send him to the bathroom to wash himself, give him food, I know, he'll grow up an ass like all the rest of them, you can't trust them an inch, but for the time being it's a pretty boy that I see, a typical Arab face but intelligent, sitting on the chair beside me, like the little grandson that I once had years ago, and there's light in the house again, I can hardly conceal my joy. He brought vegetables and eggs from his village in a suitcase, like the good Arabs, the Turks. He really makes me happy, I can give him little jobs to do. I held his hand and led him to his room, gave him a good meal. He cleaned his plate. Thank God he has an appetite, now I shall have to cook proper meals. A little man. He may be an Arab, but he's somebody at least. A quiet boy, knows what he wants, looking at me suspiciously but without fear, on his guard, knows how to defend himself, even though he doesn't respond to my teasing, I talk to him in Arabic to make him feel at home, but he answers in Hebrew, that's how far they've infiltrated us.

He cleared the table by himself, without being told, went out with the garbage and suddenly disappeared, I was afraid he might have run away but he came back. He offered to do some work in the house, I asked him to change a light bulb and I watched him as he worked, quietly, without giving himself a shock, without a lot of noise. If he stays with me till Passover he can help me remove the *hametz* and we shall make the place very kosher. He can read newspapers too. Adam has brought me a real treasure.

But when evening came and darkness filled the house, I saw that the two of us were alone here for the night and panic seized me. Suddenly I thought, he's not a little child, he's a big boy, he has a dark and dangerous face. He could steal my gold coins, attack me, if not he then his brothers, these people always have big brothers. He will open the door to them in the night. This boy has already broken into the house once. Why did I have to be so foolish, wasn't it better before, when things were quiet? Four bolts I put on the door and Mrs. Goldberg has perfect hearing. I was well protected and now I have let the enemy inside.

Strange thoughts began to confuse me.

I asked him to read me something from the paper, to see how he would read, perhaps his voice might reveal something of his intentions. I gave him the article by Dr. Rosenblum, who uses short sentences and simple ideas. He began to read, reading very clearly, and the gist of the article that we hit upon was something I have known for years, that the Arabs have no thought other than to destroy us all. That was all I needed now, to put the idea into his head. And he actually paused, thought for a moment, looked up at me and said, "Do you think I want to destroy you?"

"Of course," I wanted to say, "but you can't, thank God." But I said nothing. He was so sweet when he asked that question, full of sweetness. Again I remembered Gabriel and how he disappeared, all so quickly. Then the idea occurred to me of asking him to kiss me. Once he'd kissed me he couldn't use violence against me in the night and I'd be able to sleep peacefully, he might perhaps steal something small, but nothing worse than that. I watched him, sitting there, brooding, plotting. I said, "Come here, give me a kiss." The little bastard couldn't believe his ears, but he controlled himself, he couldn't refuse an old woman like me and he came and touched my cheek with a flutter of his hot lips. Perhaps my first kiss in fifteen years. So sweet. I sent him off to bed. I'd hidden the key to his room beforehand, so he couldn't lock himself in and make plans. He put on his pajamas, got into bed and went to sleep. I washed, put on a nightdress, switched off the lights and sat down in the dining room, listening to his breathing. Eight o'clock, nine, ships' sirens in the harbor. I went into the bedroom to look at him. He lay sprawled there on the bed, flushed with sleep. I tidied his clothes a little. Ten o'clock, eleven, and I'm still dozing in the armchair in the dining room, waiting, perhaps the telephone will ring. At eleven-thirty the lights in the bay go out, I go to his room. He's in a deep sleep, the blanket slipping off the bed. I cover him up. Suddenly I bend down and kiss him lightly. What can I do? So sad.

I go back to the dining room, still hoping for a call.

DAFI

What's the time? Nearly midnight. I've slept two hours and wakened. Dark in the house. A light and simple wakening, that's what's been frightening me lately. My sleep is like straw in the wind, leaving no traces.

Daddy's going out to work tonight, between midnight and two he must be on call. I heard it all yesterday, I know all about it. Looking for the lover at night and through the window I see the tow truck parked at the curb, the yellow crane like a finger pointing at the sky. I get out of bed and put on the clothes that I got ready during the evening. Corduroy trousers, woolen vest, warm sweater. I've decided to go with him. Hiking boots, a scarf. Winter clothes that I've never worn in winter. Just pray that some car will have an accident, or break down.

I get dressed in the dark, outside the moon moving fast against broken clouds. The water sounds in the gutters but you can't see the rain. I think of a car on its way from Tel Aviv to Haifa. I even see its shape. Its color—bright blue. I think of the driver and I see him, a young man, very sexy, in a black golf shirt, looks a bit like a gym instructor. Beside him a small woman, his wife or his mistress, very sweet. They're coming home from a play or a party, the radio plays soft dance music, he lays a hand on her shoulder, caressing her, the other hand rests lightly on the wheel. I see the speedometer–a hundred and twenty kilometers. He leans toward her and kisses her, but the lady isn't content with a kiss, she leans over and lays her head on his shoulder, distracting him. They're talking about themselves, about how charming they are, and meanwhile the rain sets in (I see it, the moon is hidden, the sky grows dark, rain lashes the windows) and he simply misses the bend, crash, the car smashes through the iron fence between the lanes, the fender is crushed, the door caves in, the lights shatter, the woman screams, the brakes squeal, the car nearly overturns but ends up on its side. They're alive. Just a few scratches and bruises. I go on quietly dreaming as I lace up my shoes. I see the man climbing out through the window and helping his lady friend to get out. Running and flagging down a car coming the opposite way, giving the details, a few minutes later the phone rings in the control room. The bored duty clerk takes down the details, looks in the register to see who's on call. I see it there, Daddy's name, and beside it our phone number. She lifts the receiver and dials.

My heart misses a beat. At this very moment the phone rings. I freeze. This is crazy. The dream is becoming reality. I run to the phone in the study. I pick up the receiver and say, "Yes?" but Daddy has beaten me to it with the receiver beside his bed. I hear the particulars. BMW, 1972 model, registration number so-and-so, three kilometers south of the Atlit intersection. Daddy writes it all down in the little notebook that I put beside the phone for him yesterday. I go into the bathroom right away, wash my face, clean my teeth and come out expecting to give Daddy a surprise but the house is in darkness, as if he's already gone. I go quickly into their bedroom, God Almighty, he's asleep again, the bedside lamp's switched off. I rouse him, shaking him roughly. "Daddy, are you crazy, have you forgotten? You've got a tow job to do." He sits up in bed, confused, bleary with sleep, he suddenly looks old. "What's the matter? What is it?" He thought he dreamed it. "Lucky that you're awake." Mommy stirs under the blanket. He starts taking off his pajamas in a hurry, stripping almost naked in front of me, completely befuddled. I run to the kitchen, put water in the kettle to make some coffee. Daddy goes into the bathroom, comes out dressed.

"Come on, Daddy, the coffee's ready."

He smiles. "Dafi, you'll make a wonderful wife."

I phone the old lady's house to wake Na'im, curious to see how he'll react to the sound of my voice, but it's the old lady who answers.

"Good evening, could you wake Na'im, please? Daddy is on his way to collect him."

"But who are you?"

"I'm his daughter, my name's Dafi."

"Dafi? What sort of a name is that?"

"Short for Dafna. Sorry, it's so late. We're on our way."

"Who is *we?*"

"Daddy and I . . . please hurry . . . wake him up and tell him to wait outside."

"All right, all right, no need to get excited, young lady."

Daddy still doesn't realize that I intend to go with him, he looks at the details written on a page torn from the notebook, his eyes half closed, you can tell it's years since he's seen what the world looks like at midnight. Drinking his coffee, smiling at me affectionately. Doesn't realize that I'm sitting beside him in an overcoat, drinking coffee, ready to leave. He puts the dirty cup in the sink, bends down and kisses me hurriedly. "There now, I'm off. Thanks for the coffee."

I stand up at once.

"I'm coming with you."

"What?"

"What difference does it make to you? I can't sleep. I'm coming with you. I want to see how the towing is done."

He's baffled.

"You've got school tomorrow. What is there to see? You want to see the towing? What are you, a baby?"

"Why should you care? Better that than wandering around the house. I won't get in the way, I promise. I'll be company for you too."

He hesitates. I know how things are, they lost control of me years ago.

"At least let's tell Mommy . . ."

"She won't wake up, she won't know."

He shrugs his shoulders, defeated.

"I warn you, we'll be back very late."

"What's so terrible about that?"

We go down to the tow truck. It's very cold outside, rain. He starts the engine, warming it up.

"Aren't you cold?"

"No."

We drive down first to the lower city, going into a little side street in the heart of the deserted market. We see a shadowy figure in a funny long overcoat. Na'im the night owl. He hurries toward us, opens the door and climbs aboard, nearly falling out again when he sees me. Even in the dark I can see his face light up, his eyes opening wide.

"Hello," I say.

"Hello," he whispers.

And he sits down beside me.

Silence. Daddy drives fast down the empty streets. The traffic lights are stuck, flickering on auburn. Na'im curls up beside me, watching me furtively. Suddenly he whispers:

"How are you?"

"Fine. How's Grandma?"

"She's all right."

And we drive on in silence, joining the Tel Aviv highway, Daddy turning his head now and then to look at the cars passing by. We pass the Atlit intersection. Daddy starts to slow down, a few kilometers farther on we see red lights beside the steel fence between the lanes and I see a car lying on its side. My heart thumps. We pull up on the roadside and climb out to look. I can't believe my eyes—a blue car. It's as if I've created this accident. The fender and the front of the car are crushed. On the opposite side of the road two cars are parked, lights dimmed. A little crowd has gathered.

The people are surprised to see Na'im and me.

"What's this, have you brought your children along?" somebody shouts but Daddy doesn't answer.

The driver, a young man, some kind of student, starts to explain what happened, making excuses, he's not entirely to blame, of course. Beside him a middle-aged woman in trousers paces around nervously, her eyes red. She's involved in this too. "What matters is that nobody's been hurt," says the young man. "What matters is that we're not hurt," he repeats in a loud voice to the little crowd of onlookers, as if he wants us to confirm what he says and share in his happiness.

Daddy still says nothing, very grim, as usual, in fact he hardly looks at the car but watches the road, watches the cars passing by, looking for something else.

At last he sets to work. Getting back into the truck, driving forward a few hundred meters till he finds a gap in the fence and crossing to the other side. Na'im strips off his coat, takes out triangles and a flashing lamp and sets them out on the road. Daddy starts giving instructions, Na'im gets out the tools and slowly they start unwinding the cable. The driver watches anxiously, the little crowd looks on with interest, I don't know why we don't sell tickets for the show. From time to time somebody shouts out a piece of advice.

I go and stand beside the woman.

"Whose is the car?"

"Mine."

"Yours? And is that your son?"

She looks at me angrily.

"Why do you want to know?"

"Just . . . I thought . . . where have you come from?"

"Why?"

"Just curious."

"From Tel Aviv."

She snaps out her answers, my questions irritate her.

"Have you been to see a play?"

"No."

"Then where have you been?"

"We are returning from a protest meeting."

"Protest against what?"

"Against all the lies."

"Who's been lying to you?"

She stares at me, can't decide if I'm trying to provoke her or just being thick.

"What are you doing wandering about at night, at your age? Don't you go to school?"

"I've skipped a grade," I say quietly. "I can afford to wander about a bit."

She doesn't know what to say, she leaves me and goes to watch Daddy working on the car. I follow her. Very interesting. Na'im crawling on the road and Daddy playing out the cable, telling him how to make the connection. Now very, very slowly they start raising the car. Splinters of glass and fragments of buckled metal fall on the road. Terrific.

The young man covers his face.

"A real smack-up," I say to the woman.

She's furious.

Now Daddy climbs into the truck and starts the engine, dragging the car away from the fence and towing it to the side of the road. Meanwhile Na'im is picking up the tools, folding up the triangles, taking the flashing light and hanging it on the back of the truck. Working quietly and energetically. Daddy wipes his oily hands, his face is covered in sweat, there's a tear in his trousers. It's a long time since I've seen him so out of breath. He tells me to take a piece of paper and write down the details. He asks them where they want the car to be towed. The woman asks his advice.

"I can tow it to my garage."

"How much will the repair cost?"

"I shall have to examine it, I can't tell you now. In the meantime there's the towing charge."

"How much?"

Daddy sends me to fetch the list of prices that the towing firm gave him, I crouch over it, lighting the pages with a flashlight. It has to be calculated according to the distances involved and the size of the damaged car. It takes me a while to work it out.

"A hundred and fifty pounds," I announce triumphantly.

Daddy checks it and agrees.

The man starts to argue, Daddy listens in silence, chewing his beard. But I get impatient.

"It's written right here, sir, what do you want us to do?"

"Shut up, girl," the woman hisses.

But Daddy says, "There's nothing you can do about it, she's right."

A police car pulls up. Two tired cops get out, start sniffing around, the man gets desperate, stops arguing. He just wants a receipt.

"Why not?" says Daddy and he tells me to write a receipt and take the money.

I take out a receipt at once, enjoying this work very much. Na'im has finished collecting the tools, he stands watching me with his mouth open. The young man holds out the money. I count it. Ten pounds short. The lady has to make it up. I'd love to know what's between them. Now the cops are in charge. We leave them to it. The money's in my coat pocket. Daddy switches on the flashing beacon on the roof of the cab and a red light flickers over the road like something supernatural. Na'im and I sit on the back seat of the truck bed, facing the hanging car, watching it and making sure we don't lose it on the way. We talk, I say something funny and he's surprised and laughs, his eyes sparkling.

Daddy drives calmly, once he stops beside a car parked at the roadside, gets out to take a look at it and then drives on. We arrive at the garage. It's huge, the cars are like horses in a stable, each one in its stall. Daddy and Na'im unhitch the damaged car, leaving it at the side. We drive on, putting Na'im down outside his house. When we get home it's already four in the morning.

Daddy says, "I'm worn out."

"I've never been more wide awake."

"How are things going to work out with you?"

"It'll be all right, don't worry."

He goes to take a shower because he's very dirty, I go and peep at Mommy, who's still lying there in the same position as when we left her, she's got no idea how busy we've been these last four hours. From there I go to the kitchen to put the kettle on for tea. Through the window, across the wadi, I see the man who types, slumped in his chair, his head thrown back, he's not usually still at it this late.

Daddy has put on his pajamas, his face is pale, he's worn out, he comes into the kitchen to put out the light and finds me sitting there, still dressed, quietly drinking tea.

"Come and drink some tea before you go to sleep," I suggest.

But for some reason he's angry.

"This is the last time I take you with me. You have to make such a big party out of everything."

"But that's life–a party . . ."

Four in the morning philosophy–

He turns away and goes to bed. In the end I go to bed too, stripping off by the open window, watching the clouds, a thin stream of light showing through. I'm not cold, the opposite, I'm all boiling hot and low down in my stomach there are dull twinges of pain, it's nearly time for my period. In the pocket of my coat, crushed, I find the money. I go quickly into Daddy's bedroom, he's under the blankets trying to sleep.

"Daddy, what shall I do with the money?"

"Put it in my wallet," he mumbles, "and for God's sake go to sleep . . . this is the last time . . ."

"All right . . . all right . . ."

I take the wallet out of his trouser pocket. It's stuffed full of bills. I count them–two thousand one hundred pounds. Why does he drag so much money around with him? I put in the night's takings, then think again, you shouldn't exploit workers even if they are members of the family, and I take out thirty pounds for myself, secretarial fees. I go to take another look at the man who types and he's disappeared. I put out the lights and disappear under the blanket, me too.

NA'IM

It isn't me who answers the phone but her, she's always awake, wandering around the house, dozing in armchairs. I've never seen her properly asleep. "How much longer do I have to live?" she says sometimes. "It's a shame to sleep."

She comes into the room and switches on the light and starts waking me up with her strange Arabic.

"Na'im, child, get up, on your feet, time to leave your dreams."

And I get up, I always keep my underwear on under my pajamas because she doesn't go out of the room while I'm dressing, you just can't get her to budge. "Don't be silly," she said once when she saw me trying to get dressed hiding behind the wardrobe door, "I've seen it all before, why should you be shy or scared?"

How did I ever get mixed up with this old woman? But I've gotten used to it, a guy gets used to anything. I get dressed, clean my teeth, put some nice scent on my face, drink some coffee and grab a slice of bread and then run downstairs to wait for them. I don't like hanging around too long in the street at night. Once I nearly got picked up by the cops, luckily Adam arrived just in time. I see the lights of the tow truck in the distance and run toward it, jump up as it's still moving, climb up, open the door and crawl in, smiling at Dafi, who makes room for me. We're like a trained team, like firemen or a tank crew. Every time I say to myself–tonight she won't come, but she doesn't miss a single night, she has such control over her father, she does what she wants.

But exactly what she wants I don't think she knows herself.

I sit down beside her, always excited, always happy like it was the first evening when I opened the door and saw her and nearly fell back into the street.

Though the seat's big and we're both small we can't help touching each other, I just pray it'll be a long journey. She's wrapped up in an overcoat, a woolly hat on her head, she's all bright and fresh. But Adam sits there at the wheel all gloomy, his heavy beard hanging down in front of him, shining in the light from the dashboard, he's tired, not saying a word, looking out at the cars passing by. Once he stopped and stared for a long time at a little Morris parked near the sea, stared and stared and in the end left it and drove on.

Dafi asks me about the old woman and what I do in the daytime and I tell her and she laughs, her mouth smells nice because she brushes her teeth before she leaves. And through her clothes I start to feel her body, I am sure to come wearing just a few clothes, trousers, a thin shirt and an open-necked sweater, so I'll feel her.

Talking and chattering, sometimes about politics, I say something about the Arab problem and she starts to argue. Neither of us knows much about it but even so we argue until Adam says, "That's enough, be quiet . . . don't make so much noise . . . watch the road and look out for a little blue Morris."

But there's no such car, I know, it's all a dream.

At last we get to the broken-down car. There were a few times when we didn't find it, because it had towed itself away and left no traces behind. But we always found a substitute on the way, we weren't short of work.

These nights I learned a lot about cars, I wouldn't have learned so much in years at the garage. Because in the garage everybody does only one job and here every car is a different problem. How to treat a fuel blockage, change broken fan belts, fix a clutch that's come loose, how to take out a thermostat that's choking the engine, how to fix torn water lines. He's got golden hands and he knows how to teach me. "Come here and see, look, come and take hold of this, tighten this, unscrew that." And I get so interested in the job I even forget Dafi, who goes and stands at the side, chatting to the driver's wife or playing with the children, entertaining them.

Sometimes I used to say to him, "Let me, I'll do that," and he let me, relying on me. Especially when it came to crawling under the car and fixing the cable, I saw that at his age this was an effort, he wasn't a young man and I used to do the crawling instead of him, I'd already learned the places to fix the cables. The first few times he used to bend down to check if I'd joined it up properly, but then he started relying on me.

And the chatter of the people around us, the advice, they never stop giving advice, everybody's an expert. The Jews are real professionals when it comes to talking. Sometimes other cars stop just to give advice. First they ask how many dead and how many wounded and then they start telling us what to do. And the guys who are hurt, standing there covered in blood, they're worried about the car, how much will it cost, whether the insurance company will cover it. There's nothing the Jews care about more than their cars.

But Adam says nothing, pretending he doesn't hear. I get impatient but he just doesn't seem to care. But when the crunch comes and it's time to fix the price, he hits hard. His prices are tough. He sends them to Dafi, she's in charge of the money. She sits there in the cab with the money box in her lap, looking so sweet, taking cash, checks, the lot. Writing receipts and sticking pretty blue stamps on them, they all ask for receipts. Some of them put them away in their pockets to show them to someone else who's going to have to pay, but there're some who throw them away in the road, taking them only out of spite, so we'll have to pay the tax.

And the money piles up. Sometimes we made five hundred pounds a night.

We made, I didn't. I went for days at a time without a cent. My wages go straight to Father, I don't know anything about it. Every night I decide that this time I shall ask him for money, but at the last moment I always lose my nerve.

In the daytime I used to walk the streets, looking in shop windows and wanting to buy all sorts of things, wishing I could go to the movies, but not a cent in my pocket.

One night after I'd been working really hard, before he put me down outside the house, I said, "Can I have a word with you?" and then I started mumbling, embarrassed at having to talk in front of Dafi, saying that my wages went straight to my father, and if I could have something . . . a loan maybe. . . .

And Dafi began to laugh. "A loan?"

And he told me to come to the garage next day, he'd tell Erlich to transfer the wages to me, but I didn't want them to take the money away from Father.

"It doesn't matter . . . doesn't matter . . ." I was getting all mixed up. "It's just . . . I thought . . ."

And he didn't understand but Dafi opened the money box and took out two hundred pounds.

"What's the point of a loan? You've been working so hard . . . do you want more?"

"No, that's quite all right," I whispered, and pulled the notes out of her hot hand.

I ran off home with the two hundred pounds, which I was sure was going to last me a long time, but after two or three weeks I was broke again, so on the sly I asked Dafi for more and she smiled and gave me more.

ADAM

Every evening I say to myself, that's enough, time to stop, it's madness trying to find him in these night excursions. But even so I can't stop. At midnight the phone rings and appeals for help come flooding in. I've already given up answering the phone, Dafi always gets there first and eagerly she writes down the details, with an enthusiasm that I don't understand, already she knows the names of the duty clerks in the control room and she swaps jokes with them. Dafi—every day I have less control over her, Asya is powerless too. I made a mistake that first night when I let her come out with me. Since then there's been no opposing her, she's got to come out with me, if I don't take her she'll go out walking in the streets. And Asya's asleep, you can't have a proper conversation with her, when I wake her up she answers me, oh yes, she talks, but she doesn't get out of bed, I just turn my back and she's fast asleep again.

And so we go out in the night, picking up Na'im and driving off to look for the nightlife Israelis who've broken down on the road. Strange work and very profitable, especially as I usually tow the cars to my own garage, picking up a flood of new customers.

Nights at the end of winter, a mixture of heat and rain, scents of blossoms. And Israel in a fitful, dreamless sleep, a moment's slumber. Looking suddenly enormous, all lit up, little villages turning into cities. And on the roads the endless roar of traffic, army convoys, private cars, trucks, hitch-hikers, soldiers appearing suddenly in the middle of an empty road, some dirty, some immaculate, returning home or to the depot. Adventurers, kibbutz volunteers from abroad, laborers from the occupied territories. Four months have passed now since the end of the war and the land is still uneasy, men wandering about in a vague search for something, for some account that remains to be settled.

And I'm in the middle of all this with the tow truck, the two children chattering happily beside me, driving along, the light flashing above my head, looking for a little old Morris, 1947 model, blue. Looking for a man who disappeared. Absurd.

And the work is hard. It's many years since I've been involved in such basic mechanical work. Repairing split rubber tubing, clearing fuel blockages, fixing loose clutches, replacing fan belts, reviving burned-out generators. Work under difficult conditions, in the dark, in the pouring rain, by flashlight, without proper spare parts, trying to improvise with steel wire, with old screws. Lucky that Na'im's there to help me, he works hard and he's learning fast. All the time I'm more and more pleased with him, he brings me the right tools and crawls under the car to attach the cables. Already there are jobs that he can do by himself and I let him. Why not? I begin to feel a new kind of exhaustion, when I have to loosen a rusty screw I breathe heavily. Contact with the forgotten nuts and bolts.

These nightlife Israelis are a people in their own right. Burly taxi drivers, young men who've smacked up their parents' cars, a tired lecturer returning from a lecture at a kibbutz, angry party officials. And women too, alone, in the small hours of the morning, coming home from a protest meeting or an adventure. And you're always liable to find a bleary-eyed soldier, a tired hitch-hiker, left to doze in the crashed car, his rifle between his knees.

And always a crowd of people gathers around you to give advice. You need nerves of steel to work in silence. They're all experts. Dafi soon gets into conversation, the girl has a light and provocative tongue. The young men swap jokes with her, attracted to her.

A girl—

Her squeals of laughter in the silence of the night—

And when at last I've succeeded in starting the engine and I'm surrounded by grateful faces, I fix the price without hesitation. Special night rates. They protest at first. But I send them to Dafi, who has written out a price list in big letters, with colored crayons, shining a flashlight on it and showing it to them with a little smile, carefully counting the money, writing down particulars on the backs of checks, taking identity card numbers, all with such solemnity, with a strange sort of happiness.

But sometimes there's nobody to take money from. Last night we were called out to a crashed car lying in a ditch at the side of the freeway not far from Hadera. A lone soldier standing beside it, waiting for us. He was witness to a ghastly accident, two parents and a child, the child killed, the parents in the hospital. The police have been there, they have taken all the details, all we are asked to do is take the car away. I flash the light on, see the smashed windows, the torn upholstery, bloodstains on the seats, a child's shoe, a little sock. Dafi and I freeze, paralyzed, but Na'im, without me saying a word to him, starts playing out the cables, crawling on the ground under the wreckage of the car, running to the winch, setting it in motion, going back to fix the coupling, back to the winch and gradually dragging the car out of the ditch. I watch him and think, how quickly he's learning, it's incredible.

And so without speaking we go back, the smashed car hanging behind us, almost airborne, just one wheel bouncing on the road. We drive slowly, a long journey, the soldier dozing beside me and the children sitting silent on the back seat, watching the car slung on the back, the rain lashing it and pouring in through the broken windows, and I drive wearily, no longer looking out at the passing traffic, forgetting to search for him. I must give him up.

ASYA

A giant Negro, very elegant, wearing a bright green suit and a fashionable tie of the same color, is leading the way. Leading me into a huge gallery full of light, the roof made of glass. He talks and explains to me the pictures hanging far apart in niches on the wall. Pictures of lush landscapes, fields, forests, villages, European landscapes but in a bracing African light. Did he paint these pictures? I ask, my eyes fixed on him, he's so tall. No, his bright, assured smile, but they are pictures of his homeland and that is why he speaks of them with such love. "How wonderful it is, how beautiful, see, the new settlements that we have built, a renewed land." And I go closer to look, seeing that these are not pictures but reality, real things, movement clearly visible, men with little carts, a plump and placid farmer plowing the earth, walking behind a beast with curved horns, a sort of roebuck. Dark people in old clothes, children in turbans at play.

"Come and see this picture," he calls to me from the end of the hall, and I go to him with a sense of exaltation, I'm at such a height and see so far, like looking down at the universe. It's a picture of fields stretching away to the blue horizon, empty of people, cut in half by a long straight channel, meandering away to the skyline. And from its center springs a bubbling mass of white foam, lava from the depths of the globe. And without a word being said I understand—this is the equator itself. I catch my breath, as if I've seen a mysterious vision. This long, obstinate and definitive line.

VEDUCHA

The Arab returns at the end of the night, dirty, his boots full of mud. He's already learned to take them off in the foyer and come into the apartment in his socks. He treads softly but I wake up.

"Well, did you find anything?"

"What?"

"What do you mean what? God in heaven, what are you doing out there all night?"

But he hardly understands what I'm saying. At first I used to run to the telephone to talk to Adam and he would say, "What do you think? If I knew anything I'd come to you."

I stopped questioning the Arab and stopped telephoning.

He's always in a good mood, this Arab, quite content, whistling a tune, pleased with himself. God, what's he so happy about? Walking around the house a little, eating a slice of bread, intending to go to bed just as he is. But I soon cured him of that.

"Shame on you, boy, we aren't in Mecca, wash first."

He was offended, going pale with anger. I had profaned the Muslim holy of holies.

"What has Mecca to do with it? Mecca is cleaner than all Israel . . ."

"Have you been there?"

"No, but neither have you."

What nerve. How does he know I haven't been to Mecca, at my age I could have been anywhere. But I said nothing, I didn't want to start a quarrel, shame on an old woman who would quarrel with a child like him, and what would Adam say, the wonderful man who is wearing himself out at night looking for Gabriel. Anyway he learned to go and wash first while I prepared him an early breakfast, and he ate and drank, thank God he didn't lose his appetite at night, wearing his strange red pajamas that always remind me of the pajamas that my late grandfather used to wear in the summer, in the Old City, when he sat on the balcony in the afternoon to look at the Western Wall.

Then he'd go to bed, tossing about for a while and making the bed creak, and then settling down. After two hours I'd go quietly into his room, covering him up well, taking his underclothes and throwing them in the laundry basket, examining his trousers to make sure there were no bombs or hashish in them. I have to keep a close watch on him. So sad. At first I used to find nothing in his pockets, not even a handkerchief, and I put in a handkerchief and a few pounds too so he could buy sweets. Later I began finding money, fifty, a hundred pounds. Adam is giving him money, he deserves it, but he's such a spendthrift, after a week it's almost all gone. Once he bought himself a big penknife. Without thinking twice I threw it away, flushed it down the toilet. We know what happens when Arabs go about with knives.

At twelve noon he wakes up, eats again, takes the garbage out, fixes a dripping tap or clears a blockage in the sink or the toilet and goes out for a walk in the city, goes to the movies. Comes back at six o'clock full of life, his eyes sparkling, sits down to read to me from the papers for a while, reading in a skeptical, scornful sort of tone, but at least he pronounces the tough letters correctly.

He eats supper now without much appetite and goes out again for a short walk, every day he comes home later, needing less and less sleep. And so the time passes. The tow truck comes in the night, returns early in the morning, and there's no sign of my Gabriel. I weep on the telephone to Adam, "What's going to happen?"

DAFI

A different tiredness now, real tiredness, no longer the empty and nervous tiredness of sleepless nights. The sweet tiredness of limbs aching from a long journey at night.

We used to arrive home at two or three in the morning and go to bed. Mommy was the first to get up and she'd rouse the two of us and prepare breakfast. It was a novelty having Daddy at home in the mornings, three of us sitting down to breakfast.

At school I moved about slowly, during recess sinking down on a stone in the playground, Tali beside me. Since what happened with Arzi they made me change places and now somebody else is sleeping there. They put me at the third desk in the middle row, right in the center of the class, exposed and helpless. I was asked questions and expected to answer, or at least to sit quietly and look at the teacher with warm puppy eyes, to smile at feeble jokes, to pay attention. The other children in the class began to bore me a bit, because at night I was seeing real life at a time when they were only playing with dreams, all of them. Even Osnat began to annoy me a bit with her constant excitement. Tali was the only one I still got on well with, she doesn't say much and keeps things to herself, doesn't get on your nerves. She always falls in with any suggestion.

In history, literature, and Bible, and even in Talmud, it wasn't too bad. Although I didn't always follow exactly what was being said and I didn't manage to do all the homework I still had good ideas, original questions to ask, and now and then I'd put my hand up and say something so interesting that the teacher was impressed and forgot all my other shortcomings. But in math I didn't have anything to say though I tried hard to think of something original. Baby Face was ruling the class now with a heavy hand and there were some of the boys who actually liked him because he used to bring along all kinds of mathematical puzzles that really annoyed me, why complicate things that are complicated enough already? We were racing through the syllabus. Before I'd managed to understand one set of exercises we were already moving on to something completely different. They'd all forgotten the teacher who was killed in the war, they betrayed him in no time. And of course I remembered him, or at least I remembered the memorial service that Shwartzy organized for him, and the poem that I recited with such feeling, in a low voice in the silent hall —*Behold our bodies laid in line, we do not breathe.* I missed him terribly, even though I wasn't sure why.

Once when I was walking arm in arm with Tali in the corridor (I was so tired I had to lean on her during the break) we came to the little sign by the entrance to the Physics Department and stopped to read the writing. The sign had already gotten tarnished and dirty. I went up to Shwartzy right there in the corridor and told him the sign needed cleaning, it wasn't to the credit of the school, and he was so surprised, he thought I was making fun of him but he couldn't think of anything to say and he really did send the janitor to polish the sign.

Baby Face knew exactly what I was worth in math but even so he wouldn't leave me alone, and when he needed some victim to amuse himself with he used to call me up to the blackboard. I'd stand up and say, "I don't know why you bother, you can give me a bad report right now if you like," but he forced me to go up to the blackboard and I was so angry I made silly mistakes that had the class in fits of laughter, and I was on the verge of tears but I just smiled a stupid smile.

Once I couldn't resist asking him what was the point of learning how to do all these sums when there are those little pocket calculators that you can take around with you anywhere, even to the desert, and he got mad, as if I were trying to do him out of a job, and he gave a long and complicated answer, not an answer at all.

And today I wasn't in a fit state for anything because last night we towed in a car in which a child had been killed and we saw the blood and the little shoe lying on the seat. I thought of skipping the math lesson to avoid any unnecessary trouble but Shwartzy was on patrol outside and in the first-aid room they were giving injections. So in the end I stayed in the classroom and Baby Face arrived, as arrogant as usual, and attacked me straightaway, as if there weren't another forty children that he could have picked on. Sometimes I think Tali's right, maybe he's a bit in love with me and he just doesn't know how to handle it. I went up to the blackboard and the trouble started. And suddenly I saw him take a familiar notebook out of his briefcase, the notebook of the teacher who was killed, with all the names and the marks written in it, they must have passed it on to him so he could compare notes. I recognized the dead man's handwriting, faint handwriting, very slanted. I felt weak, leaned against the blackboard. Terrible feelings of pity swept over me.

And Baby Face said, "I can't understand how the last teacher gave you a 'fairly good' in your report . . ."

I interrupted him.

"Don't you dare talk about him like that."

He blushed bright red, shocked. There was a deathly silence in the classroom. I should've stopped there, if I'd stopped there nothing would've happened. But I didn't stop, I rather liked the silence all around me. If I ever get to be a teacher like Mommy, there'll always be silence like this in my classes.

"Anyway, it's a pity you weren't killed instead of him . . ."

The class held its breath.

Then the silence scared me, I burst into tears and fled from the classroom, ran straight home. And they told me that Baby Face was so stunned he could hardly carry on with the lesson, he started making stupid mistakes himself. In the end he couldn't stand it any longer, he stopped the lesson before the bell and ran to the headmaster and told him everything, and the headmaster sent for Mommy at once, and then at last Baby Face found out the connection between us, and maybe he regretted being so hasty, but it was too late for regrets, both for him and for me.

NA'IM

It's great, I'm so lucky. So free. I'm not sorry anymore that I didn't stay on at school. Things couldn't be better. I'm doing real work at night, getting to be a professional. Dafi looks at me with respect when I operate the winch. Already we're real friends.

Coming back in the morning, washing, putting on my pajamas, and the old woman brings me my breakfast, waits on me like I'm a king, then going into my room and looking at the marvelous view of the bay coming to life, lying down, can't sleep for happiness and lust, jerking off and then going to sleep, I get up at midday fresh for new adventures.

Money in my pocket and I'm as free as a bird. First of all I go to a movie, a good Western, to wake me up properly. Going to look in the shops, wandering in and out looking at the goods, the prices. Sometimes buying something, a big penknife or an umbrella. Buying nuts and drinking fruit juice to build up my appetite. Coming back for supper, sitting down and making a clean plate so she won't think the food she cooks isn't good, because it is good.

I read her a bit out of *Ma'ariv,* a bit out of *Yediot Aharonot,* about how everything's getting worse, and go to bed. But lately I haven't been able to sleep in the evenings, I need less and less sleep. So what I do is take the garbage out, leave the bin in the lobby and go out to the movies again, looking for a film with less shooting and more music, and love. I'm tall enough to get into films barred to the under-sixteens without any problem, the only ones I don't manage to see are the ones where you have to be over eighteen, I get turned away by the manager or the cashier. At nine-thirty I've had enough wandering around and go home. She's already worried about me. Taking off my shoes and lying down on the bed in my clothes, waiting for the phone that I never manage to get to first, she always beats me to it.

And so I lie there in the dark, half asleep, looking out the window and seeing the city quiet down. Even in the bay the lights go dim, there're fewer cars. The old woman peeps in at me and I close my eyes so she won't think there's something the matter. Sometimes I have a dream, like yesterday, for example, when I dreamed I was walking into the university. I'd never been there but I knew it was the university. Big lecture halls and students sitting there in white coats like in a hospital. I asked where the registrar's office was and they showed me, it was like Erlich's office only a hundred times bigger, it was huge and there were maybe a hundred Erlichs sitting at little tables busy with bills. And I walk around quietly, examining the walls, noticing that where the bullets hit them there aren't holes but swellings, like wounds that've healed over and swelled up a bit. One of the clerks looks up at me, like he's asking me who I am and I answer him confidently, even though I haven't heard the question.

"I'm a Jew as well."

And I go on wandering about, touching the little swellings, like I've been sent by the security forces to check the place out. More people come into the hall and I'm beginning to feel nervous, because one of them's an Arab and he winks at me and says in Arabic, "Wake up, Na'im, the telephone has rung, they're coming, enough dreaming."

The old woman–

ADAM

The weariness gets worse. How much longer? I ask myself. Sometimes when we arrive home the dawn is already breaking. The nights are growing shorter. I get hardly an hour or two hours' sleep before Asya wakes me gently. She sees how hard it is for me to wake up and she asks, "Why don't you sleep a little longer?" but I've always been an early riser and I can't lie in bed in the morning. Strange that she never says anything about these expeditions by night, as if they're none of her business, she doesn't seem bothered by the thought of Dafi joining in the search for her mother's lover.

At first Dafi used to share with her the details of what had happened at night, and Asya listened with a frozen face. Whose car we'd towed in, what we'd seen, conversations we'd had, but after a while Dafi stopped doing this and now she just sits beside me, her head in her hands. I arrive at the garage late and everything's in chaos. I too have work to do now. The owners of the cars that we towed in during the night are waiting for me, agents from the insurance companies, sometimes the police as well. I have to fill in forms, give evidence, answer the phone, give instructions for continuing the repair work that was begun during the night. My head droops, my eyes are sore, I get confused, hurrying between the office and the workshops, my hands covered in grease and oil, explaining things to the workers. And business is booming, Erlich looks at me with love, in the repairs department we shall have to take on more workers. Night customers arrive and they refuse to speak to anyone but me, and I see the workers looking at me with awe, as if I did the towing by hand. And I'm tired and dizzy, I've split open a volcano and the lava is pouring out. What's it all for? Sometimes I go to see the old lady and she trembles, thinking I've got news for her. But there's no sign of him. Sometimes I think perhaps he never existed, it's all a delusion. I see that even she knows very little about him.

"Where's Na'im?"

"He's gone to the movies."

"Is he helping you here?"

"He's all right . . . he's all right . . ."

And the weariness grows, already I'm getting only a few hours' sleep a day. At night the phone starts ringing at ten o'clock, there are some people who phone me on their own account, they've heard from their friends about the night tow man and they approach me directly.

Must put an end to all this—

This morning I arrive at the garage exhausted. Last night we towed in a car smashed up in an accident. A child was killed in it. I've hardly gotten inside the garage when the foreman comes running up to me, all excited. He's had a wonderful idea. He shows me the smashed car that's already hanging on a sling in one of the workshops. He wants to cut it in half and join the half of it that's still intact with half of another car of the same model that we bought for scrap some time ago on his advice. A crazy and daring idea for producing a whole new car. He talks and talks, leading me around the car and showing me the possible cutting points, explaining how from two halves of two wrecked cars he'll make a new car, he'll paint it and polish it and nobody will know the difference. His eyes sparkle, there's something a bit shady about the project but a lot of imagination and clear profit, he's already had a quiet word with the insurance company, all he needs is the go-ahead from me. And I stand and listen, I can hardly keep my eyes open. The weather has suddenly turned warm, the workers walk about in T-shirts, I'm the only one still wearing an overcoat, as if I'm in another world.

I run my fingers over the wrecked car, seeing the broken windows, the bloodstains on the seats, a child's shoe and beside it a toy car of the same model and color. My head spins, my stomach turns over, I nearly faint. "Do whatever you like," I say and get into my car and drive home.

It's ten o'clock. The house is quiet. I pull down the blinds, strip to my underclothes, get into bed and try to sleep. A dim memory of a distant childhood disease stirs in me. Me, who never indulged myself this way. I lie there, my eyes closed, feeling feverish. Outside I hear the singing of children from a distant garden, the beating of carpets, somebody playing a guitar, a woman laughing. An Israeli morning. Desire growing slowly, dim, unclear, unwittingly. Outside the smell of blossoms. Something is happening to me, the exhaustion of the last few weeks is breaking something inside me, dissolving the strain of many years. I throw off the blanket, strip naked, studying my heavy body in the mirror. The front door opens. Dafi. She's on my trail too, the last few nights have turned her into an insomniac. She goes into the kitchen, opens the door of the fridge, walks about the house, comes into my room. I'm naked under the blanket.

"Daddy? You startled me. What's happened? Are you ill?"

"No, I'm just very tired."

She sinks down on the bed. Just like a little girl. Her face is sad, drawn, her eyes red as if she's been crying. I must put an end to these night trips.

"School finished already?"

"No, I just came home . . . I had an argument with the math teacher."

"What happened?"

"Nothing important. It doesn't matter."

"We aren't going out at night anymore."

"Why?" Her voice is feeble but she looks surprised.

"Enough. It's over. No point in searching anymore."

"Have you given up hope of finding him?"

"Almost."

"And Mommy?"

"She'll give up in the end too."

The seriousness and maturity of her questions–

She's silent, thoughtful. Something is troubling her very much.

"The car that we towed in last night . . . that child who was killed . . . do you know yet what happened exactly? Who it was?"

"I don't know."

She's very tense, staring into space. A new wrinkle at the corner of her mouth. Hiding something. Lately she's been getting more and more like Asya.

"Go and get some sleep."

"I can't. Too tired . . ."

"Then do some homework . . . What happened with the math teacher?"

She smiles sadly, doesn't answer, goes out of the room.

I phone the towing firm and cancel our contract.

"As from when?"

"As from tonight."

I phone the old lady.

"Where is Na'im?"

"He's gone to the movies."

"Good. When he comes back tell him he can go back to his village and come to the garage tomorrow as usual. I don't need him at night anymore, I've finished with that."

Silence–

"Mrs. Ermozo?"

"Yes."

"You'll tell him . . . ?"

Silence again. Suddenly I feel sorry for her. Her last hope. She starts to mumble.

I understand at once.

"If you'd like him to stay at your house I can leave him with you and there's no need for him to come to the garage, he can carry on helping you . . ."

Like handing over a piece of property–

Her voice shakes, as if she's about to cry.

"Thank you, thank you, let him stay a little longer, until I'm used to being alone again . . ."

"As long as you like . . ."

"Thank you, thank you, it won't be for long. God bless you. You really are a wonderful man."

ASYA

Late at night. Everyone's asleep. The house is dark. Rain and high winds outside, the wind beating at the shutters. I'm in the kitchen, cooking busily, preparing fish. Cutting off the heads, scraping off the scales, slicing the white bodies to remove the inner organs, my hands covered with blood and guts. And the fish are unusually revolting, wild fish, big fish, their dead eyes yellow, scales like feathers, hard and sharp, greenish. The pan is on the stove and the water is boiling. I must hurry.

Someone is sitting behind me at the table, I know who it is. I turn around slowly, the knife in my hand, he's reading a newspaper and eating a thin slice of bread, he's in army uniform, on his face the bristles of a black beard.

"What happened, Gabriel? Where have you been?"

He doesn't look up from the paper, turns the pages.

"But the war isn't over yet. You sent me away . . ."

"What isn't over?" I cry desperately. "It's all over and you gave us no sign. Adam searches for you at night."

"Where is he searching?"

"Look, listen . . ."

And we are silent, hearing him, hearing the heavy footsteps of someone moving about the house, opening the doors of cupboards, moving drawers.

Gabriel smiles ironically, something in his face has matured, become riper, more self-assured. He folds the paper and comes toward me, looks into the bubbling pot, turns up the flame.

"What are you cooking here?"

"Fish."

"Fish?" He's surprised. "Fish?"

I tremble, hoping perhaps he'll touch me. Should I embrace him? But he's already turning to go.

"Where are you going?"

"I'm going back."

"But the war is over . . ." I'm almost shouting.

"What's over?" he says angrily. "Look at the calendar."

And on the wall calendar the date really is still the tenth of October. "But that's a mistake, we forgot to change it." I'm laughing now. I go to the calendar and with my bloodstained hands wildly tear off the pages, crushing them savagely in my fist, but he's already gone.

DAFI

Suddenly I feel restless and I go down to the center of town to look for a swimsuit for the summer. And sitting next to me in the bus is a man with a familiar face. At first I drive myself crazy trying to identify him, it's as if he's come out of one of my dreams, a huge man with long unruly hair, forty perhaps, eagerly leafing through an evening paper. At last I get it—the man who types at night, across the wadi, he and no other.

He gets off at a bus stop and I follow at once. At last I shall find out something about him. The man who types, my night accomplice, in rumpled clothes and faded jeans, walking slowly, looking in the shop windows, the paper tucked in his back pocket. He goes into a bank and I follow, I stand in a corner and fill in some forms, depositing a million and drawing out two million. Waiting while he draws out some money (only two hundred), dropping the paper in the rubbish basket and following in his tracks. He goes into a stationery shop and I follow him, he stands there, eyes sparkling, examining wads of paper. The saleswoman asks, "Yes, young lady?" "This gentleman is before me," I reply. He looks at me kindly. "The younger generation. What manners! It's quite all right, you can go first."

"I'm in no hurry," I say. "A line is a line."

"Then what can I do for you, sir?"

A typewriter ribbon, I whisper to myself.

"Typing paper."

But he's looking for a special size and a special kind, he sends the assistant climbing up ladders and running down to the basement until she finds what he wants. He goes out. Hurriedly I buy an eraser and run after him. Fuck it. He disappears into a barbershop.

To wait or not to wait?

What can I do? Pity to lose him so soon. I find a fence with a good view and sit down on it to wait. Five minutes pass and Tali and Osnat appear, sit down beside me and start gossiping. And then he suddenly emerges from the barbershop, just as tousled as before, maybe they've taken off two hairs. I jump at once, breaking off in midsentence, and hurry after him. Now he goes into a tobacconist, I stand beside him, brushing against him. He buys tobacco, pipe cleaners, cigarettes and coffee. He touches me lightly. I tremble. He looks down at me, I smile but he looks away, absent-mindedly, not connecting me with the girl that he saw in the stationery shop. He pays and goes out. I buy one cigar and I'm on his trail again.

Now he's standing beside the fence where I was sitting, waiting for someone, pacing about idly. Watching the girls walking past, you can see how he turns his head slowly, changing his position to get a better look at their legs. I remember his bowed head, falling on the typewriter at three in the morning, nestling against the machine. He takes a little notebook from his pocket and writes something in it, some idea, I suppose, smiling to himself in satisfaction. I'm afraid he may notice me standing at the side watching him and I decide to walk in front of him. This time he stares at me intently, a penetrating look, passionate almost, the dirty old man. Suddenly, he smiles a sweet smile, his face lights up, not at me, at a little old man with a white hat, a well-known Haifa poet whose name I've forgotten. They talk for a while and then part. And he's alone again, looking at his watch all the time, until a pale young woman arrives with a little girl in a stroller. He comes to life at once, kissing the child, arguing with the woman. The three of them cross the road, stand at the bus stop.

And I follow—

Should I give up? At least let's see where he lives. Where it comes from, the light that shines on me at night. I climb on the bus behind them, but the bus is going down to the lower city, I just hope they're not going to visit somebody. They get off, start to wander about the streets, looking for a table or a cupboard, going into all the furniture shops. Leaving the child outside in the stroller and going in to look at the furniture. And all the time I'm standing in doorways and at street corners, spying on them secretly, there's a moment when I almost lose them but I find them again. They don't notice me, only the child dragged along behind them in the little folding stroller watches me in silence, with a friendly look, she's just like him.

In the end they don't buy any furniture, all they've done is confuse the salesmen. They go into a grocery and buy a kilo of garden peas, hop on another bus, going home at last I hope. The little girl must sleep sometime.

Three hours now I've been on his trail. It's evening. I no longer have the energy to hide and I sit down not far from them, tired. They're exhausted too, talking quietly, glancing at me every now and then, shelling the raw peas and eating them, giving some to the child as well, putting the empty hulls back in the bag. The bus drives into a mountain suburb that I don't recognize, though it can't be far from our neighborhood. Every hundred meters it stops and people get off, slowly the bus empties. At the terminus they get out and I follow. The street is empty, few houses. They ignore me completely, leaving the bag in a garbage can and walking fast, pulling the stroller behind them, the little girl sits there half asleep, her head nodding from side to side. I look around trying to find our house but I can't pick out anything that's familiar. An ordinary street without a view. I follow in their footsteps as if in a trance, bound closer and closer to them, really scared now, it's all growing dark around me. Streetlamps coming on. What am I doing? How shall I get home from here? Maybe at night he writes in a different house, maybe he leads a double life, maybe this isn't him but his twin brother. But suddenly the street bends sharply and they disappear into a big new apartment house that stands there alone. And all at once the view opens out, the sea appears, more housing developments, straightaway I pick out our neighborhood and I can even see our house, so close, across a narrow wadi. There's the window of my room, all dark.

I stand there looking, full of a silly joy at finding the right place.

I start climbing the stairs, just to find out his name and then go. Maybe he's a famous writer. But there's somebody moving there in the darkness, a giant shape. It's him. Waiting for me. His voice is full of bitterness, fear almost.

"What do you want, girl? What have we done to you? Who sent you to follow me? Get out of here . . . go . . ."

And before I can say a word he disappears up the stairs, fleeing from me.

NA'IM

A normal day. In the morning I get up at nine because if even at nine I've got nothing to do why should I get up at eight? Breakfast on the table but I've got no appetite, I eat a slice of bread, drink some coffee, all this in my pajamas, not shy anymore in front of this old woman, I've got so used to her I sometimes forget she's there, watching me and whining, "Why aren't you eating, you won't grow if you just eat bread." But I laugh. "No child stays a child forever."

Then she's interested in what I saw at the movies yesterday and I give her a summary of the plot. She asks questions, mainly she's interested in the actors, there're a few names that she remembers—Clark Jable, Humphrey Gumbart, somebody Dietrich, she wants to know if I've seen them and how they are and if they're still as handsome as they used to be. A real character this grandmother. But I've got no head for the names of actors, the main thing is the plot, what happens, that's what's important. One actor today, another tomorrow, what does it matter?

And she says, "You're wasting your money, you don't understand films. They'll be the ruin of you." And I laugh—

Already I'm so used to her, I don't understand how I could ever have been scared of her, like I was that first evening when she looked like a witch. I sprawl on the chair with my pajamas unbuttoned, when she tries to get at me I just laugh, what's the point in getting worked up?

Then I get dressed, take a piece of paper and write down the day's shopping list. So many instructions it's like an army operation. Every vegetable has to be bought from a different grocery store. Tomatoes here, olives there, this kind of cheese here, another kind there. She explains exactly what I've got to buy and how much and especially how much I should pay. I take the baskets and make the rounds and come back, put the shopping down on the table and the cabinet meeting begins. She examines everything, sniffs everything, puts the bad fruit aside, goes over the bill, cursing me, the storekeepers and the government, and then sends me out again to take the bad stuff back. They already know me well in the neighborhood, the storekeepers know that all this nonsense isn't my idea but hers and they don't mind me pestering them a bit.

So the morning goes by without any excitement and lunchtime comes around. I eat lunch, eat everything on the plate. Then I go out and fetch *Yediot Aheronot,* wait awhile and go out and fetch *Ma'ariv,* and then it's quiet because she sits down in an armchair, puts on her reading glasses and buries herself in the papers. I do the washing up in a hurry and go out to the movies. Luckily most of the cinemas in Haifa show movies that suit me fine. But sometimes it happens that the pictures outside give me the wrong idea and I find myself watching something really complicated, and when I come out, my eyes not yet used to the daylight, I go back to the box office and buy a ticket for the same movie, for the evening show, because there're some things I didn't understand and I've got to get it right. Why did I think he was the good guy, why did he get killed in the end?

I come back and find her dozing in the armchair, newspapers over her face and she's hardly breathing. I move the papers off her to give her room to breathe. She opens her eyes like she's being roused from the world to come, like she doesn't know me. I ask her if she'd like some tea and she nods her head. I make tea for her and for myself and without her asking me I tell her all the nasty things that happened in the movie, to cheer her up. And she listens and starts to cry. She doesn't understand anything, she thinks she does but she doesn't really. When she starts crying I take the empty tea cups to the kitchen and go to my room. This blubbering of hers isn't for me, I'm really too young for things like that. In the end she calms down, goes to the kitchen to make supper, I hear her moving the pans and the dishes around so slowly it's like her arms and legs have gone to sleep.

I don't have much appetite for supper, it's like her tears have fallen in the food and I'm swallowing them. The thought of that gives me the shivers. I take out the garbage, mend something in the house, a tank or a tap, all the pipes here are moldy. A moldy old Arab house. Then I sit down to read the papers to her, the bits in small print that her eyes are too weak for. Who's died, who's gotten married, who's been born, and then I throw in an article on the Palestinian problem, with my comments, and the big row begins, I get up and leave.

Now it's nighttime. I'm living alone, all my life I've never been so alone. Sometimes I get really homesick for the village and the fields, but I get over it in the end. I miss Dafi a lot. Some days I go up to Carmel and walk around near her house but there's no sign of her. Maybe Adam's worried about her, sorry that he let her come out with us at night. I haven't seen him for three weeks now. It was the old woman who told me that we were stopping the night work for a bit but we'd be taking it up again later and for the moment I ought to stay here, and she gave me three hundred pounds from him for pocket money.

So why should I ask too many questions?

It's a good life, really good. For the moment—

I'm independent, I don't have to work and I'm well looked after—

So long as I've got money for the movies—

I've got movies on the brain now—

I go into the first show, come out with my head in a whirl. Where's Bialik, where's Tchernikhovski, what good are they to me when the real world's so different and the real problems are so difficult?

I return home, thinking about the movie, trying to whistle the theme music. This is the quiet time in our neighborhood, the in-between time, after the traders have gone and before the hookers arrive. I ring the bell, she opens the door, her face is gray, neither of us says anything. We've done enough talking already today. I go straight to my room, count the money I've got left. Oh God, what am I doing in this house, in this strange city?

I start undressing and suddenly she comes into the room, creeping in quietly, wearing a different dress and looking all fresh, sits down on the bed. What the hell does she want?

"Well, Na'im, how are things?"

I'm here, dammit, what do you want now?

"What was the film?"

"Don't worry. The good guys won in the end and got married too."

She sighs. "You've been getting cheeky this last month."

She picks up my trousers and examines them, gets up and goes into the other room, pokes around in the drawers and comes back with an almost new pair of trousers. "Put these on, let's see if they fit you. They were my grandson's when he was your age."

I put them on. Why should I care? Put my hands in the pockets and pull out mothballs, sniff at them.

"These are for you," she says. "I was going to keep them for his son, but he isn't here and he has no son." I wonder if maybe I should say something nice to her, say maybe he'll come back and have a son, but I just say, "Thank you very much," think for a moment and then go to her and quietly kiss her hand, that's the only place where you can kiss old people and that's what they do at home in the village.

She smiles, she really likes it, you can tell.

She starts telling me stories about the Jews who used to live in the Old City of Jerusalem and how they were kind to the Arabs, who murdered them in the end. She groans and groans, then at last she shuts up and goes out.

I undress in a hurry, I get into bed but I'm not really tired. What have I done today? Nothing much. I toss around in bed for a while, remembering the movie I saw, a horrible hunchback, a magician with a burned face. Suddenly I start trembling.

I'm alone. What kind of a life is this? Stuck here in this hole. Adam's forgotten me, Father and Mother and Hamid and all the rest of them have forgotten me. I get out of bed, go to the window to watch the ships in the bay, I already know how to tell destroyers and missile ships apart. The first hookers arrive and take up their positions. A patrol car draws up, the cops get out and talk to them. It's warm outside. The window's open.

I stand there watching till my eyes start to close and I fall on the bed. In the morning I get up at nine, because if even at nine I've got nothing to do why should I get up at eight?

DAFI

I've noticed before, this isn't the first time, that I'm capable of really scaring people, even grownups, it isn't only the math teacher who's started to be afraid of me, there are others too—this disturbance gives me strength. Sometimes I follow somebody in the street. I just pick somebody out, an adult, an old man, and I follow him everywhere, relentlessly, for half an hour, an hour, until he turns pale and gets angry. It drives Tali and Osnat crazy. I can even scare myself.

Once we were sitting in the cinema at a matinee and it was a boring movie, kids' stuff. In the row in front of us there was a bald old man with a sort of beret on his head and I wondered what on earth he was doing watching a children's movie and I whispered to Tali and Osnat, "Do you think I ought to pull his ear?" and before they had time to understand what I was saying or ask why, I'd already grabbed hold of his nasty ear by the soft and hairy lobe and given it a sharp tug. This is what frightens me. I just thought of it and it was done. So quickly, no hesitation between thinking it and doing it. The old man turned around on us at once as if he'd been waiting to have his ear pulled, because he wasn't concentrating on the movie either, and he started cursing loudly in Rumanian or Hungarian in the silence of the dark cinema. He was sure Osnat had done it, he wanted to kill her. The three of us got up and fled before the manager arrived.

All that evening I was depressed. Osnat was furious with me, she didn't want to talk and she went home, only Tali, silent as usual, followed me through the streets, she didn't care about missing the film, didn't ask me why I did it, what came over me.

Anyway, what could I have said? This restlessness that's gotten hold of me lately, I can't sit still in one place, like Mommy, who's always rushing about, from teachers' meetings to seminars at the university, God knows what she's doing. But I don't do anything, just wander around from place to place, touring the city by taxi. Yes, lately I've started riding around in taxis. I've got plenty of money, at night I raid Daddy's wallet, he's got so many hundreds of pounds he can't tell anyway. There isn't much I can do with the money, if I bought a blouse or a skirt they'd notice straightaway. So I've started taking rides in taxis. I bought a street map and because it was impossible to stop a taxi, they just wouldn't stop for me, the drivers thought I wanted a free lift, I used to go to the taxi rank, get into the first one, give the name of a street and drive off. That way I started taking trips around the place, going to some hill not far away, walking about among the pine trees looking at the view or at the sunset and returning to the city. The whole round trip wouldn't cost me more than thirty or forty pounds.

At first the drivers were mostly amused, surprised at a girl going around alone like this, but in the end they got used to me. Once someone asked me before I got in, "Have you got any money?" so I showed him the hundred-pound note and said, "Yes, but I'm not going with you if you don't trust me," and I went to look for another taxi.

I always sit in the back seat, on the right-hand side, making a note of the driver's name and the number of the cab in case he tries to start something or make trouble, holding on tight to the strap and going downtown until the time clock shows twenty-five pounds. Sometimes I go down to the docks, walking for a while by the gate and watching the ships, buying nuts or Swiss chocolate, eating in a hurry and taking the bus home.

Once Mommy nearly caught me. The taxi stopped at a traffic light just half a meter from Mommy's Fiat. I curled up at once. She was sitting there at the wheel, staring up at the light as if it were a flag, awfully tense. Her face hard, thinking deeply, for a second she closed her eyes, but as soon as the light changed she jerked forward ahead of the rest and disappeared in the traffic, in a real hurry to get somewhere.

The days are getting longer, the nights crawl. Things are hard at school. Since that business with Baby Face it's as if I'm in limbo, all the time they're considering my fate, they want to throw me out. In the meantime it seems the teachers are ignoring me, even in the subjects that I've done some work for they no longer ask me questions, it's as if they're not bothering with me anymore.

And I'm beginning not to bother too. Leaving the school at three in the afternoon, getting into a taxi and going down to the lower city, no longer looking for a view but just a crowd to move about in, among the sweaty, noisy people, going into shops to finger clothes or crockery, to touch fruit and vegetables. Always being jostled, swept along in the crowd, wanting to be sick but walking on, and suddenly somebody touches me lightly, says softly, "Dafi . . ."

It's Na'im. Him I haven't forgotten.

NA'IM

All right then, they've forgotten me. It's six weeks now since we stopped doing the towing and he's forgotten me. Two weeks ago I went to see him at the garage, to clarify my position. I didn't want to go inside, I didn't want the Arabs to see me and start asking questions. I waited outside, sitting on a big stone, till he came out. He stopped his car at once.

"Has something happened, Na'im?"

"No . . . I just wanted to know how much longer I'll be staying with her . . . with the old woman . . ."

He was embarrassed, I could tell, he took my arm and walked with me around the car, explaining that it was important to stay with her, it counted the same as working in the garage. What was wrong with the place? If I was short of money he'd give me some more, and he took out his wallet and gave me two hundred pounds. That's always the easiest thing for him, giving money, just so long as I don't ask awkward questions. He gave me a little hug, said, "Don't worry, I'll phone you, I'll be in touch, I haven't forgotten you," and he got into his car.

What could I say?

"How's Dafi?" I said quickly before he moved away.

"She's fine . . . she's fine . . . she hasn't forgotten you either."

And he smiled and drove away.

That was a long time ago and since then he hasn't been in touch with me or given any sign. He's forgotten.

And the winter's over and now I spend all my time walking the streets, I've tired of the movies. Walking around the city, going up to Central Carmel, among all the Jews. Walking a lot. Once I even went as far as the university but I didn't go to the registrar's office, I went into one of the lecture halls and heard a young man talking eagerly about the habits of mice. I spent a while at the bulletin board, looking at the lecture lists. One evening I even went to a poetry recital in the basement of the Community Center. There wasn't much of an audience. Three middle-aged men, a few old women and me. We sat in a dark room and listened in silence to two young men in old clothes reading poems without rhymes, all about death and suffering. And after each poem they explained what it meant. The two men fascinated me and after they'd finished I followed them to a cafe and sat down not far from them, hearing them complain to the organizer about there being only old women in the audience. They were looking around them kind of hungrily.

And I listened. They didn't realize I was an Arab, nobody does these days, not Jews anyway. Only the Arabs are still not quite sure about me. Has something about me changed? Am I not exactly myself any longer?

Sometimes, not often, I go back to the village, to see Mother and Father, taking them presents. Once it was an umbrella, once two pairs of pajamas that I bought at a closing sale at the same shop in the lower city where I got my pajamas. And they're always pleased with me and the presents and they treat me with respect, inviting uncles and aunts to come and see me. "A great engineer," Daddy tells them all. I daren't tell them that for more than a month I haven't touched an engine, I'm just looking after an old Jewish woman.

And I carry on wandering about, sometimes getting up at six and going out into the streets, sometimes lying in bed till lunchtime. I've started sitting around in cafes, ordering beer, smoking a cigarette and listening to the conversations around me. Getting older all the time.

Sometimes I feel I'm old enough to slip unnoticed into some seedy bar late at night, sitting beside a painted woman and smiling at her politely. Until the waiter comes along, a man with an evil face, and turns me out–"Run away, little boy, and bring your sister here or your mother if she's still any good."

Filthy bastards–

There are some people I feel drawn to. Arabs from the occupied territories, real Palestinians, dim-witted laborers walking around the city looking lost, not understanding anything and not settling down. And I help them, interpret for them, show them the way. They're very surprised, they don't realize I'm an Arab too. Telling me about their problems, about the cost of living, saying something about the great Palestinian problem and crossing the road or boarding a bus. Sometimes a girl or a young woman smiles at me, saying something or other, and I think maybe the time has come to fall in love with somebody else, and I take a good look around. . . .

The old woman's getting quieter all the time. A smell of death around her. Sitting all day in a chair without moving, becoming more and more dependent on me. I asked her once, "Haven't you got any friends or relations?" but she didn't answer. Soon she'll die and I'll have to run away, they'll say I caused her death. I think of phoning Adam, but at the last moment I change my mind.

It's not so good now, I'm not enjoying it anymore. They've forgotten me. So what am I supposed to do? I go and wander about in the crowd. Not looking in the shop windows anymore, just watching the people, getting pushed around by them, studying them. Sometimes I follow a man or a boy or a little girl, walking behind them, just to see what happens to them. Sometimes I follow somebody who's following somebody else. Like today, when I started following a girl with soft legs and after a few minutes I realize–it's Dafi, she's following somebody. I hurry after her and catch up with her by a street crossing. I touch her gently. A wild sort of happiness takes hold of me.

At first she doesn't notice that I've touched her, standing there waiting for the light to change. Then she's confused, like I've wakened her from a dream. She's grown a bit taller, gotten very thin, her face is pale, black rings under her eyes.

"Na'im"–she grabs my hand–"what are you doing here?"

I don't want to say I'm just wandering about.

"I'm going to visit somebody."

"Who?"

"A friend."

"You've got friends here already?"

"Yes."

The light changes to green but she hesitates to cross, a stream of people pushes us aside. Suddenly we've got nothing to talk about, we're staring at each other, you wouldn't think we'd traveled together at night and been friends. The light changes to red.

"Are you still living with the old woman?"

"Your father asked me to . . ."

"You two are in love."

Mocking, unpleasant, her eyes glaring at me strangely. People crowding together beside us, waiting for the light to change. She seems distant, proud. My heart sinks.

The light changes to green, but she doesn't cross. People crush us hard against the iron railing at the side. No manners. She scowls at me.

"You've changed a lot."

And she doesn't say if the change is good or bad. She isn't friendly, isn't laughing. Serious.

I light a cigarette, so many things I want to say to her but I don't know how to begin. We stand there in this strange place, opposite the changing light, pushed around by the crowd crossing from side to side. I don't want to scare her, to look like I'm trying to put the make on her, though I could invite her to have something to drink, to sit quietly and talk. She's pressed hard against the railings, sad and pale. I feel dizzy with love. I'm afraid she'll go away and leave me.

"And are you still in school?" I smile.

"What can I do?" she says angrily, like I've insulted her. "I can't wander around free like you . . . without any worries . . . they've forgotten you, you're lucky . . ."

Talking so bitterly, like she wants to hurt me. What have I done to her? Why am I to blame? I feel helpless.

A taxi stops by the crossing, she grabs my hand.

"Come on, I'll take you to your friend's house."

And without asking, like I'm a baby, she opens the door and pushes me inside. I have to think quickly, make up an address, stammering a bit as I tell the driver where to go, I've never ridden in a taxi before. In the end I stop the taxi outside a house, get out, wanting to say something to her, I can see she wants to say something too, she's sorry she was so hard on me, wants to go on being with me but the taxi's starting to move, it can't stop here, and she pulls the door shut, nodding her head to say good-by. I'm left standing on the pavement. Miserable. I've lost her.

DAFI

I clutch at his hand, as if at freedom itself.

"Na'im, what are you doing here?"

That mysterious smile on his face, full of confidence. Not the same Na'im, he's taller, wearing new clothes, his shoes shiny. A handsome hustler. Pleased with himself, free of worries. No longer that awkward country boy. A different person, unbelievable, standing there by the crossing, hands in his pockets, in a hurry, going to visit a friend, he's made friends already, settled down well. Suddenly, I don't know why, I feel so sad.

He doesn't really do anything. Living with that old woman, he's got himself a meal ticket. A strange kind of work for a healthy boy. He walks around town all day. No worries. They're not throwing him out of school. He's lucky. They've forgotten him. I feel sorry for myself. He leans up against the railings, looks me up and down. I must look like a child to him now. Where's the little wet boy who came to our house that Friday night? And I was sure he was in love with me. Poor Dafi.

"You've changed . . ." I can't resist saying.

And he doesn't reply. He knows he's changed, of course. He holds his head high. He's got nothing to say to me now. He's climbed so high. He's learned a lot these last months, prowling about in dark corners, smoking earnestly. They're all of them breaking out of their shells and coming to life, to freedom, and I'm left stumbling along at the end of the line.

And what a silly place to stand, impossible to talk here, with the light changing and rude people pushing against us. I want to say to him–take me with you to your friend's house, but I bite my tongue, I don't want him to think I'm trying to put the make on him. And already he wants to get away from me, he's got nothing to say. He asks coolly, in a mocking tone, "And are you still in school?"

That really annoyed me, he found just the place to dig, my weak spot.

"What can I do? I can't wander about free like you . . . they've forgotten you . . . you're lucky . . ."

He knows he's lucky. Bows his head, wants to break off contact. And suddenly I begin to wish this silly meeting never happened, why's he so proud and puffed up? I'd take him with me, if he could forget about his friend for a bit. His freedom fascinates me. A taxi stops at the crossing and straightaway I grab his hand–"Come on, I'll take you to your friend's house"–and I push him inside. He's a bit stunned at first but he recovers himself quickly, sitting there on the edge of the seat, all excited, explaining to the driver where to go. Seems it isn't a friend but a girl friend, he's got himself a little Arab chick. We drive down a few streets and then he asks the driver to stop. He looks at me, blushing. He's hiding something. But there's something gentle about his eyes. He wants to say something, he's not proud and mysterious anymore. But the taxi can't stop there, he gets out, stands on the pavement, staring at me, looking sorry about something, maybe he doesn't want to leave me, but the taxi moves off. I've lost him.

VEDUCHA

They've forgotten him. They've forgotten me too. I'm alone here with a little Arab and that's how it will end. Strange. No family, no relations, no husband, and this is the last face I shall see before I die. For this is death, I know. A heaviness such as there has never been before. Standing is difficult, walking is difficult. Hardly eating but swelling all the time. Only the mind is clear and lucid. The body is a rag.

Na'im is a good boy. A real stroke of luck. Cleaning the floor, washing the dishes, taking out the garbage, going shopping, helping with the cooking. That's what the Arabs are really good at—housework. And the men are better than the women. They don't make a lot of noise, they're clean workers. In the days of the Turks we had a servant in the house, an old sheik, a real sheik, Masiloan. The whole house, all ten of us, he held together. But Hebrew newspapers he didn't read, no, that he didn't do.

But this little fellow reads newspapers too, entertains me. I can no longer go to the movies, he tells me about the ones that he sees. Through him I see the films. But it's not really the same thing because he doesn't understand. He gets confused, you can tell. What interests him most are the gun fights, who killed whom, who drew a gun on whom, who came up from behind, who jumped down from the tree, who fired back, and all the love interest in the film he forgets. Sometimes I listen as he tells the story and when he comes to the end I take five pounds from my purse and send him out to see the film again, this time at my expense and for my sake, so he'll get it right, who loved and who betrayed, who kissed and who disappointed, and who married in the end.

He spends long hours walking by himself in the streets. Who does he see, who does he talk to? He tells me, "Just . . . just people." What is this *just? Just* is how a boy turns into a *fatah* from too much idleness, too much thinking. The most dangerous are the ones who are forgotten.

But I can't do without him, I'm more and more dependent on him. I who was once well known as a courageous woman, a lone wolf. For ten years I was alone in this house and felt no fear, and now I begin to be afraid.

My body does not move, but my mind, thank God, is still working, working so hard it almost hurts. It's hard for me to sleep, to dream dreams. I can't allow myself to lose consciousness again. I lost it once and a war broke out and the government changed.

The situation is bad. I'm not talking now about prices, to hell with money, we'll eat onions instead of meat, but the newspapers, the pleasure has gone out of newspapers. Darkness in the eyes and where is mercy? There are too many villains, the mistakes are too great, the dead are too young. He sits there in the armchair facing me, the young Arab, the damned dog, reading quietly, and I sense his enjoyment, how can he help taking pleasure in our sufferings? He breaks off, looks up, watching me quietly as if he doesn't care and perhaps he really doesn't care. I want to weep for all the troubles, for the isolation of the state, but I control myself, why add to his pleasure? Sometimes I nearly go to the telephone to call Adam—take him away from here, let him go back to his village, I'm better alone. But at the last moment I relent. Not yet. There is time.

For he has some movements that remind me of my Gabriel. Especially when he wanders around the house at night, when he stands at the window, silent and earnest, gazing into the distance. Young and sturdy, shining white teeth. When he sits at the table with knife and fork quietly finishing his food, I think—God, here I am raising a young terrorist who will slaughter me in the end.

Adam has forgotten him and he doesn't care. They've dumped him here and he's his own boss. He's forgotten his mother and his father and his village and taken root here. He's settled down here very well, it's as if he was born here and I'm his grandmother. They also lose their roots so easily. He isn't short of money and all day he searches for entertainment. What is he thinking deep inside, sometimes I really wish I could get inside his head. In the middle of the night I go into his room, sit on his bed and look at him hard, even in his sleep he's a savage.

The beginning of summer already and it's warm outside. He still goes about in old winter clothes. I found in a wardrobe a few clothes that were Gabriel's when he was that age. I offered him a pair of trousers and a shirt. I was sure he'd refuse. But he said nothing, took it all. He didn't mind wearing somebody else's castoffs. He took off his own clothes, put on the clothes that I gave him and walked up and down in front of the mirror, smiling, pleased with himself. My heart ached at wasting good clothes like these on him, I had other dreams. Suddenly he came to me and kissed my hand. His own idea, I said nothing. I expected nothing, not even thanks. I almost died, it was so sweet. He touched me to the heart. So did we, as children, at the beginning of the century, used to kiss the hands of the old men as a mark of respect. Where did he learn to do this? The young lips on my skin, a pleasing sensation of freshness. The next day I gave him a jacket the color of Bordeaux wine. Again he kissed my hand. Ah, God, a little comfort in my last days. I almost wanted to say to him, Don't call me Mrs. Veducha Ermozo, call me grandma. But that would have been going too far.

DAFI

Today in the class that was supposed to be history suddenly Mommy came into the classroom as a substitute. Our history teacher went off to do his reserve duty two weeks ago and usually we play basketball instead of learning about the history of Jewish settlement.

Everybody looked at me and I went red, I don't know why. Mommy has never come into my class before. I thought she'd ignore me completely but the woman turned to me straightaway and asked me which page of the book we were on. I said at once that we hadn't brought any books with us because we knew the teacher was away. But it turned out that a lot of the children had brought their books along anyway. Little suckers. And then somebody told her the page and somebody else lent her a book and she looked at it for a while and went straight into the lesson.

At first she asked questions and the pupils answered. It was amazing how well she coped with the lesson, even though she hadn't prepared for a lesson with us. She ran it at first like a question and answer session and there was some noise and chattering going on, some of them tried to annoy her even though they knew she was my mother. Anyway we didn't feel like doing any work, we were a bit rusty in history. But slowly the class quieted down.

I've never seen her so friendly, so good-natured. Sure of herself, keeping control easily. Making jokes, not very funny in my opinion but the others in the class were in fits of laughter. She knew the names of some of the girls and she addressed them by name, asking them questions. She got on particularly well with Osnat, who for some reason was full of excitement, as if there was nothing that interested her more than early Zionism. Her hand was in the air all the time and that pleading voice of hers, "Teacher, teacher." And Mommy let her do nearly all the talking. Even Tali came to life a bit. The whole class was ecstatic, answering questions, making guesses, and Mommy walked about in front of them, smiling at everybody, even when someone was talking bullshit and she knew it, disagreeing politely, without giving offense.

Wearing the old skirt that I've known maybe since I was born, her hair gray, a bit ruffled. The shoes with the worn heels that Daddy's told her so many times to throw out. And I thought to myself—they're lucky they don't have to eat the tasteless food she cooks. If anyone in the class knew about her having a lover they'd drop dead on the spot. I don't mind her being so friendly in the classroom, she probably thinks she's doing it for my sake, but then why's she always so stern at home?

Anyway for half the lesson I sat there saying nothing, even though I did have things to say, because I really love history, but I decided not to get too involved with her. But in the second half I got carried away as well and I put my hand up several times but she never turned to me, as if she wanted to punish me for not bringing the book, though I wasn't the only one.

The lesson was about the period of the Second Aliya, and Mommy was trying to explain how few and isolated were the Zionists among the Jewish people, and why they thought that the only option they had was immigration to Palestine. And then I put my hand up because I wanted to say something but she wouldn't let me, she turned to others, even the ones who put their hands up after me. And I started getting really irritated, all the rest were joining in, even Zachi opened his mouth and said something silly, but she looked right through me as if I wasn't there. What's going on here? Mommy was talking about other national movements, about the differences and the similarities. Toward the end of the lesson she asked fewer questions and talked more herself. And I looked at the clock, nearly time for the bell, amazing how quickly the time had passed, and I was the only one with my hand up, I was even supporting it with the other hand so it wouldn't get tired. I was determined not to give up. Hell, what had I done to her?

"Yes, Dafi?" She gave in at last, smiling, looking at her watch. Silence in the classroom. And suddenly the bell rang and there was the usual uproar from the other classrooms, and I waited for the ringing to stop, and they were all getting edgy now, nobody likes carrying on into recess time.

And then I started to say something and suddenly I got all tongue-tied, the voice wasn't mine, it sounded thick and the words came out all mixed up. I'd waited so long to speak I was awfully nervous. And Mommy's face went white. She was frightened, came closer to me. All eyes in the class were on me. And in the end I managed to speak.

"I don't understand," I said, "why you say that they were right, I mean the people of the Second Aliya, thinking that was the only choice, after so many sufferings how can you say there wasn't another choice and that was the only choice?"

I could see she didn't understand.

"Whose sufferings?"

"Our suffering, all of us."

"In what sense?"

"All this suffering around us . . . wars . . . people getting killed . . . generally . . . why was that the only choice?"

It seemed nobody understood what I meant. Mommy smiled and dodged the question.

"That is really a philosophical question. We have tried to understand their thinking, but now the bell has rung and we won't be able to solve that question during recess, I'm afraid."

The others all laughed. I wished I could bury myself. The idiots. What was there to laugh at?

ADAM

Starting to live in real and total isolation. The family falling apart. Coming home for example on the first day of spring and finding the house deserted. Asya isn't at home, she's busy, running around and leaving no trace behind her. Her fondness for order has in recent weeks become an obsession. She washes the dishes from lunch, dries them and puts them back in the cupboard. Sometimes to know if she's eaten lunch I have to look for scraps in the garbage can. Dafi's traces are clearer, a school bag thrown down in the hall, a math book on the kitchen table, a blouse and a bra in the study. But she isn't at home either, lately she's been out walking the streets. Eating my meal in loneliness, in exile. A combination of lunch and supper. Lately the food has been tasteless, quite insipid. I've already told Asya, half in jest and half seriously, that I'm going to employ a cook. I strip off my clothes, at least that's something you can do in an empty house. I start wandering about naked, going from mirror to mirror, seeing a gloomy man, the hair graying on his chest and arms. Going into the shower and giving myself up, motionless and eyes closed, to the streams of water. Once more I'm coming home from work with my hands as clean as an office worker's hands.

I come out of the shower without drying myself. Such a blazing hot day. I put on old khaki shorts, walk about barefoot, looking for the morning paper. Going into Dafi's room and stopping on the threshold in astonishment. The room is dark, the shutters closed, on the bed a girl lying asleep. A friend of Dafi's, called Tali or Dali or something. And there was I wandering around the house naked, thinking the place was deserted. What's going on here? What liberty–taking off her sandals and stretching out like that in gym shorts and an open blouse. No longer a young girl. I catch my breath at the sight of those long shapely legs lying on the morning paper. Sleeping so soundly, and I was thinking I'd have to change Dafi's mattress because she finds it so difficult to sleep at night.

She's unaware of my presence, I retreat slowly, full of excitement. She's supposed to be really disturbed. Dafi tells stories about her, stories that I listen to attentively. Those complicated stories that Asya is always eager to hear. Broken homes, families splitting up. At least that's something we've spared Dafi.

I pace restlessly around the hallway, put on a shirt. The sight of those smooth legs laid on the morning paper gives me no peace. Fever rises in me, a choking in my throat. I go back to her, touch her shoulder gently. Her eyes open, blue, reddened by sleep.

"Excuse me"–as if I'm the intruder who must apologize–"may I take the paper?"

But she doesn't realize she's lying on the paper, and with a swift movement I lift both her slender legs and pull out the paper, still warm from the touch of her body, show it to her with an awkward smile. She smiles, closes her eyes and goes back to sleep.

I could die. I go out of the room, the paper in my hand, pace about choked with desire, it's years since I've felt anything like this, something turning over inside me, burning inside me, my eyes growing dark. I take off the shirt, crush the paper violently till it turns to a soft dough and collapse on the bed, shaking, wishing I was dead, a sensation of death mixed with desire. I must see her again, catch a glimpse of her. I get up off the bed, put on the shirt, not fastening the buttons, go back into Dafi's room not knowing what to say. She lies there thinking, her eyes open, I ask her where Dafi is.

"Dafi went out with her mom to buy a skirt and she told me to wait here."

"When?"

"An hour ago, two hours maybe. What's the time now?"

"Nearly six. Are you going to wait for her any longer?"

She sits up, her hair straggling over her face, through the open blouse I see her little breasts. She thinks I'm trying to get rid of her.

"Yes, I'll wait . . . what else can I do?"

"Are you that tired?"

"No, but I always lie down like this."

"Would you like something to drink, to eat . . . ?"

The inspirations born of desire.

"Yes . . . a little cold water . . ."

"Fruit juice?"

"No, just water . . ."

She speaks slowly and strangely, as if she has difficulty putting words together.

I go out. Passing from the dark room to the dazzling light in the apartment. I'm mad. It's as if I'm in love with her. Oppressed by sudden desire. A dozen times before she's walked around the house and I never paid any attention to her. I begin to feel afraid, perhaps I should just leave the house.

I open the fridge and take out a jug of cold water, fill a glass, look for a tray to put the glass on, the glass drops from my hand, the fragments scattering on the kitchen floor. I gather up the pieces with trembling hands. My heart beating fast. Death is upon me. Desire and death. I fill another glass and take it to her.

"Here . . ." My voice fails me.

She sits up and takes the glass, drinks half of it with her eyes closed, wipes her mouth, gives me the glass. Lies back again, as if she's sick.

"You're so kind . . ."

She fascinates me. I can't leave her now. Standing over her, trapped by desire, without shame.

"Have you done your homework yet?"

As if I care.

"That's what I came to see Dafi about . . ."

"Would you like the light on?"

"What for?"

"What do your parents do?"

"My father isn't around . . ."

Without realizing what I'm doing I drink the rest of the water from the glass in my hand, lick the rim of the glass. She watches me in silence, as if my lust shows.

"At first when you woke me I was scared . . . I thought a big wild animal had come into the room . . . I never saw such a hairy man as you . . ."

Her quiet voice and the slow intensity of her speech. This is scandalous. To die at last. I crouch over her, I can't take it any longer, my eyes going dim, wanting to bite and kiss and weep. Knowing that any moment Asya or Dafi may arrive. She puts out a thin hand to my beard and touches it. My eyes are closed. Just don't touch. The pain of not touching. Sweat breaks over me, I clench my fists, starting to come sharply, in pain, semen spurting like blood from an opened wound, without touching her, without touching me, to myself and within me without sound or movement, out of control. Death departs. I open my eyes. Her face is troubled. Realizing something has happened to me but not understanding what.

I must get out of here—

I try to smile, going to the window and opening the shutters, letting light into the room, going out in silence, into my room and locking the door, collapsing on the bed, burying my head in the pillow.

Time passes. I hear her get up, start moving about the flat looking for me. She knocks softly on the door, turns the handle, but I don't move. After a while she leaves the house.

I take off my trousers, the sharp forgotten smell. Like a growing boy. I put on clean underwear, long trousers, go to the window and look out at the reddening sky, at the street, the passing cars. She's sitting there on the step of the tow truck, small and huddled.

Waiting for Dafi, or for me—

I hesitate, but in the end I get dressed, go downstairs and outside to the truck. She stands up, blushing.

"May I ride with you?"

"Where to?"

"I don't mind."

Does she really understand? A little girl, so pretty. I can study her now coolly. She looks up at me in submission, in love. I open the door for her, she climbs in and sits there, staring at me all the time. We begin to drive in silence through the streets of the darkening city, joining a stream of heavy traffic, driving aimlessly through the streets.

"Look, there's Dafi," she cries suddenly.

And yes, that's Dafi standing there on the pavement, looking dejected. I stop. Tali leaps down and embraces her.

DAFI

Of course I can't let this pass in silence, I must get my own back. I run to the teachers' room to look for her, picking my way among the teachers drinking tea and knitting, the room full of cigarette smoke. I find her standing in a corner talking to Shwartzy and I go barging straight in, standing between them, interrupting their conversation, clutching at her skirt like a one-year-old.

"Mommy . . ."

She frowns at me.

"Just a moment, Dafi, wait outside."

But I pretend not to hear, acting stupid, not leaving her alone.

"Mommy . . ."

Shwartzy turns his back on me in disgust. Since that business with Baby Face he hasn't so much as said hello to me in the corridor, he wants to have me expelled.

Mommy draws me aside, pushes me out of the way.

"What's happened? Why are you bursting in here like this?"

"I just wanted to remind you that at four o'clock today we're going to meet downtown to buy me a skirt. So you won't forget again . . . like you always do . . ."

She's only forgotten once, but I haven't forgotten that.

She goes red with anger, she'd like to thump me, but she must keep her dignity before the other teachers.

"Is that why you came bursting in here?"

"Why not? You'll be leaving the school soon and we won't be meeting at home."

"Why does it have to be today?"

"Because that's what we arranged . . . how much longer are you going to put it off? You know I haven't got a single skirt I can wear . . . everything's too small and too old . . ."

"All right . . . all right . . . stop whining."

"I'm not whining."

"What's the matter with you?"

"What's the matter with me?"

"Why are you being so unpleasant?"

"What do you mean unpleasant?"

I know how to annoy her, how to be nasty.

"What was the question you were asking in class? What exactly did you mean?"

"Nothing."

But she takes hold of me firmly, pushes me into a corner, she isn't bothered about the other teachers seeing.

"What suffering were you talking about? What did you mean?"

"There's no suffering. I was wrong. I thought there was a bit of suffering in this country but I was wrong, everyone's terribly happy . . . I just made a mistake . . ."

She'd like to tear me apart. Her lips tighten.

"What's the matter with you?"

"Nothing . . ."

The bell rings and I run away.

Of course we didn't buy a skirt in the end. I just wanted my revenge. Anyway shopping has become a nightmare lately. She takes me to her old women's shop and the old women choose me something ancient, some shade of gray, old-fashioned length and breadth, and put great pressure on me to buy. And at the last moment when they've already put in the pins and marked it with chalk and Mommy's starting to argue over the price I object and call the whole thing off, taking her to another shop, a trendy shop, picking out of a basket some rag with patches on it that costs twice as much and insisting on it. And then she objects, and there's no way of knowing which annoys her more, the patches or the price, and so we go to a compromise shop and buy a compromise thing that neither of us likes and in the end it just gets left in the wardrobe.

And that's the way it was this afternoon too. She didn't know that really I wasn't interested in a skirt but in her, I wanted to get revenge for the way she treated me in that lesson, because she kept me asking permission to speak for a quarter of an hour and because she didn't realize that there was another possibility aside from Zionism.

We met downtown and I was a bit late, not really my fault. Tali suddenly appeared at the house to do some homework with me, I had to persuade her to wait in my room till I came back. Mommy asked me solemnly which shop I'd like to go to, to avoid arguments from the start. And I said softly, "I don't mind going to the shop you use." And this was just a trap. But she said, "Really?" and I said, "Yes, I've seen a few things in their window that aren't bad." And there really were some nice things there. Those old women have opened out a bit lately, they've realized that everything doesn't have to be the same dull color and not everything in life is symmetrical. And we really did find a nice skirt there and they were all excited. Mommy was very pleased, and then I said, "No." And there was a great fuss and an hour went by, and the old women were already falling off their feet from so much effort. And we left the shop with both of us nearly in tears and went to another shop, a new one, with red lights in the window like a whorehouse, and there I found something very expensive and said, "This one," though it was very long and made for a woman not a girl. And then she dug her heels in, and when at last she agreed and took out her wallet I decided I didn't want it after all, and she wanted to go home but then I started to whine, right there in the street, saying I was the only one in the class who could never go to parties. So we went down to Hadar and spent ages looking for a place to park, she's always afraid of getting a parking ticket. Then we walked along one of the streets in silence, going in and out of maybe a dozen shops. She stood to one side, gray and glowering, while I went and examined the dresses and skirts, not really looking at anything, just fingering the material like a blind woman. It was evening already, we'd wasted hours for nothing. The streetlamps were coming on. Exhausted and silent, we returned to the car and there was a parking ticket on the windshield and she went raving mad, nearly in tears, she tore up the ticket first, then picked up the pieces and started running after the traffic cop to argue about the twenty-pound fine. And I stood there feeling miserable and suddenly Daddy came past in the tow truck with Tali sitting beside him. Looks like Tali got bored with waiting and as Daddy was driving downtown he brought her with him. Tali jumped down and Daddy parked the truck, he always parks just wherever he feels like it.

"Where's Mommy?"

"Arguing with a traffic cop about a parking ticket."

He smiled.

That calmness of his—

Mommy came back, furious.

"I haven't the energy to cope with your daughter, you take her and buy her a skirt."

She climbed into her Fiat and disappeared.

The calming influence that he always has over me. And having Tali with me as well. Both of them looked relaxed and beautiful in the darkening street.

"What kind of skirt do you want?"

"Actually it's not a skirt I need but a blouse, I've just realized . . ."

And the three of us went to a shop that was about to close and there was a great blouse that cost hardly anything. And he took out his wallet, again I saw how swollen it was, and he handed over a hundred-pound note and said, "Perhaps we should buy one for Tali as well."

And I hugged him, it's wonderful when he's so generous, and now the two of us will look like twins. And Tali blushed bright red.

And he bought one for Tali as well and we put them on right there. And then he bought *falafel* for the three of us. And we climbed into the truck and he switched on the flashing light on the roof so the other cars would treat us with respect. Sitting there like three Afghan chiefs, eating *falafel* and looking down at the people.

Mommy—

ADAM

The look she gave me when I bought a blouse for her like Dafi's. A Russian blouse with old-style embroidery. Dafi hugged me affectionately, it's so easy to make children happy. And Tali looked at me as if I'd confessed to her. And I looked at her as if I'd already made love to her. Did she understand?

And the next day at four-thirty when I left the garage after work I saw that she understood. She was waiting for me. Sitting on a big stone outside the gate, wearing shorts and the new blouse that I bought her, reading a book. Drawing attention, excitement almost, with her beauty, her silence, sitting there so passively. Workers waiting for the bus, from my garage and from other garages, can't take their eyes off her, joking and whistling at her. And she doesn't look up, absorbed in her reading, in a sort of serene abandon. I know this abandon of hers. She doesn't even look to see if I'm coming out of the garage, she knows I'll stop beside her.

And I do stop. She looks up, the book still open in her hand, gets up from her seat, climbs into the car in silence, not saying a word, sits down, glances at me solemnly and returns to her book.

The blood rushes to my head. The looks and the smiles of the workers, understanding what I still refuse to understand. I start to drive, not toward home but out of town, to the open road. Driving slowly, almost paralyzed with fear and excitement, saying nothing. It's forbidden. It's madness. Take her home at once, or put her down here, in the middle of the road. But I carry on driving along the shore road, looking for a quiet beach. In Atlit there's a little bay where you can drive almost to the shore. I drive to the shore.

And she reading all the time, turning the last pages. I switch off the engine, get out and stand there, my face to the sea. A day of *hamsin.* The smell of the salt washes over me. My face is drenched with sweat, I bend down and wipe my hands in the sand. She's still absorbed in her reading, motionless. Not even looking to see where we are. I stand watching the waves, the sun sinking in the west. I must cool off quickly, return to my senses, but I don't want to. I look at her thin shoulders, her braids. So pretty. "Come here," I say at last in a voice that even I don't hear. I open the door. She steps out, the book still in her hand, reading the last page, suddenly moaning. Then she holds out the book to me with a movement that sets my head spinning, bending down to take off her sandals, if only I could come again without touching her.

The book is warm in my hand, I flick through it, a thin, worn volume. A tale of magic or witchcraft, a children's book. I give the book back to her, but she drops it in the sand with a weary gesture. What can I say to her? How can I explain? How can I start to speak against the murmur of the sea? A girl fifteen years old, her head reaches my chest. What am I doing? To speak would be more ludicrous than to take her in my arms and kiss her. I take her. My trembling hands caress her hair, with a false fatherly movement I kiss her face, embrace her. She's silent, a lifeless thing. I remove her blouse, stunned by the vision of purity that is revealed, the ungrown bosom of a girl just beginning to blossom. I close my eyes and bury them in this child flesh, move my lips over her hard little breasts, not believing that this is so, destroying myself. And she says nothing, she doesn't understand, she doesn't resist. The smallest shadow of resistance and I would leave her alone at once. She's staring at my beard. I hurl her down on the sand, fierce with lust, whispering, "Tali, Tali," and I see that she's listening not to me but to other voices, she says nothing but I hear them too. The laughter of children, the engine of a launch, people talking, a car starting up. There are people nearby.

Hastily I pull her to her feet, put on her blouse and tie it up, and bend down and put her feet in her sandals, fastening them for her as if she's a little girl. And all the while not daring to look her in the face. Bundling her into the car and driving inland, looking for a quiet place. But there is no quiet place. This crowded land. Roads, houses, bare fields or fenced orchards. Army units, tents, people in motion. Give up. From time to time I lead her from the car, beating a path among thorns, and she follows me obediently. Once again there is someone in my power. Once it was Gabriel, once an Arab boy, now it's a girl. People put themselves so willingly into your hands.

Wait until dark–

I stop at a little roadhouse at a *moshav*. Order cake and fruit juice for her and coffee for me.

She sits facing me, eating slowly, sucking the juice from the glass. I swallow her with my stare, my desire stretches to the sky. Twilight. Like an animal I watch my prey, her white hands, her face. This silence is unbearable, must say something. But what?

"Have you done your homework?"

"Not yet."

Silence. Again I ask her about her father. Again the same story. He disappeared years ago, they know nothing about him. I ask her about Dafi, what do they think about Dafi in the class. And she starts talking about Dafi with love, almost with admiration. A tough girl, awfully tough, the toughest. Tells everyone the truth, to his face, even the teachers. She isn't afraid of anyone.

She talks slowly, something not quite developed, almost retarded, in her manner of speech. That vague disturbance, origins unknown. My redemption will come from her?

Twilight. We sit at a broken iron table in a diner, no, in a filthy general store in some remote *moshav*.

"Won't they be worried about you?"

"No."

"Perhaps you should call your mother, tell her you'll be back late."

"No, she doesn't care anyway."

"Even so, you should phone her."

She doesn't move. She looks lost.

I go to the phone and ring home. Dafi answers. Asya isn't at home. I tell Dafi I'll be home late, I've driven to Tel Aviv.

"Still looking for him?"

"No, this is something else."

"When will you be back?"

"I'll be back. What does it matter when? What are you doing now?"

"Nothing. I've been waiting for Tali but she hasn't come."

"She'll be there soon . . ."

"Don't be late, Daddy."

A childish plea, it doesn't become her.

It's already dark. The air growing cold. I pay the bill and we're on the road again. I don't know where to drive to, just wandering about in the darkness. Still meaning to turn and drive home, but I'm trapped in something stronger than myself. Something in the surroundings looks familiar. I drive on a few more kilometers down a narrow road. From a distance I recognize the old people's home, the old hospital where the old lady was kept. I drive around the building, park some distance away. I leave the girl in the car and go into the hospital. I ask for the matron. They tell me she may still be about and I find her locking the door of her office. She recognizes me at once, her face lights up, she almost leaps at me.

"Did you hear about the miracle?"

"Of course."

She's so sorry I refused to leave my name, or an address. She wanted to give me the news herself. Just a few days after I was there.

"I know."

"And how is she? I haven't had time to contact her."

"She's fine."

She starts telling me what she's done with the money I gave her. After a lot of thought she decided to buy some pictures by a young, very promising Israeli artist. She takes me around the wards to show me the pictures hanging there, hoping I approve of them, even though I told her to do exactly as she liked with the money.

"Of course."

I walk beside her, tired, worn-out, distracted, looking at the gray, surrealistic pictures, listening to her explanations with half an ear.

At last she falls silent. I explain my request. A room for the night, or for a short rest. I'm doing some work not far from here.

The request seems a little strange to her but how can she refuse me? She'll give instructions to the Arab watchman. No problem. They'll give me supper too.

"No need."

I walk with her to her car. She shakes my hand. Only one request, that I reveal my identity.

"Never . . ." I smile. "I intend to make you another donation in the future."

She laughs, moved, shakes my hand again.

I go back to the car and find that Tali has disappeared. I start searching for her. After a few minutes I see her emerge from behind a stone wall, walking slowly back.

We wait in the car until the hospital grows a little quieter, until the evening meal is over. The lights go out. My head is bent over the wheel, sweaty, sticky. Outside a cool breeze. She still sits quiet beside me, not moving. Nothing gets through to her. An hour passes. We leave the car. The Arab watchman opens the main door, doesn't even look at Tali. He leads us down long corridors past dimly lit wards, the old people dozing after their supper, some of them moving about in their striped dressing gowns, like twisted slow-moving monsters.

The girl shudders.

At last something has gotten through to her.

He shows us into a room, not large, an operating room or intensive-care unit. In the center a big iron bed fitted with little pulleys, beside it a big cylinder of oxygen, some surgical instruments. A sink on one wall. He doesn't even ask if I want another bed. I thrust ten pounds into his hand but he refuses to accept it.

She stands in the corner like a trapped animal, terrified, not moving. But I can't stop myself, not now, one thought only in my heart. I go to her, draw her to me, suddenly she tries to resist. I lift her, she's very light, sand falls from her hair. I kiss her face, her neck, gently at first, softly, fearing the violence overtaking me. I lay her on the bed. A voice tells me to stop but I can't. I've gone too far. I take off her sandals, the soles of her feet are dirty. I go to the sink, dip a towel in water and wash her feet, her thighs, wipe her face. Then I strip her, and lie on the little naked body. She doesn't understand, she starts to cry, I kiss her until she stops. I make love to her. She begins to understand, folding her arms around my neck, closing her eyes, starting to kiss me slowly. Lying still at her side. Beginning to hear the sounds of the world around me. The voices of the old people in the nearby wards. Somebody is praying, reciting psalms. An old woman laughs. Someone groans, starts weeping. She's already asleep.

After a while I rouse her and while she still dozes I dress her, wrap her in a blanket and carry her in my arms like an invalid. The watchman opens the gate for me, I put her on the back seat. Just before midnight I arrive at her house.

Will it be possible to deny all this? I want to tell her to say nothing, but I can't. What I've lost I've lost. I watch as she disappears through the door of her house.

A small car passes me slowly. I turn to look at it, my habit these last few months. Perhaps it's him. And I too have become a lover, a lover in search of a lover.

PART FIVE

ASYA

I can't remember the beginning, the three of us are in another country, somewhere in the East, in Asia, near Afghanistan, I don't know how I know that it's near Afghanistan. An afternoon sort of country, the sun strong and low in the sky, but not a desert country, just a dry country, thousands of kilometers from the sea. Fields all around, growing corn, yellow-green, short fat stalks. What we're doing here I don't know, we're not here for a holiday but for a short stay, Adam has work to do here, but he hasn't actually started working yet, all the time he paces around the house.

We are in trouble. Dafi is pregnant. She was walking in the fields and a seed entered her. She touched nobody, nobody touched her. Not the seed of man but a seed of corn. She sat among the corn stalks and a seed entered her, something like that, vague, frightening . . . but she is pregnant. We already have the results of the tests, and now she sits before me in a wicker chair, small and pale, and I am filled with despair.

It's impossible to tell if Dafi knows the condition she's in. But I stare at her fearfully and I see that her belly is already swelling a little. It's amazing, she conceived only a short while ago, but they explained to us that this is a childhood pregnancy, very quick, and it isn't the first time this has happened to foreigners here on a visit.

Adam comes into the room with a doctor. A dark man, swarthy skinned, not black but very dark, with a little wispy beard. He's come to take Dafi away because she needs urgent treatment, an operation, an abortion, not exactly an abortion, something like that, similar, they are going to take that thing out of her womb, and they will send it to us, a field mouse perhaps, something frightful. A nightmare. Adam has settled the whole business without consulting me.

The man, the doctor, God knows what he is, comes close to Dafi and takes her by the hand, and she obeys him, rising from her seat, so miserable. And I thought I was losing my mind, I could kill Adam for submitting to this doctor, I draw him aside and plead with him, "Let's go home at once, we can take her to doctors there," and Adam listens but isn't convinced, the doctor leads Dafi to the door, stands there waiting. I talk hurriedly to Adam, and the doctor listens as if he understands Hebrew, and Adam refuses, shakes his head—"No, only they know how to do this, they will save the mouse." I'm streaming with sweat, shaking, frantic—"What mouse?" And suddenly Dafi breaks loose from the doctor, runs to me, howling, clutches at me, starts shaking both of us.

ADAM

Dafi shakes me roughly, climbing onto the bed, switching on the light, tugging wildly at my pajama jacket. "Mommy, Daddy, Shwartzy's on the phone." The light hurts my eyes, Dafi's hair is in a mess, she's all excited. "Shwartzy's on the phone, he's had an accident."

It's one o'clock in the morning.

Asya stirs slowly, sitting up in bed, her eyes closed.

The phone rang and I didn't hear it, when I stopped doing the night towing I put the phone back in the study. Only Dafi heard it. She's still awake at night. At first she thought it was a wrong number and didn't answer, but the ringing went on. She lifted the receiver and, unbelievable, she thought she was dreaming, the soft and wheedling voice of the headmaster she hates, her cruel persecutor.

She mimics him—

"Dafna? Is that you? Would you be so good as to call your father, I must speak to him."

I go to the phone.

His whispering, urgent voice, sometimes a strange laugh, even at such a late hour of the night he uses the same pompous style of speech.

A thousand pardons. A misfortune has befallen him. His car is embracing a tree, ha, ha, the hood is crushed and bent. On the road from Jerusalem, near the airport. He has been hurt too, bruises and scratches on the face. Some wonderful Jews from the *moshav* Vardim took him in, bandaged him and gave him a drink. But now he wants his car towed to Haifa, to my garage. Is it possible? Will I be prepared to receive the unfortunate car? There is nobody he can trust but me, Adam dear friend, he has no other garage but mine . . . ha, ha. . . .

Well then—

He has forgotten the address, he has simply forgotten the address, he whispers as if afraid to wake somebody beside him.

I say nothing.

"Adam?"

"Who is going to tow you?"

Nobody at the moment. His rescuers will try to find a towing service.

"Wait, I'll come and tow you in."

"Heaven forbid . . . such a distance . . . that wasn't why I rang . . ." but I detect the relief in his voice.

"Where are you?"

No, he won't tell me, he's suddenly obstinate, he was very dubious about calling, he's full of remorse, he woke the girl . . .

But I insist. Dafi's fate is in his hands. Some day soon he must decide whether to expel her from the school or not. I shall tow him in, repair his car, accept no payment, for a few days he will be in my power.

Suddenly he begins to waver. On no account does he wish to be a burden. He already regrets calling me. Besides, a special kind of tow job is required here. His car, to tell the truth, is completely wrecked.

"That's all right . . . just tell me exactly where you are, Mr. Shwartz. I won't let anyone else tow you in . . . besides, they'll overcharge you . . . do you have money to spare?"

He's taken aback.

"Adam, dear friend, what can I do? Of course I shall have to pay you . . . I shall never agree to a free job . . . and anyway, what does money matter . . . the important thing is that I'm still alive . . ."

"Pity about the time . . ."

He tells me where he is, in a devious manner, as if he's doing me a favor.

I phone Na'im. The old lady answers at once, as if she's been waiting for the phone to ring. She's an insomniac too. The wakefulness of this survivor from the last century never ceases to amaze me.

"Has something happened? News of Gabriel?"

"No . . . please wake Na'im. I shall be coming to pick him up soon, we're going to tow a car."

"I thought you'd stopped doing the night work."

"This time it's a friend of mine who's in trouble."

"Shall I make coffee for you?"

"No, thank you, I'm in a hurry."

Meanwhile Asya has gotten out of bed and is making coffee. Dafi is beside her in the kitchen, insisting on knowing all the details, disappointed that he's gotten off with just cuts and scratches.

"I wish he'd been killed, the monster . . ."

And we're so tired we don't even tell her to shut up.

"You're driving to Lod for him? What's the idea?" Asya is amazed.

"It's for Dafi . . . so he'll think twice before expelling her . . ."

"It won't do any good . . . I know him . . . he'll expel her . . . and she deserves it too."

Dafi listens in silence, quietly chewing a piece of bread, her hair falling over her face, her face puffed up, lately she's really gone to pieces.

"Pity he wasn't killed . . ." she whispers again.

"That's enough."

She's beginning to get on Asya's nerves. Asya paces about the kitchen in an old nightdress. Suddenly I remember the dream I had.

"You woke me up in the middle of a dream."

Asya looks at me.

"What was the dream?"

"I don't remember."

But as I'm accelerating down the hill, I remember the dream, I even smell it. I was in a big hall, at a sort of meeting, crowds of people were wandering about there, Gabriel among them, his head shaved, pale. I was angry with him, spoke to him harshly, he turned and went away. . . .

A thin silhouette outside the old lady's house, a flickering cigarette. Na'im is already waiting. These last months he's grown a lot taller, grown a great mop of hair, matured. Chain-smoking, buying himself new clothes, and all the time taking money from me. I don't care. A strange boy. What does he go through in the silence with the old lady, whole days? I've ruined him completely. This power that money gives me, I must put my mind to him, return him to his village.

The lights are on in the old lady's house. She's looking out of a window, her face white, like the face of a corpse come to life.

"Your sweater, Na'im," she shouts from above and throws the sweater down to the pavement.

"I don't need it," he mutters, embarrassed, angry, but he picks the sweater up from the ground.

I get out of the car, wave to her.

"She's in love with you."

He turns around to me quickly.

"Who?"

"The old lady."

"The old lady," he says softly, seriously, "is way off her rocker."

I say nothing. There's a new tone to his voice, cynical, decisive.

We arrive at the garage, Na'im jumps down to open the gate. The watchman is asleep in his shelter, the little dog in his arms is asleep too, they don't notice us coming in, changing vehicles, leaving the Dodge and climbing aboard the tow truck. Na'im loads a box of tools. Quietly we close the gate behind us, the dog opens his eyes, looks at us affectionately, wags his tail and lays his head on the watchman's chest.

A clear summer night. The sea lies calm. A gray color to the sky. The truck runs slowly. I'm very tired. Na'im is silent beside me. I ought to ask him a little about his life, but I haven't the energy to talk. Now and then I feel him staring at me. Perhaps he would like to say something to me, but he holds back.

We reach the scene of the accident after two hours. From a distance I see the headmaster, pacing back and forth on the road as if he's walking the corridors of the school, his head wrapped in a sort of white turban, a tall ghostly figure. He shakes my hand, embraces me, his torn shirt stained with blood. "Adam, dear friend, such a catastrophe, never before have I been in an accident . . ."

He shakes Na'im's hand as well, ruffles his hair, gives him a little hug, as if he's one of his pupils. He doesn't seem to realize he's an Arab. We walk together arm in arm, treading on glass splinters and fragments of metal. Where is the car? To my astonishment I find it hanging on a tree, as if he had been trying to climb the tree with it. It's incredible, I can't help smiling, it's actually hanging there caught in the branches.

I see the smile on Na'im's face.

"The car is hopeless . . ." He follows my gaze.

"No car is hopeless. Only people are."

He bursts out laughing.

Meanwhile Na'im goes to the truck and lifts down the box of tools, attends to the winch chains, lays out flashing lights on the road. There's no need to tell him anything.

Two figures appear on the dust bank at the side of the road, lean white-haired Yemenites with rifles in their hands. The night watchmen of the *moshav*. The headmaster hastens to introduce them to me.

"These dear Jews, they looked after me until you arrived . . . we had a wonderful conversation . . . didn't we? We talked about the Torah."

He hugs and caresses them too.

The two old men look a little dazed from their time spent with Mr. Shwartz. It seems he's caused quite a stir in the *moshav*. Lights are on in some of the houses, other figures appear, watching us from a distance.

"What happened exactly?"

A strange story. He was returning from Jerusalem after a long conference on educational matters. Oh, these damned meetings, the endless chattering, all so depressing. At first he intended to stay in Jerusalem overnight, but in the morning there was to be another meeting in Haifa in the office of the city architect, about the new wing that they're going to add to the school. He decided to return home. Everything was in order, the road was empty, he was quite wide awake. When he was young he used to drive for long hours at night without any problems. In England, before the war, when he was a student at Oxford. He was so engrossed in his memories of England that apparently without realizing it he began slowly straying toward the left. Suddenly a little old black car appeared in the opposite direction, with lights almost blacked out. At the last moment he recovered himself and swerved toward the right, but evidently he swung the wheels too far, and suddenly this tree, this unnecessary tree . . .

"What happened to the other car?"

Nothing, a light collision, a few scratches. If he had run into it rather than this damned tree the damage might have been less, for him that is, ha, ha, the other car would have been completely squashed, that little old tin box, to say nothing of the men within. And they turned out to be religious, these men, an old rabbi and a young man with side curls, dressed all in black, Neturei Karta or some sect like that. Like a hallucination. What were they doing driving about near the airport after midnight? They stopped, they both got out, they didn't come too close. Just checked that he was alive and on his feet.

And the old man said softly, from a distance:

"You are aware, sir, that you are to blame . . ."

What could he say to that?

"Yes, I am to blame."

Curse them. Anti-Zionists. They didn't ask him if he needed help, as if they were afraid of getting involved with him.

Na'im is already playing out the cable. This tow is going to be very complicated. A light breeze passes over us. Better get rid of the headmaster so he won't get in the way. I persuade him to go home. He's easily persuaded, he's quite exhausted. He goes to the two Yemenites, takes leave of them, writes down their names in a little notebook, promises to send them a book, his own book apparently, to continue their conversation. We flag down a car, bundle him into it and send him northward.

Now Na'im and I start assessing the situation. One of the front wheels is really embedded in the tree, wrapped around it. Na'im crawls between the tree and the crushed hood to free the wheel, I pass him the tools. A good boy. What would I do without him? For a full hour he struggles there until he succeeds in freeing the wheel, comes out covered in sweat, takes the end of the cable, ties it to his belt and gets down on the ground again, crawling right underneath the car. It's a wonder how the headmaster survived. Dafi wasn't far wrong, he could easily have been killed. He himself doesn't realize how lucky he was.

We start to move the car. Pieces fall off it, a headlight, a fender, a door handle. Na'im explains to me how the truck must be positioned, at what angle, the boy's already starting to give me instructions. But I don't care, I just want to get the job done and go home. Na'im operates the winch and starts drawing the car away from the tree, but the tree doesn't want to be parted from it, branches break off, clinging to the car. A small crowd watches us in silence. The dawn is breaking fast. Birds chirp. On the back of the tow truck hangs a wrecked car wearing a laurel of leaves. A strange sight. Cars passing on the road slow down, people stare curiously through their windows. Somebody stops. "How many killed?" he asks Na'im but he doesn't answer.

His clothes are torn and dirty, his hands cut, his face oily, but there's no denying he's learned a lot in these night trips. Now he secures the car with extra ropes and I move the truck to the side of the road.

It's already daylight. Na'im goes to collect the tools, switches off the flashing lights on the road and picks up the bits that have fallen off the car. I stand still, exhausted, smoking a cigarette, my clothes wet with dew. Na'im comes to me and shows me a piece of black metal. "Is this a part of it too?" I glance at it. "No, that looks like part of the other car." He's about to throw it away in the grass at the roadside but suddenly I stop him. Something in the shape of the metal reminds me of something. I snatch it from his hand. I recognize it at once. A piece of the fender of a black Morris. The same model. Nobody can compete with me when it comes to an eye for car parts. I feel elated. Rapidly the light grows stronger. The morning mists have gone. A day of *hamsin* ahead of us. I stand at the roadside, a piece of fender in my hand. Black, admittedly, but belonging to a 1947 Morris. Clear and living evidence. I examine it closely, turning it over in my hand, there are drops of dew on it. Na'im lies back on the bank beside me, looking at me angrily. He doesn't understand what the delay is. I examine the paint, the paintwork is crude, an amateur job.

"A small screwdriver . . ." I whisper.

And the screwdriver is there in my hand. Carefully I scrape off the layer of black paint, blue shows through underneath, the color of the Morris that I've been searching for desperately since the end of the war.

I trembled—

NA'IM

What's with him? He's got hold of a bit of metal and has fallen in love with it, doesn't want to let it go. Has he gone soft in the head? And I used to think of him as a little god.

I'm so tired. He hasn't done anything here. He doesn't work now, he doesn't bend down, doesn't move, he's even stopped giving advice. Already he's sure I can do it all without him. The cables, the hitching up, the winch. Before he has time to tell me anything I already know what he's thinking and I do it by myself. If he had to do the job by himself the car would still be hanging in the tree. His mind's somewhere else, you can tell. All the time looking around for something like he's waiting for something and he hasn't decided yet what it is.

What is this, is he sick? Fingering that bit of metal like I've given him gold. It's morning already, what does he think he's doing? How much longer are we going to stand here? I'm nearly asleep on my feet. This is the hardest tow job we've had yet. That old man planted his car in the middle of that tree, smashed it up, I still don't see how he got out of it alive. And I've got myself torn and scratched all over, crawling under the car. Who for? What for? If only Dafi was here. God, sometimes I miss her terribly. But she's not here, she's finished with me, no point in trying anymore.

What does he want now? He's off his head. What's he thinking about? He might at least give me some money. He's got so much money and I've done a real professional job for him here. He reckons if he gives me a hundred pounds now and then that's enough. What's a hundred pounds these days? I can spend twenty or thirty pounds in just one outing, quite easily. An average sort of meal, the movies, a few nuts and a pack of Kent and I'm on my way home with only coins in my pockets. Lucky I'm not smoking cigars yet or inviting some lady out to dinner. Give me some money at least. Once I used to take it carefully, shyly, now I just grab it off him and stuff it straight in my pocket. So what? I haven't yet seen him empty his wallet for me.

When will we be finished here? Why doesn't he take this bit of metal home with him and think about it there? Why waste all this time? The smashed-up car is hanging on the winch all covered with leaves. No wonder they're all slowing down on the road and staring at it, looking for blood.

"How many killed?" somebody shouts.

That's all they're interested in. Corpses. I don't answer, I'm not getting involved with anyone here. The car's no loss to anyone. The insurance company will pay, why should anyone worry? And they'll repair it. I've seen cars in the garage in a worse state than this one, seen them cutting them in half like a cake, getting a complete half from another wrecked car and stitching the two halves together and making a new car. It's like a real ceremony in the garage, everyone standing around and watching them weld the two halves together, slap on a fresh coat of paint and there's a new car ready to be sent to the dealers in Tel Aviv.

I shall sleep here on this bank. I wish now I hadn't given him that bit of metal that I asked him about. Now he's whispering to himself, the man's gone bananas, he's asking for a small screwdriver.

What does he want with a screwdriver?

Here take this screwdriver, I hope it makes you happy, just make up your mind and move.

He starts scraping paint off the metal. He's gone right off his head. I'm going to have to leave him, I'll have trouble from him yet. Maybe I should go back to the village, persuade Father to send me back to school. I've missed only a year.

A twig fell on . . .

On what?

Sometimes I wish I was dead.

The piece of metal isn't black anymore but blue. Big deal. But this scraping of his has got him all excited. He jumps into the truck and shouts at me.

"Hey, let's go, what are you waiting for?"

Go fuck yourself, it's not me who's holding things up.

I'm getting out—

DAFI

What's this? She's not going straight back to bed. What's the matter with her? Sitting in the kitchen beside the empty coffee cup and losing her sleep. Mommy's wide awake at two o'clock in the morning. Incredible. The house is full of light, Daddy's gone to rescue Shwartzy, poor man, all for my sake. And Mommy's in no hurry, not tired, giving me an understanding look, studying me as if she hasn't seen me for a long time. Touching me, trying to start a conversation, smiling.

A wild happiness takes hold of me.

"You woke me in the middle of a dream . . ."

Strange to think of her having dreams, but, I suppose, why not?

"What was the dream?" I ask politely.

"A real nightmare. I dreamed about you."

"A nightmare? What was it?"

"A strange dream, awfully confused, we had gone to some far-off country and you were sick there."

And suddenly she pulls me to her and hugs me. I really like this dream of hers, about me being sick. I hug her in return. Her stale old smell. She's not turned completely to stone after all.

"A serious illness?" I ask.

"No," she says hastily, hiding something, "what does it matter . . . it was just nonsense . . . were you awake when the headmaster called?"

"Yes."

She shifts out of the embrace, very slowly.

"Still can't sleep at night? What's the matter with you?"

"Nothing. I just can't sleep."

"Are you in love with somebody?"

"No. Why do you say that?"

"Nobody?" She smiles at me so sweetly. "That's impossible . . ."

"Why's it impossible?"

"Because there are some very nice boys in your class."

"How do you know?"

"I taught in your class once, didn't I? I saw some . . . really charming boys."

That's what she thinks–

"Who?"

"I can't remember . . . I was just struck by some of the faces."

"But who?"

She's still stroking me, absently.

"It doesn't matter. I just said . . . I was joking . . . so what do you do when you can't sleep, do you read in bed?"

"No. I walk about, eat something, listen to music . . ."

"Music? In the night? I never hear anything."

"You and Daddy sleep like a pair of corpses, if somebody blew up the house you wouldn't notice."

"That's odd. In the daytime I don't notice that you're particularly tired. It amazes me how you get through the night, all alone like that. I wish I could do with less sleep . . . but don't you get bored by yourself in the dark house . . . time creeping by so slowly . . ."

"It's not that bad . . . sometimes when I go out for a little walk it's really very nice . . ."

"What?"

"You heard me . . ."

"You go out of the house at night? Are you crazy? You know what can happen to a girl walking the streets at midnight . . ."

"Two o'clock in the morning, not midnight. There's nobody around then . . ."

"Dafi, you must stop this . . ."

"But why all the fuss? What can happen? Everything's quiet . . . and there's the civil patrol . . . nice old men . . ."

"Dafi, that's enough, no arguments . . ."

"What can happen to me? I don't go far. Down to the corner where Yigal was killed and back again . . ."

She goes pale. The hand lying on the table clenches to a fist . . . she wants to say something but the words don't come. I shall have to help her.

"But you told me . . ."

"Who told you?" she snaps.

"Daddy."

"When did he tell you?" She's all on fire.

"A long time ago."

She starts biting her nails, in agony, bewildered. I carry on in an innocent, patient tone.

"But what is there to hide . . . why am I not allowed to know? Daddy said he was killed at once and didn't suffer."

She doesn't answer, looks at her watch, groans, doesn't want to answer. I've ruined everything.

"Do you think he did suffer?" in a soft, distant voice. Sometimes I can be dreadful, unbearable, I know.

"What does it matter now . . . enough, Dafi."

She won't be drawn–

Silence. A clock ticking. A clear summer night. The house all lit up. Bread crumbs on the table. Mommy sits there frozen, her eyes hard. Tense as a spring. Now and then she looks at me, her sweet smile has gone. Night crickets. Poor Daddy, driving with Na'im to Lod. He was so tired, he didn't want to wake up, I really dragged him out of his sleep.

"I wish he'd been killed," I say quietly, thoughtfully.

"Who?"

"Shwartzy."

"That's enough, Dafi . . ."

"Why not? He isn't a young man . . ."

"Enough, Dafi . . ."

She's pleading–

"All right then, not killed, just badly hurt, a few months in the hospital."

"Enough!"

"O.K. then, no blood even, just concussion, paralysis from the neck upward, so he won't be able to talk . . ."

And then I get a hard slap on the cheek. She hits me, the first time she's hit me in seven years maybe. And I fall silent, it's easier now. My cheek burns, tears spring to my eyes, but this blow has cracked something inside me, weariness, something dissolves in me. A stupefying sort of blow. I don't move, don't jump up, just slowly put a hand to my cheek to feel if the skin's been torn.

She's more shocked than I am, she clutches at my hand, as if she's afraid I'm going to hit her back.

"I said, enough," she almost whimpers.

"Will he expel me from the school?" I ask quietly, not saying a word about the slap, feeling quiet, relaxed and tired, a sweet tiredness, the tiredness of immediate sleep.

She's still holding my hand.

"I don't know."

"But what do you think?"

She starts thinking.

"Do you deserve it?"

"I deserve it a bit . . ."

"What do you mean, a bit?"

"I deserve it."

"Then it looks as if he will expel you. It's not so bad, we'll find you another school."

And I stand up, tired, I've never felt so tired before, yawning a big yawn . . . so drowsy . . . my other cheek is burning as if it's been slapped as well, I go stumbling to my room and Mommy comes with me, supporting me. She puts me to bed, covers me up, puts out the light. My room is dark and the rest of the house lit up, as it always used to be, as it should be. She sits on the bed beside me, as she used to years ago, and I say to myself, a pity to sleep now, and with this thought, as I'm still thinking it, I go to sleep.

VEDUCHA

Is this how it will end? For weeks now I've seen my body depart from me. There's no taste in food, it's like putting plaster or absorbent cotton in my mouth. I cover my food with salt and black pepper and red pepper and it makes no difference. All the taste has gone. And Na'im is a fool, he burns the food. Much too hot. "Are you in love with somebody?" Little swine. And I'm afraid to tell him that I'm going to die because if he thinks this is the end he'll run away and I can't be left alone any longer.

He's so jittery. Impatient. They've forgotten him, it's true. He's become a real delinquent. His bed in a mess, socks thrown on the floor, chain-smoking the whole time, I run around after him checking the ashtrays. I must sniff them to make sure there's no hashish there. You never know, anything is possible.

He doesn't even want to read the newspapers. He just tells me what the headlines are and says it's all lies, all nonsense, you shouldn't believe what they say. What is this? We've gone back to Turkish rule. He does as he pleases. Once I thought of phoning the police, telling them to keep an eye on him.

Adam has forgotten him, but apparently he's giving him money, otherwise how could he go out to the movies every evening, two movies in an evening. I say to him, "At least tell me what you've seen, tell me the story. I'm so bored here. And I know about films, when I had a good pair of legs I used to go to the movies in the afternoon." But he refuses–"What is there to tell? Leave me alone, these movies aren't your kind, all kissing and cuddling and guns, you wouldn't understand."

He's learned how to talk–

Hooligan, bastard–

Fatah–

Sits in the armchair, pretty boy, all sweet and laughing.

What can I do?

I'm completely dependent on him, I can't move much now, just go from chair to chair. If he wasn't buying the food and taking out the garbage, things would be very bad here.

I bring out old clothes and give them to him, emptying the wardrobe, and he takes them and says nothing. He's bought himself an old wardrobe and he's started filling it. And already I'm forgetting that I have toes on my feet, they've disappeared. It's a sign of the end. I can't stand up from my seat any longer. He has to pull me to my feet.

In the middle of the night Adam phones to call him out on a tow job. At first I thought it was news of Gabriel but I was wrong. Sometimes I say to myself, Gabriel did not return, not he, and if he did return then he really is dead.

The Arab puts on working clothes, clothes that he hasn't touched for a long time. I said, "These clothes suit you better than those silly clothes you buy. Now you only need a haircut and you'll look like a human being again." But he didn't answer, he just scowled at me and left, leaving me in the armchair.

And so I'm stuck here all night, unable to stand. My legs are like torn absorbent cotton. And outside it slowly becomes light. They don't come back. Must be a difficult job. I try to stand and sink back again. All the windows are open, he forgot to close them. Suddenly it's cold. I'm in a thin nightdress, as if I've just gotten out of bed. The cold enters the dry bones. I bend down, start picking up the newspapers scattered around me, papers that I haven't read, papers that I so much wanted to read, stories about this unfortunate government, I start covering myself with them, stuffing them behind my head, behind my back, at my sides, no longer knowing which is *Yediot Aheronot,* which is *Ma'ariv,* tucking in here and tucking in there, a little comfort and warmth for the grieving body.

And at the window—the sun rising. Hands slowly sinking. No feeling in the fingers, as if the wires inside have burned out.

This time it's the opposite . . . the body perishes and only the mind remains.

ADAM

And I'm still standing there, on the road, deep in thought, smoking cigarette after cigarette. The piece of metal has turned blue in my hands. An endless flow of traffic passing on the road, the first planes taking off with a roar from the airport. The tow truck at the side of the road, the headmaster's car covered with leaves hanging on the back. Na'im sits on the dust-bank, his eyes closed, his head in his hands, waiting for me in silence.

So the Morris exists. It hasn't been dumped in a wadi, or buried in the sand. They painted it to conceal its identity. Perhaps they stole it. But who? The religious Jews?

At last I make a move, climb into the truck and drive to the first gas station. I phone Erlich, getting him out of bed and telling him to send Hamid to pick up the truck from here. I tell Na'im to wait for him, giving him fifty pounds so he can eat at the diner nearby. I cross the road to the bus stop and take the local bus to Jerusalem. I've forgotten what a bus looks like from inside, it's thirty years perhaps since I've traveled by bus. I sit by the window, the torn piece of metal on my knees, convinced now that I'm going to find him.

I'm shown the way to the religious quarter and I begin slowly combing the streets, studying the parked and passing cars. No sign of the little Morris but I have a vivid feeling that I'm close to it, that it's only a matter of time. I choose a busy intersection in the heart of the religious quarter and stand there watching the passing traffic. Before long a crowd of children with long side locks gather and stand watching me. Suddenly somebody touches me, a religious Jew with a broad felt hat.

"You are waiting for somebody, sir?"

"Yes."

But I say nothing more. I decide not to ask any questions about the car, if word gets around that I'm looking for it it may vanish again.

At midday I go to a little restaurant at the corner of the street and order lunch. I'm the only nonreligious one in the place, and the proprietor discreetly lays a skullcap beside my plate. I put the cap on my head and eat, my eyes straying all the time through the window to the street outside. The proprietor realizes that I'm looking for somebody.

"You are looking for somebody, sir?"

"Yes."

"May I be of assistance?"

I want to ask him, his face inspires confidence, but I stop myself, they all belong to one sect here.

"No, thank you."

For some reason I'm absolutely sure I'm going to find him. I have no doubt. I don't know where this certainty comes from. I pay and leave. Exhausted. I've been awake since two in the morning and excitement is sapping my energy. A blazing hot day in Jerusalem and I walk around the dirty little side streets, already feeling dizzy. I start looking for garages, perhaps they've left the car to be repaired somewhere. There are several small garages there, or rather shops converted into garages. Workshops really, men repairing ovens, children's carriages, bicycles, and a car standing there in the middle, beside it a mechanic with long side curls arguing with somebody. I approach and look to see if the Morris is hidden there behind the rusty scrap metal and the junk.

"Looking for something . . . ?"

I don't answer, take a look and walk on.

My movements become heavy. I'm attracting attention with my persistent patrolling of the religious quarter, with my big tousled beard, my uncovered head and dirty overalls. I decide to leave this area, to search in the streets nearby, finding myself turning toward the Old City, jostled in the crowd. I who have forgotten what walking is, walking on and on, following in the tracks of religious Jews, I never knew there were so many of them, young and old, a black river sweeping me along the streets. Sometimes I have to rest, leaning against a wall, take a break, looking them full in the eyes, studying them closely, but they don't seem to mind, staring back at me with a proud and empty look, passing me by hurriedly.

In the end I reach the square in front of the Wall. The place has changed a lot since I last visited it. White all around. The sun burning down ferociously. I go close to the great stones. Somebody stops me and thrusts a black paper skullcap into my hand. I go and stand by the Wall itself. Just standing there. Looking at the crevices. A piece of paper falls at my feet. I pick it up and read it. A prayer for the return of a faithless husband. I pocket it. Dazed by the heat, the commotion of prayers around me. Somebody starts to wail. Somebody shouts. A crazy thought occurs to me. The religious ones killed him and stole the car.

I leave the place, the light skullcap still on my head, forcing my way against a mad stream of people. I reach the New City, find a public phone and call Asya.

"I'm in Jerusalem."

"Have you found him?"

Straight to the point, without unnecessary questions. My heart misses a beat.

"Not yet. But I think I'm close behind him."

"Do you want me to come?"

"No . . . not yet."

I return to the religious quarter, combing the streets in a wide circle. It seems there's something special in the air, the shops are closing, people walking about in linen shoes. As if there's a festival or a fast. Toward evening I find myself outside the little restaurant again. I go in. Nobody there. The tables clean, the chairs upturned on them. The proprietor appears at an inner door. He's surprised to see me.

"You haven't found him yet?"

"No."

He says nothing, embarrassed.

"Could you serve me the same meal . . . as at lunchtime?"

He hesitates, looks at his watch, then goes to the kitchen and brings me a full plate and a slice of bread. I start to eat, almost falling asleep, my head bowed over the plate. He touches me.

"Sir, you must hurry . . . before the fast . . ."

"Fast?"

"Tomorrow is the seventeenth of Tammuz . . . you must hurry . . ."

"Seventeenth of Tammuz? What's that?"

"The day they breached the wall."

"The wall?"

"The wall of the Temple."

I touch my head, the skullcap is still there, stuck to my head, I take it off, put it back, carry on eating, but my eyes close again. I've never known such a deep weariness.

"Do you wish to sleep, sir . . . ?" I hear him say.

It turns out he's willing to let me sleep at his house. I go up the stairs with him. It's six o'clock, the day is fading. The house is full of blond-haired children, he clears them out of one of the rooms and leads me in there, goes away to fetch clean sheets but I'm already lying on the bed fully clothed, on a threadbare silk blanket. He tries to rouse me, touches me, but I don't move.

I sleep in the daylight, a fitful sleep, hearing the sounds of the street, the chatter of children, seeing the light turn to a limpid darkness. Dirges rise from a nearby house of prayer.

At about midnight I wake up. A small light burning in the house. People talking, the voices of children. I go out into the corridor, my clothes crumpled, an attractive young woman sits calmly on the floor, reciting dirges in a low voice. Still murmuring the prayer, she points the way to the bathroom, I turn on the tap and drink water.

Evidently her husband is in the synagogue. I stand in the dark corridor waiting for her to finish, but she doesn't look up from the book. I take out a hundred pounds from my wallet, go into the room and lay the money on the top of the cupboard, she shakes her head as if to say, there's no need. "Give it to somebody who needs it," I whisper, and leave the house.

I resume the search, revived. Religious Jews pass through the streets, passing from one synagogue to another. I've noticed that these people are constantly, restlessly in motion. Again I comb the streets thoroughly, examining the cars. Strange, how sure I am that I'll find it, this stubborn search looks a bit like a sort of madness.

About three in the morning and all is quiet. The houses of prayer are silent, the streets deserted. I start exploring the courtyards of the houses, the inner courtyards of big yeshivas, inspecting car after car. At four o'clock I find it. Parked in a corner. The engine still warm, apparently it has only recently returned from a journey. Part of the front fender is missing. With my fingernail I scrape some paint off one of the doors. In the clear night light the original blue beneath is soon revealed. Inside is a black hat and some newspapers. I take a small screwdriver from my pocket and pry the window open, looking for clearer signs of him but finding nothing. The kilometer gauge shows thousands more than before. I find a hiding place nearby and sit down to wait.

With the first signs of dawn, once more the religious people begin to emerge from the houses. From the synagogues rises a plaintive, monotonous chant. Church bells ring softly. At five-thirty a party of young boys arrives, chattering excitedly, and stands waiting beside the Morris. A few minutes later he arrives, walking slowly, a religious Jew with long side curls, a cigarette in the corner of his mouth, and stands beside the car, running his hand over the damaged fender.

The lover transformed into something unlike a lover—

I leave my hiding place and approach him. He sees me, smiles sadly, as if to apologize. I stare at his changed face, at his black side curls. He's very fat, a big paunch flops over his belt.

"Hello . . ."

A faint reek of onions.

I touch him.

"So you didn't make it to the front."

GABRIEL

But I did get to the front. Hardly twenty-four hours had passed since you sent me away, and there I was in the middle of the desert. They pushed me out there so fast I couldn't think straight, and not because they needed me, but because they wanted to kill me. I tell you, they wanted to kill me. Just that. It had nothing to do with the war. And they really did kill me, and this is somebody else.

I thought—it's nothing more than a formality. Is there anyone to whom I'll be of any use in this war? I shall present myself at some office and say, "Well, here I am. I belong here too. Include me in the list of volunteers and don't say I didn't close ranks in time of trouble." I had no wish to be a partner in victory, much less in defeat, but if my presence was so important to them, I didn't mind standing for a day or two beside a roadblock, guarding an office, even carrying equipment. Something symbolic, for the sake of history, as they say. . . .

I didn't know somebody was going to snatch me up and send me straight into the inferno. I say it again—they simply wanted to kill me.

At first things happened casually. By the time I found the camp it was already midday. I parked the car in the parking lot and looked for the gate, but there wasn't a gate, just a broken-down fence and a lot of confusion. People running backward and forward among the barracks, army vehicles racing about, but behind the mask of feverish activity a new and unfamiliar lethargy prevailed. The system breaking down. Ask a question and nobody listens. Everywhere you're pursued by the voice of the transistor, but it gives no news. Even the old marching songs have no spirit left in them. Suddenly, folly.

It was obvious, I saw at once, they didn't know what to do with me. Aside from a passport, I had no document that could have given them something to work on. They sent me from hut to hut, they sent me to the computer building, perhaps the computer would come up with something about me. And the computer did come up with something–not me but an old Jew, about fifty-five years old, living in Dimona, perhaps a relative of mine.

Finally I wandered to a hut at the edge of the camp where all the doubtful cases were assembled, most of them citizens who had just come back from abroad, still with their colored suitcases, crouching on the withered grass. And a ginger-haired soldier, she was stunted and ugly, was collecting the passports. She took mine as well.

We waited.

Most of those waiting were Israelis who had returned. When they heard that I'd been abroad for ten years it was as if their eyes sparkled. They thought I'd returned especially for the war. I didn't mind them thinking that, if it was good for their morale to see that even after so much time the Israeli still belongs.

From time to time the ginger-haired girl would come out, call out the name of one of those waiting and lead him into the hut, and after a while he would emerge with a conscription order. At first they were dealing with us as if we were a nuisance, as if they were doing us a favor in drafting us, in taking the trouble to find units for us. As if there was nothing to be gained by all this conscription, as if the war was already over. But as the light faded around us their attitude began to change. The rhythm of recruitment intensified. Suddenly we became important. They needed everyone. The ranks were thinning out. From the transistor there rose a smell of death. Between the lines, among the slogans and the vague reports, it seemed something had gone wrong.

Gradually the crowd around me dwindled. Men who had arrived

after me were being called into the office and dispatched to their units and there was no sign of my case becoming any clearer. I was already famished. Aside from that piece of bread that you'd given me in the morning I'd eaten nothing all day. Suddenly I got tired of waiting. I walked into the office and said to the ginger-haired girl, "Well, what about me?"

She said, "You must wait, we have no information about you."

"Then perhaps I can come back tomorrow?"

"No, you must stay here."

"Where's my passport?"

"Why do you want to know?"

"At least let me go and find something to eat . . ."

"No, you must stay here . . . don't start making trouble now."

And with the first twilight a new party of officers arrived at the camp. I never knew we had officers so old. Some white-haired, some bald, fifty, sixty years old and more, wearing uniforms from different periods, medals on every chest. Some of them lame, leaning on canes. Captains, majors and lieutenant colonels, survivors from another age. Coming to the nation's rescue, to shore up the tottering, baffled command.

They dispersed among the huts. Now everything was dark. Blankets had been hung over the windows to black out the lights. And on the edge of the camp I suddenly found myself alone, even the sounds of the transistors had died away. A smell of orchards all around. I wanted to call you but the public phone that had been working all day was now dead. Darkness and silence all around. Even the whine of aircraft and helicopters had grown faint. Only a distant siren, perhaps in Jerusalem, passed over like a hushed wail.

At last the little ginger-haired girl came out, it was already nine o'clock, perhaps later. She called me and led me to a room inside the hut. Waiting for me there was a giant major, about fifty years old, completely bald, a red paratrooper's beret tucked into his epaulet, his uniform newly pressed, he seemed fresh, he even smelled of after-shave lotion.

He stood leaning on a chair, one hand in his pocket and my passport in the other hand, the clerk sat down at the table, already pale with exhaustion. For some reason she seemed confused by the appearance of the major in the office.

"You arrived in Israel four months ago?"

"Yes."

There was something urgent, intense in his voice. He clipped his words sharply.

"You should have presented yourself within two weeks. Did you know?"

"Yes . . ."

"Why didn't you?"

"I didn't expect to be staying . . . as it happens, I was delayed . . ."

"As it happens?"

He took a short step toward me and then back. Then I observed a small transistor protruding from his shirt pocket, a thin white flex connecting it to his ear. He was dealing with me and listening to the news at the same time.

"How long have you been abroad?"

"About ten years."

"And you never came back here?"

"No . . ."

"Didn't you care what was happening in this country?"

I smiled. How could I reply to such a question?

"I read newspapers . . ."

"Newspapers . . ." he echoed me scornfully and I saw that he was full of anger, a vague, menacing anger.

"What are you? A deserter?"

"No . . ." I began to mumble, thrown off balance by these savage questions.

"I just wasn't able to come back . . ." I paused for a moment and then added, I don't know why, in a low voice, "I was ill, too."

"What was wrong with you?" He spat it out harshly, with venom.

"The name of the disease would mean nothing to you."

He hesitated, looked me over carefully, glanced angrily at the clerk, who was sitting there baffled, not knowing what to write, a blank sheet of paper in front of her. He listened to the transistor plugged into his ear, some important news. His face grew dark.

"Are you all right now?"

"Yes."

"Then why didn't you present yourself in time?"

"I told you. I didn't expect to be staying."

"But you stayed."

"Yes . . ."

"Something suddenly caught your fancy?"

There was something obscure about these questions. A hidden, relentless provocation.

"No . . . I mean . . . nothing like that . . . I was just waiting for my grandmother to die."

"What?"

He took a step toward me, as if he didn't believe his ears. It was then that I noticed an ugly red scar on his neck. And the hand that was hidden in his pocket was motionless, lifeless, or maybe artificial.

"My grandmother became paralyzed . . . she lost consciousness, that is why I came home."

Then began a personal, intimate interrogation, as if he wanted to prepare a list of charges against me without knowing of what crime I stood accused, probing, trying from every angle. We stood facing each other, he like a wildcat poised to spring at me, relenting only at the last moment. The ginger-haired girl listened as if hypnotized, scribbling in pencil on an army form the mass of personal, intimate details, details of no relevance at all to the army.

But he, incredibly alert in that stifling, airless room, with old army blankets hung over the windows, shutting off the world outside, carried on the interrogation while listening to the stream of news bulletins that we did not hear, dragging out of me information that only increased his fury, mingling with the news of serious developments. For example, that I was a fourth-generation Israeli. I told him about the years in Paris, about the years before that, about my broken home, my father who disappeared, about the studies that I attempted. A year here, a course there, nothing regular, no degree completed. Then my loneliness, my confused life, were examined in depth. I even said something about the car, unintentionally. But I said nothing about you, I didn't mention you once. As if you didn't exist, weren't important. I had no intention of handing you over as well.

And he listened to it all with supreme, tense attention, dragging the facts out of me with such relish, almost madly, but a different kind of madness, his was, quite different from mine.

At last the interrogation came to an end. I felt strangely relaxed. He gathered up the papers that the ginger-haired girl had completed in round, childish handwriting. He read through them again from the beginning.

"I shall have to make a decision about you, it's a pity it's so late. We'll straighten it out after the war, when we've won. Now we must get you into uniform as soon as possible. It's because of men like you that our army is so understaffed."

I thought he was joking, but the clerk was hurriedly filling in the documents, a recruitment order and vouchers for the stores and the armory.

"Who to inform if anything happens?" she asked.

I hesitated, then gave the address of my landlady in Paris.

Now at last I shall get away from him, I thought, but he showed no sign of leaving me alone. He picked up my documents and led me to the stores. It was nearly eleven o'clock, the camp was quiet. We found the stores locked and in darkness. I thought at least we'd postpone this business till tomorrow, but he had no intention of giving up. He set off to look for the quartermaster, going from place to place, I following him. I noticed that with other people too he behaved in a high-handed manner, with a tone of authority. At last he found the quartermaster in the clubhouse, sitting in the dark watching television. He ordered him out of there. A short, swarthy soldier, apparently rather stupid. First of all he made a note of his name and number, to bring him up on charges. The quartermaster was stunned, he tried to say something in his defense but the officer silenced him harshly.

We returned to the stores. The quartermaster, resentful and nervous because of the charge he was threatened with, began tossing out the items of equipment.

"I'll show you what's urgent," hissed the major, still not mollified, making sure I was left short of nothing. Belt, straps, ammunition pouch, three knapsacks, a bivouac tent with posts and pegs, five blankets. I stood there dumbfounded, watching the pile of equipment grow on the dirty floor, things in which I had not the slightest interest. He stood to one side, grave, stiff as a post, the weak lamplight shining on his bald scalp.

Suddenly I felt desperate.

"I don't need five blankets . . . two are enough for me. It's summer now . . . autumn. It isn't cold . . ."

"And what will you do in winter?"

"In winter?" I laughed. "What has winter to do with it? In the winter I shall be far from here."

"That's what you think," he whispered scornfully, without even looking at me, contemptuous, as if the whole time he was collecting evidence against me.

Meanwhile the quartermaster, silent and scowling, was laying out eating utensils, greasy mess tins, a bayonet.

"A bayonet? What's this bayonet for?" I was laughing almost hysterically. "This is a war of missiles and you're giving me a bayonet."

He didn't answer. He stooped and picked up the bayonet, and gripping it between his thighs he drew it from the scabbard, ran his finger lightly over the blade, took off some black oil, sniffed it with an expression of disgust, then wiped the blade on one of the blankets and without a word put the bayonet back in its scabbard and tossed it onto the pile of equipment.

I signed a long list, running into two or three columns. I had forgotten my army number and I had to look again at the draft form to be reminded of it. But he already knew it by heart and corrected me disdainfully.

Finally I wrapped everything up in one giant bundle. The quartermaster helped me to fold the ends of the blankets while the officer stood over us giving advice. Then the quartermaster loaded the bundle onto my back and we went out into the darkness. It was nearly midnight. I staggered along under the crushing load while he strode in front, bald, thin and erect, the dead hand in his pocket, a small map case slung on his shoulder, the little transistor beaming its broadcasts direct to his ear, dragging behind him his very own soldier, his personal man.

He led me to the armory. I was already on the verge of collapse, hunger turning to nausea, to the need to vomit up something I hadn't eaten. A sour, bitter taste in my mouth. The load grew heavier on my back. Suddenly I realized how close I was to tears, real tears. At the door of the armory I collapsed, my equipment scattering.

The armory was open, lit up. Men were standing in line, most of them officers drawing revolvers and submachine guns. He by-passed the long line and went straight in, glancing at the rows of rifles and machine guns as if they were his personal property.

Finally he called me to sign for a bazooka and two containers of bombs.

"I've never touched a weapon like this," I whispered, afraid of annoying him.

"I know," he replied with sudden warmth, smiling to himself, amused at the ingenious idea of saddling me with a bazooka.

Now I was so laden with equipment I couldn't move. But he had no intention of taking me anywhere.

"Hurry up and sort out your belt and knapsacks. I'm going to find transport to take us down to the front."

And suddenly, with despair, I understood, in the dark it came to me in a flash what he intended, this aging officer who still reeked of after-shave lotion.

"You've decided to kill me," I whispered.

He smiled.

"You haven't heard a single shot and you're already thinking about death."

But stubbornly, angrily, I repeated what I'd said:

"You want to kill me."

But he was no longer smiling. Dryly he said, "Sort out your equipment."

But I didn't move. Something was broken inside me. A spirit of rebellion seized me.

"For half a day I've eaten nothing. If I don't get some food I shall collapse. I'm already seeing you double."

He said nothing, not batting an eyelid. Still that arrogant, empty look in his eyes. Then he put his hand into the map case, took out two hard-boiled eggs and gave them to me.

At one o'clock in the morning I was already in uniform, shod in heavy boots and lying half asleep under the open sky, in the growing chill of the night, my head heavy on the big knapsack that was stuffed with blankets and my old clothes, my feet propped up on the bazooka and the bombs. White egg shells scattered around me. The belt harness, which was spattered with bloodstains, I'd never have managed to put it all on by myself, without the help of the ginger-haired girl who had taken pity on me. She too was being harassed and hounded by the officer, who gave her endless instructions, sending her running from one end of the camp to the other. Now I saw his silhouette flitting about like something from a dream. He was searching in vain for transport to take us south, to the desert.

At two o'clock, when he'd given up hope of getting there, he remembered my car and decided to commandeer it.

I leaped to my feet, suddenly alert.

"But the car isn't mine."

"So why should you care?"

And he sent the clerk away to fetch new forms. I watched as he took the documents and without a moment's hesitation signed each one, easily and with complete self-assurance. He gave me a receipt and took the keys.

"After the war, if you return, you can reclaim what's left of it."

And he went to the parking lot to fetch it. Old though it was, he took an immediate liking to it. He treated it as if it was his own, lifting the hood, checking the oil and water, kicking the tires. He was as awake as the devil. He sent the clerk, who was already collapsing from exhaustion, to find paint and a brush to dim the headlights, and she, efficient as always, brought a large tin of black paint. He began enthusiastically smearing the lights, front and back, then adjusted the driver's seat, moving it back from the wheel to make room for his long legs. Then he watched as I loaded my equipment into the back. We set off.

He was driving with one hand, but with absolute control. I'd never seen such an enthusiastic driver. It was as if he owned the car, the road and all the transports he was overtaking right and left, maneuvering adroitly in the dark, in the weak light that filtered from the headlights, accelerating among the long convoys of tank transports and ammunition trucks. The Morris dared much in his hands. And I sat beside him, exhausted, as if I'd already been at war for days, looking at the melonlike head, my own personal major, all the time absorbing his own personal news bulletins, his face contorting from time to time.

"But what's happening there?"

"They're fighting," he replied laconically.

"But how's it going?"

"It's hard, very hard."

"But what's happening exactly?"

"You'll see for yourself soon enough." He was trying to shake me off.

"Have they fixed us?"

"Now you're starting to squeal as well. Go to sleep." And he broke off contact.

I was suddenly alone, on the road to war, resting my head on the windowpane, looking out at the dry, sun-scorched fields, the sweat already dry on my face, breathing in the cool autumn air, gradually falling asleep, dreaming dreams to the hum of the engine, dreams that led me to Paris, home, walking late at night in the bustling streets beside the Seine, little alleyways, brightly lit cafes, chestnut stalls. Going down to the Odéon station. The authentic smell of the Métro, a sweet tang of electricity mingling with the stench of the crowds that have passed through these tunnels during the day. I walk about on the empty platform in the bright neon light, hearing the roar of trains from distant stations, drawing nearer, dying away. The train arrives. Immediately I leap into a red first-class compartment, as if somebody has pushed me there. And at once, among the few passengers, I recognize my grandmother, sitting in the corner, on her knees a basket of crisp, fresh-baked croissants. She eats them delicately, picking up the crumbs that fall on her printed dress, her old best dress. I'm filled with joy, the joy of meeting. So she's regained consciousness at last. I go and sit beside her. I know she won't recognize me immediately, and quietly, speaking softly so as not to alarm her, I say with a smile, "Hello, Grandma." She stops eating, turns to face me, smiling absently. And I realize, suddenly I know it instinctively, she's already divided the inheritance, she's run away, traveling incognito in Paris. "Hello, Grandma," I repeat and she sits there, looking confused, mumbling, "Pardon?" as if she doesn't understand Hebrew. I decide to speak in French, but suddenly I've forgotten the language, even the simplest words. I feel a longing to take one of the golden croissants. I say again, almost in despair, "Hello, Grandma, don't you remember me? I'm Gabriel." She stops eating, a little alarmed, it's obvious she doesn't understand a single word. The language is quite strange to her. The train slows, approaching a station, I look at the signs. The Odéon again. The station that we started from.

And she stands up quickly, wrapping up the croissants in the basket. The doors open automatically, she steps out onto the platform, trying to slip away from me. But there are only a few people around us, and I walk close behind her, doggedly, patiently waiting for my memory of French to return. Opening the glass doors in front of her, climbing the stairs, pushing aside for her the low iron turnstiles. She's smiling to herself, a smile of tolerant old age, constantly mumbling, "Merci, merci." She doesn't understand what this young stranger wants of her. We come out into the street. Already it's first light. Paris at dawn, moist, misty. It's as if we've been traveling on the Métro all night.

And there, parked at the roadside, is the blue Morris, just as it is, the headlights dimmed, only the Israeli license plate has changed to French. Grandma fumbles in her bag for the keys. And I stand beside her, still waiting for my French to return, searching for some first words of communication. I'm desperately hungry, real spittle at the corners of my mouth. She opens the car door, puts the basket of croissants down beside her, sits at the wheel. It's obvious she's impatient to break off contact. She's smiling now like a young girl, enjoying the attention. She says "Merci" again and starts the engine. I catch hold of the car as it moves away, putting my head inside, leaning on the windowpane, saying, "But just a moment . . . wait a moment . . ." As if detached, my head starts to move with the car.

My head against the windowpane, leaning out. In the sky the first light of day. No longer were there fields around us but sand dunes, palm trees and white Arab houses. We were standing still, the engine switched off, bogged down in a giant multiple convoy. Trucks, armored troop carriers, staff cars and civilian vehicles. The noise was deafening. The officer stood outside, wiping the dew from the front windshield. He didn't seem tired from the long drive. There was only a hint of red in his eyes. I wanted to get up and out of the car but something held me back. I found that in my sleep he'd tied me to my seat with the seat belt. He came and released me.

"You really go wild in your sleep . . . falling against the wheel all the time."

I stepped outside, my clothes crumpled. I stood beside him, shivering in the cold. My stomach was turning over, I was so hungry. The third day of the war and I had no idea what was going on. More than ten hours since I'd last heard a news bulletin. I looked at the earplug still in his ear.

How mean of him, keeping the news from me as well.

"What are they saying now?"

"Nothing. Now it's music."

"Where are we?"

"Near Rafah."

"What's going on? What's new?"

"Nothing."

"What's going to happen?"

"We're going to smash them."

Short, self-assured answers. That arrogant look in his eyes, glancing over the convoy that stretched from horizon to horizon as if it was he who was leading it. Now that I was already his prisoner, I wanted to know at least a little about him, to try breaking through this blown-up shell.

"Excuse me," I said with a smile, "I still have no idea what your name is . . ."

He looked at me angrily.

"Why do you want to know?"

"Just curious . . ."

"Call me Shahar."

"Shahar . . . what's your job, Shahar? . . . I mean in civilian life . . ."

He was annoyed.

"Why do you want to know?"

"Just . . . just curious . . ."

"I work in education."

I was so surprised I nearly fell over.

"Education? What kind of education?"

"Special education. In a home for juvenile delinquents."

"Really? An interesting profession."

But he showed no inclination to prolong the conversation. And standing there beside me, as I was still fumbling for words, with one hand he unfastened his trouser buttons, took out his big erect dick and pissed straight ahead of him on the dry ground, standing there stiffly, legs wide apart. Drops fell on my boots.

On the truck in front of us, the soldiers were watching him. He'd attracted their attention too. They laughed and shouted jokes. He, quite unabashed, his dick still hanging out, rose to the challenge, and raised his hand like a priest blessing the congregation.

In the big canteen at Rafah I fainted, quite unexpectedly, without warning. It just happened, as I stood there in the line of soldiers by the counter, waiting my turn to get at the trays of sandwiches and the little containers of chocolate milk, surrounded by the smell of food and the racket of transistors. First I dropped the bazooka, then myself. It seems he was afraid they'd take me from him, he slipped away from the group of officers that he'd been talking to, dragged me outside to a water tap, laid my head in a pool of mud and poured a stream of water over my face. I heard him talking to the soldiers gathered around us. "It's fear," he said, and tried to move them aside.

But it was hunger. "I'm so hungry," I croaked as I woke up, sitting on the ground, pale, with mud in my hair. "Since last night I've been trying to tell you."

Again he took two hard-boiled eggs out of his map case and gave them to me.

And so at midday he brought me to the heart of the Sinai. I didn't believe we'd make it. The little Morris ran beautifully. You did a fine job, Adam, she was starting up at the first touch. The battered old lady obeyed him, he hypnotized her too, and she made a hundred kilometers per hour.

There were military police roadblocks on the way, trying to stop all kinds of adventurers from entering the war zone. But he outwitted them all, pretending to ignore them, pressing on and passing them by. He wasn't stopped once. And if they came after us, he'd stop the car some distance farther on, leap out of the little Morris like a long thin flame and stand waiting, wearing his red paratrooper's beret, on his chest medals of previous wars. When the military police caught up with us, panting and cursing, he'd say calmly:

"Yes? What's your problem?"

And they'd retreat.

But at Refidim we had to stop. Nobody was allowed to pass beyond that point. From far away came the echoes of explosions. The sounds were muffled as if they came from deep down inside the earth. Shrieking aircraft wheeled in the sky. We were directed to a wide-open space full of civilian cars, like the parking lot of a concert hall or a football stadium. Men were flocking to the war as if to some great spectacle. He told me to unload the equipment and I put on my harness, donned my helmet, picked up the bazooka and started to follow him, searching for a unit that would accept me.

We marched through a cloud of dust, all around us half-tracks and lumbering tanks. And the people in the sand, a nation sinking in the desert. Here it was born, here it shall perish.

And yet in spite of all the noise and confusion we were attracting attention. The one-handed major, tanned crimson by the sun, sweat gleaming on his bald scalp, leading me, his own personal soldier, as if I were a whole squad, marching behind laden with equipment, bound to him with an invisible rope. Men would pause for a moment to look at us.

Eventually he stopped beside a column of half-tracks parked at the roadside, stretching away to the horizon. He asked for the commander and they pointed to a short, lean youth making coffee on a camp stove.

"When are you moving?"

"Soon."

"Are you short of a bazooka gunner?"

He was astonished. "A bazooka gunner? I don't think so . . ."

But the officer was insistent.

"You mean your outfit is complete?"

"What do you mean?" The youth was utterly confused.

"Well then, take him into your unit." He pointed at me.

"But . . . who is he?"

"No buts. This is an order," he snapped, and signaled to me to climb aboard the nearest half-track.

And I began to strip off my equipment and pass it to the young soldiers, who tossed it up inside the vehicle, they were amused by the vast load that I'd dragged along with me. Then they held out their hands and pulled me up onto the steel car, which was all blistering hot from standing in the sun. Meanwhile the major was making a note of the unit commander's name and the number of the unit. He even took the number of the half-track, making sure that I'd be taken into battle, that all avenues of escape had been blocked. Finally he made the commander sign for me as if he was taking delivery of a load of supplies.

"Make sure he fights properly," he shouted. "He's been out of the country ten years . . . he tried to run away."

They looked at me.

"You must be crazy," somebody whispered. "What a time to come back!"

But I didn't answer, just whispered, "Have you got a piece of bread or something like that?" and somebody passed me a big slice of yeast cake, it was sweet and delicious and I bit into it at once, gobbling it up with great relish. Tears rose to my eyes. Suddenly I felt at ease. Perhaps it was because of that sweet home-baked cake. Perhaps it was because at last I'd gotten away from him. And so, perched on the half-track, surrounded by soldiers, leaning against the hot fuselage and swallowing cake, I looked down at the bald officer, who was still, standing there cockily, grilling the young commander about the plans for the offensive. The latter was quite baffled, didn't know how to answer. In the end the major sent him off, disappointed. For a while he hesitated, as if he found it hard to be parted from me, he stood there alone, looking about him with his empty, arrogant glance. Suddenly I was struck by the pathetic nature of his madness and I smiled down at him from my perch on the high vehicle, out of his clutches now.

Suddenly, decisively, he turned to go. I called out, "Hey, Shahar, good-by." He turned around. Even as he looked at me for the last time, there was hatred in his eyes, he raised his hand with a weary gesture, a sort of half salute, murmuring, "Yes, good-by . . . good-by . . ." and he set off toward the headquarters along the crumbling path, the path ground to dust by the endless stream of tanks. For a while I watched him, striding along with slow, measured, provocative gait, the tanks avoiding him carefully, right and left.

And now I was surrounded by young, boyish faces, a close-knit band of regular soldiers. They looked excited, eager to go into battle. Laughing at their private jokes, talking about people that I didn't know. The young commander called me over to his jeep, he asked me to explain quietly who I was and how I'd come to be in the hands of the major. So in the middle of the desert, amid the crackling of radio sets and the roar of engines, once again I told the whole story, adding some superfluous details, getting entangled in a strange confession, about my grandmother, about the legacy. A man standing before a silent youth, telling the story of his life. I thought perhaps he'd want to get rid of me, send me away. I even told him that I had no idea how to use a bazooka and that war in general wasn't exactly for me. But I could see he had no intention of getting rid of me. They'd foisted me on him, so he'd find a use for me. He heard me out, not saying a word, just smiling faintly from time to time. Then he called to one of the men from the platoon, a soldier with glasses who looked like an intellectual, and told him to give me a quick lesson on the use of the bazooka.

The soldier made me lie on the ground, put the bazooka in my hands and started lecturing me on sights, trajectories, varieties of bombs, closed electrical circuits. And I was nodding my head but only half listening. Only one thing stuck in my head, the backlash that recoils on the gunner. The bespectacled soldier warned me repeatedly about the dangers of the backlash, apparently he himself had once been burned by it. And in the middle of this strange private lesson they called us to eat. They brought out a stack of tinned foods. I was the only one with an appetite. They were a bit astonished at my ravenous hunger. They opened tin after tin, tasting it and passing it over to me, watching in amusement as, spoon in hand, I polished off one after another, in any order, tins of beans, grapefruit salad, meat, halva, sardines, and pickled cucumber for dessert. I gobbled up everything. And among the empty tin cans the radio crackled constantly, and at last I heard the news that had been kept from me the previous day. Hard news, dark news, dressed up in new words—defensive strategy, battle of attrition, holding operation, regrouping of forces. Jargon designed to soften the truth, the burning reality into which I was now so deeply sunk.

And suddenly alone, very much alone. An empty space in my heart. Imagine me in the middle of all this confusion. Sitting among the soldiers, beside the chain of the half-track, hiding in a scrap of sweltering shade, in the sickening stench of burnt gasoline. My clothes so filthy you'd think I'd gone through two wars already, seeing all the preparations being made for my death. Troops milling around us endlessly, encircling us. Tanks, half-tracks, jeeps and artillery, the crackle of radio sets, the shouts of soldiers hailing their friends. I begin to understand, I won't leave this place alive. Shut in from every side. A nation ensnaring itself. Suddenly I wanted to write you a postcard, but already urgent orders were arriving, we must prepare to move immediately.

We moved on a kilometer or two, advancing in a broad formation, then they halted us. We waited there, trussed in our belts, helmets on our heads, drivers at the wheel, for four long hours, watching the dim, threatening horizon where the battle was noiselessly in progress. Watching the plumes of dust rising in the distance, the smoke of distant fires, signs that my companions interpreted eagerly. Slowly the desert turned red about us and suddenly, on the dusty skyline, the ball of the sun caught fire, like a flare thrown up from the burning canal, a weapon of war, a part of the battle. And as evening came the sun began to disintegrate, as if it too had been caught in the cross fire, and our faces, our vehicles, the weapons in our hands were painted purple.

And in that same place, still deployed in advance formation, we waited two days, as if frozen where we stood. And personal, linear time, the time that we knew, was blown to bits. And a different, collective time was smeared over us like sticky dough. Eating and sleeping, listening to the radio and pissing, cleaning our weapons and hearing a lecture from an eccentric instructor who came to us with a little tape recorder and played us rock music. Playing backgammon, huddling together in tight circles, leaping onto the half-track at false alarms, watching the aircraft going out and returning. And somewhere else, beyond us, there were sunrises and sunsets, twilight and darkness, burning noons and cool mornings. They cut us off from the world so they could kill us more easily, and I, a stranger twice over, or, as they called me, the runaway who returned, I wandered about among the young men, hearing their foolish jokes, their childish, adolescent fantasies. And they, not knowing how to deal with me, still impressed by my ravenous hunger of the first day, would offer me slices of cake, biscuits and chocolate, which I took absent-mindedly, munching moodily among the armored half-tracks. Once, in the middle of the night, I thought of trying to escape. I took some toilet paper and started walking toward a distant hill that I thought was deserted. To my surprise I found troops dug in there as well. The whole desert was alive with men.

At last we began to move, slowly, like struggling out of quicksand. Already exhausted, advancing a few hundred meters and stopping, stopping and advancing. Moving south, then north, then east, then turning back to the line of advance. As if some moon-struck general were controlling us from far away. Suddenly, without warning, the first shells fell among us and somebody was killed. And so the battle began for us. Lying flat on the ground, scratching trenches in the sand, then up again onto the transports and moving on. Sometimes opening fire with all weapons at sand-colored targets. They too were wandering like sleepwalkers on the dusty horizon. I didn't shoot. The bazooka was slung over my shoulder all the time but the bombs were tucked away under one of the seats. I sat there huddled, the helmet over my face, turning myself into something inert, an object without will, a lifeless creature, only at intervals looking out at the nearby scene, the endless, never-changing desert. Our unit was changing all the time, disbanding and regrouping. The boy-commander had been killed, another, an older officer, had taken over. The half-track broke down, they put us aboard another. Changes all the time, handing us over to somebody new, taking us away from him. Sometimes under bombardment, short or prolonged, hiding our heads in the sand. But advancing, that much was clear. Men trying to whip up enthusiasm. Victory, the breakthrough, at last. But a hard, bitter victory. One evening we arrived at an important field headquarters. We were set to guard a staff officer who was sitting among a dozen radio sets, surrounded by wires and receivers. A tired man, his eyes narrowed by long days without sleep, sitting on the ground, taking up receiver after receiver with endless patience and fearful slowness, in a sleepy voice, sending out orders to faraway units. All night we sat around him. I tried to follow his conversations, to understand the course of the battle, but it seemed that matters were growing always more complicated. In the morning twilight, in a brief lull, I plucked up my courage and approached him, asking when he thought the war would be over. He looked at me with a fatherly smile and in that same sleepy voice, very slowly, he began to speak of a long war, a matter of months, perhaps even of years. Then he picked up a receiver and in a weary voice gave the order for an assault.

Now the young men around me were beginning to look like me. Aging prematurely. Hair white with dust, beards unkempt, faces wrinkled, eyes sunken through lack of sleep. Here and there, bandages around filthy heads. Already we could see in the distance the sparkling waters of the canal. They ordered us down from the transports and set us digging deep into the ground, each man his own grave.

And then I heard the singing. Chanting, prayer, live voices, not from the transistor. It wasn't yet light, just the first flutterings of dawn. Shivering with cold, wrapped in our blankets, wet with dew, we woke up to find three men dressed in black with side curls and beards, leaping and dancing, singing and clapping hands, like some well-trained dance troupe. They came closer, touching us with warm, thin hands, rousing us from our sleep. They came to cheer us up, to restore our faith, sent by their yeshiva to circulate among the troops, to give out prayer books, to bind *tefillin* on the young men.

Already some of our men had joined them, drowsy, bedraggled soldiers, laughing nervously, rolling up their sleeves and repeating the words of the prayer. They were blessing us. "A great victory," they said. "Another great miracle, by the grace of God." But it seemed they weren't sure, their voices lacked conviction. This time we'd disappointed them a little.

The morning came and quickly the air grew warm. Men started to prepare breakfast, smoke rose from campfires. Transistors broadcast the morning news. And they, having finished their mission of awakening, folded up their equipment, the *tefillin* and the rest, sat down on a hillock, took out little cardboard boxes from their jeep and laid out their morning snack. We invited them to take breakfast with us, but they refused politely, bowing their heads, smiling to themselves. They had their own food. They were even afraid of touching our water bottles for fear of contamination. I went closer to them. From among their sacred objects, among the prayer books and tassels, they took out bread, hard-boiled eggs, tomatoes and giant cucumbers. Sprinkling them with salt and eating them complete with the skin. From a big red thermos they were drinking some yellowish liquid, apparently cold tea that they'd brought with them from Israel. I stood and watched them, more and more fascinated. I'd forgotten that Jews like this still existed. The black hats, the beards and the side curls. They took off their jackets and sat in their white shirts, patches of color not of this world. Two were adults, about forty years old, and between them sat a pretty youth with a sparse beard and very long side curls. He seemed a little shy and ill at ease in the middle of all the bustle, picking with a pale hand at his breakfast, which was laid out on an old religious newspaper.

I didn't move away from them. They could feel me watching them. They smiled at me kindly. I took the tassel they offered me and put it in my pocket, still standing close beside them. They were eating, swaying backward and forward and chattering in Yiddish. I didn't understand a single word but I could tell they were talking about politics. And I, a dirty, unkempt soldier, with a ten day growth of beard, staring at them hard. I was beginning to make them uneasy.

Suddenly I said, "May I have a tomato?" They were astonished, they thought I'd gone mad. But the eldest recovered his composure and handed me a tomato. I sprinkled salt on it, sat down beside them and began asking questions. Where had they come from? What were they doing? How did they live? Where were they going from here? And they replied, the two older men, swaying all the while as if their answers too were a kind of prayer. Suddenly a thought struck me. These men are so free. They don't really belong to us. They come and go at will. They have no obligations. Moving around like black beetles among the soldiers in the desert. Metaphysical creatures. I couldn't leave them alone.

But the religious-affairs sergeant, who was acting as a sort of impresario for them, came to move them on. A bombardment was expected soon, they'd better leave. Immediately they stood up, buried the remains of their food, tied up their boxes with string and at fantastic speed mumbled the grace after meals, then they climbed into their jeep and disappeared from sight.

And on one of the rocks I found a black jacket that one of them, apparently the youngest, had left behind. I picked it up. It was made of good thick material. The label was of a tailor in Geulah Street, Jerusalem, guaranteed pure wool. It gave off a faint smell of sweat, but a sweat different from that of the men around me, a sweet smell of incense or tobacco, a smell of old books. For a moment I thought of throwing it back, then suddenly, without thinking, I put it on. It fit. "Does it suit me?" I asked a soldier who was passing. He stopped and stared, I could see he didn't recognize me. Then he grinned and started to run.

And now there fell around us a bombardment unlike anything that we'd known before. We crouched on the ground, curled up like embryos, desperately scratching at the dry earth with our fingernails. The shells groped for us blindly, pounding angrily and accurately a crossroads only a hundred meters from us. Such a tiny miscalculation. For hours on end we lay in the sand, shells exploding all around us, eyes closed, dust in our mouths, beside us a burning half-track.

Toward evening, silence returned as if nothing had happened. Deep silence. They moved us forward five kilometers, to the foot of a hill, and once again we spread out our blankets to sleep.

And at first light, as if time were repeating itself, again we woke up to the sound of chanting and prayer and rhythmic hand clapping. The three of them had returned, as if they'd sprung from the ground, and they were trying to rouse us.

"You were here before! You were already here! You gave us prayer books!" They were silenced by the hostile reception. The three of them were frightened, froze where they stood and then retreated in confusion, mumbling among themselves in Yiddish. But one soldier leaped from his blankets and ran toward them, rolling up the sleeve of his left arm with an expression of pain, as if expecting an injection. Encouraged, the three men began binding *tefillin* on his arm, opening the prayer book in front of him, showing him what to read, tending him as if he were sick. Leading him a few steps forward, a few steps back, making him sway in unison with them, turning him toward the east, to the rising sun. We lay in our sleeping bags and watched them. From a distance it looked like they were praying to the sun.

They finished, and once again they sat down to eat, as on the previous day, groping in their cardboard boxes and again bringing out eggs, cucumbers, peppers and tomatoes, as if they'd picked them in the desert. But this time they were no longer the center of attention. The men had lost interest in them, still shaken by the bombardment of yesterday. Slowly I approached them, glanced in the open boxes. These no longer contained sacred objects, they'd given everything away yesterday. The boxes were full of booty they'd picked up, army belts, ammunition pouches, colored pictures of Sadat, souvenirs for home.

And again, I was amazed at their freedom—

"How are you? Are you well?" I smiled at them, trying to start a conversation.

"The Lord be praised each day," they replied. I could see they didn't recognize me.

"Where are you going from here?"

"Home, with God's help. To tell of the miracles and wonders."

"What miracles? Don't you realize what's going on here?"

They were unmoved.

"By God's grace, everything is a miracle."

"Are you married?"

They smiled, surprised at the question.

"Praise the Lord."

"Praise the Lord yes or no?"

"Praise the Lord . . . of course . . ."

Suddenly they recognized me.

"Have we not spoken with you before, sir?"

"Yes. Yesterday morning. Before the bombardment."

"And how are you, sir?"

"So-so . . ."

I sat down beside them, in my hand the small knapsack in which the young man's jacket was hidden. They shifted away slightly.

"Have you lost your jacket?" I asked the young man, who hadn't spoken yet. He was wearing an Egyptian combat smock that he'd picked up somewhere.

"Yes," he replied, with a thin, charming smile. "Perhaps you have found it?"

"No . . ."

"It doesn't matter, doesn't matter, you are forgiven," the older man reassured him.

And all the while they were eating with such ease, such assurance. I felt a growing attraction to them, it was painful.

The young man with the pretty face was daintily chewing his bread, ignoring me, picking up the crumbs with his thin delicate fingers, still reading that old religious newspaper spread out in front of him. They no longer had tea. They were passing a bottle from hand to hand, manna perhaps, or dew that they'd collected on their way. It was obvious they were content with little. Again I felt an urge to take something from them, a vegetable or a piece of bread. But in the end, without asking permission, I picked up the young man's hat, which was lying in the sand, and put it on my head. Then, to a rhythm of my own, I started swaying. They smiled, very embarrassed. Their faces went red. I could see they were a little scared of us, a little wary.

"Don't you find it hot in these hats?"

"Praise the Lord."

"Does it suit me?" I asked childishly.

"With God's help . . . with God's help." They forced themselves to smile, bewildered, uncomprehending.

"Maybe we should exchange hats," I said to the young man. "That way I shall remember you."

He was utterly dumfounded. Already he'd lost his jacket. Now somebody wanted to take his hat as well. But the eldest of the group gave me an intelligent, perceptive look, as if he'd grasped my intention even before I'd made up my own mind.

"By all means take it, sir . . . it will bring you good fortune . . . you shall return safely to your wife and children . . ."

"But I'm not married. I'm a lover." Brazenly I challenged them. "I'm a lover of other men's wives."

The man of God didn't lose his composure, but looked at me as if seeing me now for the first time.

"Then may you find your counterpart . . . return home safely."

On the horizon plumes of dust were rising. A moment later, as if unconnected with them, came the boom of artillery. The start of the working day. Men began running. Again the shells came groping for me, trying to destroy me. The religious-affairs sergeant came running to move his party, to get them away from here. The camp was struck in haste, covered over with earth. At the side stood a party of soldiers starting to dig in. I hadn't even had time to say good-by.

Now I knew what I must do. I must escape. I could do it. I

thought of nothing else all that day, crouched in a corner inside the half-track, keeping quiet, avoiding all unnecessary contact with the other men, trying to efface myself. It was a day of blazing heat, a thick dust cloud shut out the sky. The sun was hidden. Visibility, hopeless. All day the radio sets crackled as units tried desperately to locate one another. And covering everything, the yellow, menacing dust. We were advancing on the canal. They'd broken through to the other side and we were to join forces with the troops who were crossing the strip of water in a continuous column. Toward evening we dipped our hands in the bomb-racked waters. New officers arrived and told us what was planned for tomorrow.

But I was already well advanced in plans of my own. Clearly this was a war without end. What could I do on the west bank of the canal? Even on the east bank I'd found nothing useful to do.

So, stealthily, I made my preparations. I packed into a small knapsack the sacred objects that I'd collected over the last two days. Hat, black jacket, tassel. I prepared meat and cheese sandwiches, filled two water bottles. And in the night, in the last watch, when the time came for me to go on sentry duty, I took my equipment, went to the edge of the camp and slipped away behind a hill. I dug a shallow pit and buried the bazooka. I stripped off my army clothes, tore them to shreds with the bayonet and scattered the shreds in the darkness. I took from the knapsack my white civilian shirt and my black woolen trousers, put on the tassels and the stolen jacket, put the hat down beside me. I had a fortnight's growth of beard, and from my tousled hair, which had grown wild, I could make rudimentary side curls.

So I sat in a cleft of the rock, not far from the canal, shivering with cold, watching the dim skies, which were lit up from time to time by explosions, waiting for the dawn, hearing them rouse the men of my unit, moving them on. I listened hard to hear if they were searching for me, if they were calling my name. But I heard nothing, only the hum of engines starting up. Nobody had noticed my absence.

For a moment I was astonished at being obliterated—

But I didn't move from my hiding place. I sat and waited for the first signs of light, greedily finishing off the sandwiches that I'd brought with me for the next day. At last the light came, creeping around me like a mist. A rainy dawn, almost European. I hid the last remnant of my army life, the knapsack itself, shook the dust and sand from my clothes, trying to straighten them, to put some shape into them. Then I put the hat on my head and started walking out of history. Heading east.

Soon I found myself on a road, and before long there was the sound of a vehicle approaching from behind, a bullet-ridden water carrier, water still streaming from the holes. I was still hesitating, wondering whether to flag it down, when the vehicle stopped beside me. I climbed in. The driver, a thin Yemenite, showed no surprise at the figure clad in black who sat down beside him, as if the whole desert were full of religious Jews, springing out from among the hills, just like that.

Oddly enough he didn't speak to me, not a single word. Perhaps he was running away too, perhaps he'd just now come under fire and was returning the way he came. I don't think he even noticed what kind of person he'd picked up. The roadblocks gave us no problems. The military police didn't even glance at us. They were busy with the transport coming from the opposite direction, with men trying to get through to the fighting zone, to the western shore of the canal.

In Refidim I got out, didn't even have time to thank the driver. The confusion there was even greater than before. Men running, vehicles traveling in all directions. And I, so light I was nearly floating, already feeling the effects of freedom, began wandering about the base, quietly looking for the way north. But I noticed that people were turning their heads to stare at me. I was attracting attention, even in the crowd. Perhaps there was something unreligious in my bearing, or in the way I wore the hat. I grew more and more apprehensive, walking at the side of the road, shrinking, trying to keep out of sight among the storehouses and tank shelters. And suddenly, on one of the paths, there, straight in front of me, like in a nightmare, was the tall, bald-headed officer, erect as ever, thin as ever, still with that arrogant and empty look in his eyes. I nearly collapsed in front of him. But he passed by without recognizing me, continuing on his way with that same slow, provocative walk.

So I must have really changed, a change that I myself had not yet grasped. I stood hiding in the shadow of a wall, trembling with shock, watching him as he crossed to one of the shelters. Something blue caught my eye. Grandma's car. I'd almost forgotten it.

Suddenly I resolved to liberate the car as well. Why not? I'd wait till it was dark and take the car with me. I made a mental note of my surroundings, so I could find the place again, and went to look for a synagogue in which to hide until evening.

The synagogue was deserted and dirty. It looked as if a squad of soldiers had been billeted there a few days before. Ammunition pouches were scattered on the floor. The ark was locked but there were a few prayer books lying on the shelves and in a little cupboard I found a bottle of wine for Kiddush.

And there I sat all day, alone, sipping the warm, sweet wine, glancing through a prayer book to familiarize myself with the first rudiments of prayer. My brain grew hazy, but I didn't dare go to sleep, somebody might come in and surprise me. Toward midnight I left the synagogue, carrying a nylon sack full of prayer books. If anyone challenged me I could say I'd been sent to distribute prayer books to the troops. The base was quieter now, people moving about with less animation. I even came upon a soldier and a girl-soldier embracing. As if there were no such thing as a war.

The Morris was parked between two battered tanks. It was covered in dust. The doors were locked, but I remembered that one of the windows had a defective catch. And so I succeeded in getting inside. My hands trembled as I held the wheel, resting my head on it. It was as if an eternity had passed since I'd been parted from the car, not just a few days of war.

I'd already prepared a piece of silver paper taken from an old cigarette packet, and just as in the past, when I was taking the car at night without grandmother knowing, I bent down beneath the wheel and found the point of contact of the ignition wires. And the battery, the new battery that you'd fitted for me just a few weeks before, Adam, it responded at once to the light touch and set the engine in motion.

And so I began to move—north, east, God knows. I had no sense of direction, I was just looking for signposts. I'd stop and ask which was the way back to Israel.

"Which Israel?" the military police would reply with a laugh.

"Doesn't matter, doesn't matter, just get me out of the desert."

The bulk of the transport was moving in the opposite direction. Tanks, artillery, giant ammunition trucks. A khaki river roaring along with dimmed lights. And I in the little car running against the tide, moving aside to the edge of the road and even so upsetting the smooth progress of the convoy. I heard the muffled curses—"Holy bastard, chooses this time to tour the Sinai"—but I didn't respond, just smiled pleasantly, weaving in and out of the traffic, never pausing but pressing on all the time, as if possessed, speeding along the battered roads, away from the desert.

In the morning I reached the big canteen at Rafah, exhausted by the long drive but drunk with freedom. I went in to buy food, and went cavorting from counter to counter, drinking soup, eating sausages, munching chocolate and candies. Then among the crowd I saw a group of religious Jews, men dressed in black like myself, watching me curiously, astonished to see me eating so wildly, so anarchically, prancing from meat counter to dairy counter and back again. I decided it was time to leave. But at the door one of the religious Jews stopped me, clutched my shoulder.

"Wait a moment, we are forming a *minyan* for the morning prayer . . ."

"I prayed yesterday . . ." I broke away from his grasp and ran to the Morris, started the engine and fled, leaving them to their astonishment.

A few kilometers farther on, the desert ended abruptly, there were palm trees at the roadside, white houses, sand dunes ringed by little orchards. Israel. A wonderful smell of the sea. I slowed down, stopped. So–I'd escaped. Now I felt the full weight of my weariness, I felt dizzy, could hardly keep my eyes open. I left the car, breathed in the morning air. The smell of the sea enticed me. But where was the sea? Suddenly I wanted the sea, I needed to touch it. I waved down the speeding car of a tall senior officer who drew up beside me. "Where is the sea?" I asked. He was incensed at the question. But he showed me the way.

And I found a pure, clean beach, silence all around, like another world. No country, no war, nothing. Just the murmur of the waves.

I lay down under a palm tree, facing the sea, and went to sleep at once, it was as if I'd inhaled ether, I could have lain there for days. But the setting sun broke into my sleep and I woke up, stretched out in the sand. A little sand hill moved above me and sheltered me. Such a pure kind of warmth. I dozed again, enjoying the sea breeze, turning over in a bed of sand, and still lying there I stripped off my clothes, the black coat, the tassels, my trousers, underwear, shoes and socks. I lay naked in the sand for a while, then rose and went to bathe in the sea.

How wonderful it was, solitude all around. To be alone again after long days among crowds of people, quite alone. The gentle silence. Even the whine of the aircraft was swallowed up by the murmur of the waves. It seemed the local Arabs were afraid to leave their homes because of the war. I put on my underwear and strolled about the beach as if it were my own private shore. Time came back to me. Sunset approaching. The sun, a Cyclops' eye on the horizon, watching me calmly.

I went back to the Morris, which was standing faithful and quiet, its face to the sea, and I had a sudden shock. Inside the car was all the officer's luggage. He'd been using my car as a storage cupboard. Some folded blankets on the back seat, a small bivouac tent, even his mysterious map case was there. I opened it nervously and found that it really did contain maps, a stack of detailed maps of the Middle East, Libya, Sudan, Tunisia. In a little box were the new insignia of a lieutenant colonel. He was expecting promotion. There was also a white linen bag containing two old, cracked, hard-boiled eggs, their shells turning pink. Without thinking twice I peeled them and ate them hungrily, while reading an interesting document that I'd found. It was a sort of will that he'd written, addressed to his wife and two sons, written in elevated tones and a poetic style, something about himself and the people of Israel. It was a strange mixture–destiny, mission, history, fate, endurance. A bloated anthology of righteousness and self-pity. A chill passed through me as I thought of the rage he'd fall into when he discovered that the car had gone. He wouldn't rest till he'd found me. Perhaps he was already in pursuit, perhaps not far behind. He hadn't seemed really involved in this war.

I took all his maps and papers, tore them into little pieces and buried them in the sand, threw the empty bag into the sea and cleared the car of all the rest of his property. In the trunk I found a large can of paint and a brush that had been left there after the lights had been blacked out, back in the base camp.

I had a sudden inspiration–

I'd paint the car black, change its color.

I set to work immediately, stirring the paint to thicken it a little, and in the dim afterglow of sunset, with brisk brush strokes, I painted the car jet black. Standing in my underwear as the light faded, turning my car into a hearse. And I was adding the last touches of paint, humming an old French song to myself, when I sensed that I was being watched. I turned around and saw on the little sand hill behind me a number of shadowy figures. A little group of Bedouin in flowing robes, sitting there, watching me at work. I hadn't heard them approach. How long had they been there? The paint brush fell into the sand. Now I wished I hadn't discarded the bazooka. I had only my bayonet.

I could see they were fascinated by me. For them I was a real event. Perhaps they were considering my fate. I'd fallen into their hands, such an easy prey.

But they apparently sensed my fear, and with a slow movement they raised their hands high to greet me, a sort of half salute.

I smiled at them, bowing slightly from a distance, then turned to the heap of my clothes and dressed in a hurry. The shirt, the tassels, the trousers, the black jacket, the hat. Suddenly it occurred to me that in these clothes I was sure to be safe from them. And they, following my movements, were astonished indeed. I saw them stand up to watch me more closely. Hurriedly I gathered the rest of the things together and buried them in the sand, in the dark, knowing that anything I hid would be unearthed the moment I left. I leaped into the car and tried to start the engine. But it seems that in my agitation I missed the point of contact and the engine just groaned.

After a few moments of futile attempts I saw them approaching, standing in a circle around the car, a few paces distant. They watched me fumbling under the dashboard. They were certain of one thing at least, that I'd stolen the car. I kept smiling at their dark faces, groping again feverishly for those goddam wires. At last I succeeded, bringing the engine to life and breaking the silence, switching on the lights, sending out twin beams of light onto the dark sea, starting to move, turning, sinking in the sand, the wheels digging deep.

Meanwhile the crowd of onlookers had grown, like a flock of birds settling at night. Children, youths, old men springing up from the folds of the sand. I bent down to examine the tires stuck in the sand, returned to the car and tried again. The engine cut out. I started the engine again and sank farther.

Then I turned to the silent shadows and wordlessly appealed for help. They'd been waiting for this sign. Instantly they leaped at the car, dozens of hands sticking in the wet paint. I felt the car moving, hovering in the air, carried up to the road. The wheels touched firm ground. I drove forward a short distance and stopped. Climbed out and looked back at the group of shadowy figures standing silent on the road, took off my hat and waved it in an elegant gesture of thanks. I heard a mumbled response, something in Arabic, presumably a farewell.

I went back to the car and set off.

To Jerusalem.

Yes, to Jerusalem. Why Jerusalem? But did I have an alternative? Where else could I go? Where could I hide till the storm blew over? The ginger-haired girl had all my personal details recorded in her files. The one-handed major would be searching for the car. Could I have gone back to grandmother's house, a fugitive from the war, a deserter, a wanted man?

Or perhaps you think I could have returned to you. To live with you, to be more than a lover, to be one of the family. Was that possible?

But why not carry on with the destiny chosen for me. The first step had been taken, I'd escaped from the desert, crossed the border into Israel. I was wearing black clothes, tassels and a hat. I'd grown accustomed to the smell of the sweat of the holy man. My beard was flourishing, I didn't object to the idea of growing a side curl or two. The Morris had turned black, was well disguised. Why not carry on with the adventure?

Also the money that you'd given me, Adam, was running out. I had somehow to get through a difficult period, until the war was won or died down. Why shouldn't the religious Jews take me in? They seemed quite good at that sort of thing, at least to judge by their emissaries in the desert. It seemed that somebody looked after them.

Such were my thoughts on the night journey, in the pale light of the waning moon. Passing through the settlements of the south, reaching the coastal plain, driving slowly to conserve fuel. I didn't even know the date, much less what was going on in the world.

And so, cautiously, in a dark land, at three o'clock in the morning, I began climbing the road to Jerusalem. From time to time I left the main highway and took to the side roads, to throw any pursuers off the scent. Looking out at the dark, rocky landscape, hearing the crickets. Since returning home I hadn't visited Jerusalem, I'd been so busy with my grandmother, with the legacy, with the lawyers, and with your love. So that when with the first light of dawn I entered the city, dirty and deserted though it was, with sandbags piled up around the houses and shabby civil defense personnel patrolling the streets, I was startled, overwhelmed, by the stark beauty. And in the approaches to the city, like an omen, my last drop of fuel was used up. I left the car in a side street and set out to look for them.

They weren't hard to find. Their quarter was in the suburbs. They were already out in the streets for their early morning shopping, baskets in their hands. Men and women. A light rain falling and a smell of autumn. Another world. Shops open, business as usual, a smell of fresh-baked bread. Here and there a huddled group, talking excitedly about something. Strange signs on the walls, some of them torn.

I followed them, followed the black drops that became, as I watched, a black stream of pious Jews, hurrying inside, into the heart of the religious quarter. When I saw the big Sabbath hats of tawny fox fur I knew I'd reached the end of my journey, nobody would find me here. There was a group of them standing on a street corner. I went to meet them, to make contact.

They knew immediately that I wasn't one of them. Perhaps it was the shape of my beard, the style of my hair, perhaps some more intimate sign. There was no deceiving them. At first they were shocked at the idea of somebody appearing among them in time of war, disguised in their clothing and their likeness. Quietly I asked, "Is it possible to be with you for a while?" I didn't tell them that I'd come from the desert, I said that I'd just arrived from Paris. They looked at the dust and sand on my clothes and at my boots and said nothing. In silence they listened to my confused words. Clearly they thought me a madman or a dreamer. But to their credit they didn't turn me away, they took me lightly by the arm and led me slowly and tenderly, while I was still talking and explaining myself, through alleyways and courtyards to a big stone house, a yeshiva or a school, teeming like an ant's nest. They took me into a room and said:

"Now, start from the beginning."

I began by bending the facts, changing dates, jumping from topic to topic, telling them about my grandmother lying in a coma and about the car that I was willing to hand over to them. My head was spinning from weariness but slowly a story began to take shape, a story from which I was never again to deviate. But, just as in that night interrogation by the officer, I made no reference to you. Again I saw how easily I could wipe you from my past.

They brought in a blond, heavily bearded Jew, with the clear features of a goy hidden beneath beard and side curls. He spoke to me in French, questioned me with a perfect Parisian accent about the French details of my story. He asked me about streets in Paris, about cafes, varieties of cheese and wine, names of newspapers. I gave detailed replies in fluent French. I felt inspired.

When they saw that I really did know Paris, they asked me to undress. For a moment they were in doubt as to whether I was Jewish at all. I could see that they were quite baffled, not knowing why I'd come to them or what I really wanted. They repeated their earlier questions from a different angle, but I kept to my story.

Finally they held a brief, whispered conversation among themselves. They were afraid to come to a decision of their own. They sent a messenger to make some inquiry and he returned, nodding his head. They led me to their rabbi. In a little room I stood before a very old man, wreathed in cigarette smoke, reading a newspaper. They told him the story that I'd told and he listened, all the while his eyes fixed on me, studying me with a kindly, good-natured expression. When he heard about the car that I wanted to make over to them, he turned to face me directly and, in Hebrew, began asking me detailed questions about it. The date of manufacture, the capacity of the engine, the number of seats, its color, finally he asked where it was parked. He was delighted at the idea that I was bringing the car with me as a kind of dowry.

Suddenly he began scolding his men.

"He must be given a bed . . . can't you see he's tired? He's come a long way . . . from Paris"–he winked at me–"first of all find him a place to sleep . . . you are hard-hearted Jews."

And he gave me a playful smile.

At last they were satisfied. They led me through the courtyard, before the curious gaze of hundreds of inquisitive students who felt instinctively that I was putting on an act. They took me to a room that served as the yeshiva guest room. A humble room, with old furniture, but pleasant enough and clean. I was already growing accustomed to the light, religious smell of the objects around me. A blend of old books, fried onions and sewers.

They made up one of the beds and went their way, true to the rabbi's instructions. It was eleven o'clock in the morning. A faint gray light in the world outside. Through the embroidered lace curtain, a curtain fit for a king, there appeared at my fingertips the Old City, which I'd never seen before.

A startling, breath-taking view of the lovely old wall, the towers of churches and mosques, little stone courtyards, olive groves on the mountain slopes. For a long time I stood beside the window. Then I took off my boots and lay down fully clothed on the bed. There was something in the air of Jerusalem that kept me awake, though I was exhausted and almost feverish.

At first I had difficulty sleeping, I was dirty as well, my hands stained with black paint, my hair and beard full of sand. An eternity had passed since I last slept in a bed. I began to doze. The murmuring voices of the yeshiva students, their intermittent shouts blended with the sighing of the waves, the roar of tank engines, the crackle of radios.

Soon after, while I was still dozing, my roommate came in. A little old man, elegantly dressed, with a red silk skullcap on his head. He stood at my bedside and looked down at me. When he saw I was only dozing, he began chattering at me gaily in Yiddish, trying hard to communicate with me. He couldn't believe that I didn't understand Yiddish. He began telling me about himself, things that I couldn't understand precisely. I only grasped that he'd come here for a matchmaking, that he was going to take some girl abroad with him, and meanwhile he was undergoing a series of tests–physical or spiritual, I wondered.

He went prattling on, pacing about the room, playful, making jokes, as if there were no war, no other reality. For some reason he was convinced that I too had come here to find a match and he tried to give me some cunning advice. As if through a mist I remember my conversation with him, sometimes I think perhaps he was just a part of my dream, because after he'd undressed, paced about the room in his shining white underwear, sprinkled some perfume on himself and put on a dark suit, he disappeared and I didn't see him again.

Slowly I sank into a bitter, fitful sleep.

When I woke up there was darkness all around. It was nine o'clock in the evening. Through the magnificent curtain, stirring lightly in the evening breeze, the Old City was dark. Utter silence. I was still exhausted, shivering with cold, as if I hadn't had a moment's sleep. Suddenly I felt a strange longing for the desert, for the faces of the men of my platoon, now fighting on the other side of the canal. I opened the window. The air of Jerusalem, pure, intoxicating, unfamiliar. Now I know that I really was feverish, running a high temperature, falling sick. But at the time I thought the pain was the result of hunger, my excruciating, maddening hunger. I put on my shoes, too weak to lace them up, and went in search of food. The yeshiva was silent and in total darkness. I wandered from floor to floor, corridor to corridor. Finally I opened a door and found myself in a tiny room, full of cigarette smoke, the blinds closed. Two students in thin shirts, sleeves rolled up, were bent over enormous volumes of the Talmud, disputing in whispers.

They seemed annoyed at the interruption. They told me the way to the dining room and immediately returned to their studies. The dining hall was empty, the benches were stacked on the tables. A young woman in a gray dress, a kerchief around her head, was washing the floor.

She almost cried out when she saw me, as if she were seeing a ghost.

"I'm new here . . ." I mumbled. "Is there anything left to eat?"

Disheveled from sleep, my army boots unlaced, clad in a mixture of secular and religious clothing, my head uncovered, I made a startling impression on her, but she recovered her composure and set a place for me at one of the tables. She brought a big spoon, a dish and slices of bread, discreetly and without a word laid a black skullcap beside them, and then she brought in a dish of thick, oily soup, full of vegetables, dumplings and pieces of meat, a hot, spicy mixture. My first proper meal for two whole weeks. The pungent spices brought tears to my eyes. The soup was delicious. At the other end of the room she carried on with her work, stealing furtive glances at me. She came and took the empty dish and refilled it, smiling pleasantly to herself at my effusive thanks. A good-looking woman, so far as it was possible to tell. Only her hands and face were uncovered.

At last I stood up unsteadily, left the table without saying grace and groped my way back to my bed. Entering the room I was surprised to find that the Old City, which had been in darkness when I went out, was now all lit up. And in the yeshiva as well, shutters were opening one after another and lights were appearing.

Excited voices talking about a cease-fire, students appearing from every side, shirts unbuttoned, milling about noisily in the courtyard, as if a battle has just ended. It seems I was hasty in my flight. The war is over.

A sort of inner peace descends on me. I take off my clothes, strip back the bed, gather together all the blankets from the other bed and wrap myself up tightly. I'm ill, a mighty pain hammering in my head.

For two weeks I lay in bed with a strange disease. High temperature, aching head and inflammation of the intestines. Cowpox was the diagnosis of the doctor who treated me. Apparently I'd caught it from some cow shit on the beach. They tended me with great devotion, even though I was a stranger and a puzzle to them. One day they were thinking of transferring me to a hospital, but I asked to be allowed to stay with them. They granted my request, even though I caused them a lot of trouble and considerable expenditure on medical fees. At night, youths studying Torah and reading the psalms kept watch at my bedside.

It was the illness that smoothed the transition from secular life to life with them, that took away the need for superfluous questions. Physical contact with the hands that fed me, that smoothed the bedclothes beneath me, made them all more human for me. And after two weeks, when I rose from my bed, weak but well, my beard thick and matted, I became one of them without too many formalities. They gave me another set of black clothes, old but in good condition, pajamas and some underwear. They showed me how to use the prayer book, taught me two or three chapters of the Mishna. Meanwhile they had keys cut for the Morris. I observed how efficient they were, how well organized, how disciplined.

And so it was that I became the driver for the yeshiva, in particular the driver for the old rabbi who'd taken me in on the first day. I used to deliver oil for memorial lamps to synagogues, take little orphans with long side curls to pray at the Western Wall, drive a *mohel* to circumcise the son of a pious family in one of the new suburbs, or join the long, slow-moving funeral cortege of some eminent rabbi whose body had been brought from overseas. Occasionally I'd make the drive to the coast, to the airport, with an emissary going abroad to raise funds. Sometimes, late at night, driving quietly and with dimmed lights, I was chauffeur to zealots sticking up posters and daubing slogans against licentiousness and frivolity.

I got to know all their little ways. They lived a life apart in the land, in their closed order. Sometimes I wondered if they obtained even their electricity and water from private, kosher power stations, reserved for them exclusively.

I settled down well among them. They knew as well as I did that at any moment I might leave and disappear just as suddenly as I'd come. In spite of this they treated me with affection and didn't question what they didn't understand. They never gave me money, even gasoline I used to buy with coupons that they provided. Otherwise they supplied all my needs. They washed and mended my clothes, they gave me more suitable shoes to replace my army boots. And above all I had plenty of food. The same oily soup that I'd enjoyed so much the first evening was served to me every night without exception, though not always by the same woman. The women took turns serving the yeshiva students.

And gradually my side curls grew. Not that I made any special effort, they just grew of their own accord. The barber who came every month to cut the students' hair used to cut mine as well, but he didn't dare touch the curls. At first I used to hide them behind my ears but eventually I abandoned this too. I used to look in the mirror and see to my surprise how much I was beginning to resemble them. They too were aware of this and it was pleasant to see that they were gratified.

But only so far. No farther. They had no success with me in deeper, spiritual matters. I didn't believe in God, and all their observances seemed pointless to me. The amazing thing was that they were well aware of this, but they put no pressure on me and cherished no false hopes. In the early days I used to ask them questions that shocked them and turned their faces pale. But I didn't want to upset them and I began keeping my thoughts to myself.

I used to avoid morning prayers somehow or other. But I'd attend evening prayers, the prayer book open in my hands, my lips moving, watching them swaying and groaning, and sometimes as the sun went down they'd beat their breasts as if in pain or yearning for something, the devil knows what, exile perhaps, or the Messiah. And yet they couldn't be called unhappy, far from it. No, they were free men, exempt from military service and affairs of the state, making their way with dignity through a united Jerusalem, looking down with scorn and strangeness on the secular people, who constituted for them a kind of framework and a means.

The winter was already at its height, and there was a lot of work to be done. The old rabbi was always rushing from place to place, he was lucky to have a car and a chauffeur at his service. I used to drive him from place to place, to deliver sermons, to mourn at funerals, to visit the sick or to meet members of his flock at the airport. Moving around Old and New Jerusalem, from west to east, north to south, I got to know all its nooks and crannies, growing ever more attached to this strange wonderful city, of which I still hadn't yet had my fill.

When I drove him to some yeshiva to deliver a sermon, I wouldn't stay to listen to him. I never could understand what he was getting at, he always seemed to me to be caught up in imaginary problems. I'd go back to the car and drive to a place of which I was growing increasingly fond, above Mount Scopus, near the church of Tora-Malka. From there not only was the entire city visible, but also the desert horizon and the Dead Sea. From there I could see all, perfectly.

I'd sit in the little car, still marked by the handprints of the Bedouin from Rafah, rain lashing the roof, flicking idly through *Hamodia,* a newspaper that was always finding its way into the car, as it was provided free by the yeshiva. And through partisan, religious eyes I learned of outbreaks of fighting, prolonged exchanges of fire, precarious truces, weeping and mourning, anger and arguments, as if the war that was over was still festering and fomenting and from its rotting remains a new war was emerging.

If so, what's the rush–

At last the rain would stop, the skies would clear. I'd throw down the newspaper and leave the car, strolling by the wall of the church, between the puddles, through a cypress grove, the black hat from the desert tilted back on my head, tassels stirring in the breeze. Watching the scraps of fog drifting across the city, bowing slightly to the Arabs watching me from the dark interiors of their shops. I'd noticed that they showed less hostility toward us, the Jews in black, as if we were more naturally a part of their landscape, or maybe just less dangerous.

Bells ringing, monks hurrying by, nodding their heads in greeting. I too, so they think, am a servant of God, in my own way.

Arab children following in my footsteps, amused at the sight of the figure dressed in black. Silence all around. At my feet the gray, wet city. The black car lying at the roadside like a faithful dog.

So why should I make a move? Where should I go? To the ginger-haired girl, who has the list of equipment for which I signed and which I threw away in the desert? To the officer, still no doubt searching for me furiously? To my grandmother, lying in a coma? (Once I called the hospital to hear of any change in her condition.) Or perhaps to you? To hide in your house, not as a lover but as one of the family, living on your charity, a slave to mounting desires.

Yes, desire has not died. There have been some hard days. I haven't ignored the stealthy glances of the girls of the community. I know that I have only to give a hint to the old rabbi and he'll arrange a marriage for me. They're waiting only for a clear sign on my part that I've linked my fate to theirs.

But this sign I still withhold.

NA'IM

I'm getting out. I tell you I've had enough. I can't take it anymore. I'm splitting. Leaving me the whole morning with a tow truck in a gas station and running off to Jerusalem. What am I, a dog? No work no hours no life. He's stuck me with an old woman who's dying and when she dies they'll say I killed her. It's no good. I'm only a kid and he's made a loner out of me. A real loner.

At eleven o'clock Hamid arrives and finds me curled up in the back of the truck. Even the great silent one takes pity on me.

"What's the matter with you?"

"What's the matter with me?"

"Why are you lying here like this?"

"What else can I do?"

"Where is he?"

"Gone to Jerusalem."

"Why?"

"Just like that . . . he's off his rocker . . ."

But Hamid won't hear a word said against his boss.

"Have you started towing again?"

"Don't know . . . this is the car of a friend of his . . . an old man who ran into a tree."

Hamid looks at the car hanging there, checks the cables.

"Who fixed it like this?"

"I did."

He doesn't say anything, just operates the winch and lowers the car to the ground, unties the cables.

"What's this?" I ask angrily. "What's wrong with it?"

"It won't hold like this."

He works in silence, on his own. Thin and dark, looking for other ways to fix it. I stand and watch him like Adam watched me. Stubborn Arab.

In the end he finishes, we climb aboard and head north.

"What's new in the village?" I ask.

"Nothing . . ."

"How's Father?"

"All right."

"Tell him I may be coming back to the village."

"What will you do there?"

"Nothing . . ."

He doesn't look at me, driving sort of dryly, easily, changing gears so quietly you'd think it was an automatic. There's no mechanic like him.

"Is Father angry that I'm not sending him any money?"

"Don't know . . ."

By the time I've dragged an answer out of him I'll be dead.

Now and then I see him looking at me suspiciously, like he's angry.

"What is it?"

Suddenly he says, "Why don't you get a haircut?"

"This is how they all go around now."

"All who? Only the Jews . . ."

"Arabs too . . ."

"The crazy ones maybe . . ."

"Why all the fuss?"

But he doesn't answer. We drive into Haifa, I ask him to drop me off at the old woman's house.

"You're still living with her?"

"Yes."

He smiles a nasty smile to himself, puts me down at the corner of the street and goes on to the garage.

I go up the stairs, ring the bell because she's never given me a key. Is she asleep? Impossible, she's always up waiting for me. I knock hard. No answer. Suddenly I get worried and start kicking the door. Silence. The neighbor comes out and looks at me, I want to ask her something but she closes the door straightaway. I start to get really nervous. Going down and seeing the windows open, up again, knocking, going down.

I start walking in the crowded street, beside the stalls in the market, tired and worried. Maybe she really is dead. I look up, maybe she'll appear at the window. I must get into the house, into my room, sleep in my bed. I cross the street, go into the house opposite. And from the stairs I try to get a glimpse inside the old woman's apartment. The windows are wide open, the curtains moving slightly in the breeze. There's my room, the bed all messed up like I left it at night and on the chair in the living room I see her sitting . . . and from where I'm standing on the other side of the street it looks like she's smiling to herself, or I'm so tired I'm seeing things.

I'm going nuts, I cross the street in a hurry, run up the stairs and knock, screaming out, "It's me, Na'im, open up," but the door doesn't open.

I'm in the street again, pacing about nervously, and suddenly I decide to climb up the drain pipe, like that night when we broke in the first time. I look at the people around me but nobody's interested. I get a grip on the stones, on the drain pipe, and start climbing, exactly the same route as before, looking down all the time to see if anybody's shouting at me, raising the alarm, but people aren't interested, they don't care about me breaking into a house in broad daylight, and I'm already at the window, jumping inside. I find her sitting in the chair, very white, she really is smiling a bit, a frozen sort of smile, like she's been crying. Dead, I think and I tremble. I take a sheet and put it over her like I've seen them do in movies. I go to the kitchen, drink some water to steady myself, decide to take another look, pull away the sheet, touch her hand, it's very cold. But something moves in her eyes, the pupils. She gives a little groan. I talk to her but she doesn't answer.

She's lost the consciousness that she found—

I'm getting really desperate, sometimes I forget I'm only fifteen years old. Putting me here to look after a dying old woman a hundred years old. What is this? Where's the justice in it? Going off to Jerusalem like that. I must get away from all this. I'm getting out. I've been thinking about this all day but nobody listens. I go to my room, almost running, start to pack my things, stuffing the suitcase with the clothes she gave me. I go to the kitchen, something's cooking on the stove, burned to a cinder. I try a bit of it, because it's burned it tastes good. I scrape it out of the pan and eat the lot, burning my mouth. I go back to the old woman and she really is looking at me, watching me, I try talking to her again, in Arabic this time, she moves her head a bit like she understands but she doesn't say anything . . . she's lost her voice.

I phone the garage and ask about Adam. They don't know anything. I phone his house, no answer. I go to my room and close the door. I'm afraid. God, I must get out of here but where can I go? I'm so tired, a final nap at least. I close the shutters, get into bed with my clothes on and go right to sleep. I wake up and it's night already, eleven o'clock. I've slept ten hours straight.

I go into the living room. She's still sitting there, looking just the same. Somebody's pushed today's *Ma'ariv* under the door. I'm off,

I'm going. There's a poem I learned once, I can't remember how it goes, just the first line–"Son of man, go flee." I've forgotten the poet's name.

I phone Adam's house. His wife answers. He isn't back from Jerusalem yet. She's expecting a call too. I tell her about the old woman and she says, "Don't leave her"–she's handing out orders too–"when Adam arrives we'll come over right away . . . we may have found her grandson . . ."

I go back to the old woman, sit beside her, talk to her, pick up *Ma'ariv* and read her something about a terrorist attack, maybe that'll revive her.

This is crazy. All night I stay awake. She's breathing, alive, even smiling at me, understanding what I'm reading, looking at me, watching me. I go to the kitchen and bring some bread, stuff it into her mouth so she won't die of hunger. But the bread won't go into her mouth.

In the end she'll choke and they'll say I strangled her. . . . It's light outside, morning. I must escape from here. I'm leaving, that's what I've been trying to say all day but nobody listens.

DAFI

"Dafi, my dear, it's you, you're still awake, be so good as to wake your father. I must speak to him. My car is embracing a tree . . . ha . . . ha . . ." I'm in the school playground, in the morning, with a bunch of children from my class and other classes, standing there imitating the old fox with his soft, oily voice. And they're all delighted to hear about the accident, they don't get any free time out of it, because he doesn't teach anyway, but if he's out of the way for a while it'll add to the general freedom, go nicely with the disorder of the school year's end.

So everybody's surprised to see him arriving in a taxi during the second recess, his head bandaged it's true, his face scratched, limping a bit but quite lucid, bossy as usual and giving out orders, coming in at the main gate, walking slowly and painfully, collaring children on the way and telling them to pick up shells, paper, chalk, clearing the path in front of him. Sure that the school will collapse if he doesn't turn up.

But the silly fool was too embarrassed to walk around the corridors during the break or to go pestering the teachers in the staff room, he shut himself up in his room, and because after his adventure during the night all he could think about was me, he sent his secretary to fetch me in the middle of the third class.

It was a literature lesson, one of the last of the year. We were reading Ibsen's *Peer Gynt.* We weren't studying it, or interpreting it, just reading it around the class, each of us taking a part. It was great. I was reading the part of Solveig. Not a very big part but very significant. It was quiet in the classroom, we were really enjoying the reading even though we didn't understand it all. And suddenly the poor unfortunate secretary came into the room and spoiled it all. I was just in the middle of reading:

Winter shall surely turn and spring shall follow
And summer shall pass away too and autumn in turn
But I know, one day you will return to your home
And I shall wait for you.

And suddenly she came in.

"The headmaster wants to see Dafna."

The literature teacher was annoyed and asked if it couldn't wait till after the lesson.

But the secretary said, "I think not . . ."

She knows her boss–

And I understood–the time of departure has come.

Today of all days, the morning after Daddy went to his rescue in the night, just now when Daddy's repairing his car. Just a few days before the end of the school year. I closed the book.

The secretary said, "Bring your satchel with you, please."

The teacher was surprised. "Why?"

He knew nothing.

I felt suddenly desperate, alone. There was a murmur in the class, they realized what was going to happen to me. But nobody moved.

I walk down the empty corridors following the little secretary, knocking at his door, going in, standing at a safe distance from him, the satchel lying at my feet. He's bent over his papers, his head wrapped in a white turban. A strange man. Why did he have to come to school today?

Silence–

I stand there in front of him but he ignores me, rummaging among his papers, reading something, screwing up a piece of paper into a little ball and throwing it into the basket.

"How are you?" I say almost inaudibly.

After all we were in contact during the night–

He's startled by the question, looks up at me, his eyes bright, smiling a thin smile, the bastard, nodding his head slowly, somehow he can't believe I'm really concerned about his health.

"We were sure you wouldn't be coming to school today," I add boldly. What do I care?

"Perhaps you hoped I wouldn't be coming . . ."

"No . . . what an idea . . ."

He lets out a quiet little laugh. It looks like it really amuses him to think how unpopular he is here.

Silence–

Oh hell, what does he want?

I notice they've sprinkled a sort of disgusting yellowish powder on the cuts on his cheek.

And then quietly, in that soft sickly voice of his, he starts lecturing me about my crime. A public insult to a young teacher who ought to be respected all the more . . . saying to him "Why weren't you killed?" A disgrace . . . in a land where people are being killed all the time . . . an unnecessary, unprovoked attack . . . the teaching committee is shocked (what teaching committee?) . . . quite out of the question for me to remain in this group . . . especially seeing that my achievements so far have been so poor . . . no alternative but to transfer me to another school . . . a technical school . . . cooking or needlework . . . there's no need for everybody to be a professor in this land . . .

After a sermon lasting a quarter of an hour the old devil comes to the point at last–since there are only a few days left before the end of the school year, and this business has gone on quite long enough . . . and there's a suspicion that all this has come about as a result of there being close relatives in the school . . . and the injured party is seeking damages . . . therefore an immediate, even a symbolic, expulsion is essential, otherwise the whole business will lose its point . . . it will look as if I'm simply leaving . . .

He mumbles toward the end, a bit embarrassed, still not daring to look me in the face.

Throwing me out just a few days before the end of the year–

"Of course, there will be a report," he adds.

To hell with the report. Tears rise in my throat but I hold them back . . . I mustn't cry, mustn't cry.

"When must I leave the school?" I ask quietly.

He still doesn't look at me straight.

"Now."

"Now?"

"Yes, from this moment."

An icy chill in my heart. I stare at him with all my strength. Goodby, Solveig. But no pleading, mustn't demean myself. I pick up the satchel, walk up to his desk, deciding to change the subject.

"Did my father arrive to rescue you in the end?"

This time he's taken aback, he blushes, recoiling.

"Yes, your father is a wonderful man . . . a quiet man . . . he helped me a lot . . ."

"And your car was pretty well smashed up?"

"What?"

"Anyone killed?"

"What? What are you saying? Enough!"

He's almost shouting.

"Then you can have this . . ."

And I hurl the satchel down on his desk and hurry out of the room, seeing the secretary sitting there, all attention, and in a corner, somehow I didn't notice him before, little fat Baby Face blushing bright red. I run to the gate and away from the school, the bell ringing behind me. I don't want to see anybody. I stop a taxi and say to the driver, a fat man with a funny yellow beret on his head, "Drive to the university, or rather, above the university."

And he's a bit dumb, a new immigrant from Russia, he doesn't know the way, I have to explain it to him. We go up and up, to the top of the mountain, driving along little forest tracks. I stop the car, get out, walk among the pines, crying a bit. The driver stares at me. In a moment he'll start crying too. I go back to him, give him fifty pounds and ask him to return here at four.

"Yes, madam," he says.

Madam–

I stay in the woods for a long time. Lying down on the dry ground and getting up again, walking about and going back to the little road. My eyes already dry, relaxed, just beginning to feel hungry, forgetting the headmaster, the school, *Peer Gynt,* Daddy and Mommy, and just thinking about food. At a quarter to four the taxi arrives. Unbelievable. The fat, bald driver stands waiting, quietly cleaning the front windshield. He sees me running to him through the trees, laughs, smiles at me.

At four-thirty I'm already home. The satchel lies there beside the front door. Mommy's very tense.

"Where have you been?"

"Just walking about . . ."

"How are you feeling?"

"I've been expelled from school."

"I know . . . they told me. Where have you been?"

"Just walking, I cried a bit . . . but it's over now . . . I've calmed down."

"Tali and Osnat were here."

"What did you tell them?"

"That they should leave you alone today."

"Good. You did the right thing."

"Have you had anything to eat?"

"No . . . nothing . . . I'm awfully hungry . . ."

"Then come and sit down."

"Where's Daddy?"

"In Jerusalem."

"What's he doing there?"

"He went straight there . . . it seems he's getting close to him . . ."

"Close to whom?"

"Him . . ."

Ah . . . that's why she's so tense. The light in her eyes. An aging woman. I feel empty and depressed.

I sit down to eat, she cooks french fries and meatballs, these are the things she cooks best. I eat and eat, a sort of lunch and supper combined. She walks about nervously. Every time the phone rings she rushes to it. But it's always friends of mine, expressing sympathy, and Mommy answers for me, I don't mind.

"Dafi's not at home, she'll be back later, phone tomorrow. I'll give her the message." My secretary. And I go on eating and eating, chocolate pudding and fruit cake, with Mommy all the time reporting the phone calls to me, surprised herself at this show of solidarity from the children in the class.

At nine o'clock I run a hot bath, lie down in the bubbly water and sing to myself. Going to bed, finding the satchel already in my bedroom, it's been following me around all day, without me touching it. I open it, take out *Peer Gynt,* open the book at the place where I was interrupted and quietly go on reading to myself:

May God bless your path wherever you go
And blessed you shall be if you pass through this land
If you come to my house I shall welcome you here
And if not, we shall meet above.

And I put out the light—

Mommy's still pacing, wandering around the house, after a while she goes to bed, but she can't sleep, I'm an expert on insomnia, she tosses about in her bed, gets up to go to the bathroom, comes back, the light goes on and off. At eleven o'clock the phone suddenly rings, but it isn't Daddy. Sounds like it's Na'im. They're talking about the old lady, Mommy's asking him not to leave her, since it's possible Gabriel's been found, he should stay put till Daddy gets back from Jerusalem.

I'm already hearing this through a dream. Asleep and not asleep, but I don't get out of bed. A whole night passes in sleep and short wakings and then sleep again.

Early in the morning the phone rings again . . . Mommy's talking, a few minutes later she's standing by my bed, already dressed, talking to me. She's going to Jerusalem, I must phone the headmaster and tell him she won't be coming to school today. I nod my head and go back to sleep. Waking up at eight. The house is empty. I get up, pull down all the blinds, take the phone off the hook. No school, no parents, no nothing . . . I go back to bed and sleep again. Sleep has come back to me. Good morning.

ADAM

This slow movement. It seems to me I'm hearing soft music. I just begin walking slowly to get him away from there and he trails along behind me, his hat slung back, talking and telling his story, and I'm still afraid he may suddenly pick up his heels and run. I keep close to him, touching his shoulder lightly and leading him away. Full daylight already, in the streets people hurrying to pray. More than anything I'm careful not to scare him. Three children trail along behind us, disappointed, anxious about the morning trip that's been interrupted, but it's as if he's forgotten them, carried away by the current of his words, and already we're outside the religious quarter, walking through the New City, in old Mamilla Street, beside the ancient Muslim cemetery, and the children are afraid to leave their quarter, they stop and call out to him and he waves his hand to shake them off—"Later, not now"—and he walks on with me.

And now I start telling him about my search for him, about the army authorities who knew nothing about him, still not saying a word about the grandmother who came to life, not mentioning Asya by name. Telling him only about my wanderings at night in search of him. And he listens to these stories with great enjoyment, smiling to himself, his eyes bright, laying a hand on my shoulder as he follows me along.

We pass by the King David Hotel, carry on through the gardens of the YMCA, going down a little side street to the Hotel Moriah, and through the big windows I see the tables being laid for breakfast. A faint smell of coffee and toast. We stand beside the main entrance, by a glass revolving door. I say to him:

"But your grandmother has recovered in the meantime . . . she has come home . . ."

He clutches at the wall, almost collapsing, bursts out laughing.

"And I was in such a hurry to get back . . . that silly legacy . . ."

Through the door comes the sound of soft music, light morning music. I touch his arm.

"Come inside, let's have something to drink."

"They won't let us in."

And the doorman really does stop us—two odd-looking creatures, not fit for such a smart hotel, a religious Jew dressed in black with side curls and a beard, wearing sneakers, and a heavily built laborer in dirty overalls. I take out a hundred-pound note and give it to the doorman. "We only want a light breakfast." He takes the note eagerly, leads us in by a side entrance, calls the headwaiter, who comes hurrying toward us, hastily takes another bill that I offer him and without a word leads us to an ornate little room with soft carpets and closes the door on us.

This breakfast costs me three hundred pounds but I stopped thinking about money long ago. He claims that he isn't hungry and I don't press him to eat. Sitting beside me, chewing his side curls and watching me gobbling up the fresh little rolls, gulping down cup after cup of coffee. Absently he puts out his hand and starts picking up the crumbs from the table cloth, playing with them.

"What is this fast?" I ask.

"The seventeenth of Tammuz, the destruction of the Wall."

"But they built it again." I point through the curtain at the gray wall of the Old City.

He doesn't even look, just smiles uneasily.

"Not that wall . . ."

"And is that why you're not eating?"

He smiles, that weak enchanting smile of his, shrugs his shoulders, mumbles something about not being hungry. And suddenly he starts taking an interest in Asya, at last, I was thinking he'd forgotten her. Asking how she's been getting on during the time he's been missing, and cautiously I tell him about her work, about her longings, he listens, his eyes closed.

"But how did you find me?"

I put down on the table the crumpled piece of blue metal, it's been handled so much it's going soft. I tell him about the accident.

He remembers the accident. He smiles. That old man nearly killed him–

On the other side of the fence, behind his back, to my surprise I see the three little orthodox children peeping through the bushes, waving their hands, calling out, throwing gravel at the windowpane. I get up quickly, go to the main entrance, find the doorman, give him fifty pounds and tell him about the little nuisances. From the lobby I phone home. It's six o'clock. The ringing's hardly begun and Asya picks up the receiver. I tell her what's happened, she decides to come at once. I go back to the little room and find him munching the half roll that I left. At once I order another breakfast. On the other side of the fence, the doorman collars one of the boys, snatches his hat, takes care of him cruelly.

He gulps down his coffee, eats two soft-boiled eggs.

"And I thought you'd given me up . . ."

And suddenly I realize, he's clinging to me just as much as I am to him, he's afraid I may take him back there. I rush out to the desk, order a room, again handing out money, needlessly, to the waiters and the doorman. I go back to the little room to fetch him. He's already devoured the lot, as if he's been fasting for days, he's licked out the butter dish and the little pots of jam, there are yellow egg stains on his beard. I lead him out, passing through the lobby that's crowded with American tourists who stare at us curiously, following us with their smiles. The headwaiter shows us into a room on the third floor. Gabriel flings himself down in one of the armchairs, sighing with relief.

"I'm escaping again . . . like before, in the desert . . ."

Through the window an impressive view of the Old City. The furniture is upholstered in a pleasant shade of gray, the carpets are gray, the curtains gray. He takes off his black frock, removes his shoes, starts walking about in his socks, goes into the bathroom, washes his hands, dries them on a scented paper towel, he turns on the radio and music swamps us.

"What a wonderful room."

I ask him if I should fetch the possessions that he left behind at the yeshiva. He shrugs his shoulders, there's nothing of any value.

"But the car . . ."

Oh, he'd almost forgotten it. He hands me the keys, better not to go himself, he couldn't stand their disappointment and sorrow.

He strips off his shirt, picks up a magazine and starts leafing through it, looking at the pictures.

I lock the door on him, go downstairs in a hurry and return to the quarter, getting a bit lost on the way but finally arriving in the courtyard of the yeshiva.

The children rush at me.

"Mister, where have you taken him?"

But I don't answer, I get into the car and try to start the engine. The battery's very weak, the engine coughs loudly.

The children call to some students who surround the car at once.

"Where are you going, mister? Where do you want to take the car?"

At last I succeed in starting the engine, I must have been a bit flustered. I don't say anything, but my silence only adds to the anger around me. They take hold of the car and won't let it move. I'd have thought that as they were fasting they'd have no strength, but the hunger only increases their vigor. The car won't budge, although I put it into gear and press the pedal hard.

An old man comes out to see what's happening. They tell him something in Yiddish.

"Where is he?" he asks me.

"He's a free man," I reply. "He doesn't owe anybody anything."

The old man smiles.

"What is a free man?"

To hell with it, I say nothing.

Meanwhile three students get into the car and sit in the back. A crowd gathers around us. I switch off the engine, get out, to hell with the car, why fight over it, I put the keys away in my pocket, let them tear the bloody thing apart.

The old man still stands there watching me.

"Tell me, sir, what do you mean, a free man?"

I say nothing. Tired and worn out. Almost on the brink of tears. A man of forty-six. What's happening to me?

"Do you, sir, consider yourself a free man?"

Theological arguments now–

I open the door of the car and find the registration certificate, show him that it's signed in the old lady's name, explain that I must take the car back to its owner.

One of the students takes the license, glances at it, whispers something in the old man's ear.

"So the gentleman wishes to take the automobile, let him take it, only let him not say that there is one free man in the world."

I stare at him, nodding my head as if hypnotized, take the license and get into the car. The students idly leave the back seat, the way is open. I drive away from the quarter, arrive at the hotel, leaving the car in the parking lot. I enter the hotel, standing at the desk I see Asya, distraught, the reception clerk knows nothing.

When she sees me alone she goes pale.

"Where is he?"

I take her by the arm. She trembles, light to my touch. We climb the stairs to the room, she leans on me. I take out the key and open the door, curious to see if he's still here or if he's already flown away through the window.

NA'IM—DAFI

I know there's nobody in the house but I ring the doorbell anyway wait ring again wait ring for the last time and there's no answer. Ring for the very last time and still no answer, knock a few times, no answer. I put the key in the lock, one last ring and I open the door. The house is dark, all the blinds closed like they've all gone out and they're not coming back for a long time. I'll write him a note and go. First let's just go to her room, have a look at it, lie down for a while on the beloved bed, and go . . .

There's a ring at the door. Who can it be? Another ring. I don't feel like getting up. If it's the postman he can use the letter box. Another ring. He's persistent. Now he's knocking. Maybe I ought to get up. Suddenly it sounds like somebody trying to put a key in the lock. . . . A short ring and the door opens. Who is it? Somebody walking into the house. Light footsteps. A thief in the morning? Now he's coming straight into my room. Oh, help . . .

But there is somebody here . . . Dafi lying in bed in a dark room. Her head on the pillow, her blond hair all over the place. She's alone in the house. Too late to run away.

"It's only me . . ." I mumble. "I didn't think there was anyone at home. Are you sick?"

But it's only Na'im. So what? Daddy's given him a key to the house. He's surprised to find me here. The sweet little Palestinian Problem blushes, says hurriedly, stammering:

"It's only me . . . I didn't think there was anyone at home. Are you sick?"

"No, I'm not sick . . . just lying down . . . did Daddy send you to fetch something?"

"Yes . . . no . . . not exactly. I'm looking for him . . . hasn't he come back from Jerusalem yet?"

"No . . . why?"

"I wanted to tell him something."

"Tell me."

"No, I'm not sick . . ." She goes all red, wrapping herself up tight in the blanket, maybe she's naked underneath. "Just lying down . . . did Daddy send you to fetch something?"

What can I say? They're sure to find out about the key and then I'm fucked.

"Yes . . ."

But she'll find out in the end that it's a lie.

"No . . . not exactly . . . I'm looking for him . . . hasn't he come back from Jerusalem yet?"

"No . . . why?"

"I wanted to tell him something."

"Tell me."

She smiles such a sweet smile.

What can I say to her? Lying there in those flowery pajamas. What can I say to her? I love you. I've always loved you . . .

"The old woman's dying . . . and I came here to say I'm resigning . . ."

"Resigning from what?"

"I'm resigning from the job . . . I've got no strength left . . ."

"Strength for what?" She smiles with disdain.

All these cursed questions–

"Strength to look after her. She's really dying."

"I thought she was looking after you . . . that's what Daddy said . . ."

"What's that? It isn't true . . ."

That really annoys me. And suddenly I feel all weak. My breath stops short. Her feet are peeping out from under the blanket, she sits up a bit . . . her blouse is open . . . no bra . . . I see something soft and white, her feet disappear again . . . I start to shake inside . . . I shall kill her . . .

How serious he is, this boy, you could die. Blushing all the time. Anyway he's changed an awful lot. That thick mane of curly hair and those clothes. Who bought them for him? Glaring at me so fiercely you'd think he wanted to kill me. Staring at me, studying me, those hot Arab eyes, something a bit foggy about them. I just hope he doesn't run away suddenly.

"The old woman's dying . . . and I came here to say I'm resigning."

What a crisis. The Prime Minister's resigning.

"Resigning from what?"

"I'm resigning from the job . . . I've got no strength left . . ."

Strength for what? You'd think he'd been working hard lately. He's funny, and so serious and grim. I wish he'd give me just a little smile.

"Strength for what?" I smile at him.

It's obvious these questions are annoying him, but what can I do, otherwise he'll run away from here.

"Strength to look after her."

The swine! He's looking after her? And Daddy said she was looking after him, she was in love with him.

"I thought she was looking after you."

Now he really gets mad. I've offended him.

"What's that? It isn't true . . ."

I sit up in bed. His eyes are blazing. That voice of his, a bit hoarse, that cute accent. He'll catch fire in a moment. The poor schmuck is in love with me, I know. But he's worried about his pride, their famous pride. I must hold him, get his rocks off before he goes.

"Why don't you sit down for a bit, if you've got time. You can resign later."

A smile at last. He looks around for somewhere to sit, but the only chair's covered in clothes. He comes to the bed and sits on the edge. Something warm and solid in the distance.

Silence. I watch him all the time. He sits there, his head bowed, trying to think of something to say.

"School finished already?" he asks suddenly.

"For me."

She doesn't understand anything. She never will understand. What's hurting me. How lonely I am. With her mother and father in this lovely house. Lying there in bed with no worries. What does she know about anything? And suddenly she smiles at me, a long, nice sort of smile. I love her more and more. Maybe there's hope after all.

"Why don't you sit down for a bit, if you've got time. You can resign later."

So sweet—

I look for a place to sit. The chair beside the table is covered in clothes, a blouse, a little bra, underwear, things I don't know anything about. In the end I decide to sit on the bed, I sit on the edge, feeling her legs move, something warm and soft. I stare at the floor, at her slippers that I wore once, they've gotten a bit tattered since then. She's looking at me all the time and smiling. What does she want? She'd better stop smiling like that or I'll kiss her so hard she'll be sorry. What's she doing? Her legs move underneath me. It's quiet. So quiet.

"School finished already?" I ask her, to keep the conversation going.

"For me," she says, still smiling. "They expelled me."

"What? They expelled you?"

"You heard me. I insulted one of the teachers and the headmaster expelled me."

"How did you insult him?"

And she tells me what happened. Very strange. She's really a bit unbalanced. I've noticed it before.

"Why didn't you say you were sorry?"

"I was crazy."

The warmth that she gives off. Her flushed face. This smooth skin. Tits, yes, real tits, little ones, peeping out through her sleeve. I must be strong, not give up. The time has come, the main thing is not to lose the conversation. Suppose I just take her and kiss her. What could happen? Anyway I've already resigned.

"They expelled me," I say and he's astonished, doesn't believe it.

"What? They expelled you?"

"You heard me. I insulted one of the teachers and the headmaster expelled me."

And I tell him about it, the whole story from beginning to end, and he listens with such concern, as if I were his daughter, trying to understand and not understanding. But suddenly I myself don't understand why I was so obstinate. The whole business seems pointless when I describe it now.

"Why didn't you say you were sorry?"

"I was crazy."

And really, why not? A simple apology. That would've been that.

And he's very close to me, he's got a smell like straw. Smooth swarthy skin. All it needs is a bit of strength. Mustn't give up now. Suppose I take him and kiss him. What could happen? He's already resigned, hasn't he? The main thing is not to lose the conversation. A wave of heat within, this is desire. Let him take me, embrace me, let him be strong. Suddenly I need to piss. Need it badly. "Just a moment," I say and jump up all at once, the blanket flies off, I run to the bathroom half naked, close the door and sit down, burning inside and pissing noisily, like a cow. What a relief. What's going to happen? Just so he doesn't escape. I wash my face, brush my teeth and quietly, barefooted, I go back to him, finding him in the same place, sitting on the bed, thinking hard, only his head's drooping, lying in the hollow that I left in the crumpled sheet. He doesn't notice me coming in. He jumps up at once, blushing bright red.

"I must go."

"Why? Wait for Daddy . . ."

"But he isn't coming . . ."

"He'll come . . . eat here, I cooked you a meal once before, was it so bad?"

I'm pleading with him.

He agrees. I put on a dressing gown and go to the kitchen, he goes into the bathroom.

I'm just about to touch her but she gets excited, jumps out of bed, scared, the blanket flies off, she runs out of the room, locks herself in the bathroom. That's it, Arab. Go, go. *Son of man go flee.* Never. Say good-by because in a moment she'll scream. I'm desperate, I want to stand up but I can't. The warmth of the bed that she's left behind. This warmth at least. Here on the sheet there's a little book–*Peer Gynt.* I don't know it. I'm fed up with these poems. I put it back. I can't get up. Looking at the hollow that she's left in the bed, in the crumpled sheet. Putting my hand there, wanting to kiss it. My prick's burning, hard as stone, in a moment I'll be all wet. Just get off and get out of here, that at least. I lay my head down. Must get out of here, before I make a fool of myself. But I've made a fool of myself already. Here she is, coming in quietly. She's combed her hair, she looks new and fresh, her face washed. I jump up, to flee.

"I must go."

"Why? Wait for Daddy . . ."

"But he isn't coming."

"He'll come . . . have something to eat, I cooked you a meal once before, was it that bad?"

She's desperate but she's hoping too. She's really pleading. "O.K.," I agree, proudly, like I'm doing her a favor. She puts on a dressing gown and goes to the kitchen and I take *Peer Gynt* and go to the bathroom, a long slow piss, wetting my prick with a bit of water and giving it air and waiting for it to get back to its normal size. Meanwhile I read a bit of *Peer Gynt* but I don't understand a thing. I've gone really dumb. Looking at the dark face in the mirror, washing my face, pressing toothpaste on my finger and brushing my teeth a bit, combing my hair, putting on a bit of scent. And thinking suddenly, maybe she's a bit in love with me, why not?

A decadent meal. We ate in the dining room, on a white cloth and with the best china. I lit a candle on the middle of the table like I've seen them do in movies. And I cooked farmhouse pea soup and made a big tomato and cucumber salad, well seasoned. And I made a sauce too. And I fried four meat cutlets that were already half prepared, and I opened a tin of pineapple and put ice cream on the pineapple and pieces of chocolate on the ice cream. And then he helped me make the coffee and I brought in some nice biscuits. And he ate the lot and really liked it. And he asked me about *Peer Gynt* and I told him the plot, as far as we'd gotten in class.

And she gave me pea soup and salad and sauce and cutlets and fried potatoes and pineapple with ice cream and bits of chocolate. And I helped her to make the coffee and there were some really nice cookies. And it was all very tasty. We sat in the dining room at a table laid out like in movies, with a candle burning in the middle of the day because it was a bit dark with the shutters still closed. And I asked her about the play she was reading and she told me all about it. It was marvelous listening to her and eating the food that she'd cooked. I know I'll never forget her to the day I die. And then there was a ring at the door and I thought–this is the end, but it wasn't the end.

And suddenly at the end of the meal there's a ring at the door. I go to open it and nearly drop dead. Shwartzy, large as life, still with the white bandage on his head, a bit dirty now. Smiling pleasantly, the fox, he wants to push his way inside but I hold the door, so he won't see Na'im and the table.

"Dafi, are you sick?"

Him as well. If so many people think I'm sick maybe I really am sick.

"No . . . what's up?"

"Is your mother at home?"

"No."

"Where is she?"

"She's gone to Jerusalem."

"To Jerusalem? What's happened?"

"I don't know. She went early in the morning. Daddy's there."

"Oh, I see. They told me at the garage that he was away yesterday and today too. Has something happened?"

"I don't know."

"I was just worried. Your mother didn't come to school today and she didn't send any message, this has never happened with her before. We tried to phone here and there was no answer. When did you come back?"

"I didn't come back . . . I've been here all the time . . . I just left the phone off the hook."

"Oh . . ." He smiles at me playfully. "Why? If I may ask . . ."

You may, you may–

"I just did . . ."

I'm out of your jurisdiction, mister, out of your power. You insisted on expelling me before the end of the school year. Now you shall pay.

But he's still trying to get inside, pressing forward all the time.

"I hope nothing has happened . . . I was really worried . . . didn't she tell you to give me a message?"

"I think there was something, I remember now, it was so early in the morning . . ."

"What did she say?"

"That she wouldn't be in school today."

"Then why didn't you phone?"

"I forgot."

Straight to his face.

"You forgot?"

"Yes."

Out of your jurisdiction, mister, you're not my headmaster any longer, you can't do anything more to me.

He doesn't go. Astonished, red with anger. He waves his cane in the air and puts it down again.

"There's something wrong with you . . . something really wrong . . ."

"I know." I look him straight in the eyes.

Silence. Why doesn't he go? Na'im is in there listening quietly, suddenly he moves a chair.

"But there is somebody in the house." All at once he comes to life, pushing me out of the way and storming into the house, he bursts into the dining room, sees the table with the remains of the meal, and Na'im standing there all tensed up in the corner.

"Who are you?"

"I'm Na'im," he replies like an idiot, as if this is his headmaster.

And Shwartzy catches hold of him, grabs his arm, the same way that he catches hold of children during recess, all excited.

"I know you from somewhere . . . where have we met?"

"That night. When your car got smashed up. I came to tow you in . . ."

"Ah, you're his assistant?"

"Yes."

"So what are you doing here?"

"Waiting for him."

Shwartzy seems satisfied, walking about the room, examining the table and the cutlery, behaving as if he's in school. I could shoot the man. Tears spring to my eyes.

"Tell your mother to contact me."

I don't answer.

"All right?"

I don't answer.

"I'll tell her," Na'im chips in.

Shwartzy smiles to himself. And I nearly faint.

And she goes to open the door and I hear a familiar voice. It takes me a while to remember who it is, that old man, we towed his car in the night before last, he's talking to Dafi at the door. And Dafi answers him rudely, again I'm impressed, she really has nerve. He asks her about her mother and father and she answers him with a lot of nerve. And the man gets really up-tight, starts talking sort of poisonously, in that soft voice of his. In the end he forces his way into the house, she's got him really worked up. Walking about with a cane, he sees me and grabs me. I'm terrified, I don't know why this old man with the white bandage on his head should scare me.

"Who are you?"

"I'm Na'im," I say right away.

He catches hold of me roughly.

"I know you from somewhere . . . where have we met?"

He doesn't recognize me.

"That night, when your car got smashed up. I came to tow you in."

"Ah, you're his assistant?"

"Yes."

"So what are you doing here?"

"Waiting for him."

And then he walks around the room a bit, like it's his house, taking a look at the plates on the table, smiling to himself a bit. Then he says to Dafi, "Tell your mother to contact me."

But she doesn't answer.

"All right?"

She still doesn't answer. Answer for God's sake. Why is she provoking him like this? But she doesn't answer, and he isn't going to budge.

"I'll tell her," I say, just to get rid of him.

And he went. Leaving the door wide open. I went to close it. Dafi didn't move, standing there staring at the wall. I went to her, touched her.

"But who was that?"

And she didn't answer, just stared at the wall, pale. He made a good job of scaring us. And suddenly she turned to me, I think she grabbed me and then I grabbed her, embraced her I mean, and then we kissed, I don't know who was first, I think it was both of us together, at first we fumbled a bit, but then we kissed full on the mouth, with the tongue, like in movies, only in movies there's no taste, and I tasted the coffee and the cake on her lips, and a deeper smell, and it was a long kiss and suddenly I saw that I couldn't stand it any longer, I'd die if I stayed in that kiss, and I fell on my knees and started kissing her feet, for so long I'd been wanting to do that, but she lifted me up and pulled me into the bedroom, and she was almost naked, and then she tore off my shirt and said, "Come and be my lover."

And then Na'im came to me, miserable and broken and said, "Who was that?"

And I didn't answer. I felt so sorry for him. The way that bastard interrogated him, and the way he co-operated, so humbly, so wretchedly. And I grabbed him because I was afraid he'd leave me and he hugged me and suddenly we were kissing, I don't know how it happened, who was the first, I think it was both of us together. And a deep sort of kiss, like in movies, and the taste of pineapple and chocolate on his lips, sucking at my tongue. And suddenly he let go of me and fell down on his knees and started kissing my feet, like a madman. And I saw he was afraid to stand up and he wanted to stay there on his knees, so I lifted him up and he pulled me into the bedroom and opened my dressing gown and pajama top and then I tore off his shirt so he wouldn't still be in his clothes when I was almost naked.

It's wonderful. Already, so quick. But is this all? I'm really doing it, God, this, this is it, this is the real thing. These little tits, like hard apples. A little girl. And that cry. What am I doing? Inside, really inside. Inside her. Just like I thought it would be but different too. Her eyes are closed. Why doesn't she say something? This is happiness this is the highest happiness there's nothing greater than this there couldn't be . . . and then I start sighing terribly . . .

I said, "Come and be my lover," because I didn't want him to hurt me. But he did hurt me. There was no stopping him. Enough, stop now, it's so sweet, oh God. There's no stopping him. This is it. I'm sure I'm the first of all the girls. If only Osnat and Tali knew. That it's good, it's like a dream. Na'im inside me, awesome, this smooth movement. All terribly serious. And suddenly he starts to sigh, like an old man, like somebody else inside him. Sighing in Arabic . . . from pleasure or pain there's no way of telling.

"What are you thinking about?"
"I'm just not thinking."
"That's impossible, you must be thinking about something."
"Good for the old woman."
"What about the old woman?"
"She must be dead by now."
"How old is she?"
"Over ninety. I wish I could live that many years."
"Did he offend you?"
"Who?"
"The headmaster . . ."
"That was the headmaster. . . . No, why, what is there to be offended about? I was just scared."
"Were you scared?"
"Yes, he really scared me . . ."
"When did Daddy give you the key to the house?"
"He didn't."
"But you had the key today."
"It's my key . . ."
"Yours?"
"I got a duplicate of the key he gave me, that time he sent me here to fetch his case . . . when I saw you . . ."
"So long ago . . ."

"Yes."
"Why?"
"I just wanted to have a key to this house."
"But why?"
"I just did . . ."
"Because of me?"
"Because of you too."
"Because of who else?"
"All right, only because of you."
"But they can put you in jail for that."
"Let them. . . . Somebody's coming into the house."
"No!"
"Listen . . . people coming in . . ."
"Then get dressed . . . hurry . . . I'll hide you . . . it's Daddy and Mommy and I think there's somebody else."

ADAM

Stretched out weakly, dozing on the broad bed, his head on a heap of pillows that he's put together, the strong light of a Jerusalem morning filling the room. The music still playing, a lively march. She clutches at me, she stumbles in the doorway. I didn't expect her to be so shocked at the sight of his black beard, his long side curls, the tassels straggling carelessly from his clothes, and the hat of tawny fox fur that lies menacingly on the table, beside the telephone.

"What happened?" she whispers.

He opens his eyes, looking at us, still lying there, a thin smile appearing on his face, as if he's enjoying her astonishment, as if the whole sequence of his actions has been aimed at this moment.

"How are you? Mrs. . . ."

And she can't even answer, the words stick in her mouth, is she afraid that the lover is no longer a lover, that the lover has gone mad?

The love of an aging woman—

"But why?"

He rises slowly, sitting up, still smiling with a sort of happiness.

"They wanted to kill me, I had to escape. Praise the Lord, what matters is that I'm alive."

And he starts pacing about the room, going to the window to look at the wall of the Old City, its towers and turrets. She watches him as if every one of his movements has a deep significance. Still afraid to approach him, still nervous of him.

He notices the Morris in the parking lot.

"So they've given me up? Wonderful people . . ."

I don't answer. Speech has deserted me. He continues pacing about the room before us, his hands clasped behind his back. He's grown accustomed to slow, elderly movements.

"But what will happen now?"

"God willing, we shall return home. Grandmother is alive, let us bid her good-by. Receive her blessing. Now there is no legacy, that was a dream and is no longer. Let us sit and wait. Really, why should we hurry? I have time . . ."

Praise the Lord, God willing, these phrases fall from his lips without a thought, naturally, or is he trying intentionally to provoke us? Walking about the big, pleasant room, at some distance from us, lightly touching the furniture, picking up an ashtray to examine it, standing in front of the mirror and studying his reflection, lightly touching his curls.

"You won't believe it, but I've hardly seen myself these last few months. They don't have mirrors."

And he sinks into a chair.

Somebody knocks at the door. The hotel reception clerk appears, staring at us so hard you'd think we were standing there naked. He can't quite get the words out. It's twelve o'clock, he's afraid, he says, we must leave the room, today some congress or other is convening here.

I'm still silent. Asya doesn't know what to say. Gabriel stands up, taking the initiative.

"We're leaving."

The clerk bows to him slightly and closes the door.

A few minutes later the three of us are walking down the stairs. I go to the desk and pay a hundred and fifty pounds for the use of the room. "We don't have hourly rates," the clerk apologizes, but I'm not asking for such a rate, I hand over the money (my wallet has become light, crumpled, I've never known it so flabby). The delegates to the congress stand in a line in front of a hostess who's sticking name tags on the lapels of their jackets. They watch the three of us curiously. Gabriel makes a great impression on them with his black clothes, his curls, the broad fur hat. A flash bulb pops, somebody has taken his picture.

We get into the Morris, I at the wheel, leaving Jerusalem at last.

A blazing hot day. The car goes slowly, thirty to forty kilometers an hour. Everything overtakes us, even little motorcycles, drivers turning to us with a friendly smile as if we're young adventurers. The very presence of such a car on the roads deserves respect.

On the ascent to Castel the Morris starts to cough, the engine making a strange ticking noise like a rusty machine gun, a light report responds from behind. But with one leap we reach the crest of the hill. But after Sha'ar Ha'gai on the sharply winding road a long line of cars starts to trail along behind us, unable to overtake us because of the oncoming traffic. Like a little black beetle with a trail of big colored beads. A traffic cop on a motorcycle stops us, asks us to pull over to the side to free the clogged traffic. We do as he asks. Before we return to the road he checks the documents, my mechanic's license reassures him.

And again a long column of traffic builds up behind us, and again we pull over to the side of the road and the line of cars breaks through.

We reach the Tel Aviv–Haifa freeway after five hours driving, as if we've come from another continent. Before Hadera we stop at a roadhouse, fill up with gasoline and go inside for a meal. Curious stares follow us all the time, something in the combination of the three of us arouses great interest.

We eat. Or rather, Gabriel eats, devouring course after course, as if he has some ravenous hunger to satisfy.

We leave to continue our journey. It's four o'clock. We stand in the parking space beside the car, looking at the sea sparkling nearby, around us the movement of people and cars. We don't speak. All the time followed by curious stares, smiling eyes. Gabriel turns toward a little shop, souvenirs and camping equipment, we follow him, still afraid he may try to escape.

Among the objects in the display window his reflection appears.

"She'll be shocked to see me like this . . ." he says as if only now he realizes the effect of his remarkable appearance.

He takes off the big fur hat, stands there bareheaded, takes off the black coat, touches his side curls.

"The time has come."

He goes into the shop and returns with an old razor in his hand.

We turn to the sea, to the beach. He sits on a big stone and Asya bends over him and cuts off his curls. Two long thin locks, shining from endless fingering. She gives them to him, he's about to throw them away but changes his mind, finds an old tin can lying on the beach and puts them in it.

Asya feels easier, she begins to smile. He takes off his tasseled apron, folds it and puts it into the can. Asya starts trimming his beard with the rusty razor, they laugh. I walk back and forth along the shore, my head bowed before the dazzling brightness of the waves. Tired, numb, only one thought in my head, to get home.

We go back to the car. People no longer stare. We drive on for about an hour and a half, the rusty ticking stops, instead the engine begins to creak, I have no idea what's going on inside there.

We arrive at the house. He's decided to come in with us and phone her first, so she won't be startled by his sudden appearance. I can see how concerned he is about her, looking forward to the meeting with excitement.

I go up the stairs first and they follow. My shoes battered, my legs like jelly, I'm encrusted with sand and oil. It's been a long journey. The apartment is dark, on the table piles of plates and cutlery, as if there's been a banquet. A big candlestick stands there with the flickering remains of a candle, shadows on the walls. Dafi's dressing gown and pajama top lie scattered on the floor. Suddenly I feel terribly afraid. Something has happened to the girl.

VEDUCHA

So now it's the reverse the body is lost and only thought remains the hands have gone the legs have gone the face is going can't move but I think of what I want to think knowing it all my name and my parents' name and my grandson's name and my daughter's name remembering them all recalling all I was a stone a frog a thorn bush all is clear how can death come when I'm thinking with such power no pain but no feeling and I don't want to die no no why if I've lived so long why not a few more years I was born in the nineteenth century sometimes I'm astonished when I remember but soon this century too will be over no pity I could have lived a little into the next century too at least the first years two thousand and one two thousand and two the fullness of light it's all gone so fast this century so quickly a dark and fast century not like the last years of the century that went before full of sun in Jerusalem when Jerusalem was great full of fields when I was married it began to grow dark nineteen hundred already twilight.

The bastard came in through the window they aren't as stupid as they were when the state began he thought I was already dead the little Arab he put a sheet over me lucky there was one more tear left and it fell he would have choked me little *fatah* animal then he tried to feed me put bread in my mouth so kind and I had a daughter and I had a grandson it's all a disappointing dream without a true end.

No hunger no thirst no feelings I'm only thought the brain works very clear there's even a whistling in the mind I can think of what I like but of what?

The boy has gone left fled good if he had stayed longer in the house I would have given him it all as a present terribly sweet when he reads the papers sweet and dangerous but why should he take this house?

Oh Lord of the Universe the eyes sink in darkness the cupboard before me goes black the corners turn and split farewell cupboard farewell table darkness approaches black mist quickly quickly farewell carpet farewell chair I am going and peace all around good at last I shall think in peace but of what?

The cars have gone from the road farewell bus what's this the siren of a ship like the wail of a little cat hearing nothing seeing nothing farewell street enough street and suddenly a little bell a whistle oh the telephone is ringing like a little lamb beside me someone is calling wants me weaker and weaker not a bell but the whistle of a dying wind I know but do not hear too bad too bad about me too bad for I am dead too bad, for I am not

ADAM

What is this? What's going on here? Who's here? The whole place is dark. Pulling down the blinds in the middle of the day. These new ideas. Na'im standing there in a corner dressing.

"Daddy don't do anything to him he isn't to blame Daddy have mercy on him." Why's she yelling at me like that? Dafi's completely disturbed. I shall have to do something about her. I hardly understand what's going on here. I'm the one who needs pity, not him. I've spent two mad days on the road. I go closer to see if it really is Na'im and what the hell he's doing here and he tries to slip away or it looks as if he's trying to, and I catch him by the shirt, the shirt that's already torn, and he dangles in the air, either he's very light or I've forgotten the strength in my arms that've slumbered for so many years, there was a time when I used to lift engines, turn cars over, bend steel pipes and put doors straight.

Now I just hold him for a moment in the air, by the shirt that I haven't torn, in the dark room, and he's sure I'm going to strangle him and he shakes all over. I'm shaking too, I'm capable of anything. And Dafi leaps up, throwing off the blanket, getting dressed, quite hysterical. I've never seen the girl in such a state, so aggressive. Na'im is silent, I'm silent, only Dafi speaks.

"Leave him alone, he came to say he's resigning."

And Na'im, still suspended in the air, repeats after her in a choking voice, "Yes, I'm resigning . . ."

"Resigning from what?"

"From everything . . . from working with you."

I drop him on the floor. This is crazy.

"You're not moving from here now even if you have resigned, do you hear?"

"I hear . . ."

"Tell me exactly what's happened to the old lady. Where is she? I rang and there was no answer."

He looks at me, very quiet.

"I think she's already dead."

"What?"

"Since yesterday she's been paralyzed. She doesn't talk, doesn't answer, doesn't eat."

"Then why did you leave her?" I yell, suddenly I feel like stamping on him.

"But he's resigning . . ."

Dafi again. I go to silence her once and for all, but she slips away. Asya is in the doorway, looking in silence at the chaos of the darkened room, the blankets on the floor, the crumpled sheet, Dafi's clothes. Na'im hurriedly buttons his trousers, puts on his shoes. From the living room comes the sound of the television. Gabriel is attacking civilization. Now we shall lose him again.

"What's happened?" she asks.

"We're going down to see the old lady, come on you . . ."

Gabriel's sprawled in an armchair, he stares at the little Arab, who stares at him. We leave the house. A drizzly summer evening, the *hamsin* broken. I have great difficulty starting the Morris, it's exhausted after the long journey. The battery's almost dead. I jump out and go to Asya's car, quickly remove her battery and throw it onto the back seat of the Morris, in case of need. Also, I think, better they shouldn't follow us there.

Na'im curls up in the seat beside me, scared by the little black car that looks like a coffin. The sight of the tasseled apron, the fringes, the tin can with the severed side curls, the big fur hat and the other ritual objects scattered about the car, all perplex him. He's careful not to touch them. He wants to say something but before he can open his mouth I say, "Shut up."

We drive fast to the lower city. The gear box shakes, the engine goes on bubbling and shimmying, the whole thing's falling apart, but I hurry on, cutting the corners, the sea on our left, the bay all green and red, a strange sick color.

"What's this? What's happened to the sea?"

I'm talking to myself, he looks at the sea, he's about to say something.

"Be quiet, it doesn't matter . . ."

We go up to the old lady's apartment. A heavy twilight. I've forgotten this apartment, so long since I've been here. We find her in the armchair in the big room, leaning forward a bit, dead. The telephone on a little stool beside her. She's still warm, she died just a few hours ago. I take a sheet that's lying beside her and spread it on the floor, I say to him, "Come on, we'll lay her on the floor," and together we lift her. Newspapers start falling from her, scattering and drifting. Copies of *Ma'ariv* and *Yediot Aheronot* sticking to her body, she's upholstered with newspapers. I've never seen such a mass of newspapers. Na'im looks at me, wants to say something, but he's afraid.

"Well?"

"She loved newspapers . . ." An evil smile twists his mouth.

I pick up the phone, to pass on the news, but suddenly I change my mind and put the receiver down again. I don't have the strength now. Let's give her one night at least.

It's seven o'clock, still traces of light outside, but in the room it's dim. Na'im lights himself a cigarette, offers me one, with an adult sort of gesture, I take it, he gives me a light, I look at him, now I begin to realize what's happened between him and Dafi. I sit in the old lady's chair, seeking a moment's rest.

The old lady lies there in front of me in the clear light of evening. Through the open window–the sea, endlessly changing its colors.

"Pack your belongings and bring them here," I tell him quietly.

He goes to his room and returns with two big cases.

So, he really did mean to leave–

And with property–

We go out, closing the door behind us, leaving the old lady lying on the floor, covered with a sheet, newspapers scattered about her. For a moment it seems there's a slight movement there, but it's a newspaper stirring in the breeze. The Morris sinks under the weight of Na'im's cases. The engine won't start, but I keep on trying, playing with the gas pedal. At last I get a spark and start the engine.

But what to do now?

Where to?

A gray evening in spite of the clear skies, thin smoke covering the town, a *hamsin* wind. We're still stationary, the engine running, charging up the almost dead battery. Na'im sits beside me, listening to the engine. What's he thinking? He's a stranger really, another world, and I thought he was close to me. No, I'm not angry with him. From his point of view, why not? And anyway, what use are words, I must just get him away from here.

But where to?

"How long has this been going on with you and Dafi?"

I don't look at him.

"Only today . . ."

"Did you sleep together?"

He doesn't know . . . he thinks so, isn't sure, doesn't know . . . this was the first time in his life . . . if that's what they call it . . . he isn't sure . . . he thinks so . . .

He stammers, his voice shaking, as if he's about to burst into tears. I remember how he stood and cried outside the bathroom.

He's become a little lover in the course of the year–

I feel a sudden stab of pain. Must get him away from here at once.

I switch on the lights, the engine falters, coughing.

The lights are weak but I start to drive. I feel something mechanical in my movements, something perverse, I'm about to do something stupid, so I drive very slowly, very carefully.

"Where are you taking me?" he asks.

I don't answer.

This car's going to fall apart under me and yet I can't bring myself to leave it. I've spent too much time searching for it up and down the land.

At a gas station I fill the tank, my wallet almost empty, I've been spending money like water these last few days. I buy a map as well, unfold it on the wheel and calculate the distance to the border.

Lunacy, a stupid idea, to throw him across the border. And yet I drive north, passing through Acre and Nahariya, following the road north.

The night grows clearer, the headlights are dim on the narrow road. Suddenly there are searchlights, roadblocks, half-tracks, machine guns and soldiers, the frontier guard, Circassians, Druzes.

"Where are you heading?"

I look at Na'im.

"Peki'in," he says.

"You're on the wrong road. Get out of the car!"

They search us thoroughly, everything arouses their suspicion, me, Na'im, the car, they shine their flashlights into the car, taking everything out, searching under the seats. Everything is stripped, the suitcases are opened, old clothes from generations past are scattered on the road, they're astonished to find the big hat, they examine the tassels, the severed side curls.

"But who are you?" they almost shout.

Na'im pulls out his identity card, I search for mine.

In the end they send us back, showing us the way to the village. After half an hour, the road stops, on the hillside the dim lights of a little village.

"This is it . . ." he says.

I put him down.

"Go to your father's house. Tell him you've finished working for me."

And then he starts quietly weeping, explaining that he's willing to get married, not just to be in love.

In love? What's he talking about, the world's gone mad. How old are they?

"In our village . . . at this age . . ." he tries to explain, the tears still flowing.

I smile.

"Go, go, tell your father to send you to school . . ."

He really does love her. He fell in love quietly and I didn't sense it.

He starts to go, carrying the two cases. The headlights lose him, he disappears around a bend in the road, I try to turn the car but the engine goes dead. The lights fade. The battery is absolutely dead.

I take Asya's battery, lift the hood and change the batteries, unfastening and replacing the screws with my fingers. But even now there's no response from the engine, her battery too has gone dead these last months, I hadn't noticed.

A smell of fields around, the sky full of stars, a broken side road. Somewhere in Galilee.

Old lives, new lives–

He will go and I shall have to start from the beginning.

My state of mind–

Standing beside a dead old car from '47 and there's nobody to save me.

I must look for Hamid–

But still I don't move. Silence envelops me, deep stillness, it's as if I'm deaf.

NA'IM

He could have killed me but he didn't kill me, didn't strike me, didn't touch me he was sorry or he was afraid back home in the village I'd have bit the dust.

Great God, thank you God–

It was so sweet, only now I understand how good it was. Honey and butter to the very end and at once how wildly she kissed how she tore my shirt. Dafi Dafi Dafi Dafi I could shout your name all night and how I suddenly sighed what happened to me such shame sighing and sighing and she just gazing at me my love–

I fall at your feet–

This warm dust the smell of the village and down below a new desire awakening–

I kneel before you God–

It was so good and wonderful so good Dafi Dafi Dafi

Now to go home to the village and say to Father "I have come"

To say hello to the donkeys

What do I care if they don't let me see her I shall remember her a thousand years I shall not forget

I miss her already—

I've been burned with kindness—

And he doesn't move from there. He's switched off the lights. From behind a fence of cactus I see him lift the hood and try to start up. Not moving . . . a big tired shadow . . . stuck . . .

Let him work a little, he's forgotten how to work—

"Go back to school" he said and I've forgotten what school is. A good man, a good and tired man, and they got on poor Adnan's nerves so—

It's possible to love them and to hurt them too—

He's stuck there he can't do anything. But if I go back to help him he'll attack me better to go and rouse Hamid.

The people will wonder what's happened to Na'im that he's suddenly so full of hope.